THE
FIRST
KING

THE ANOINTED, BOOK I

JACOB A. WELDON

Printed in the United States of America
Anointed Book, LLC
Paperback ISBN: 979-8-9926555-0-6
Ebook ISBN: 979-8-9926555-1-3

AUTHOR'S NOTE

This series is based on the stories of 1 and 2 Samuel from the Hebrew Bible / Old Testament. While the author has made every attempt to ensure that the storyline is true to the Word, fictional backstories, characters, and dialogue have been added to the biblical framework. Any and all artistic license has been taken with the goal of supporting and bringing to life the biblical stories from scripture. Readers are encouraged to read the corresponding scriptures which are provided at the beginning of many chapters. I hope you enjoy this book and that it leaves you with a deeper understanding of God's Word.

ACKNOWLEDGMENTS

I want to thank my wife, Sarah, and daughters, Seanna and Scout, for the countless hours they have sacrificed for this book.

Many thanks to my editor, Susan Hendricks, my father and mother, Michael and Mickie Weldon, who gave their time to review multiple revisions of this work.

I could not fail to mention the influence of my brothers, both in blood and in service, which influenced many of the stories that fill the pages of this work.

So many of the positive influences in my life have come through Rock Springs Church and my Pastor, Benny Tate. Thank you, Benny, for your guidance and influence during our trip to Israel in June of 2023. Thank you, Rock Springs staff and members, for your support, friendship, encouragement, and sharpening.

Thank you, Christopher Young, for pointing me to God's word when the going got tough.

I thank God for this calling, your patience, your gentle correction, and your numerous affirmations throughout the process.

CONTENTS

CALL TO WAR

1095 BC Ammon (modern-day Jordan)

On this condition will I make a covenant with you, that I may thrust
out all your right eyes, and lay it for a reproach upon all Israel.
I Samuel 11:1-2

Far east of the confluence of the Jabbok and Jordan rivers, an army formed into ranks in the dim blue hue of the early morning sky. Their king and general stepped purposefully to the high place, an altar atop a wooden platform constructed there amid the arid and rocky landscape. Starting to his right, officers reported their numbers as they each saluted. Nahash, King of the Ammonites, stood tall and proud before the largest Ammonite force ever assembled.

In total, they were five hundred thousand strong, though the logistics of maintaining such an army in this climate necessitated their division. Those present would be the first to begin their conquest, the sickle's edge as the army swept westward towards the Jordan.

Nahash surveyed the impressive array of warriors assembled before him.

"For generations, the sons of Jacob have been a thorn in our flesh," Nahash shouted to the men. "They came unprovoked! Like a devouring plague of locusts, they caught us unawares. They stole what was ours," he shouted jabbing his finger toward the dirt below, "the land of our forefathers Ammon and Lot. To this day they deplete our land and desecrate it with their presence. Uprooted and forced from our homeland, our grandfathers and fathers fought, bled, and died so that a remnant would survive, grow strong, and somehow multiply here in this unforgiving place," he shouted. "For far too long, we have been exiled from the land of forefathers, forced to carve out what we might in this wilderness. But Milcom did not forget his people! Our trials have strengthened our resolve!" Nahash shouted as he lifted his powerful arm high above his head.

The troops shouted their affirmation in unison, "AHU, AHU!"

"We have gathered here not to steal as the Hebrew, not to take what we do not rightfully own, but to recover our inheritance, the land of our people. For some of you, the lush and fertile land of your childhood. Do you remember it?"

A roar went up from the assembly. Despite the hour, the men were roused by their leader's energy and fervent call to arms.

"When we fight, think not of yourselves, but of your children and your wives at home. The Hebrew will not stop," Nahash continued, pacing the platform. "Your homes are next. There is no border they will not cross; there is no amount of land that will satiate their lust for more. If we do not take back what they have stolen, they will come for more. They will make slaves of your wives and children! The wells you hacked out of this dry and rocky dirt, your gardens, your vineyards which you have sweated and bled for will feed and profit their offspring."

"NEVER," the men shouted back.

Most had heard accounts of the Hebrew invasion, eerie tails of woebegone widowed grandmothers and gray-haired men. While many in the assembly had never actually seen a Hebrew, their hatred was no less ardent. They'd heard of the slaughter at Jericho since their youth and other firsthand accounts of the Canaanite caravans, widows and fatherless children passing in droves. The stories they'd heard by firelight as children instilled deep within them a hatred and loathsome fear of their Hebrew neighbors to the west. They were determined that their own families would not suffer the same fate. Since the death of the long-haired judge, the one called Samson, they'd been decades without a real leader. They'd grown weak and complacent.

Many years ago, Ibrahim, an Ammonite officer, had witnessed the aftermath of Samson's murderous tantrums firsthand. "No more," he thought. He and his sons were prepared to fight. Hammurabi, the oldest of his sons, was present. Ibrahim watched with pride as Hammurabi shouted in unison with the other soldiers at Nahash's calls for blood and vengeance.

Since their youth, Hammurabi and his brothers had been trained to wreak havoc among the Hebrews. They sabotaged fields and vineyards, stole livestock and tools, anything they could do to make life more difficult in the neighboring Hebrew villages. It was the favorite pastime of their childhood. As adults, it would be their life's mission to take back what had once been Ammonite land or die trying. Though still a teen, Hammurabi was tall, strong, and mature. Through their family's success in breeding horses, Ibrahim had secured a position as commander of the Ammonite cavalry. Their horses were said to be the best from Egypt to Chaldea. Wealth had its privileges and he'd appointed Hammurabi as the leader of a small section under his command.

"The Hebrews will serve us tribute," Nahash continued. "Those who oppose us will be cut down. We will put out the right eye of every man until none remains able to oppose us. This will be a disgrace greater than death. They will be our slaves and they will suffer as we have suffered!" Nahash concluded.

"AHU, AHU!" The soldiers shouted, pounding the shafts of their spears against shields. Hammurabi's heart pounded in his chest. The excitement was contagious. He wanted more than anything to fight, to test and prove himself in battle. Soon, he would make his father proud. Soon, his spear would be red with the blood of the Hebrew.

DEFACED

1095 BC, Bezer, Reuben, Israel (modern-day Jordan)

Shiza glared at the glowing red iron just inches from his right eye. The events that led up to this moment flashed through his mind in quick succession: the farmers and herdsmen flooding into the city only days ago, the Ammonite encirclement, and finally, the gruesome proposal. Die or submit to Nahash your right eye. Then came the infectious fear that had spread through Bezer like a cancer. He'd wanted to fight. He'd tried to convince the elders and fathers of the village that if they fought, God would go before them. "Was this not the land God had promised their fathers?" He asked them. It was no use. He remembered the immovable faces of men he'd once respected as they sat listening to Shiza and the other "zealots."

They'd come for him at night. The Ammonites poured into his small home without so much as an alarm from the guards atop the wall. As he and the other holdouts were rounded up, it became clear that the Ammonites had not invaded the city by force; they'd been escorted in. Shiza didn't have to see their faces to know who'd betrayed him, those men who clung to their little fiefdoms. Shiza and those like him would be the first to lose their right eye, their dominant eye, and with it, the ability to accurately aim a bow, sling a rock, and many other skills required of a soldier. At least, that was the idea.

Snatched from their homes in the dead of night, Shiza and the others who'd wanted to fight were forced to watch as their families were violated and beaten. The rest of the city would go willingly, like sheep to the shearers. "Cowards," Shiza thought. "You deserved this, not me, not my family." Every inhabitant of Bezer would now serve the Ammonite King Nahash. "Fools!"

Now here he was, on his knees in the dirt, his arms firmly barred by Ammonites on either side of him, barely able to maintain consciousness from the tight and choking grip of the soldier behind. His hair was pulled rearward, lifting his forehead and brow. A hand stained with dark coagulated blood pressed against his face, prying the eye wider as the red-hot iron hovered briefly above. His eyes shifted to the right, where a team of Ammonite soldiers held his wife and daughters hostage just a few yards away. His teeth clenched. He could feel the heat of the iron before it touched his eye, simultaneously piercing, burning, and searing the tissue. The stench of his own burned flesh filled his nostrils as his chest heaved. He did not writhe or cry out, refusing to add to the agony his family had endured through the night and doubtlessly felt watching him now.

With marked efficiency, the Ammonites completed their task. Shiza gasped for air as the arm around his neck slackened. A foot placed squarely between his shoulders sent him face forward into the dirt. Unable to open his remaining eye, Shiza searched the ground for his son. He wanted to place a hand on him if he could not see him.

"Adina," Shiza called out.

"I'm here Father," Adina said. Shiza forced the left eye open. The look of terror on his son's face was far more painful than what he'd just endured. He reached and placed his hand on his son's as the men repeated the grisly procedure. Adina screamed in pain as his small hand clenched tightly around his father's thumb. The men released him, and he fell into his father's arms. He was barely five years old.

Shiza struggled to see with his left eye as he stood and scooped up his son. Adina held both hands tightly over the wound, wailing in agony. Shiza looked to the men who'd held his wife and daughters at the points of their swords. The men withdrew their weapons and shoved the girls towards him. Shiza's wife ran to his side, touching his face, and embracing her son's head. The girls clung to his waist. He wanted more than anything to be able to lift them all, to hold them, and take them away from this place, this so-called city of refuge, this "promised land."

They walked back to their home, passing neighbors who watched from within darkened doorways and windows. This was their example. This is what happens to those who resist.

They passed the home of a city official, one who oversaw the watchmen and gatekeepers. Evil and merciless thoughts ran through Shiza's mind as he considered how he might repay the man for his betrayal. They passed more homes, each inhabited by those he'd once called friends. There was not a face to be seen. They'd all been complicit, he thought. Hatred and contempt boiled within him. He wanted to leave this forsaken city.

"Not yet," Shiza told himself. The worst had come and Bezer was the safest place for his family, for now. Ammonite platoons scoured the land and Bezer was still encircled. Any attempt to leave would likely subject them to worse treatment than what they'd just endured. The rest of the consenting sheep would now receive similar treatment, though their families would remain unharmed.

When the time was right and under cover of darkness, they would leave. He would take them across the Jordan and warn the other tribes. Reuben and Gad had been caught unprepared. Shiza would make sure that the other tribes were not. Maybe Samuel or one of his sons would have the courage to stand against the Ammonites.

As they entered their home, Shiza laid his son on the table, as the youngest daughter fetched a pillow for his head. His eldest daughter went to work preparing bandages and a poultice of healing herbs. He walked to the hearth and leaned against the wall. His eye, or what used to be his eye was throbbing. His head pounded and the anguish of the day and previous night's events flooded over him. What could he do now for the family that he'd failed to protect? What use would he be now? How had he let this happen to them? His body shook as the flood of tears finally came. It made the wound burn all the more. His battered wife went to him and embraced him.

"I'm sorry," was all he could say.

She brought him over to the table and began working on his wound, cleaning the blood from his face and beard.

"You did not do this to us," she said. "You'd be no better than the ones that did if you had given in." She placed her hands on each side of his face and pulled his attention to her. "I am proud of you," she said.

The words both stung and lifted him. He bowed his head and sobbed openly now. How could she be proud of him, he thought.

"You trusted God to deliver us. I know you trust Him still. I know that God sees you. He sees us. He will have the final say. We cannot accept the good from Him and not accept the bad."

His own words were being used on him now. His wife was quoting what he'd used countless times with his children whenever things did not go their way. Words from his favorite story in the Holy Scriptures. The story of Job, the incorruptible man. Like Job, Shiza had been tested. His faith, though shaken, held strong.

"I don't deserve you," was all he could say.

Regaining his composure he stood and returned to his son's side. He sat next to the boy and ran a hand across the boy's hair. Shiza lifted Adina's head under his arm and put his forehead to his son's.

"They made a terrible mistake leaving us with two good eyes my son."

CORRUPTION

1095 BC, Beersheba, Simeon, Israel

And his sons walked not in his ways, but turned aside
after lucre, and took bribes, and perverted judgment.
I Samuel 8:3

A crowd gathered before the court at the gates of the outer wall surrounding Beersheba, a village in the southernmost reaches of Israelite territory. Abijah, the Levitical Priest and Judge, second son of Samuel the prophet, would be hearing cases that tribal judges either found too difficult to decide or for which there existed some perceived bias for one of the parties. Israelites traveled for hours, sometimes days, and waited to present their cases, seeking what little shade the walls and trees provided. Those fortunate enough to find shelter from the sun held their positions like statues. It was already a hot day in Israel, and the sun had barely risen. Young and old, they milled about, waiting for the judge to begin hearing their cases.

"Where is he?" They muttered to one another.

"Is it not custom to begin court at sunrise?" One litigant asked a court official.

"Abijah must come a very long way to be here," was the man's reply.

"I saw him in town last night," one man grumbled.

"Many of us have traveled farther," shouted another.

"What do you want me to do about it?" The official said loud enough to address the crowd, dismissing them with a wave of his hand.

It was near midday when a group of six well-adorned men trickled into the courtyard. One of them took a position on the steps and scanned the crowd till his eyes met those of an elderly couple on the opposite side of the courtyard. A proud smile formed on his neatly manicured face. The old woman looked away, disgusted, but the old man held a disdainful gaze, which was finally broken by the judge's sudden call to order. Everyone in the courtyard who was not already standing sprang to their feet.

Abijah had already taken his place on the elevated platform on the north side of the courtyard. "I'll hear one case at a time," he said. "Do not speak unless I address you first. I'll hear only one of you at a time. If your opponent is not here, I will not decide until he has also been heard unless you can prove through two other witnesses or his acknowledgment that he was informed of his need to be here today. Plaintiffs should be to my left, defendants to my right. If you are charged with a crime and do not wish to admit your guilt, your case will be tried by me and I will sentence you today!"

Abijah's tone suggested that guilt was a forgone conclusion. As his clerk began calling the list of criminal charges, the various municipals came forward and presented their cases.

Defendants who admitted their guilt were sentenced and punished swiftly. Their sentences were frequently only slightly less severe than their accusers requested.

The first trial lasted only minutes. A man was accused of having false weights and thus cheating his accuser of some trifling amount of silver. The accuser, a merchant of Beersheba, and a Beersheba city official testified against the defendant, a man of some small Simeonite village. Abijah asked questions of the accusers that were suggestive of the answers he sought, then cut the defendant short when he attempted to defend himself. The official was called to produce the confiscated weights. A hush fell over the crowd as the allegedly diverse weights were placed upon the scale with the court's. A silent moment passed before the faintest tilt could be observed in favor of the accused man's weights. Abijah found him guilty and sentenced him to forty lashes and a fine seven times that which the accuser claimed he would have been deprived. The man was laid on his back in front of the assembly with his hands and feet bound to a plank, then whipped with cords of braided leather.

There were no more trials requested by the accused after this occurrence, but it was still well past mid-day when the clerk began calling the civil cases.

The first plaintiff was a very old man, apparently of little or no status. He stepped forward as quickly as his tired legs would allow. A younger man who appeared to be his son or relative assisted him.

"Your Honor," he began, "I am Zachariah, son of Shimea, son of Jehud, of the tribe of Judah. I have a small matter to present to you today. I am not a rich man, I own very little. But what little I own, I care for diligently," Zachariah said as his voice wavered.

"What's that? Speak up! I can barely hear you," Abijah shouted irreverently.

"I have no children, only a wife to care for. I have no livestock except a female goat, which my wife and I use for milk. I raised this goat from birth. Never has it strayed from my small parcel lest I was there to tend it and watch over it. I kept it tied close to my home under a tree for shade so that if any predator might come I would be near to defend her. Having no children to care for, my wife and I merely wished to live out the remainder of our days in peace."

Abijah interrupted again, "Am I to hear your complaint today or just this goat's life story? Get to the point. Why are you here?"

"My apologies, your Honor, I am here because this man," he said, his hand shaking as he pointed to the defendant to his left, "took my goat. This man's children constantly molest my wife and me. Often have I caught them stealing from my garden and often have I traveled the distance to his home to address the issue. He has done nothing about it. Eight days ago, I arose on the Sabbath to check on the goat. I found that she had been untied. There were two sets of adolescent tracks along with hers leading away from the tree towards my neighbor's property. This man's property," he said, pointing to the defendant again.

"It being a great distance to any other neighbor who might be witness to this, my wife accompanied me as I followed the tracks onto my neighbor's property and to the ground where my doe had been slaughtered, still wet with her blood and entrails. When we approached my neighbor's home the delinquents were out in the yard. One of the youngsters looked at me and rubbed his belly and licked his lips." At this he paused and turned his attention to the defendant as he spoke. "I proceeded to the home and called for him. I informed him of everything that had happened. He called the youths to him and questioned them. Of course, they denied any involvement. I know what I saw and I know what they did." The old man continued, "he said I had falsely accused his sons of being liars and thieves. He threatened that if I should ever enter onto his property again, I would soon regret it."

"And what other evidence or testimony do you have to support your accusations," Abijah asked.

"Just that of my wife and this man," he said gesturing to the young man who'd accompanied him.

The young man stepped forward. "I am Jehoiada son of Ethan of Kabzeel of the tribe of Levi. Both of these men are my neighbors. The accused is, in fact, my cousin. I know his character and that of his children. I have also seen the doe that this man speaks of and knew it to be his and where he kept it. I know him to be an honest and trustworthy man as he has employed my children from time to time and always dealt with them fairly. I cannot speak the same of my relative here and would go further in saying that I will not allow my children to mingle with his."

At this, the defendant smirked.

"And you witnessed this man or his children take the she-goat?"

"No your honor, I did not witness the theft, but my children heard their cousins speak of tormenting this man. They are his nearest neighbors and when he says he and his wife followed the tracks to Jett's home, I believe him. I believe everything else…." Jehoiada was cut short by Abijah's interruption.

"I will hear no more of your bolstering the complainant's testimony. You either witnessed the theft or you didn't. You've stated that you did not." Abijah turned his attention back to Zachariah. "Is there any other witness you intend to put forward or do you stand alone in accusing this man?"

Jehoiada spoke again "You didn't let me finish! His sons confessed to the…" Again he was interrupted.

"One more outburst from you and I'll have you beaten," Abijah yelled. Two guards moved closer to Jehoiada, one of them drawing a small wooden club.

"Just that of my wife, who witnessed all of which I've already stated," said the old man.

"A woman!" Abijah shouted contemptuously. "You expect me to rule against this man based on the testimony of a woman? Even a layperson such as yourself should know better."

"What else would you have me do? What other option do I have? What.." Again the judge interrupted, speaking loudly to drown out Zachariah's appeals.

"I will not make your case for you, sir. Do you have any other witnesses?" Abijah asked, waiting briefly for Zachariah to speak.

Jehoiada spoke up, "Your Honor, I have studied the law, there is nothing which prohibits this man's…"

Again, Jehoiada's words were cut short, but this time by the flick of Abijah's wrist, which was instantly followed by the thud of a wooden club against Jehoiada's skull. One of the guards nearest him had struck him hard sending Jehoiada to his knees.

"I warned you," Abijah scolded.

Jehoiada glared at the man who'd just struck him. He glared brazenly back, confident in the fellow guards who'd now moved into place behind him.

Turning his attention back to Zachariah, Abijah asked again, "Do you have any other witnesses?"

Zachariah looked at his wife and to Jehoiada.

"No? Very well." Abijah slammed his gavel. "Case dismissed. Sir, you would do well to familiarize yourself with the law. It requires the testimony of two or three witnesses. One witness is not enough to convict any man." Looking to Jett, "You and your sons are free to go."

"You didn't let me finish!" Jehoiada shouted before he was struck across the temple with the club wielded by the guard.

Holding his aching head, Jehoiada looked menacingly at the guard who'd struck him. The man was now flanked by two others, one of which had his hand on the hilt of a small blade tucked into his belt.

"Thank you Judge," said Jett. "Your wisdom truly surpasses that of your father," he said as he and his sons turned to Zachariah with contemptuous smirks on their faces. Jett gave a proud tug on his garment, straightening his ornate robe, then turned and left.

Jehoiada turned back to the judge. He held a furious gaze, hoping to provoke the judge. Abijah ignored him and called the next case. Jehoiada listened one by one as each case was heard until late in the evening. His mind churned and boiled as he heard each unjust decision spill from Abijah's lips.

Abijah's uncontrolled outbursts and rants seemed directed at only the most lowly and defenseless parties. It appeared almost without fail that the accuser or accused with the most status or wealth would win his case. The most egregious was that of a man who claimed his daughter had been raped. The young man accused of the act had fled to Hebron where he could stay without concern for reprisal by the young girl's family. It was clear to Jehoiada that the accused man's family had been in prior discussion with the judge.

"Am I to understand that this young woman is completely blameless?" Abijah asked.

Her father looked back indignantly at the judge. "She was raped," he said. "She came home from gleaning in the fields scratched and bruised. What are you suggesting?" the man shouted.

By the time Abijah had heard the man's case, he'd all but accused the poor girl of being a prostitute. His ruling was no less egregious. The young man would pay a dowry to the father of the young girl and he would remain at Hebron for another year before being allowed to return.

The girl's father was irate, but he knew there was nothing more he could do. His daughter, who'd stood quietly at his side throughout the proceeding, sobbed. He gave up his verbal attack on the judge to console her and they shrank back into the crowd.

Jehoiada was sure that one accuser, a man with a long black and gray beard, had won his case solely on account of a beautiful young woman who'd accompanied him to the court. It was not clear if she were his daughter or his slave. With her face turned downward, she'd not made eye contact with a single person so far as he could tell. Abijah stared at her nearly the entire time the accused man argued his case. At one point, she'd raised her head enough to notice Abijah's lustful gaze, then quickly lowered her eyes again. From that point on, she could have been made of stone for she did not move a single muscle.

Finally, as the sun began to set, Abijah stood and addressed those who remained. "That will be all today. I will return in two months and hear the rest of your cases then. This court is adjourned." Abijah gave one more glance at the accuser with the beautiful young woman and turned to leave. The man took the girl by the arm and exited.

Jehoiada hurriedly tried to leave the court, but was stopped by one of the guards. "Only the judge may leave this way."

"What?" Jehoiada asked, surprised. "And how about that man?" He shouted and pointed in the direction of the long-bearded man.

"What man?" The guard asked indignantly, refusing to turn his head. Jehoiada turned to leave through the opposite side of the courtyard and hurriedly ran around the structure in an attempt to confirm his suspicions. As he rounded the corner, he saw the accuser with the long black and gray beard mounting a small donkey. Jehoiada looked around for the girl, only to realize that he and the bearded man were the only two souls on this side of the structure. He looked down the end of the street just in time to see the fleeing judge, mounted on a horse with a single passenger as he disappeared down an alley. Jehoiada looked back at the long-bearded accuser to be sure he wasn't mistaken. The man was departing, alone.

Jehoiada stood there outside the court square, head spinning and furious. Remembering the strike from the guard, he moved his hand to his head and rubbed the egg-sized lump that had risen there. He heard a motion to his left and turned to see a small group of men on camels emerge from an alley near the court. One of the men, exhausted and filthy, dropped from his camel and staggered towards the entrance. Leaning in, Jehoiada heard the man gasp.

"No, no! They've left. We've missed them," the man said frantically as the others dropped from their camels and ran to his side.

The cloaked man appeared to search around for anyone who could give him some direction or confirmation. Jehoiada continued watching the men until the cloaked man turned in his direction, appearing to notice Jehoiada for the first time. The man staggered towards Jehoiada with his arms outstretched followed by the other men who appeared less disheveled.

"Did I miss the judge? Is he near? Where can I find him?"

"You just missed him," Jehoiada replied. "As to where you can find him, I doubt he'll accept visitors."

"Where has he gone? Can you show me the way?" the man pleaded as he collapsed to his knees at Jehoiada's feet.

Moved by the man's plea, Jehoiada knelt down to lift him along with the others who'd accompanied him.

"Are you alright? I'm afraid I don't know where to find him, though I don't know how much good it would do if I did."

As he lifted the man, his marred face became visible for the first time.

"Good heavens! What happened to you?" Jehoiada asked. As the man struggled to find his voice, Jehoiada turned to the other men. He noticed nothing out of the ordinary about their appearances.

"Ammonites," the man finally gasped. As he began to speak, his voice strained, "My village! My family," he croaked. As his face twisted, Jehoiada couldn't tell if it was more from physical pain or mental anguish.

One of the men spoke up for him. "He staggered into our village days ago. His name is Isaac, a Gadite. He's from a village southeast of Jabesh Gilead. They were attacked by Ammonites. As you can see, he took a strike to the head. They must have mistook him for dead on account of the injury. When he awoke, his family had been murdered, his home and village in ashes."

The man shook and wept as he stammered, trying to communicate the events at his village. "My family," he cried but was unable to speak

any further. Frustrated by his inability to communicate, he finally collapsed to the ground.

"I don't think he's eaten in days. When he arrived at our village,
Middin of Judeah, he was exhausted and nearly dead from lack of water.
We gave him some wine and water and tried to feed him, but he insisted
on coming here and seeing Abijah. That was yesterday. We've traveled
without stopping. He wants Abijah to assemble a force to attack the
Ammonites before they can cause more harm," the man said.

Jehoiada studied the broken man on his knees in the dirt, staring up
at him with bloodshot eyes. He was sure he could see the man's skull
from the gaping head injury. Blood caked his face and neck.

"We need to see to that wound my friend," said Jehoiada.

"We tried," said the man of Judah. He wouldn't let us touch it. All he
wanted to do was get here, to see Abijah."

"I'm afraid I won't be of much help. I'm not from here either. We'd
better find someone who knows their way around," Jehoiada said, not
hopeful that they'd get any help from Abijah even if they could find
him. He was, however, eager to see what the corrupt judge might do.

As they proceeded in the direction he'd seen Abijah leave, Jehoiada
caught a passerby.

"Shalom," he said, "pardon, but we need to find the judge, where
might we find Abijah this time of day?"

The Simeonite laughed, "You don't!"

"I understand, but we really do have a matter of the utmost impor-
tance. We must find him immediately."

"Look, I'm not going to go out of my way and anger the judge for a
few out-of-towners," the man said as he turned to go.

"What's your price you jackal?" one of the men of Judah shouted.

The Simeonite stopped.

"10 shekels," he replied.

The men scoffed. "I'll pay you two," said one man.

The Simeonite turned to leave but was met by the disfigured face of
the Gadite.

"Where is he?" The Gadite shouted as he shook the now frightened man by the shoulders. The man gave a startled shriek and fell backward. The Gadite pressed him. "Where is he? TELL ME NOW!" he said raising his fist.

"Don't touch me! I'll tell you, I'll tell you!" The man shouted as he shielded himself, fearing his attacker was a leper.

"No," said Jehoiada. "You'll take us."

STIRRING

1095 BC, Kabzeel, Judah, Israel

Joanna watched her husband and children from the window of their home. The children played in the yard with a pair of baby goats as Jehoiada sat in the shade with his back against a solitary tree, apparently deep in thought. He'd been distracted ever since he'd returned from court in that matter with the neighbors. Jehoiada was known to be a contemplative man, it was one of the reasons she'd come to love him in their youth. People respected him and often looked to him to mediate their disputes. For as long as she'd known him, he'd studied the law and read the scriptures day and night. She was convinced, as were many others, that no one knew the law better. He was, after all, a Levite, the tribe chosen by God to serve as His priests to the nation.

Only days earlier his countenance had changed from the hopeful man she knew. For the past few days he'd barely spoken a word. She knew that court had not gone well for their neighbors, but she was surprised at how deeply her husband had been affected by it. As she walked out to speak with him, he appeared not to notice.

"What troubles my beloved so?" She asked as she sat down beside him.

"Just thinking," he said.

"That's obvious," she said with a smile. "Have you come to a conclusion, or do you intend to keep your troubles all to yourself?"

"The matter with Zachariah and Naomi was not the only injustice I observed." He paused. "I stayed and listened to all of the cases presented to Abijah that day." He said, shaking his head. "It was a complete disgrace," he cried. "How can God allow such injustice and corruption to reign among His people," he said, his voice cracking as he spoke. "I expected more of Samuel's sons, but they are no better than Hophni or Phineas. They are leading us to destruction." He paused and lowered his head. "How can we expect God's protection with such men ruling our people?"

"God has always protected the righteous," she said in reply. "When Hophni and Phineas met their fate, our people endured. And God did give us Samuel and Samson before that and Gideon before him, and Barak and Deborah before that. God will provide another leader."

"Samson. Warrior yes, righteous, no." He paused to think a moment. "At least he defended his people. That's more than we can say about Abijah and Joel." His elbows rested on his knees, Jehoiada pressed his face into his hands. "There's more," he said as he lifted his eyes to meet Joanna's. "I'm concerned for our children. Nahash is assembling a vast army to invade our lands." He let the words sink in. He had not wanted to disclose the matter of the Ammonites, but the rumors were becoming more and more eminent. He stood and pulled her close. She had to know in order to understand what he was about to do. Joanna stood motionless as Jehoiada recounted the story of the ill-fated Gadite man, how they'd been dismissed by Abijah, claiming the man to be a crazed lunatic.

"Samuel is too old to lead our people in combat. He's a man of God, not a general. His sons are corrupt beyond measure and they are certainly no warriors."

He could tell the magnitude of the situation was beginning to sink in.

"Joanna," he said, "we need a king."

She stood silently reading her husband's eyes. The idea had not been well received in the past. Those in positions of authority, local judges and priests, had always eschewed any talk of creating a centralized government capable of curtailing their small piece of the pie.

Seeing that she was hesitant in her response, Jehoiada explained.

"The law provides for a King. I found it in the scripture, in the fifth book of Moses. I'm convinced that the Priests and Judges don't want anyone to know about it. The law given to Moses states that once we come into possession of the land, we may choose to set a king over us, one whom the Lord God will choose. I'm convinced that if more people knew of this, they would support it."

Joanna sighed. "You won't be making any friends in high places."

"That may be the best proof that it's the right thing to do."

***

Jehoiada's campaign began the next morning. He set out to the surrounding homes of his tribesmen, telling each of them the things he'd seen and heard at the court in Beersheba and the story of the one-eyed Gadite. Many had already heard similar stories or experienced them firsthand. Some were far worse.

At each home, the latest intelligence of the Ammonites circulated. King Nahash's great army seemed to grow with every home and tribe he visited. With every elder, with every family, one question would eventually come, "What do you propose we do?"

Some, suspicious of his intent, suspected Jehoiada wanted to build an army of his own. Some were eager to fight. Others, struck with terror, were ready to bow down. Some suggested that they seek protection from other nations. "We could make a treaty with Egypt," they suggested.

"And who would negotiate this treaty?" Jehoiada would ask. "The same corrupt judges that exploit our poor and accept bribes to sate their own lustful desires. With what profit will we entice the Egyptians to risk their lives for ours? The Moabites already have a longstanding relationship with the Amalekites whose hate for us is nearly equal to that of the Ammonites."

The tide of Jehoiada's movement grew exponentially as other influential men joined in his efforts. In a short time, he would arrive at a town already engrossed in the discussion of how they would fend off the Ammonites, who would lead them, and in what way they should deal with Samuel's corrupt offspring. In each successive village and town the people would inevitably look to the elder or some revered leader of the area for the final decision. The conclusion of the elders was consistently the same. Israel would have a king. With the elder's blessing, so too went the clan and the tribe until nearly every Israelite was in agreement that a king was the answer to the problems they now faced.

The word spread that the people, represented by the elders of each tribe would come together to discuss the matter and present their case to the man of God at Ramah.

DEMAND

1095 BC, Ramah, Benjamin, Israel

And when you saw that Nahash the king of the Ammonites
came against you, you said to me, 'No, but a king shall
reign over us,' when the Lord your God was your king.
I Samuel 12:12

If there were a heart or center of the long, but narrow territory occupied by the children of Israel, it was Ramah. Conveniently located in the southern portion of Benjaminite territory just near the border with Judah, it was also home to the seer, Samuel. He was long past his prime and possessed an impatience that was typical of seers, though not as eccentric as most. The growing frustration with his sons, as well as the fear that had spread among his people, had not eluded him. Ramah itself was full of talk and rumors of the coming invaders. Here too, the fear had spread. Everywhere he passed in the village, there were hushed conversations and awkward exchanges. Even those he regularly interacted with, which were few, had begun to withdraw from him. Wherever he went, people scattered like rodents.

Finally, the day had come. Ramah had been bustling with visitors for days. Samuel knew he would not be called until all of the tribes were sufficiently represented and prepared to confront him. His young apprentice kept him informed of the latest news. Samuel was enjoying the morning breeze from atop his home when the young man approached to summon him.

"What is it Nathan?"

"The elders are ready to see you," shouted the young man.

"Then see me they shall."

Samuel descended from the rooftop and proceeded from his home down the hill to the town center where he knew they would be expecting him. The youth hurriedly walked alongside him, nearly running to keep up. Along the way, the streets were empty and silent. As they approached the amphitheater, a hush fell over the crowd. The young apprentice halted nearby as Samuel proceeded to the front where twelve of the wisest men in Israel sat before the assembly, each the most revered man of his tribe.

Samuel entered the open space in front of the twelve gray-haired men.

"You summoned me," Samuel said loudly.

The twelve men exchanged glances as if they had not decided who among them was supposed to speak.

"Yes," replied the elder of Judah finally.

"Well," Samuel said, "here I am."

For a moment, no one spoke, then the elder of the tribe of Simeon spoke up.

"As you must know by now, that your sons, much like your predecessor's, have not followed in your ways." The elder paused. "You have grown old, and your sons do not administer justice the way that you did."

The young apprentice couldn't help but see the irony in the man's statement. These elders looked ancient. Though Samuel was not a young man, his mere presence commanded respect. Unlike any of these men, he had the appearance of someone most men did not venture lightly to offend. Somehow, the seer still possessed greater strength and stamina than most men half his age.

The elder continued.

"Not only this, but surely you know that the Ammonites stand at our border, ready to destroy us. We need someone to lead our young warriors and to protect our people. We have come together here that you may appoint a king to rule our people as the other nations."

Samuel lowered his head and stroked his long beard. He began walking slowly from side to side in front of the assembly.

"You have spoken true of my sons. However, there are others capable of judging you. There are just, trained, and godly men who would take their places."

"We are resolute in our determination," the elder of Reuben responded. "Are your young protégés prepared to lead the fight against the Ammonites?" The elder asked.

Nathan began to speak up, but was cut off by the elder of Gad.

"Did you not train your sons in the ways of the Lord as well? Look at them!"

"But a king," Samuel replied, "a king would be different I suppose?"

Irritated by the prophet's mockery, the elder of Reuben shouted back "YES! We will have no more judges to be bribed and swayed. No more conflicting and inconsistent rulings with no one to enforce them. We will have a King! A king has no need of bribes. A king would answer only to God. A king would form and lead an army. A king would lead us in battle and defend us against our adversaries. We will have structure and order like the other nations. We will no longer settle for life as the nomads who fled Egypt only to be pillaged and abused by those who surround us in this 'Promised Land.'"

"FLED?" Samuel shouted the question. "Our people did not flee Egypt! We were led out by the one true God, the God of the covenant, the God of our forefathers. He who provided for our ancestors in the wilderness, the same ancestors who worshiped a golden image made from their own hands. Still, God forgave them. He is quick to forgive if you will turn away from this madness and trust Him. He is the same God who watches over you now and has consistently provided deliverance when our people had need of it."

"Then He is capable of doing the same with a king," shouted the Gadite. Many in the assembly nodded and voiced their agreement. Others continued, "Give us a king," they shouted.

Speaking over the crowd, Samuel shouted, "If it is structure and an army you want, the same could be achieved without a king."

"And yet we have neither!" responded an elder of Ephraim. "Do you not see that our destruction is at hand if we do not act now? If we do not move quickly and decisively?" The people trumpeted their support of the elders. The crowd's temper had reached a fever pitch.

Emboldened by the crowd's support, the elders refused to reign in the mob. Things were getting uncomfortable for the young apprentice, though it seemed Samuel hardly noticed. He strode back and forth slowly before the assembly, considering the matter. He'd been praying for guidance for months now regarding the Ammonite threat, for years concerning his sons.

"You fail to comprehend the gravity and consequences of your request. Nevertheless, I will consult with the Eternal One last on your behalf in this matter. I suggest you all do the same. You will have your answer tomorrow." With this, Samuel turned and proceeded back up the hill as the people slowly began to disperse. His apprentice sprinted to catch up.

What Samuel feared most had come to pass. He knew well of his sons' corruption, but he had not anticipated the full impact it would have and how they would turn the hearts of people. Despite his warnings, despite his prayer and fasting, his sons had become no better than Eli's. 'How had it come to this?' He thought back on how he had despised Hophni and Phineas, their desecration of the temple, how they'd lost the Arc to the Philistines, and how Israel had suffered during those many years of its absence.

Samuel was back home before he'd realized it. His mind still turning over the matter, he'd all but forgotten his young apprentice was even there, watching and waiting for direction. He could give none at the moment. In times like these, there was only one thing to do. He dreaded the long night that lay ahead of him, but knew that his broken heart would not allow sleep to come.

Samuel thought on the consequences of the people's request. To request a king was to reject God's rule over them. Moreover, he knew that it was due in large part to his own sons.

"Where did I go wrong?" Samuel thought aloud. He began to weep. He thought of his sons as infants and toddlers, how he'd watched them in his wife's arms. How precious they had been to him in their youth. He thought of how he had trained them. All those years at his side watching as he rendered judgment and led the people. All those years at his side as he prayed to the Lord. How could they not hear His voice as clearly as Samuel had? How could they not tremble at the thought of perverting judgment?

Nathan watched as Samuel proceeded onto the roof and followed him up. There they remained in prayerful contemplation as the sun set. All night, Samuel wept and prayed for his sons' repentance and his people's deliverance. Prostrate, Samuel poured out his heart. As the morning sun rose, Samuel knew the Lord's answer.

Nathan had been at his side the entire night. Though he'd dozed off several times, he'd awoken each time to find his master praying and earnestly tried to do the same. Finally, he sensed the prophet beginning to stir. Nathan straightened and watched as Samuel slowly rose to his feet.

"Has God answered your prayers?" Nathan asked.

ANSWER

1095 BC, Ramah, Benjamin, Israel

A s Samuel and Nathan proceeded down the hill, they could already hear the clamor of the people. There was even more than the day prior. A hush fell over the people as the prophet entered the amphitheater. Samuel walked to the center and looked at each of the elders already assembled before him.

"God will give you what it is that you desire, only you shall receive it with the full knowledge and understanding of the consequences of your request. Therefore, you shall not be ignorant when these things come to pass."

"Let it be so," cried one of the elders.

"These will be the ways of the king who will reign over you," Samuel said solemnly. "He will make your sons drive his chariots, be his horsemen, and go ahead of his chariots. Your king will select commanders over one-thousand and commanders over fifty. He will make some of you plow his fields and collect his harvest. Some of you will forge his shields and swords for battle and outfit his chariots. He will force your daughters to make perfumes, to cook, and to bake. He will seize the choicest of your fields, vineyards, and olive orchards to give to his courtiers, and a tenth of your grain and your vineyards to give to his court eunuchs and servants," Samuel said to the crowd gathered behind him."

"This king will take your slaves, male and female, and put the choicest of your donkeys and your young men to do his work. He will take a tenth of your flocks. You will become his slaves!" Samuel said with a wave of his hand over the whole assembly. "One day you will cry for mercy from the Eternal One from this king you have chosen for yourselves, but He will not hear you on that day!" Samuel shouted.

The elder of Ephraim looked to the elders of Reuben and Gad. They each nodded their assent.

"We have decided that we will have a king who will rule over us," said the Ephraimite. "So that we will be like all the other nations and will have someone to judge us and to lead us into battle."

"Very well," Samuel said, dropping his head and nodding, "very well." Raising his eyes, he examined the faces of the elders in front of him, then the great mass of people behind them. He felt the weight of his failure to lead his people. He feared what would come of his sons. Pushing these thoughts from his mind, he remembered the words God had spoken to him in the still of the morning. He closed his eyes momentarily, focusing on the words. A peace came over him.

"God has heard your pleas. He will give you a king. Go back to your cities until I call you together to anoint the king He has chosen."

Samuel turned and left the people to celebrate in his absence. Nathan lingered in the amphitheater and watched as the elders congratulated each other. They laughed and talked of whose son would be chosen among them. Nathan noticed for the first time, some of the men who'd accompanied the elders. It was clear that these were the eldest or most impressive of their sons. Some were dressed as though they were prepared to be anointed right then. Several looked disappointed. These were haughty men, accustomed to ease and comfort.

"Human peacocks," Nathan said to himself as he watched them strutting about vying for positions which were not yet theirs to give. Whoever the king would be, Nathan hoped he would not be chosen from among this lot. Turning, he realized Samuel was already a long way up the street. Nathan sprinted after him.

As they reached the prophet's home, he asked, "What happens next?"

"Rest for now, our work has just begun."

WAYWARD

1095 BC, Gibeah, Benjamin, Israel

There was not a man among the people of Israel more handsome than he. From his shoulders upward he was taller than any of the people.
I Samuel 9:2

East of Ramah, a sturdily built, middle-aged man watched proudly from the edge of his field as his eldest son drove a plow pulled by a team of oxen. He leaned against the wooden fence and remembered what it was like being young and strong. God had blessed him. While he didn't have many sons like some, this one was worth the five others he didn't have. The same could be said for his nephew, also at work in the field.

Kish admired his son's prowess as he watched the young man work. He was by far the largest and fittest man of anyone in their village, perhaps even their tribe. His long wavy black hair, pronounced jaw and eyebrows made him both attractive and intimidating. He was a near replica of Kish in his prime, albeit a larger version.

"Saul," Kish called out, waving him over. "Come here. I have more pressing business for you."

The young man lifted the plow from the dirt and steered the oxen over to his father with ease.

"Good morning Father."

Kish nodded.

"We have a problem. It looks like someone set the donkeys loose last night. There's no sign of them anywhere. I need you to take one of the young men and go look for them."

"I didn't hear anything unusual last night, but then again I was sleeping pretty hard after finishing the barley field yesterday. Another band of Philistine teenagers you think?"

"Don't know. All I know is they're gone along with whoever took them. We need to find them and quick. Looks like they went north towards the Shiloh. Your mother and Ahinoam are packing provisions now. Abner will help me here. We'll be fine till you get back."

"I'd best be off then," Saul said, turning over the reins to his father. "Don't work him too hard," he said with a smile.

Kish laughed. "I don't think that's possible anymore," he said as his nephew steered a team of oxen towards them on the opposite end of the lane. He too was an imposing presence. While of average height, his frame was thick and solid. Abner reminded Kish of the tales and drawings of travelers from the south. They told of black fur-covered creatures that inhabited the jungles and walked like men with long arms and brawny chests. They could have been describing Abner.

As Saul walked over to meet his cousin halfway, Abner stopped the oxen.

"You're making me look bad," Saul said.

"Ha!" Abner replied as he wiped his brow. He knew Saul was being generous. Not a man in all of Israel could match Saul at the plow. A man had once joked that Saul looked as if he could pull the plow all on his own, without the ox. The comment stuck with him.

"Did you hear anything last night?" Saul asked. "The donkeys are missing."

"No. What happened?"

"We don't know. Probably Philistines again. I have to go find them."

"Better you than me," Abner said. "Maybe I'll have the fun stuff done by the time you get back," Abner said sarcastically. "Happy hunting."

Saul made a beeline for the house. Jabir, his father's servant, met him in the yard.

"You get the word?" The servant asked as he strode up to Saul.

"Yes, we're leaving as soon as everything is ready. Do you have your things together?"

Turning to the servant as they reached the house, he realized the man had in his possession the only necessity he ever traveled with. A single buckskin hide rolled tightly around a leather strap which was draped over his shoulder.

"Got all I need right here."

"Alright then."

Grabbing their provisions and a cowhide leather pack, Saul kissed his wife.

"Please be careful," Ahinoam said as he turned to leave.

Saul nodded. "Nothing could keep me from returning to you my love. Pray we find them quickly," he shouted over his shoulder as they departed on foot.

ANOINTING

1095 BC, Benjamin, Israel

[T]he Lord told him, "Here is the man of whom I spoke
to you! He it is who shall restrain my people."
I Samuel 9:17

Northwest of Ramah, Saul and Jabir continued their long trek, circling back around into Benjamin after venturing deep into the mountains of Ephraim. It had been days since they'd seen the last of the tracks, which had become obscured over rocky ground speckled with pockets of dense vegetation.

"How much further do you reckon we should go?" The servant asked his master's son.

"Until we find them." Saul replied as they crested another hill. "We've been gone too long already, but to return without the very thing we set out for, well…"

"You don't think they will be concerned for us? You know, being gone this long without word?"

"But I guess you have a point. If we continue for much longer, father will stop worrying about the donkeys and become worried about us."

They gazed out across the valley to the city on the hillside opposite them.

"So that's Ramah?" Saul asked.

Jabir nodded.

"Ever been there?"

"A long time ago," Jabir replied.

The two men stood, watching the city for a moment when something occurred to the servant.

"Look now," he said excitedly. "There is in this city a man of God, and he is an honorable man," he sputtered. "All that he says surely comes to pass. So let us go there, perhaps he can show us the way that we should go."

Saul considered this. This must be the same man of God that had prayed with them at the battle of Ebenezer, he thought. Indeed, they'd encountered many on the road who were on their way to Ramah. Not long ago, a man from Judah had come to speak with his father Kish. He'd tried to persuade Kish that Israel needed a king. The man had informed them of a gathering at Ramah of the tribes to discuss the matter and petition God to anoint a king. It occurred to Saul that the people had chosen Ramah because of the seer. Kish, never one to involve himself in politics or social gatherings, had declined the offer. Their small family farm did not afford the luxuries of frequent or lengthy travel.

Jabir stepped off toward the city.

"But look," Saul said seizing the servant's arm. "If we go, what shall we bring the man? The bread in our vessels is gone, and there is no present to bring to the man of God." Setting his pack on the ground, Saul asked, "what do we have?"

"I have one-fourth of a shekel of silver. I'll give that to the man of God to tell us our way," said Jabir.

"Well done," Saul said with a smile. "Come on then; let's go."

The two men descended into the valley and up the hill to Ramah. As they went, they passed a group of young women heading down to the valley to draw water. Jabir, never one to pass up an opportunity to speak with a beautiful young woman, greeted them.

"Shalom! Do any of you know, is the seer here?"

"Yes, there he is, just ahead of you. Hurry now; for today he came to this city, because there is a sacrifice of the people today on the high place."

Another of the girls continued. "As soon as you come into the city, you will surely find him before he goes up to the high place to eat. For the people will not eat until he comes, because he must bless the sacrifice, afterward, those who are invited will eat."

"Now therefore, go up, for about this time you will find him," the first damsel concluded.

Saul and Jabir thanked them and quickened their pace up the hill. As they were entering through the city gates an old man was approaching them. The crowd in front of him seemed to part and watch as he walked. He had a white beard, was balding on the top of his head which was red and freckled by the sun. He had a strong, stout build and walked with purpose. The man's eyes were set on Saul.

As he approached, Saul glanced behind him to see if there were something else that the man was focused on. Seeing nothing, he turned to the man.

"Please tell me, where is the seer's house?" Saul asked, unnerved by the man.

"I am the seer," the old man answered. "Come, go up before me to the high place, for you shall eat with me today," he said, placing a hand on Saul's shoulder and extending the other up towards the hill. "And tomorrow I will let you go and will tell you all that is in your heart. But as for your donkeys that were lost three days ago, do not be anxious about them, for they have been found. And on whom is all the desire of Israel? Is it not on you and on all your father's house?"

Confused, Saul tried to process the seer's words as he returned the old man's stare. Behind the seer stood an entourage of bystanders all seemingly waiting for Saul to follow the prophet's instructions. Saul's face became flush. He looked to Jabir, who nodded towards the hill.

Saul, turned and proceeded up the hill as he'd been instructed, his mind swirling with the seer's words. Saul remembered why all the people had been congregating at Ramah. They said they wanted a king.

The seer walked just behind as they strode up the hill.

"Forgive me sir, what was it you said back there? I think you may have me confused with someone," Saul said as he stopped and turned toward the seer.

The seer gave a patient grin. "My son, there is no mistake."

"Am I, am I not a Benjaminite," Saul stammered, "of the smallest of the tribes of Israel, and my family the least of all the families of the tribe of Benjamin? Why then do you speak like this to me?"

"Come with me," Samuel responded, taking his arm and turning

Saul back up the hill. Together, the two proceeded to the large hall atop the highest point in the city. An attendant opened the doors as they approached. Saul and Jabir exchanged a curious look as they entered.

Samuel instructed them to sit in the place of honor, at the head of the table among the thirty or so other persons. Samuel sat to his right.

"Bring the portion which I gave you to set apart," Samuel instructed one of the priests.

So the man took up the thigh with its upper part and set it before Saul.

"See, what was kept is set before you. Eat because it was kept for you until the hour appointed that you might eat with the guests."

Saul sat, dumbfounded by this turn of events. Neither Saul or Jabir had ever taken part in such a feast. Samuel called the group's attention and began with a prayer. The prayer was brief but within it, Saul caught the words "we thank you for your anointed and for a righteous man to lead your people."

They each lifted their eyes as Samuel concluded the prayer. Saul looked at the others around the table. No one stirred. Every eye was upon him.

Jabir touched his arm under the table.

"I think they're waiting for you to start sire."

Saul fumbled for the knife and began cutting a piece from the large hunk of meat before him. The other attendants continued to stare. Jabir looked to the man next to him and gave an understanding nod. Finally as Saul raised a piece of meat to his mouth, the rest of the people began eating and conversing around the table.

Saul was at once received.

Jabir was too busy eating to be all that concerned about the strange circumstances for their current fortune. He was slowed momentarily when a man to his left struck up a conversation.

"What brings you to Ramah?" The man asked.

"My master's donkeys were lost. We've covered a lot of ground searching for them and ultimately ended up here. The seer invited us to join as we entered the city."

"Hmm, and so, you found what you were looking for?"

"The seer?" Jabir asked and he turned to look at Samuel across the table.

"Your donkeys," the man responded.

"Ah! He informed us that they have been found, but no, we found not a hide or hair of them in the past several days."

The man nodded then turned to his neighbor and engaged in an apparently more interesting conversation.

Saul felt out of place here among these people. He was a farmer. These were city folks, not to mention the fact that he and Jabir had been walking for three days and sleeping in the dirt. If he looked anything like Jabir, he was far from presentable at present, even by a farmer's standards. Saul was sure they stunk, though by this point he and Jabir had become immune to their own aroma.

Jabir didn't appear to care either way. He was gorging himself on the feast in front of him.

Still, Saul was enthralled by the conversations around him. He listened as the people voiced their troubles, concerns, and complaints – all of which were directed at the seer. The man took them in stride, answering them calmly and tactfully. Saul liked the man instantly. His words were few, but thoughtful and discerning. It was as if he only said that which was necessary to address the concern and in as few words as possible.

Each time, Samuel's attention turned back to Saul. "Tell me, how is your father?"

"He is very well, strong as an ox. Do you know my father?" Saul asked.

"Surely you know of his exploits at Aphek when the Ark was taken?"

"I know it was a terrible battle. I know many Israelites died that day, but he has never spoken much of the event" Saul replied.

"Yes," Samuel nodded, "though if we'd had more men like your father, things may have been different. He slew many Philistines that day. It was not for lack of courage or will to fight by men like your father that the Ark was taken. Men like your father can often steer the course of battle. The reason for our loss at Aphek was poor leadership. Eli's sons were foolish to bring the Ark into battle when their hearts were not right. You remember the second battle, the battle of Ebenezer was much different."

"Yes," said Saul, "the Lord went before us that day."

"Experience has shown me that these things are easily forgotten. You would do well to remember these things. God favors those who revere Him."

Saul smiled and nodded. "Now I know where my father must have gotten that saying. I've heard it my entire life."

"Apparently your father does not forget so easily."

"Not as easily as I would have liked as a boy," Saul replied.

Samuel laughed. "I imagine not."

When the meal was finished, Samuel called Saul and Jabir to accompany him to his home. In not so many words, the old man insisted that Saul and Jabir would be staying with him that evening. Saul agreed that they would stay the night and leave the following morning. When they arrived, Samuel instructed Jabir to make himself comfortable on the main floor, then led Saul up to the roof.

As the two men talked, Saul wondered when the man of God would finally explain himself. The old man would never initiate the conversation, but simply waited for Saul to speak. The old man answered his questions and then it would be over. When Saul could stand it no longer, finally he asked, "what did you mean about me and my father's house being the desire of all Israel?"

"Do you not know why the people of Israel came to me a short time ago?"

"A man came to our home. He said that the tribes were assembling here to petition the Lord for a king to rule and to judge our people."

The seer was silent.

"Is that what you mean?"

Still, he did not answer.

"I... I am a farmer. What do I know of the law? What do I know of leading men? My tribe is the smallest, my family is one of the poorest of my tribe, why would you choose me?"

The old man stood silently and leaned forward with his hands rested against the parapet. They both watched as the last rays of sunlight faded on the horizon.

"God often chooses the lesser things of this world. The weak he uses to defeat the strong. The foolish he uses to confound the wise, so that in this, His hand may be seen and the proud may be humbled."

Saul pondered the statement. No one had ever called him weak or foolish before, at least, not in a very long time and certainly not as an adult. Somehow he was strangely comforted by the statement, though only for a moment. The old prophet placed his hand upon Saul's shoulder.

"You have a long journey tomorrow. You should get some sleep. My apprentice has prepared a place for you there," pointing to the spot on the roof where two pallets and blankets lay neatly folded. "We'll talk more in morning," he said as he departed.

A short while later, Jabir joined Saul on the roof. "Good talk?"

Saul nodded solemnly.

"If you don't mind telling me, what's all this about?"

"I'm still trying to figure that out," Saul said as he laid down on one of the pallets. "Let's get some rest."

Saul was thankful for the exhaustion he now felt. Despite the thoughts swirling through his mind, sleep would come easily.

***

The next morning Samuel awoke before the dawn, as was his custom. He prayed for his people and the young man on the roof. There would be court in Ramah today and there was not much time to tarry. He called up to the men on the roof "time to get up, that I may send you on your way before I must leave."

Jabir grunted and sighed as he stood and stretched.

"They've got some strange manners here," he said. "Oh, been on the road? Come in and sit at the place of honor for dinner and a sacrifice. Weary from your travels, come stay at the Seer's Rooftop Inn, just hope you don't mind getting rushed out the door before the sun is fully up."

Saul chuckled at his sarcasm.

"What are you complaining about? Back home you'd have already yoked the oxen by now."

"Back home, yes. Guess I just expected a bit more leisurely morning after our royal treatment yesterday."

Royal treatment, Saul thought. If he only knew.

Moments later the men appeared outside where Samuel waited. The light of the rising sun was just beginning to turn the sky a pale blue.

"I will accompany you a short ways, but then I must return to the court," he said, then turned abruptly and began walking.

Saul hurried to catch up. Jabir, still irritated by the interruption of what would have been a decent night's rest, lumbered on behind them.

"Thank you for your hospitality," Saul said as they walked along. The old man simply nodded.

Shortly after they exited the gate of the city, Samuel stopped. "Tell the servant to go on ahead of us. You and I will stand here awhile, so that I may announce to you the word of God."

As Jabir caught up to them and Saul told him "go on ahead. I'll catch up."

"Thank you for your generosity," Jabir said with a smile.

Again, the old man simply nodded and Jabir was on his way.

Once he was out of hearing, Samuel turned and instructed Saul to kneel as he removed a flask of oil from his coat.

Saul complied, bringing him to just below eye level with the prophet. Samuel took the oil and poured it on Saul's head, then kissed the top of his head.

"What does this mean?" Saul asked.

"Is it not because the Lord has anointed you commander over His inheritance?" Samuel asked.

Saul's mouth opened, but no answer came.

"Look for these things to confirm what I have told you," Samuel began. "When you have departed from me today, you will find two men by Rachel's tomb in the territory of Benjamin at Zelzah and they will say to you, 'The donkeys which you went to look for have been found. And now your father has ceased caring about the donkeys and is worrying about you, saying, 'What shall I do about my son?' Then you shall go on forward from there and come to the oak of Tabor. There, three men going up to God at Bethel will meet you, one carrying three young goats, another carrying three loaves of bread, and another carrying a skin of wine. And they will greet you and give you two loaves of bread, which you shall receive from their hands. After that, you shall come to the hill of God where the Philistine garrison is. And it will happen, when you have come there to the city, that you will meet a group of prophets coming down from the high place with a stringed instrument, a tambourine, a flute, and a harp before them, and they will be prophesying."

The seer placed his hands on Saul's shoulders. "Then the Spirit of the Lord will come upon you, and you will prophesy with them and be turned into another man. And let it be, when these signs come to you," Samuel said as he held three fingers up with this right hand, "that you do as the occasion demands, for God is with you."

"You shall go down before me to Gilgal and surely I will come down to you to offer burnt offerings and make sacrifices of peace offerings. Seven days you shall wait, till I come to you and show you what you should do."

As Saul listened to all of these instructions, he felt as if he were dreaming, as though he were watching this happen to someone else. Surely this is not real, he thought to himself. When the man of God had finished his instructions, Saul remained speechless. It was too much to take in. Why me, Saul thought. He simply could not believe all that the prophet had just told him. Me? Prophesy? It sounded ridiculous.

"Go with God my son. I will be praying diligently for you and will see you in eight days." Then the prophet turned and walked back to the city. Saul stood and watched him leave. Looking to Jabir in the distance, he slung his pack and walked away from the city of Ramah.

FULFILLMENT

1095 BC, Benjamin, Israel

As Saul and Jabir continued on their journey back to Gibeah, Saul ruminated on the seer's words. Though it was a beautiful day and the morning air was cool and pleasant, he was anxious and troubled as they approached Rachel's tomb, the matriarch of his tribe. Looking ahead, he saw Jabir a good distance down the path speaking with two other travelers. Saul had been too preoccupied to notice until this point.

Could these be the men the seer spoke of? He wondered.

As he approached, one of the men addressed him.

"Is your name Saul by any chance?" Asked one of the men.

"Yes," Saul responded, "do I know you?"

"They weren't kidding about him were they?" Saul heard the man say to his traveling companion. "We're from Mizpah. I traveled here to visit Rachel's tomb with my son," the traveler explained. "We encountered a young man on the way named Abner. He was looking for you. The donkeys your father sent you to look for have been found and now he has ceased to care about the donkeys and is worrying about you, saying, 'What shall I do about my son?'"

Saul was speechless when the man spoke the words exactly as the prophet predicted. Was this a ruse, he wondered.

"Thank you," he finally said. "Yes. We've been looking far and wide with no success and well, now we know why."

"I suppose so. How far have you gone?" The traveler asked.

"We made a large circle around the hill country and eventually went to Ramah. We stayed there last night."

"Well, at least it's a good day for a walk," remarked the traveler. "Sounds like you'd better be on your way."

"Yes, thank you for letting us know," said Saul as he and Jabir bid the men safe travels and continued on the journey back to Gibeah.

"How about that?" Jabir exclaimed as they continued on. "I'd like to beat those donkeys for all this trouble," he said with a chuckle.

When Saul didn't respond, Jabir looked at him wryly.

"Say, if you don't mind me asking, what did that seer say to you that has you so worked up? You've been acting strange since last night. Stranger still today."

"Just ready to get home I guess," Saul deflected.

"I guess I can understand that," Jabir responded. He knew his master's son well enough to know he wouldn't get any more information. "I've enjoyed this little adventure though. Haven't you? Seeing new places. Living with just what's on our backs."

Saul appeared deep in thought again, not at all focusing or listening to what the servant had asked. Seeing he would get no response, Jabir walked on ahead, irritated.

A short while later, Saul could see the great oak tree ahead. Drawing closer, there appeared three men sitting on the ground conversing in the shade of the tree. As they approached, the party began to stir, repacking their various belongings on the ground. They each slung their parcels over their shoulders, but continued to converse as Saul and Jabir drew near. One of the men had three small goats in a sack hanging over his right shoulder, their white and brown heads protruding from an opening at the top.

"Look," Saul heard one of the others say to the man with the goats, "we've eaten our fill and don't need anymore bread. Why don't I take one or two of them from you to lighten the load?"

"Sure," responded the young man with the goats. "These little guys get heavy after a while."

Seeing Saul and Jabir approaching. The men turned and greeted them.

"Shalom!"

"Shalom!" Saul and Jabir responded.

"Where might you be headed?" Asked one of the two younger men.

"Home to Gibeah. We've been on a long and fruitless journey looking for my father's donkeys, which apparently have already been found," Saul replied. "We spent the night in Ramah."

"You've covered some ground today," the man exclaimed. "Look, we've just eaten and I need to use my sack to help lighten my brother's load here. Would you two like some bread?" The man asked, producing a loaf from the sack and holding it out to Jabir.

Almost as soon as the man had stretched out his hand, Jabir accepted it.

"Yes, thank you!" Jabir exclaimed instantly. It was now mid-afternoon and the two had been walking all day. They were both famished.

The man smiled and produced a second loaf from the sack and held it out to Saul.

"Certainly," Saul said as he accepted the bread with both hands. "Thank you very much for your generosity. This will sustain us for the rest of our journey today. What are your names?"

"My name is Elnaam. This is my younger brother, Joshua, and our father Korah."

"I am Jabir, servant of the house of Kish of Benjamin. This is my master's son, Saul."

"Pleased to meet you," said Korah as he produced a large bottle of wine and offered a drink as the two younger men redistributed the three small goats between themselves.

Saul took a small sip of wine, sufficient to wet his mouth, then handed the bottle to Jabir and thanked Korah.

Jabir took a long pull from the bottle.

"Ahhh! That is refreshing," he said, handing it back to the man. "Thank you," he repeated several times.

"I'm sorry we have nothing to offer you in return," said Saul, feeling sheepish.

The man smiled and shook his head.

"It is a blessing to be able to help a fellow Israelite in need," he replied. "Think nothing of it."

Content with the new distribution of weight, the two younger men donned their loads.

"Well, we'd best be on our way. Safe travels," said Elnaam.

The three men bade farewell and renewed their journey.

Jabir took a bite from the loaf of bread as they watched the men leave.

"Well that was nice of them," he said with a mouthful of bread before turning to leave.

As they continued their trek, Saul tore off small pieces of the bread and ate slowly, trying to make the bread last as long as possible. Once again, the seer's prophecy had come true. There was one more sign left to confirm what the seer had said. Could this be? Saul thought to himself. He lacked any training or formal education. The more he thought about it, the less adequate he felt to the task of leading an entire tribe, much less the whole of Israel. How many people would that be, he wondered. He'd never even seen much of Israel apart from Benjaminite territory. In fact, this recent journey was nearly the farthest he'd ever gone from home.

Soon they could see the hill Gibeath-elohim on the horizon. Saul's mind raced with anticipation.

"Would you mind if we stopped by the market? I have an old friend here I'd like to check in on," Jabir asked.

To the left, Saul could see the nearby Philistine garrison and ahead, a number of tents occupied by the usual mixture of merchants selling small animals, meat, fruits, vegetables, wineskins, and other necessities. The afternoon crowd of patrons bustled about, crowding the small bazaar.

"Sure," Saul replied. "You go on ahead. I'm just going to wait out here. Find me out here when you're finished in the bazaar."

Saul stopped as Jabir nodded then waded into the crowd. Not seeing anything out of the ordinary, Saul listened for a moment, remembering the seer's prophesy. Turning toward the hill used for sacrifices, he could just begin to hear the faint sound of music above the crowd. There was a small group descending the hill towards the city. His eyes opened wide.

As the procession approached, Saul could begin to make out the words of one of the men in the group. Others gathered around them listened intently to the speaker in addition to a far younger man as musicians played and sang all around them. Those at the center of the group were dressed in priestly garments. The two at the center looked towards the sky as they spoke and walked in Saul's direction. They appeared to be in pursuit of a fleeting vision in the clouds and paid him no attention at all as the crowd swallowed him.

"Hyenas from the east leave a path of destruction. A great wolf rises up and battles the hyenas in the east. He prevails over them and the hyenas flee. The wolf turns to the west where he is opposed by a great leopard..." the priest paused. "They battle but neither prevails. The wolf then turns his gaze to the south. He seizes a jackal... the jackal is wretched and emaciated. He shakes it and injures it severely, but not to death. The wolf is joined by others... his pack leaves a trail of destruction...."

The crowd around the prophets listened intently. Saul stood among them watching the two men describe the visions before them. Other priests scribbled furiously on their parchment as they tried to capture every detail of the prophecy.

As Saul listened, his heart beat faster and faster within his chest. Others around him worshiped and prayed as the prophets spoke, and the musicians continued playing. He was exhilarated by the energy of the worshipers, the music, and the prophets' words. All his life he'd heard of the prophets of old. Now, at thirty years old, he was witnessing it firsthand. Samuel's words still ringing in his ears, Saul was overcome with emotion. The crowd suddenly stopped moving around him as the prophets fell silent.

The two priests who'd been prophesying looked to each other and those around them. Suddenly a bright light pierced the clouds. Saul raised his hand to shield his face from the brilliant light as the sky began to change. Awestruck, he lowered his arm and gazed at the wondrous and terrifying sight. His knees felt weak. His scalp tingled and the hair of his neck stood as he watched the sky appear to split and peel open from the light. Saul dropped to his knees with his face to the sky.

"Look," said one of the prophets as he pointed to Saul. A hush fell over the crowd and musicians as they parted around him.

"The Spirit is upon him," the younger priest exclaimed.

His eyes to the heavens, Saul appeared not to see the crowd around him. The prophets gathered near Saul, holding their arms out so that no one would touch him or disrupt the vision.

Saul gazed to the sky in wonder.

"Tell us what you see!" one of them finally shouted.

Saul gasped in awe at the vision he alone could see in the heavens.

"I... I see the great wolf and his pack. He is battling with the leopard and its kind. The battle is fierce. I see a young lion appear alongside the great wolf to fight the leopard... he prevails against it! The wolves nurture the lion as their own. He lives and sleeps in the wolf's den as one of the pack. But the great wolf turns on the lion and pursues him... the lion flees to the wilderness. The great wolf searches for him... but does not find him."

The scribes continued hastily writing Saul's words as the two priests listened intently.

"The lion grows strong in the wilderness and many others come to join him, even some from the wolf's pack.... Now I see again the great wolf battling the leopards with his pack. The leopards prevail. The wolf is slain along with many others..." Saul fell silent as he tried to understand the events unfolding before him.

"What do you see?" one of the priests finally said. "Tell us what you see!"

"The lion takes up the battle with the leopard while those with him battle what remains of the pack... the lion prevails... the lion's pride grows and his offspring multiply. They grow powerful and strong... they are... they are fighting amongst themselves. One prevails over his brothers and grows in stature. He rises up against the lion who is now old.... There is a great battle within the pride, but the old lion prevails, aided by two other lions and a leopard. His offspring is slain in the battle and torn open by one of the lions... the old lion grows weary. One of his offspring, a young cub, grows and takes his place. His mane has the likeness of gold! He is radiant and his radiance shines on the rest of the pride...." Then, as suddenly as he began, Saul fell silent. His eyes, once fixed upon the sky, now searched the faces of those around him, darting about from side to side.

"Go on," one of the priests said. The crowd remained quiet and a moment passed in silence.

Saul blinked his eyes as he searched the sky and the faces of the men all around him.

"The vision has ended," said the older of the priests. "Help him up," he said motioning towards Saul.

Several of the priests took him by the arms and lifted him.

"Come! Come with us," the older priest insisted as he led them up the hill towards the altar and small priest's quarters there.

The others ushered Saul up the hill.

"Where are we going?" Saul asked.

"We have questions," the young priest said. "It's not every day these things happen you know."

That's quite the understatement, Saul thought to himself.

"My name is Ahimelech, and that is my father Ahitub," the young priest said, pointing up to the silver-haired priest as they followed behind.

"I'm Saul, son of Kish."

"Where have you come from?" The young man asked.

"I'm from Gibeah."

"Ah! So, not far. You're a Benjaminite, correct? What were you doing when you came upon us today?"

"We just came from..." Saul paused. "We were looking for my father's donkeys which had been lost."

"Did you find them?"

"We were informed that they had been found, so we were on our way home," Saul replied.

"Oh, is there someone with you?" the priest asked. Concerned, he stopped and looked down the hill. "I will go get them."

"Ah, yes, but he's on an errand," Saul quickly replied.

"Very well," the priest replied and started back up the hill.

"Look, I have been gone for several days looking for these donkeys," Saul said. "What questions do you have for me? I... I really must be getting back."

The priests alongside him exchanged curious glances, then turned back to Saul.

"You act as if this is some common occurrence," one of the priests stated. "Do you prophesy often?"

"It is important that we get all of the details," Ahimelech added. "We must accurately record and preserve what you saw and heard," he explained. "This... can take awhile."

They entered the small outpost, just slightly below the crest of the hill. Ahitub showed Saul to a spot for him to sit while the scribes and other priests took positions around him. There were several short writing tables for the scribes who began setting up parchment and ink immediately.

"This is Saul, son of Kish, a Benjaminite," Ahimelech said introducing their guest.

"I am Ahitub, chief priest of the school at Nob. These men are my students. The scribes need to accurately record everything concerning the visions we saw today. Please be sure to speak clearly and accurately to make things a bit easier for them," Ahitub instructed. "Now, as I recall...."

The priest began a recitation of the earlier events of the day in minute detail. The procedures for the sacrifices, the words and events as they'd unfolded after, when the vision had come upon him, how it had passed to Ahimelech and then to Saul.

As the minutes turned to an hour, Saul's patience grew thin.

"Look," he said finally as he stood. "I'm sorry to interrupt, but I really must be going."

Ahitub jumped to his feet.

"My boy, this is a very important matter, a very important matter indeed! Do you understand that you may never have an experience like this again? I bid you, do not take it lightly," the priest warned.

"I can return later and answer all of your questions another time," Saul replied then turned to leave.

The priests exchanged bewildered looks as Saul fled the small structure.

Ahimelech ran after him.

"Wait!" Ahimelech shouted as hurried to catch up.

Saul had left in such a hurry he hadn't noticed the small column of Philistines returning from patrol and nearly waded into their formation. Ahimelech stopped him.

They both stood motionless watching the soldiers pass before them.

"They've been camped here for over a month," Ahimelech remarked. "About forty-five of them."

Their leader walked alongside the squad as they passed near Saul. Noticing the two Israelites staring at them, the commander called his men to a halt.

"Column left," he shouted in Greek.

Each of the Philistine soldiers pivoted left to face Saul and Ahimelech.

The commander lifted his leather ephod, exposing himself to the Israelites and began to relieve himself.

Saul boiled with anger at the provocation. He felt a rush of furious energy welling up inside him.

"Filthy uncircumcised!" Ahimelech said, loud enough for the Philistine to hear. "One day, God will send someone to remove them from our lands."

Without hesitation, Saul had started toward the Philistine, but was seized by the young priest.

"What? Wha-what are you doing?" The priest asked in a low voice. "They will kill you," he exclaimed as he took hold of Saul.

Indignant, Saul glared at the Philistine commander, who stood defiantly waiting to meet Saul's challenge. Saul pulled his arm free from the priest. Samuel's words echoed in his mind, "Do as the occasion demands, for God is with you." His hands curled into fists. He started again towards the Philistines when another hand took hold of him.

Enraged, Saul spun to address the priest when he was met by Jabir.

"There you are! I've been looking all over for you," Jabir exclaimed. "What's come over you? It looked like you were about to go smashing into that gaggle of Philistines over there."

Saul looked past the servant to see a group of familiar spectators nearby.

"Everyone was talking about you back at the market," Jabir explained, "what is going on?"

Saul looked back to the Philistines.

The commander smirked, then turned and ordered the column to resume their march. The tension of the moment had passed, but somehow Saul felt an opportunity was slipping through his fingers.

"You feeling alright?" Jabir asked.

"Fine," Saul responded curtly.

"Come on," Jabir said starting towards Gibeah. "Let's get on back home," Jabir insisted.

"Wait," Ahimelech said following after them. "Your presence is needed here... what could possibly be more important than this?"

"Look," Saul responded. "He's right, we have been gone long enough. I am an only son. I am needed at my father's house, you can come find me there."

"I thought for a moment that you were about to take on those Philistines back there and now, you're in a rush to get home and catch up on your chores? You are a strange man Saul, son of Kish."

"I... I don't know what came over me back there. It wasn't what you think," Saul said as he quickened his pace. "We really must be getting back."

Several familiar faces passed as they walked along the city's perimeter. They seemed to lower their voices as they approached, eyeing Saul suspiciously.

"Is Saul now one of the prophets?" he heard one young woman ask another.

Looking over his shoulder, he recognized two cousins of Ahinoam.

"What has come over him?" he heard her companion ask.

Saul's face became flush with embarrassment. The tenacious priest still walked abreast of them, quite unsure what to make of the large man's strange behavior.

"Stop following us!" Saul finally said sternly.

It was clear that nothing the priest could say or do would persuade the man to stay or turn back. Ahimelech finally stopped his pursuit and watched the two strangers depart.

Returning alone to the small sanctuary as the sun began to set, the young priest tried to reconcile the events that had just played out before him. He recounted the events to his father and the others in attendance.

None could make sense of it.

"Tomorrow we will report these things to Samuel at Ramah," Ahitub finally concluded. "Perhaps he will know what to make of these things."

RELUCTANT

1095 BC, Gibeah, Benjamin, Israel

Saul sat in silence, reflecting on all that had occurred. The day was breaking and he knew he should be getting the oxen ready for the work that lay ahead, but he'd been up for hours and was already exhausted. A moment had not passed since his conversation with Samuel that he did not think on the old seer's words. Why did I entertain that old man's crazy rambling? Saul thought to himself. Merely days ago, he'd been happy and content to work the fields, to drive the oxen, to be the son of Kish. The old man's words had changed everything.

If I'm supposed to be the king, why did he tell me in private? Saul thought. "What am I supposed to do now?" he prayed aloud. Part of him wanted to believe that it had all been a dream, just an elaborate concoction of his own mind. Surely this cannot be. Surely, I am not fit to be a king. Who am I to lead God's people? The questions swirled in Saul's mind.

The prophet had instructed him to go to Gilgal and wait there. But there was so much to be done at home.

What had the prophet meant when he said I would be turned into another man? What had he meant when he said to do as the occasion demands? Saul thought back on that moment when he'd prophesied.

"What does it all mean?" he cried aloud.

He could not leave without some valid reason or explanation for his father. He couldn't be expected to just leave his family, not with so much work left undone. The fields would not plow themselves and he couldn't very well leave his father, Ner, and Abner to do all the work themselves. Saul thought of ways to explain the whole ordeal to his father. He considered excuses to sneak away to Gilgal by himself. There was simply no question about it. The work could not be completed without him.

He remembered the faces of those who had seen him prophesying. Their surprise. Their doubt. They couldn't believe he'd prophesied, even when they'd witnessed it with their own eyes. Just imagine what they would think if he told them he'd been chosen as the first king of Israel. Who am I among the great and intelligent men of Israel? Saul thought again.

Saul remembered the way he'd felt when he'd seen the vision, then the strength that had surged through his body when the Philistines had taunted and mocked him. A wave of shame came over him.

"Fool," he confessed aloud and pressed his face into his open palms. And so Saul continued at Gibeah as the date of his appointed meeting with Samuel came and went.

WAITING

1095 BC, Gibeah, Benjamin, Israel

It had been weeks since his visit to Ramah, depression still loomed over Saul like an overcast sky. After a particularly grueling day in the fields, he was physically exhausted, though his mind still churned. Saul stood at the window of his home peering out at the fields. There was still so much work to be done. The sun's last light could be seen on the distant horizon. There were so many things he needed to do, so much requiring his attention, and yet, his mind was completely absorbed by the words the seer had spoken to him.

Saul wished he'd never met the man, he wished he'd never heard the words Samuel had spoken. At least he'd been happy before. Saul had always been content as a farmer. It was his station, it was what he'd always known and what he was good at. Why did this seer have to meddle in his life? Had any of it really happened? It all felt like some sort of vivid dream, some temporary break from reality. 'Why couldn't he have called me to be a warrior? To use my physical strength. Why a king?'

Saul heard several soft steps approaching from behind. Ahinoam stood behind him and wrapped her arms around him.

"What is it that has consumed your mind since you returned from Ramah? Won't you please tell me?" she asked.

"It's nothing," he said as he turned and embraced her.

She knew he was lying. She leaned into him, enjoying the warmth of his vast embrace. "You are different. You have hardly spoken since you came back. What happened?"

"It's really nothing. It's just that," he paused, choosing his words carefully. "I wonder if there is something more I should be doing... if God might have some greater plan for my life."

"What do you mean?"

Saul considered how to answer the question. What if Samuel's words never came to pass? His own wife would think him a fool, he thought. "I don't know," he answered. "Forget I asked."

"I have no doubt that God has a special plan for you," she said as she looked up to see his face. "I've always felt that way about you. I've never met someone so kind and humble, yet there is not a man in all of Israel more capable than you. You are smart, strong, handsome. Other men might be prideful or arrogant, but that's not like you," she said as she leaned her head against his chest. "I believe you will do great things."

Her words seemed to lift him momentarily. "I want to believe that," he said. "But who am I?"

He was, without doubt, the largest man in the tribe of Benjamin. But, it had not always been so. He was in his early twenties and just a few years earlier, he'd been a much smaller man. His personality had been formed and solidified well before his size was able to contribute substantially to any aspect of it. He'd grown so quickly in the past few years that he felt oddly unfamiliar with the large space he'd come to occupy. At times, it made him feel clumsy and awkward.

As a child, he'd always had to deal with the boys from neighboring families. The ones who smirked at him over the dirty condition of his clothing or poor quality of his family's land. Most of it came from the ones just slightly better off than himself. It felt as though he were the only single child in all of Israel. He'd hated this in his youth. It seemed every challenger always had a brother, someone to turn the tide if things weren't going their way. Until Abner came along, he'd been the only one to assist his father and uncle in the fields. Suddenly though, as his stature had increased, the comments and challenges from other young men became less and less frequent.

Ahinoam was not used to hearing her husband speak this way. She wanted to encourage him.

"We are still very young," she said. "Who knows what lies ahead?"

Saul did not want to push the matter further. Ahinoam did not understand. How could she? He'd not spoken a word of anything Samuel had said to him. He was the only one who knew and even he doubted whether it had actually happened at all.

"Perhaps you're right," Saul said as he kissed her.

***

It was almost noon the following day when Saul observed the runner approaching from the southwest. Not recognizing the man, Saul led his team of oxen over to the hitching post at the end of the field and began walking toward the man to meet him. Ner had seen the man approaching from an adjacent field and was already ahead of him. Saul watched as Ner intercepted the man and the two began conversing. As he grew nearer, Ner motioned for him to quicken his pace.

"This is my nephew Saul," he said to the man.

The man, who Saul observed now to be quite small, looked excitedly at Saul. "Land of Goshen! He's as big as the Nephilim! Look at those hands! Were you steering that plow or pulling it?"

A moment of awkward silence passed as neither Saul or Ner laughed or responded to the comment.

"He's come to tell us and spread the word that the prophet Samuel has called the people together again. This time at Mizpah. Everyone is gathering there in five days to hear who God has chosen to be the King of Israel," said Ner.

"That's right. We're going to have a king! Can you believe it? Hundreds of years and now our generation will get to be there when Israel has his first king. I wonder what tribe he'll come from, and what he'll look like! I hope he gives those uncircumcised heathens the thrashing they deserve!" The young man said excitedly. "Samuel has asked that everyone you can spare be in attendance."

"Samuel is calling all of the tribes to be there?" Saul asked.

"Everyone," the messenger exclaimed.

Saul considered this. The city would be wall to wall and overflowing with people five days from now.

Perceiving there were no more questions for him, the messenger finally spoke up again. "Well, that's it, I best be on my way before this one gets hungry," he said jokingly as he pointed to Saul, "I've got a lot of ground to cover."

"I pray God speed your journey. Can we give you anything before you leave?" Ner asked.

"Nope, best I travel light. I appreciate it, but I've got everything I need right here," he said patting the bladder and small leather bag slung over his shoulder. "I would appreciate it if you pointed me in the right direction. I've just come from your neighbor, Simon's. I'm spreading the word around Benjamin, then headed east to Judah and down to Simeon. Where might I find the next homestead?"

"Tuvya lives just about eight stadion that way," Ner said, pointing east. "Once you crest the second hill, you'll see their home. Just follow that path there over the hill and you can't miss it. We'll spread the word around here."

"Thank you for that. Maybe I'll see you in Mizpah," the messenger said and trotted away.

As the man departed, Saul could feel the blood leave his face. He felt nauseated.

"How about that? The people asked for a king and now they'll have one," Ner said, shaking his head. "Cursed fools," he said before turning and heading back to the oxen.

CHOSEN

1095 BC, Mizpah, Northern Benjamin, Israel

Now Samuel called the people together to the Lord at Mizpah.
I Samuel 10:17

S aul had never seen so many people in one place before. The sight was overwhelming. Mizpah was packed with Israelites and they weren't even inside the city yet. Many had gotten there early after the messengers started spreading the word. Every inn at Mizpah had been full for days. Saul wondered at how they would even get to see or hear Samuel with this multitude in attendance.

There were so many Israelites crowded near the gate, Saul couldn't tell if anyone was going in or coming out. The anxiety that had come over him after the messenger's visit just five days ago was excruciating. His stomach felt twisted to the point that he'd barely eaten anything since. As he, his father, Ner, and Abner approached the crowd, Saul doubled over and vomited.

The three men turned to look at him, surprised.

"Are you alright son?" Kish asked.

Spitting the remaining filth from his mouth, Saul raised his head and nodded. "Must be the smell," he replied.

They all nodded. "I doubt that Mizpah's sewer system was prepared for anything like this." Ner said.

"Cities always stink," Kish responded. "I can't understand why anyone would choose to live so close together."

Ner and Abner agreed.

Saul straightened and followed behind. As they approached the crowd, they could begin to hear an official near the gate.

"Leave all your belongings over there please!" The man shouted above the crowd. "There isn't room enough inside the city for everyone's baggage and there is nowhere left with any room to accommodate travelers. Please, everyone, leave anything you don't absolutely need in the tents over there." The man was pointing to several tents that had been erected for the purpose of securing visitor's belongings. There were officials from Mizpah taking an inventory of travelers' things and handing out receipts.

The heat was making Saul's nausea even more unbearable.

"Why don't you all hand me your things? I'm going to go and sit in the shade for a while," he said. "You all go on ahead."

Observing his distress, the three passed him their bags.

"We'll come find you at the tents later," Kish said.

Saul nodded. Kish, Ner, and Abner turned and walked to the city gate where the mass of people trickled into the city.

Saul walked over to the nearest tent and approached the official.

"Shalom! Name?" The official asked.

"Saul, son of Kish, son of Abiel, tribe of Benjamin."

The official took inventory of the baggage and their distinguishing characteristics, then wrote "Saul, Kish, Benjamin" next to it.

"Got it. Just find a spot back there and make sure to remember where you leave it," the official said, looking up from his parchment. "Are you all right? You don't look so well."

"Must be the heat. Would it be alright if I went inside the tent to get out of the sun for a while," Saul asked.

"Yeah, you know what? Why don't you go back there and get off your feet for a bit. If anything comes up missing, I know who to blame," the official said with a smile.

"Thank you," Saul said and stepped inside. Surely Samuel would choose someone else when he realized that Saul was not among those inside the city. He looked down at his shaking hands. His whole body seemed to quake and tremble. "You're no king," he told himself.

***

Several hours had passed since Kish, Ner, and Abner entered the city. It was extremely crowded and despite the excitement, everyone was starting to grumble.

If there were any benefit to visiting the city, it would have been for food and drink. Crowded as it was however, it was nearly impossible to gain entry into any of the local establishments. Even then, they promised only shade, as most businesses had long since been depleted of their wine or food.

"I think Saul was smarter to stay outside," Abner said.

Ner and Kish laughed. Suddenly the noise and commotion of the crowd began to still and quiet like a wave coming from the court.

"Samuel is speaking," someone said, before being hushed by those around him.

Kish and Ner could hear a faint voice in the distance, then another, then another, each voice getting louder as the speaker grew closer. There were men positioned atop the houses echoing the Seer's words.

"Listen to what the Eternal One, the God of Israel, has to say to you," the closest man shouted.

Again, they could hear another message, faint at first, then louder and louder until the announcer closest to them shouted at the top of his lungs.

"I brought Israel up from Egypt and rescued you from Egyptian bondage, and then I delivered you from all of the nations that sought to burden you," the man shouted, then paused again and listened for the next statement. "Today, though, you have rejected the true God who has saved you from every disaster and distress." Another pause. "And you have asked for a king to rule over you." Silence again.

Abner looked at his father. "That's what you said," he whispered.

"The Lord has granted your request." The next message was not a direct statement from the seer, but an explanation of what the crowd nearest him could not see. "The elders of the tribes are now drawing lots." Again there was silence.

"The king will be of the tribe of Benjamin!" The man shouted.

There was a loud commotion among the crowd. Many grumbled angrily and turned to leave.

"Benjamin for heaven's sake," one man shouted and fumed as he made he way toward the gate followed by several grown sons. "The smallest tribe in all of Israel!"

"All Benjaminite clan representatives should move to the front of the assembly" the announcer shouted over the grumbling masses. "If you are a Benjaminite clan elder or representative, go that way," he said as he pointed to the court.

"Should we go?" Abner asked.

"No need unless our clan is called. I don't want to have to wade back through this on our way out. The closer we stay to the gate, the better," said Kish.

About an hour later a hush came over the crowd again before the next announcement. "The Matrite clan has been chosen!"

Ner's eyebrows raised.

"Aphiah was an only son, was he not?" Kish asked.

Ner nodded in agreement.

"Should we move closer now?" Abner asked.

"I reckon so," said Kish.

"Saul is missing all the excitement," Abner said.

"Lucky him," Ner replied as they squeezed past throngs of men, many more now headed in the opposite direction towards the gate.

Every head turned and watched as the three men passed, moving towards the court.

"They're trying to figure out which of us will be their new king," Kish said.

Some of those nearest them laughed. Others scowled as they passed.

As they entered the court, Kish and Ner were greeted by cousins, uncles, and the last remaining great-uncle.

"Welcome to the winner's circle," the old man said straining to speak above the commotion. He waved a small river rock between his thumb and forefinger – no doubt, the winning lot he'd drawn.

"Where is Saul?"

"He wasn't feeling well and decided to stay outside the gates," Kish responded.

The old fellow nodded and turned to Samuel.

"That's everyone," he said.

Samuel's apprentice reviewed the names of the sub-clans with the elder, checking each off of the list written on parchment, then held out the bag of small round stones. Samuel announced the number for each of the sons of Becorath as the elder drew the small round stones from the satchel. An official recorded the number next to each family name.

"Zeror has been chosen of the children of Becorath!" Samuel announced to the crowded court.

Kish and Ner's uncles stepped forward to draw lots according to their birth order. Kish stepped in line as the eldest of the two brothers to represent their father, Abiel, the youngest of the children of Zeror. They each stepped forward and drew a stone from the satchel then showed it to Samuel. Finally, Kish reached in and drew his stone.

"Thirty," Samuel announced, reading the number inscribed on the rock. The highest number thus drawn.

Ner and Abner's eyes widened. Now it was down to the four of them.

"The sons of Abiel!" Samuel announced to the murmuring crowd.

Ner joined Saul to draw lots without exchanging a word. This was getting serious. As the eldest, Kish reached in and drew out a rock inscribed with the number twenty-four. Ner followed and drew a number two from its contents.

Samuel looked to Kish. "You have but one son, the man Saul, is that correct?"

Surprised, Kish responded, "Yes."

"And where is the man?" Asked Samuel.

"He's outside the gate tending our things," Kish responded.

"We have city officials performing that service."

Kish leaned closer to the old seer. "He wasn't feeling well," Kish said in a hushed voice.

"I see. Very well, draw a stone for yourself first and a second stone for your son."

Kish nodded. He reached inside the bag and drew a stone. He looked at the number engraved into it.

"Five."

Kish reached into the bag a second time and drew another from within, his heart pounding in his chest. He opened his fist and examined the small stone in the palm of his hand.

"Six."

Unmoved, Samuel leaned forward with his hands rested on his knees.

"Perhaps we should have someone find the young man," he said to Kish. Turning to one of the officials, he said, "Call for the man, Saul, son of Kish, to be brought forward."

The man shouted the message, "Saul, son of Kish, come forth!"

The announcement was echoed through the crowd. Moments passed. The official next to Samuel gave an inquisitive look to the man on the roof nearest to him. The man looked down the street then back and shrugged. "Perhaps he has not arrived yet," the man shouted. Samuel looked to Kish, whose flushed face betrayed his embarrassment.

Samuel could see this was not getting off to a good start.

"Let us inquire of the Lord where the young man might be found," Samuel said. He moved from his seated position to his knees, then lifted his eyes to the sky with his palms upwards. Quietly, he inquired of Saul's location and requested the Eternal to give courage to His chosen king. When he'd finished praying, he stayed there kneeling in humble deference to the Lord. A few moments later he straightened and stood.

The old prophet turned to his young apprentice and leaned close to one ear.

"Why don't you go check the baggage tents near the southern gate," he said just loud enough for the boy to hear.

Nathan nodded and disappeared into the crowd.

Samuel turned to Kish. "Not to worry."

***

Nathan squeezed through the crowded street. One of the announcers on the rooftop saw him struggling to get through.

"Make way!" he shouted and pointed at the boy. "You there! Make way for the boy!"

Suddenly Nathan could see a path open up before him. He ran through the crowd and finally emerged from the city gate. He ran to the nearest tent and looked inside.

"What's going on Nathan?" Asked the official standing guard.

"I'm looking for our new king. Is Saul, son of Kish, here?"

"What?"

"The man chosen by lots. I'm looking for him."

"Saul, you say?" The office scanned his list. "I don't see one by that name." The man turned to the other officials standing watch over their own tents. He shouted to them. "Any of you seen a "Saul, son of Kish?"

The official at the end of the row of tents motioned for the boy to come over.

Nathan ran over and walked into the tent with the official. They walked around a table loaded with baggage and found the man knelt with his face to the ground. He appeared to be praying. Sensing their presence, he looked up at them and straightened.

"Have courage," the boy said. "The Lord your God is with you. He has chosen you as King. Samuel requests that you come with me."

The official knelt and bowed his head, "God be with you."

Nathan looked down at the man, then back up at Saul. Was this to be a new custom? Bowing to men? Nathan thought to himself.

"They're waiting for you," he said jovially, then turned and headed out of the tent. He stopped at the entrance and waited for Saul.

Saul followed the boy to the gate and through the crowded street as the onlookers watched them pass by. Silence spread like a wave through the crowd as it opened up before them. As they walked down the dusty street, some bowed their heads in deference to their chosen king, others just stared.

"How can this man save us?" One man shouted.

"Coward!" Shouted another man. "What king hides himself among the baggage?"

Others in the crowd hushed them.

Saul could be seen approaching well before he'd reached the court. Though he'd heard it said many times, Saul realized for the first time that he truly was the largest man in all of Israel. As Saul emerged from the crowd onto the platform, his father embraced him, then kissed his hand.

"My king." Kish said.

Abner and Ner repeated the gesture.

Samuel stood to address the crowd.

"Do you see the man whom the Eternal One has chosen?" Samuel shouted. "No one else among the people can compare to him!"

Once again, someone shouted above the crowd, "how can he save us?"

There, in the midst of the crowded court, Jehoiada shouted above all the other voices.

"LONG LIVE THE KING!"

He pumped his fist into the air as he shouted again.

"LONG LIVE THE KING!"

Abner was the first to join him.

"LONG LIVE THE KING! LONG LIVE THE KING!"

Kish, Ner, and others from their clan joined in, followed by others in the court until the chant spread through the city until the place shook from the chorus.

Samuel quieted the crowd with the aid of the announcers positioned on the rooftops.

"Now hear this," Samuel said. "As your king, this man has certain rights. He is now your governor and judge. You shall pay him a king's wages which is to be taxed from each family. He alone may appoint judges and delegate this responsibility among the people. And, should he deem necessary, he may recruit or conscript an army as he sees fit." Samuel continued addressing the people, explaining what the Eternal expected of them regarding their king. He then turned and addressed Saul in front of the people.

"With these rights and privileges comes a great burden for to whom much is given, much is expected. You shall be their commander and shall lead the Lord's people in battle." Turning back to the people, Samuel said, "as king, he shall be in need of protection and assistance. Whoever will accompany him and see to his protection should commit themselves now."

Several men came forward from the crowd and stood before Saul and Samuel.

"May the Lord protect you and bless you in this," Samuel said to the men. "As for everyone else, God has given you the king as you asked, now go, return to your homes and pray for your king, for there is much that will be required of him."

At this, the crowds began to disperse. Many of the people came forward to get a closer look at this impressive figure that would be their commander and leader. Some presented gifts, others simply offered their prayers and blessings.

The men who'd stepped forward at Samuel's invitation presented themselves and pledged their service to Saul. Many of them were powerful men, men known for their deeds in past battles and actions against Israel's enemies.

Ner leaned over to Abner, "that's Tzuriel," he said quietly pointing to one of the men who'd come forward.

Abner instantly recognized the name. Tzuriel, one of the volunteers that now stood before Saul, was a man well known for his courage and exploits. It was reported that he'd led a group of men to ambush an Ammonite patrol after it pillaged a Reubenite village, taking several women and children captive. As the patrol egressed back to Ammonite territory, they crossed the Jabbok River. Just prior to reaching the northern bank, a barrage of arrows took out most of the Ammonite warriors from concealed positions in the woodline. Several of the survivors fled back across to the southern bank but were met in the water by Tzuriel and his men. The entire patrol was exterminated.

Kish, Ner, and Abner observed the whole procession in quiet amusement.

Saul had never seen so much gold and silver. He was given beautiful horses, mules, oxen, and fine garments. A beautiful purple mantle had been placed upon him by a wealthy Asherite from the northern coast of Israel. A golden ring with a large ruby was placed on his finger by a Simeonite merchant.

Slowly, the remaining crowd began to dissipate. The last of the people passed by and presented their gifts to Saul and blessed him. Saul's new devotees had already loaded the gifts onto wagons, which were also gifts from one of Mizpah's prosperous citizens.

As the last of the people came and went, Saul turned to Samuel.

"Return to your home," Samuel instructed. "The opportunity to lead your people will present itself soon enough. Take no mind of those who have complained today. The same who reject you as their king rejected the Eternal God of Heaven."

So Saul, Abner, Kish, and Ner returned to Gibeah, accompanied by thirty men who'd pledged themselves to his protection and service. Several of them had wives and female family members or servants who followed along. As they headed south, Saul wondered how he would manage such a large group once they finally arrived home.

Then there was the matter of paying them and caring for their needs. Taxes would need to be collected. Men would need to be selected to collect the taxes. How much should the taxes be? What would be reasonable for a new kingship? All these things and many more swirled through his mind.

CASUALTIES

1095 BC, Near the Wadi Jabesh, Gad, Israel (modern-day Wadi Yabis, Jordan)

Hammurabi stared blankly at the ground as he wiped the blood and grime from his hands.

"I'm going to go relieve myself," he said to the sergeant standing nearest to him.

The young Ammonite had seen more than he'd bargained for today. The nauseating smell of seared flesh and blood lingered in his nostrils. Trails of smoke streaked the air and made him cough as he passed through the street, seeking a place to conceal himself from the men of his squad. His eyes burned from the constant haze that draped the villages they'd ravaged. He'd seen the men from his unit commit unspeakable acts. Men, women and children, young and old, boys and girls, no one was safe from the ravages of the Ammonite army. He'd been invited to join in. Much to his surprise and dismay, his own father and acting commander had encouraged the behavior.

Hammurabi had a knot in his stomach. He felt anxious, like a child with a terrible secret about to be found out and punished severely. This was a far cry from the valiant battles that had played out in his head. These people looked helpless. There was nothing exciting or honorable about conquering and maiming an already defeated people. They were nothing like the stories he'd heard about the sons of Jacob. Only moments earlier, he'd held men and boys as their right eyes were gouged out. Young boys' eyes were burned while helpless fathers, mothers, and siblings watched. Even toddlers and infants. The fresh memory of an especially young boy made his stomach turn again until the nausea was overwhelming. He ducked inside a dwelling and vomited just inside the threshold.

When his abdomen stopped convulsing long enough to straighten, he looked up to find the terrified occupants of the home huddled in a corner. A wrinkled old woman watched him indifferently along with a distraught and red-eyed middle-aged woman clutching her young daughter. The girl's face was buried in her mother's bosom. Hammurabi straightened himself and wiped the vomit from his lips and beard, then returned to the street. His squad was nearby rounding up the last of the men and boys from the village.

They didn't even have real weapons. There had hardly been a sword among them. How were these the same people that had conquered and oppressed his ancestors, he thought. How could these be the same people he'd been taught to hate and fear his entire life?

His thoughts were interrupted by the sound of a familiar shout.

"Hammurabi!"

It was his father. He spit the remaining taste of vomit from his mouth, then using the bladder tied about his waist, rinsed his mouth and face before running in the direction in which he'd heard his name being called. The other squad leaders were already present, along with Shihon.

Shihon, a Hittite and his father's most trusted servant, had been Hammurabi's constant companion since he'd begun training to become a soldier and long before that even. There was no one Ibrahim trusted more with his son's life. Truth be told, there was no one Hammurabi trusted more either.

Shihon, who despite his age was still as strong as an ox, was also cunning and adroit. Though he was merely a servant, Shihon enjoyed the respect of their family and any who knew him. He'd looked after Hammurabi as a boy, trained him to ride, and later to fight.

"You all will take your men and scout a route for our movement to Jabesh Gilead. Once our work is finished here, Nahash has ordered that we take the city."

Ibrahim could see that Hammurabi was surprised.

"This is a great honor, my son," Ibrahim said. "Nahash wants to ensure that not a single Hebrew man this side of the Jordan retains both eyes. Jabesh is the last remaining stronghold east of the Jordan and many have fled there for safety. While I do not expect you to encounter any resistance, you are not to engage. You are only scouting the route and best crossing point for our infiltration. We will be right on your heels, so you must make haste and avoid detection. I want you two," Ibrahim said pointing to Hammurabi and Salim, one of the other squad leaders, "to find the best crossing for the horses. You will find the best place for us to position the cordon on the southwest side of the city."

"Nahash wants to know the lay of the land around the city, their defenses, gates, walls, the best approach, and activity coming into and out of the city. He wants to know if they are reinforcing or evacuating," Ibrahim instructed. "Hammurabi, you and your men will stay behind and keep your eyes on the city until we link up with you. It is important that you not be seen. You will assist in moving the cordon into place around the city. Salim, you will report back to me before sunrise. Shashek, you and one of your teams will stay back with me. Your other teams will go with Hammurabi and Salim."

Ibrahim turned back to Hammurabi and Salim. "There will be other reconnaissance sections south and east of the city. You are to approach west of the city and keep west until you find a sufficient position of observation from the north. The second division will be closing the cordon from northeast of the city in one to two days. Do you have any questions?"

This was what Hammurabi wanted most to hear. A real mission, and he would be on his own with his men overnight, in enemy territory, ahead of the army. He tried to conceal his excitement.

"No sir."

"May Milcom protect you and give you strength," Ibrahim said. He looked over his son briefly once more and nodded his approval.

***

The two reconnaissance sections moved north abreast of one another, far enough to conceal their numbers, but close enough to provide aid should one group get into trouble. They crossed a landscape of rolling hills, spattered with scrubs and groves of olive trees. The land itself reminded Hammurabi of the surface of a melon or dried fig. Its wavy hills separated by deep draws, all leading to the Jordan River or Wadi Jabesh. As they drew closer to the large wadi, the vegetation grew thicker, making it easier to conceal their movements. So far they had not encountered any Israelites and had only seen a few abandoned homes. The Israelites that normally dwelt in the sparse countryside had clearly fled to walled cities seeking protection.

Hammurabi and his men were the first to reach the river. The men stayed hidden among the vegetation as they waited for Salim's squad. Hammurabi saw one of Salim's men approach the river from about one hundred cubits downstream. He signaled for Salim to meet him then moved back into the vegetation and started walking upstream.

Salim was a far older and more experienced soldier and leader. Hammurabi knew that the only reason he was in charge of this mission was because his father was the one calling the shots. Still, he would prove his worth and show himself capable of the task.

Hammurabi had nearly covered the entire distance between the two squads when he came upon Salim.

"I think we've got a good crossing point downstream. The river is shallow there and thin. We haven't run into Israelites and we haven't observed any activity on the far side. It's pretty thick down there. I think it's safe to cross now. From the looks of it, if the army stays west of that bend, they shouldn't have any problems getting across," Hammurabi said as he pointed upstream. "What do you think?"

"Whatever you say," said Salim. "You want us to follow you?"

His contempt was not lost on Hammurabi.

"After we get out of the thick stuff on the other side let's stay within sight of each other and find a good observation position northwest of the city."

"You're the boss," was Salim's only reply. Then he turned and disappeared into the thick vegetation.

Hammurabi watched him go before turning his back to the man. He did not like the way this was shaping up. No matter, he thought. He was confident that he would earn Salim's respect in battle. He proceeded back along the river until he reached his men.

"Alright, everyone got plenty of water?"

They all nodded.

Hammurabi pointed to his archers. "You two, take up positions on each side of us and cover us as we cross. Once we get to the other side, you'll be the last ones to come over." He pointed to two others. "You each watch their backs."

The two archers exchanged looks of contempt as the rest of their squad crossed the small intermittent stream. Given the lack of resistance encountered during the entirety of their campaign thus far, such by-the-book maneuvers seemed entirely superfluous. It was, in their minds, proof of their leader's inexperience.

They crossed the brook without incident and began their trek through the dense foliage on the north side of the wadi. Jabesh would be close now. The undulating terrain and dense vegetation concealed its high southern walls on the side closest to the wadi. If Hammurabi had planned it right, they would emerge southwest of the city.

Though his map was crude, he had a profound understanding of the lay of the land. Growing up wealthy and with horses, he'd seen far more of the Jordan River Valley than many of his fellow Ammonites. He and his father had visited Jabesh before and the knowledge served him well on this occasion.

If the Israelites were preparing for a fight, reinforcements would come from the west, across the Jordan, where the vast majority of their fellow Israelites dwelt. The main forces of the Ammonite army would approach from the east, but his father's men and their division would proceed along the route they'd just taken and set a cordon on the western and southern sides of the city before the main body arrived with heavy infantry. The city would be surrounded before its citizens had an opportunity to escape.

Before long, they had left the dense vegetation of the wadi and could see the walls of Jabesh peaking over the crest above them. They were now moving on the western side of whatever hills, draws, ridge lines, and vegetation they could use to conceal themselves from the city's watchmen.

Well before nightfall, they'd reached their objective: an outcropping of rocks at the top of a tall hill northwest of the city. He had a perfect vantage point of the northern third of the western wall and almost the entire northern wall. He could position one team to watch the upper portions of the western wall and serve to guide the rest of their division into position. It was perfect. His father would be very proud. Hammurabi congratulated his men for their pace.

"We are the tip of the spear," he reminded them. His men were a mixture in age and background. Most of them grew up as farmers or shepherds, but some had come from artisan families. Over half of them had served more than five years with the army and had even seen combat. All of them were far less privileged than Hammurabi, and he knew it. He'd pushed them hard at every opportunity, hoping to overcome any thoughts that he might be weak or soft.

Hammurabi divided the men into pairs to keep watch and observe the city's activity in shifts throughout the night. Some Israelites could be seen pouring out of the city loaded down with their most precious belongings. Still, if the Israelites knew how soon the Ammonite army would be upon them, there would be a mass exodus far greater than anything Hammurabi was seeing now. As they watched, they could see a steady flow of civilians entering the city, families from areas outside of the walls. Poor souls, he thought. You've gone out of the pan and into the fire.

All that was left to do was link up with Salim and his squad, go over the lay of the land and position their teams at various points along the route to observe until they could link up with their sister division. They hadn't seen Salim or any of his men since leaving the river. He began to wonder what could be holding them up.

"I last saw them just before that small farm we passed," the rear guard reported.

Leaving his senior team leader in charge, Hammurabi collected Shihon to go in search of their missing section.

Shihon slowly rose from the spot he'd carved out as his resting place for the night, slung his shield and bladder, then picked up his spear.

Another man moved into the space. "Have fun," he said as he crawled into the now vacant stop which Shihon had already smoothed and cleared of sharp rocks.

Hunched low behind the rocks, he crept slowly behind Hammurabi down the path they'd ascended only a short while earlier. Once they were low enough for the hill to conceal their movements, Shihon stood up straight and stretched his aching back.

"You all right old man?" Hammurabi asked.

"Fine." Shihon replied in his Hittite accent. "Just don't get us into more trouble than I can outrun."

"Let's move to the other side of that crest and see if we can get an eye on Salim or his men. I don't see how he could have gotten any further off course than that. If we're going to find them we have to do it fast."

Shihon nodded and they began moving quickly across the depression between the hills that possibly concealed the other section. The sun was nearly on the horizon as they crested the ridge. They could make out a small farm at the far side of an open field.

"You don't think they got held up over there do you?" Hammurabi asked.

"I wouldn't put it past Salim to help himself to whatever spoils he might get his hands on before the rest of the army gets here."

They moved quickly towards the small mud brick home on the far side of the parcel. There was smoke coming from the vent of the oven and they could see movement within as figures passed by the the dim light inside the home. Finally, as they reached the last concealment offered by the terrain or vegetation, they could hear the sounds of human voices within.

"Does that sound like Lashak to you?" Hammurabi asked. Lashak was one of Salim's team leaders and a veteran Ammonite.

"It's an Ammonite is all I can tell," Shihon replied.

"What the hell!" Hammurabi muttered in a hushed voice. "Father said to avoid any contact." There was nothing else to do but get a closer look. "I'm going to see what's going on. You stay here. If I run into trouble you can get the others."

"I don't like this," said Shihon grabbing his arm. "Let me go."

"Don't worry. I've got it," Hammurabi said, unslinging his shield and grasping it in his left arm. Before Shihon could raise any further objection, he quietly dashed across the open yard to the closest corner of the house. Creeping around to the next corner, he vanished from Shihon's sight.

As Hammurabi neared the door of the home, he heard the challenge of an Ammonite from one of the darkened windows of the home. He froze instantly and replied with the password, knowing he likely had a cocked arrow aimed for his heart. He could hear Salim's voice along with several of his men. They were laughing. Hammurabi paused to listen at the door.

"Come on in Hammurabi," he could hear Salim say from within.

Hammurabi pushed the door open and could see Salim standing in front of the fireplace. Several of his men were seated around the room. On the ground near Salim were two female Israelites with gaunt faces and torn clothing. A beautiful young girl whose face was streaked with tears was held by a middle-aged woman whose face was buried in the young girl's hair. Hammurabi's eyes moved over the room to the body of a middle-aged man on the floor near where he stood. His garments were stained red with blood in the middle of his belly.

"The best thing about scouting is that you get to enjoy the unspoiled fruits of war," Salim said. "Have your pick my friend," he said, waving his hand over the Israelite prisoners. "We were just finishing up, but I'm sure we can spare a few minutes for the son of our Captain. The girl's younger brother is currently detained, but will be available shortly if that interests you. We don't judge," he said as he lifted his hands. Salim lifted a jar of wine from the mantle and poured himself a cup before topping off one of his team members.

Hammurabi's heart pounded in his chest. What have I walked into? Hammurabi thought to himself.

Salim's men sat silently waiting for his reply.

"We don't have time for this! Ibrahim said not to engage. We need to position the men and send word back to him now," Hammurabi said sternly.

Salim nodded then looked around the room.

"Hammurabi," Salim said, shaking his head. "Hammurabi," he repeated, slowly drawing out the name. "I know this is your first time and all, but if you really want to develop a taste for war, you have to try it first."

One of Salim's men emerged from a room to his right leading a young boy by the neck. The child's head hung low so that Hammurabi could not see his face. The soldier shoved the naked boy towards his sister and mother, who quickly embraced him and tried to cover him with some of her own torn garments.

Hammurabi's blood was boiling now. He could no longer restrain his anger.

"You are disobeying a direct order from the Captain! Get your men together, we have a mission to complete," Hammurabi commanded.

"Very well," Salim said as he dropped his head. "Chophi," he said, then nodded towards Hammurabi.

Before Hammurabi could react, one of Salim's men, seized him from behind, trapping his arms to his side. The others quickly sprang to their feet and wrestled the spear from his hands. Moments later, Hammurabi was pinned face down to the floor. He struggled and fought with every ounce of energy until his arms and legs were sapped of strength. They bound his legs and feet together with his hands tied tightly behind his back while Salim watched calmly from the fireplace sipping his cup of wine.

Salim walked over and crouched next to Hammurabi.

"It was a mistake to challenge me Hammurabi. You had your chance to be one of us. Now," Salim sighed, "well now, you will be like one of them," he said nodding towards the Israelites. Salim stood and addressed one of his team leaders. "Chophi, go and link up with Hammurabi's men, tell them we spotted an Israelite patrol that slowed us down. We had to split up and I sent you ahead to link up with them. Take their report and meet back up with me at the rally point by the large cypress tree."

"What about him?" Chophi asked, nodding towards Hammurabi.

"You didn't see him," Salim replied. Chophi smiled and turned to leave.

Salim turned to Hashem, one of the other team leaders.

"I'm going to go position the over-watches. You and your men finish up here and clean things up. No blood. No bodies. The well is over there," he said pointing outside of the dwelling. "Be quick about it. I'll need you to link back up with me before I can head back to the main body."

Salim crouched next to Hammurabi's face.

"So long Hammurabi," he said, patting Hammurabi's upturned cheek. Salim turned back to Hashem as he stood. "Ah! I almost forgot. Chophi saw that Hittite slave with him earlier. He's out there somewhere. No doubt he'll try to make a move once we leave, keep him alive," he said pointing to Hammurabi, "until you have the Hittite. The old man will not leave as long as he knows his master is still alive. Make sure he meets the same fate as the rest of these. Don't leave a mess! Ibrahim's orders, remember?"

Hashem nodded stoically. Salim departed, leaving Hammurabi and the Israelites alone with Hashem and his team.

Hammurabi knew there must be two more outside. Shihon would have to get past them and soon if there were any chance of his survival. Hammurabi's mind raced as he tried to think of ways to free himself. The ropes that bound him would not budge. His hands and feet throbbed from the tight cords around them. The more he struggled, the more excruciating the pain. His legs seized and cramped, pulling rearward on his arms and shoulders. All hope began to fade from his mind. He could hear the Israelite woman sobbing and muttering something in Hebrew. It occurred to him that she must be praying.

"Baalis, you heard him, make it quick," the Hashem instructed.

Baalis, one of the soldiers who'd tied Hammurabi, walked over and seized the young girl by the arm and yanked her to her feet. She clung to her mother who tried to pull her back to the ground when Baalis struck the woman hard across her face. She fell to the ground with a cry of anguish as her son clung to her torso. Baalis disappeared into the room with the young girl as she sobbed and pleaded for her mother. Hashem lifted his spear then walked over to the fireplace and sat against the wall opposite Hammurabi.

The only sounds now were the sobs of the Israelite woman and a muffled commotion in the adjacent room. Suddenly an abrupt cry was heard from outside of the dwelling followed by an indistinct rustling. The team leader rose to his feet and went to the door, then disappeared.

Hammurabi watched him go. He quickly scanned the room, then turned to the woman.

"Hey. Hey woman. Untie me!" Hammurabi pleaded frantically, hoping not to alert the soldier in the next room.

She did not move from her position, clinging tightly to her son, rocking back and forth.

"Hey," Hammurabi said louder, wiggling as much as he could to try and catch her attention. "Untie me," he pleaded again. When the woman looked up, her eyes met Hammurabi's. She quickly looked around the room. Seeing they were alone, she scrambled over to him. Frantically, she struggled to untie him.

"My spear," he said, twitching his head towards the weapon propped against the mantle. She looked and saw the weapon then sprang to her feet and seized it. Returning, she began frantically cutting at the ropes as Hammurabi pulled at the cords with all his strength. He could hear commotion in the room behind him. Finally, the ropes around his hands snapped and his legs straightened. Hammurabi rolled over to his back and sat up in time to see the Baalis emerging from the room.

Baalis quickly ran towards them as the woman jumped to her feet and met him, clawing at his face and eyes. Hammurabi grabbed his spear and severed the ropes around his feet. Baalis struck the woman hard sending her sprawling to the floor just as Hammurabi rose and thrusted the spear into his ribs. Baalis let out a gurgled cry as Hammurabi yanked the spear rearward. Bright frothy red blood bubbled from his wound as he sank to the ground. Hammurabi thrust the spear again, driving Baalis onto his back on the hard dirt floor. Hammurabi pulled the spear free and ran to the doorway. The fading sunlight revealed another life and death battle.

Shihon was struggling with Hashem in the open yard. The lifeless body of another Ammonite soldier lay on the ground behind them.

Hammurabi sprinted towards them with his spear, but before he could reach the fray, Shihon was struck in the teeth with the shaft of Hashem's spear. The Hittite stumbled rearward as Hashem cocked for a killing thrust of his spear. Mid-run, Hammurabi desperately hurled his own spear at Hashem. It flew through the air and pierced Hashem's back just as his spear jutted forward barely missing Shihon's ribcage and slicing the flesh on his right side and arm. Hammurabi ran to Shihon as blood poured from the Hittite's side.

"Look out!" Shihon shouted.

Hammurabi spun and saw another soldier running towards them, his spear raised. Suddenly, the attacker was struck by the Israelite woman as she slammed into him with the full weight of her battered body, sending them both tumbling to the ground.

Hammurabi seized Hashem's spear and started towards them. The Ammonite recovered quickly and grabbed the spear from the ground as the woman rose and came at him again. With one hand, he thrust the spearhead deep into the woman's torso. She screamed as he pushed her back with his left hand and pulled the spear from her falling body, but Hammurabi had closed the distance. Hammurabi thrust his spear into the Ammonite's sternum, driving it deep through his back and all the way to the ground. Hammurabi shouted wildly as he placed his foot on the man's chest and ripped the spear from the his body, then plunged it again into the man's writhing torso. Hammurabi's arms and lungs burned from exhaustion as he finally collapsed to the ground.

Surprised by movement to his left, Hammurabi spun around to see the Israelite children as they ran to their mother's body on the ground behind him.

"Eema! Eema!" he heard them crying.

The girl lifted her mother's head as she tried to speak.

Instinctively, Hammurabi scooped her up and began to carry her into the home. Shihon walked slowly behind them, holding his side tightly with both hands. Blood ran down his injured side and down his right leg.

Hammurabi laid the woman down near the fire and pressed his hand to her wound. He knew it was no use, her injury was fatal.

Shihon pressed his back against the wall next to the hearth and sunk to the floor.

The woman looked at Hammurabi and placed her hand atop his own. She began speaking to him in Hebrew, her voice faint, but urgent.

"I'm sorry... I, I'm so sorry," he said turning to the children. They paid him no attention and buried their faces into her arms. Hammurabi looked to Shihon.

The old man's face was twisted in a painful but attentive stare. His eyes were on the woman and appeared not to hear Hammurabi.

Her eyes shifted to her daughter as she lifted the girl's face. She spoke something in faint Hebrew and the girl acknowledged, nodding her head and slowly turned to look up at Hammurabi. She turned back to her mother and nodded her head.

The woman touched the young boy's head and he lifted his eyes to meet hers. She caressed his soft black hair as she spoke to him.

The boy shook his head vehemently.

"No, no. Eema! Eema, no!"

She was growing weaker by the moment. Mustering her strength, she interrupted him. "Bani," she said as loud as she could.

The boy fell silent and listened as she spoke to him slow and deliberately. Finally, he nodded as well, turning to look at Hammurabi as the girl had done.

"Towda," the dying woman said to Hammurabi.

He shook his head. "Thank you," he replied in his native tongue. He felt so foolish. He'd come here to kill and enslave these people. Now, he owed his life to this battered and dying woman.

"What can we do for her?" Hammurabi asked Shihon.

"Nothing my boy. She is not long for this world."

Shihon looked at the boy and said something in Hebrew. The boy disappeared momentarily and returned, clothed, to his mother's side.

Hammurabi looked back to Shihon and noticed the blood pooling on the ground where he sat and realized for the first time the extent of Shihon's injuries.

Seeing the young man's concern, Shihon was the first to speak.

"It's ok. I'll be alright," he lied.

"What do you need? What can I get you?" Hammurabi asked.

"Help me wrap this wound. I don't think I can get it tight enough on my own."

Looking at the young girl, Shihon spoke something in Hebrew. She stood and disappeared into an adjacent room, then returned with a thin sheet. She laid it next to Hammurabi then gently moved her hand in place of his over her mother's wound.

Hammurabi shredded the cloth into long strips and began tightly wrapping Shihon's torso when he heard the young girl begin to cry.

"Eema, eema? Eema?" the girl pleaded for her mother to awaken as her young brother rocked back and forth pressing the palm of his mother's hand to his face.

Shihon secured in the last strip of linen by tucking it tightly into the folds of cloth wrapped around him. With apparent difficulty he stood and placed his hand on the girl's shoulder. Quietly, he spoke something in Hebrew. It appeared to Hammurabi to be a prayer. Shihon turned to Hammurabi.

"What are you going to do?" Shihon asked.

"Salim must pay for this," Hammurabi said. "Father must hear of what he has done."

"What about these?"

The days and events that had led them to this point flashed through Hammurabi's mind. The village, the smell of burning flesh, the women and children cowering in their home. All of the destruction had been overseen and led by his father. Everything he'd heard about war had all been a lie. These people were not the monsters he'd been told they were. Their homes looked like Ammonite homes. The only men he'd fought with up until this point had been his own. This broken and battered creature, his enemy, had twice saved his life today.

"Blood for blood," Hammurabi replied.

Shihon nodded. "We owe her that."

Hammurabi thought of how Salim's men had turned on him so quickly, how they were prepared to bury him along with the Israelites. He looked up at Shihon.

"What did she say to them? What did she say to me?"

"She asked you to protect them. She said their God, the one they call Yahweh, He watches over you. She told them to follow you and do as you say."

Hammurabi's eyes welled with tears. He forced them back as he shook his head, struggling with the decision before him.

"Why would she do that?"

"Maybe she saw something in you," Shihon replied. "But what other choice do they have at this point?"

Hammurabi considered this. She'd paid for his life with her own blood. There was the ancient and sacred law which eclipsed all others. The debt must be repaid.

"Let's get them out of here."

REFUGEES

1095 BC, Jordan River Valley, Israel

The sun beat down on the weary bodies of the beleaguered group. They'd walked throughout the night and all that day. Hammurabi was only vaguely familiar with their general location. Shihon was more familiar, but even so, neither could guess at who or what they would run into first, whether friend or foe. They had no friend that they knew of now. The rest of the army surely knew they were missing and there was no telling what sort of story Salim had conjured up to explain his missing men. No doubt he'd fabricated a story with Hammurabi at its center and responsible for the deaths of his men, a crime punishable by death no matter who Hammurabi's father was.

He and Shihon would not be considered mere deserters, they would be deemed traitors. If they encountered Israelites, they'd surely be killed in their weakened condition. As they approached the outskirts of a small village, Hammurabi turned to see Shihon collapse beneath the shade of a lone tree. The old man could walk no further. He sat down upon a large rock and spread his bed roll on the ground and motioned for Hammurabi to lay the boy down on top of it. The young girl crumpled to the ground next to him, exhausted.

They'd been moving hard all day. Hammurabi laid the child on the mat and examined Shihon's injuries. They were worse than the old Hittite would acknowledge. His lower rib was exposed and the wound was starting to smell. For the first time, it occurred to Hammurabi that the wound might be fatal. The old man never once complained.

"I didn't know it was this bad," Hammurabi said excitedly, "I'm sorry we've been moving so hard, I..."

"It wouldn't have changed anything," Shihon interrupted. "We had to get away from there."

"You wait here. I'll try to go get some water from the village. I'll be back."

Hammurabi looked at the girl on the ground next to her brother. Without moving her head, her eyes glanced up at him pitifully. Hammurabi collected up the empty bladders.

"Do not risk it for me," Shihon said grabbing Hammurabi's arm as he reached for the bladder. "Wait till it gets dark."

"Will you be alright if I do?"

"Water will not make much of a difference at this point I'm afraid."

Hammurabi sunk to the ground in front of the old warrior.

They sat in silence. Enjoying the protection from the sun offered by the tree.

"We were once a great people you know? My grandfather told me the history of our tribe when I was a child. The sons of Heth, the son of Canaan, son of Ham, son of Noah. We were a numerous people when the Hebrew chieftain Abraham came and settled among us. We lived peaceably with him, his son Isaac, and grandson, Jacob, who was also called Israel. His sons made a treaty with our people. Then, when famine struck our land, they left for Egypt and were gone for a very long time. Our people stayed and endured. Times were hard, but there was peace in those days. After the famine, the land began to prosper again. My people prospered. But they began to quarrel among themselves over petty differences and offenses, things that do not matter in times of war and hardship. The giant kings of the south and north left us to ourselves in the highlands. Many years had passed without war in our land when the descendants of Jacob returned."

"Because of their differences, the chieftains refused to make an allegiance with each other. One by one our cities and villages fell. Those who survived were scattered to whatever places they found refuge. The remnants of my people still survive in the hill country, some in Jebus, some in Hebron."

"In my youth, I cursed their God. I thought him unjust for favoring the Israelites." He paused in reflection. His expression changed and his tone softened. "I had two children of my own, a boy and a girl," he said. "As they grew, my heart became knit to my daughter's in a way I cannot express in words. Since they were taken from me, it is my little girl that I see in my dreams." Shihon paused. "If we cannot control to whom our heart belongs, perhaps the gods are the same. If it is, as they say, that there is only one God, would it be wrong for him to show himself faithful to those who are faithful to Him?"

Hammurabi sat in silence, listening to the old Hittite. It dawned on him that as much as he cared for and respected this man, he knew very little about him and his earlier life. Till now, he'd denied having any family and Hammurabi had never known the man as anything other than a warrior and quiet, faithful servant. It changed everything he knew about the man to think of him as a father of two children, with a wife and a home of his own.

"What happened to your people, your family?" the young Ammonite asked.

"I have not spoken of my family in many years," he said solemnly. "We lived there in the hills not far from where we are now," he said pointing west. "One can find solitude there as it is not good for farming, nor grazing. One day, I traveled to the market at Jebus. When I retuned, I found my home had been raided. My wife and children…." The Hittite paused as he closed his eyes and a solitary tear ran down his cheek.

"I don't know how much time passed before I came to your father's land. He took me in. He gave me a home and a purpose. You were so young then. You reminded me of my son. I have rarely allowed myself to think back on these things. I blamed the Hebrews for my loss. I focused my hate on them since I had nowhere else to put it. Recent events have forced me to see that, in truth, I do not know who took my family. When I saw what was done to these, all of my rage was rekindled." Shihon shook his head. "Evil does not have a tribe or people. It is everywhere," the Hittite said with disgust. "It is there, in all of us. The best one can hope for is to live a little while and raise his children up strong enough to endure."

He looked over to the two Hebrew youths.

"What will you do with these?" he asked.

"What do you think we should do? Shouldn't we return them to their own people?" Hammurabi asked.

The Hittite sat up a little. "I am old. I have been to many places and seen many things, but I have never seen an orphan treated as anything more than a slave in their master's house. Your old life is gone, as is theirs. I will not be with you much longer," he said looking down at his wound. "It's up to you where you go from here. Their fate is in your hands."

***

It had been at least an hour since Hammurabi had seen anyone at the well. It was dark and the moon had not yet risen. Seeing his opportunity to approach, he emerged from the hiding place and moved quickly and quietly to the well. Feeling in the darkness, he lowered and lifted the bucket and rope, filling the bladders as quickly as he could while trying not to alert anyone in the village to his presence. The people were clearly uneasy. He could see in the daylight their endless hurrying back and forth throughout the village, many of them leaving hurriedly with small children and their most precious belongings. He hoped it would make his task easier.

With the skins full, he shouldered them and hurried back to the thicket where he'd left Shihon and the Hebrew children concealed. Feeling in the darkness, he called out to Shihon. No response. Again he called out, "Shihon," then listened intently. Again, no reply.

"Shihon!" he said louder. Finally, he heard the female voice of the young girl reply in Hebrew. He quietly made his way towards her.

"Shihon?" he called out. Again he heard the faint reply of the girl.

Finally reaching her in the underbrush, she turned and made her way back through the dark animal path to Shihon and the little boy. The boy was asleep. The day's struggle having finally overtaken him in merciful rest. Barely able to see, Hammurabi dropped the skins of water and knelt down beside the old man he'd come to love like a father.

"Shihon," he said, his voice betraying the emotion welling up inside him. "Shihon," he said again, gently shaking the Hittite's shoulder. He placed his hand near the old man's face, hoping to feel breath on his skin. He moved his ear to the man's chest, searching for signs of life. He wanted to cry out in the darkness. It was all he could do not to. He dropped back on his haunches then buried his face in the Hittite's chest and wept.

The young girl came and knelt beside him and placed a hand on his shoulder. Hammurabi could feel her hand trembling, reminding him of the great loss she'd also suffered the previous night. Despite this, she had the strength to try to comfort him now while her own loss was so close at hand. Hammurabi collected himself and sat up. He grabbed a skin and handed it to the girl.

"Drink," he said, "you need to drink."

She accepted the skin, took it to her sleeping brother, then gently patted him.

"Bani, Bani, wake up, drink," Hammurabi heard her say.

The boy awoke with a start and began to cry. His sister quieted him there in the darkness, patting and reassuring him until he finally calmed and took a long drink.

The girl sat down next to him and cradled his head in her lap until he fell asleep again. Hammurabi felt she was looking at him though he could not be sure in the darkness.

"Thank you for the water," she said in her own tongue as she held up the skin.

It was not extremely difficult to interpret the language given its similarity to his own.

"You are welcome," he said. They sat in silence for a moment before it occurred to him that there had been hardly a word spoken between them the entire day.

"What is your name?" Hammurabi asked.

"Hanna," she said, placing a hand to her chest. "Ammurabi?" she asked pointing to him.

"Ha-Hammurabi," he replied.

"Hamm-ur-abi" she said.

"Hanna," he replied. He could see her smile in the dim starlight as she nodded. "Bani?" he asked pointing at the boy.

She nodded in affirmation, then looked over to the lifeless servant laying near them in the dark. "Shihon?"

Hammurabi nodded. "Shihon."

SHOWING PROMISE

1095 BC, Gibeah, Benjamin, Israel

Now, behold, Saul was coming from the field behind the oxen.
And Saul said, "What is wrong with the people, that they are
weeping?" So they told him the news of the men of Jabesh.
I Samuel 11:5

S aul watched the sun sinking in the western horizon as he and
Abner led the teams of oxen in from the fields. So far, the life of
a king had not proven entirely different from being a farmer. He
did not feel like much of a king, the leader of a small village perhaps,
but not a king. Apart from paying the men in his service, Saul had not
touched any of the gifts that were presented to him at Mizpah and he
had not used any of it to improve his own circumstances.

He'd settled a few quarrels here and there regarding somewhat triv-
ial matters and had sentenced a few criminals. He'd begun studying
under various teachers who'd volunteered their services. He was learning Phoenician, the language of trade, as well as Egyptian, military history, and strategy. Abner especially was enjoying his education. Adriyel,
the head of his guard was training them daily in hand to hand combat
and fighting with a staff, club, or mace.

Adriyel was an Asherite. He'd grown up on the coast of Israel in a
fishing village near Tyre and had regular interactions with Macedonians,
Egyptians, Arameans, and all manners of travelers and merchants.
Adriyel's father, an industrious businessman, insisted that his children
learn the various trade languages so that they, like their father, would
profit from trading with these foreign visitors. Adriyel had not been
content to merely learn their foreign tongues. He engrossed himself in

the cultures of these foreigners, their practices and traditions. He loved visiting foreign ports and their trading partners across the sea. Most of all, he studied the various forms of martial arts practiced by them. From his youth, he'd studied fighting and honed his body to peak physical fitness after he and a younger brother were pummeled relentlessly for sport by a group of marauding teenagers. After the beating, they'd vowed to never fall victim again. They never did.

Saul was exceedingly grateful for Adriyel and the others who'd pledged their allegiance to him. Apart from their presence, little else had changed. Saul's Benjaminite neighbors seemed the least receptive to his new status. Many had openly expressed their disapproval of Saul as king, but none more so than the wealthiest men of his own tribe. It seemed that those Israelites from the furthest reaches of Israel, like Adriyel, were the most supportive of him.

As they walked towards home, Saul and Abner could see a large group of visitors. They seemed more agitated than the crowds he'd become accustomed to seeing in the short time since his anointing. Adriyel, never far from the king's side, was met by Nuri, who gave them a quick summation of the situation.

"Gadites from Jabesh Gilead. The Ammonites have the city surrounded. They've come seeking help."

Saul tied the oxen to a nearby post and hastened his pace to greet the refugees. They each bowed to one knee as he approached.

"Come, come sit down," he said and ushered them to a covered outdoor table. Their humble dwelling could not comfortably accommodate the visitors. Ahinoam and the other women were already fetching water and tending to the travel-weary men. Each of the men sat down with the exception of one man whose face was marred by a scabby wound where his right eye should otherwise have been.

There were eight of them. All distraught and weary save the one-eyed man who stood quietly behind them. One of them spoke up.

"Saul, my king, we are all of the tribe of Gad, save this man," he said motioning to the one-eyed man. "We have come from Jabesh Gilead to seek your help. King Nahash's army has surrounded the city. Each of us left wives and children behind to seek your assistance. This man came to us from a village to the east outside of our walls. He warned us of what was done to his family, his daughters and wife," the man said glancing back at the silent one-eyed man. "How they put out his eye and his son's eye while the Ammonites held their blades to his daughters' throats."

The man paused and lowered his head. "We could not accept this fate, but we lack the strength to defeat the entire Ammonite army. Our leaders tried to negotiate with them." His eyes met Saul's. "King Nahash actually said he would wait to attack the city while we sought help from our countrymen. He does not think anyone will come to our aid. He does not fear the God of Israel."

"What is your name?" Nuri said, looking at the one-eyed man.

"Shiza, of Reuben."

"Tell us in your own words, what happened to you?"

As Saul listened to the man recount his story of the events that had transpired only days prior, he could feel his muscles grow tense. Listening to the horrors this man and his family had endured stirred in him a hatred which began to manifest itself physically. Saul's face reddened with anger.

When the man concluded, an elder of Manasseh who'd accompanied the travelers from Bezek turned to question Saul.

"What will you do about this oh king?"

Another Benjaminite elder blurted out before Saul could respond, "surely, this great wealth you've amassed would be sufficient to gain King Nahash's favor. We could offer it as a peace offering." Several others nodded their approval, including two of the men from Jabesh.

Saul looked to the one-eyed Reubenite. The man stood quiet and unmoved. His silence said enough.

One of the Benjaminite elders spoke out.

"That is what we must do. We will make a peace offering of these treasures. Surely King Nahash will withdraw from our lands once he sees such a great offering."

"That's not a decision you can make," Nuri asserted.

Saul could hear no more of it, he turned abruptly and walked purposefully towards the oxen and untethered them. Pulling them back
to within meters of the crowd, he drew a sharp knife from his belt and
severed one of the oxen's jugular with a swift stroke of the blade. The
surprised animal fought and pulled against the yoke which bound
him to the other beast. Saul moved to the second ox and severed
its artery. Both animals moaned and pulled against the lead rope
clutched firmly in Saul's left hand. Blood spurted from the animals'
necks with each heartbeat. The first beast went to its knees, followed
by the second. Soon, they both slumped to the ground as the blood
slowed to a trickle.

Saul went to work, quickly and skillfully slicing through hide, muscle, and sinew. He quartered the animals, then removed the heads. His
hands, arms, and torso were smeared with gore when he turned and
addressed the warrior Nuri.

"Have ten messengers each take a piece of these oxen," he said and
pointed at the pile of quarters and heads. "Each messenger will go to
one of the ten tribes west of the Jordan." He looked at the Benjaminite
elder. "They will tell the people, 'whoever does not go with Saul and
Samuel to battle against the Ammonites, so it shall be done to his oxen.'
We will assemble at Bezek of Manasseh in four days."

Nuri turned and called for a young urchin they called Tzevi, who'd
joined the men on the route from Mizpah. He instructed the boy to go
and summon ten men. The boy immediately ran off towards the tent
where Saul's devotees resided.

The Gadite messengers each exchanged glances, then hastily nodded their affirmation. They watched the eldest among them walk slowly
toward Saul and embrace him.

"Thank you," he said. "Thank you."

Seeing this, the Benjaminite dissenters murmured amongst themselves, fearful of openly expressing any disapproval and thereby questioning the resolve of their new king or, moreover, Nuri's willingness to
carry out his orders.

Saul looked to the one-eyed man named Shiza, whose face was still without expression. Shiza bowed his head slightly in deference. Inwardly, Shiza could not have been more pleased with the king's response. "Finally," Shiza thought to himself. "Someone willing to fight."

GATHERING

1095 BC, Bezek, Manasseh, Israel

When he mustered them at Bezek, the people of Israel were three
hundred thousand, and the men of Judah thirty thousand.
I Samuel 11:8

N uri's runners dispersed the message throughout Israelite territory, aided by other runners picked up along the way. They covered hundreds of miles on foot in a matter of days. Men arrived in Bezek from the surrounding tribe of west Manasseh, then Ephraim, Benjamin, and Judah. Others began to appear from the more distant tribes of Asher, Zebulon, and Naphtali in the north, then Simeon and Dan from the south and everywhere in between. Some from Gad, Reuben, and east Manasseh poured in as well, each of them bearing the same wound where their right eye had once been. After ushering their families safely across the river, they'd found welcoming Israelite families to provide shelter while the men answered Saul's call to war.

These men stood out from the rest. While most of the new arrivals were excited, almost giddy, those from across the river were quiet and resolute. Though just as eager to fight, they were not unfamiliar with the toll of war and death like most of the young men present. The pain showed in their faces. The stares cast by their one good eye told the story of what they'd each seen and been through.

Nuri, Adriyel, Tzuriel, and the other warriors who'd pledged their service to Saul broke the men into units of one-thousand, or "elephs"[1]. There was no lying about, no idle time in Bezek. New arrivals, weary from

---

[1] A battalion or unit of roughly one thousand men.

travel, were recorded in the ledger, listing their origin, tribe, father, and grandfather, then immediately assigned to one of the elephs.

With no time to waste, their training began instantaneously. Martial arts were the primary focus. The men learned how to parry attacks with their makeshift shields, how to attack and counterattack with the farm implements or improvised weapons they'd each brought. Most had clubs of some sort which could be wielded in one hand while they held a shield in the other. Others had spears made either from sharpened shafts of wood or tipped with rock spearheads. Others had stone hammers, axes, and maces, or javelins carved from wood which could be used for stabbing or clubbing, but entirely incapable of cutting, slicing, or piercing armor. Based on reports from encounters with the Ammonites, they drilled attacks that focused on weaknesses in the enemy's armor, predominantly the face, neck, elbows and knees. When time permitted during short lulls in the rigorous training, they learned how to treat their own wounds quickly and efficiently by applying pressure and binding.

Tzuriel had the idea of mixing the divisions so that each was representative of the entire nation of Israel. Others wanted to organize the divisions by tribe. Tzuriel submitted that men, knowing their brothers, cousins, or fathers to be fighting elsewhere, would be less likely to desert or retreat en masse and would be quick to rally in support of a neighboring force in need of reinforcement or aid. He argued that separating families in this way also decreased the chances that all the males of one family could be exterminated in a single battle. Saul agreed.

It had been five days since the men from Jabesh Gilead had arrived in Gibeah and several hundred thousand men had already arrived. More were still pouring in from the outskirts of Israelite territory.

As Saul walked through the camp viewing the men, he felt a surge of energy and pride well within him. During the short breaks in their training, the men joked and exchanged stories of battles fought many years earlier. Men who'd never met began to regard each other as long-forgotten friends and brothers. Shepherds, city officials, tent makers, bakers, carpenters, masons, fishermen, and merchants slept, ate, and trained alongside each other. They heckled each other about accents and upbringing. No topic was sacred. They laughed and jested heartily. No tribe exalted above another. For the first time in decades, they were one people.

**

It had been seven days since the messengers left Jabesh. Saul gathered them to his tent just after sunrise.

"You see that our numbers are great. Three hundred and thirty elephs have assembled here to redeem their brothers across the Jordan. Go back to your city and thus shall you say to the men of Jabesh Gilead, 'tomorrow, by the time the sun is hot, you shall have salvation.'"

"What do you plan to do?" Manasses asked. "What is your plan of attack?"

"I'm sorry, but if you are taken captive and questioned by the Ammonites on your return to the city, it is better that you know nothing," Tzuriel replied.

"I see. I was foolish to ask," Manasses acknowledged. "I will inform the men of Jabesh as you have said. If it pleases you, the others and I thought it might be wise to add a bit of a ruse. We could tell King Nahash that we will surrender the city on the second day of our return. This way, he might not anticipate a fight or attack the city before your arrival."

The men looked to Nuri who nodded his approval.

"Go and do as you have said. May God protect you and give us victory."

"We will remain watchful for your arrival and prepared to join the battle when the time comes," Manasses assured them.

The messengers from Jabesh, accompanied by Shiza the Reubenite, mounted their horses and exited the camp. They would have to pass through the Ammonite line in order to reenter the city. While Nahash promised safe passage upon their return, the risk of capture, interrogation, and torture was considerable. However, if it meant he could take the city without prolonged or costly effort, Nahash would likely welcome their return.

"What shall we say if we are captured," asked one of the Gadite men. "We must be of one accord if we are interrogated. Even if every one of us were to die, we must not let them know that this army exists."

"We will tell them that we met with King Saul," Shiza responded. "That he sent out a call to arms, but after six days, only three hundred and thirty responded."

The men of Gad laughed and shouted, "Three hundred and thirty!"

**

That night, as the Gadite men approached the Ammonite cordon, they were met by a captain of the Ammonites. Dismounting their horses, they were blindfolded then led to a large tent on the East side of the city. One by one, they were separated and brought before King Nahash.

As Shiza's blindfold was removed, he saw the interior of the king's tent. It was adorned with golden lampstands and blue and purple tapestries. King Nahash was dressed in an ornate robe and sat atop a throne elevated several cubits above the ground. There were two of the largest men Shiza had ever seen posted on either side of the tent and several gray-haired warriors, adorned with the finest armor he had ever seen.

"Ah, the Reubenite, and what have you to report to your king?" asked one of the gray-haired soldiers.

"We appealed to King Saul at Gibeah. He put out a call to arms, but it seems the reports of your great army preceded them," said Shiza.

"And why did you return then," asked another of the generals.

"Where can I go that King Nahash's reach does not touch?" Shiza responded.

The general gave a proud smirk and looked at his King. Nahash sat up straight in his chair, clearly pleased with this response.

"It was good that you accompanied them," Nahash said. "You are a witness to my abundant mercy. Here you stand, humbled, but able to serve and care for your family. Go now. You have done a service to your people."

They dismissed him and called the next messenger to be questioned. Each man was questioned by the king's officials about what had transpired. To a man, they reported as they'd rehearsed, withholding nothing except the vast array of men assembled at Bezek.

Satisfied that the city would be surrendered without a fight or loss to his forces, King Nahash released the men with the instruction, "Give your report to the people of Jabesh. Tell them that they will surrender tomorrow morning or the city will be burned to the ground."

The men left Nahash's tent and approached the city gates. The guard atop the wall recognized them and called down to the gatekeepers. Inside, the large beam which barred the doors was lifted and carried to one side. The men entered with their horses and the gate was shut and barred again. A crowd waited within the walls. Families with small children, young girls and boys, fathers and mothers, waited for the messengers to give their report.

All hope subsided when the people of Jabesh saw the faces of the messengers. With the exception of Shiza, whose stoic demeanor never wavered, their countenances were grim as they made their way through the crowd.

"What happened?" they asked.

"Did you speak to King Saul? Is he coming?" others asked.

The messengers did not respond. No one made eye contact.

Rafael, the city's chief official ushered them past the crowd and to his home. Many of the city's elders and prominent men followed inside.

They took up places around Rafael's table and waited for him to secure the door. Shiza took up a place to one side of the room and waited. Barring the door, Rafael turned and addressed the messengers.

"Thank you, men, for what you have done. I'm sorry that you must bear the burden of delivering a disappointing message, but you have done a great service to our city. You could have chosen not to return. You are men of honor and courage, and we are indebted to you."

Manasses placed a hand on the official's shoulder.

"Don't sound so downhearted my friend. Before sunrise tomorrow, a force of Israelites, the likes of which have not been seen since the days of Joshua, will descend upon King Nahash."

Seeing the smile on Manasses' face, Rafael's countenance immediately lightened.

"But I thought…"

"We could not let the people know just yet," Manasses interrupted. "King Nahash thinks we will surrender the city. If we told the people that an army was coming to our aid, the Ammonites would surely have heard the commotion. No doubt, there are spies within our walls. We must not impede our brothers tomorrow by putting Nahash on the defensive."

Sighs of relief echoed around the room. The men restrained their excitement and listened for further instructions.

"Before the sun is hot tomorrow, Saul promises to attack the Ammonites. There were 330,000 Israelites in the camp before we left. Many of them traveled great distances to get there and must come further still before sunrise tomorrow. We must be prepared to render aid to our brothers and support the attack. We should prepare our homes to welcome and treat the wounded. They will need water and bread following the battle."

"Are we to sit inside our walls while the other tribes fight this battle on our behalf," asked one of the men.

"No, we will join them as soon as the fight begins," answered another.

One by one, the other men around the room expressed their agreement. The men, frightened and downcast only moments earlier, now seemed filled with energy. It was as if a dam of dread and despair had broken, pouring courage, hope, and action into the men.

The men of Jabesh continued as Shiza listened on. How defeated and hopeless they'd all seemed only minutes ago, thought Shiza. He considered this abrupt change in the men. A month ago, he would have called these men cowards, but now he merely contemplated the matter without criticism or judgment. He was thoroughly captivated by the change he'd just witnessed. Why was it that, at one time, he would have harbored contempt for these men, but now he felt only pity. How fickle man is, he thought to himself. Must one's mindset always be captive to his circumstance, ever-changing with the turmoil of life? Certainly not, he thought to himself.

There was a lesson here though, one he dared not dismiss or overlook. He considered his own circumstances. He'd always been ready to fight. His confidence was not in himself but in God. His neighbors back at Bezer talked of what they'd lacked. Shields, spears, and swords. They focused on the enemy's strengths. They focused on their own weaknesses. It was their own mindset that made the leaders at Bezer weak. Why then was his own outlook so much different, he considered. Choice. Merely choice, he concluded. His attention was brought back to the present.

"I will announce from the wall that we will come out and submit to the king's will. I won't say which King's will," he said with a smile. "Spread the word carefully among the people. No one goes in or out. No one is allowed on the wall, save the guards. No fires. No means of signaling can be permitted," he instructed. Turning to the captain of the guard, he added, "Only your most trusted men on watch tonight. We cannot risk Nahash finding out our true intentions. The Ammonites won't expect a fight. When they are attacked from behind by the other tribes, we will be prepared to join the battle."

RETRIBUTION

1095 BC, Jabesh Gilead, Gad, Israel
(vicinity of modern-day Wadi Yabis, Jordan)

Saul put the people in three companies. And they came into
the midst of the camp in the morning watch and struck
down the Ammonites until the heat of the day.
I Samuel 11:11

"Thank the heavens for such a clear night," Pinochos said as they trudged through the darkness. They'd been marching at an incredible pace for hours, and there were still seven hours before daybreak.

"Shhh," another man hissed. "Nuri said complete silence."

Pinochos shot him a contemptuous glance.

"You think anyone could hear us over this wind?" he asked.

The moon was at its fullest. Indeed, none of the men could recall such a night when the moon had shone brighter. A strong, unseasonably cold east wind whipped through the long columns of men as they marched. They'd been moving for so long and at such a pace that no one seemed to mind however, for without it, they would have been miserably hot. The hunters among them thanked the Lord for His provision as the wind aided their efforts to remain undetected during the long and arduous movement.

The line ahead began to slow until the men were bunched up. There was a murmur ahead of them that began to spread its way rearward.

"We've reached the Jordan," one man whispered ahead of them.

The announcement was repeated on down the thick column of men.

"Thank God! My feet are killing me. How much further have we got?"

"About sixty to seventy stadion," his companion answered, "didn't you listen?"

He was referring to Nuri's brief given prior to stepping off on the march towards Jabesh. Saul had divided the men into three divisions. Nuri was the leader of their division. They'd been assigned to maneuver far north of Jabesh and attack southward from northeast of the city. Their mission was to strike King Nahash's camp and cut off his communication with the rest of the army, disrupting any hopes of providing reinforcements that might be positioned east of the city.

Saul's division, along with Mordecai, would spread north of the city and attack south as well. Tzuriel's division would be attacking from the northwest. The terrain and vegetation south of the city did not lend itself to maneuver of such a large force at night and it was unlikely that the Ammonites would have any significant numbers there given the steep slopes of the Wadi Jabesh from which the city derived its name. It was a simple plan, however physically demanding. The northeasterly path from Bezek to Beth-shean then east to the Jordan and Jabesh was well over two hundred stadion.[2] It was a grueling, but necessary task if they were to catch the enemy by surprise. If all went according to plan, the Ammonites would be caught by surprise and pushed against the walls of the city, making them vulnerable to attack from the wall. It also meant Nuri's division had to travel the furthest in the same amount of time as the other two.

As Pinochos approached the water's edge, he noticed men removing their sandals and followed suit.

"Seventy more stadion," he said aloud. "Impossible! I'm a young man and a runner. There's no way most of these men can make it that far and still have any fight left in them. This is crazy."

"You'll see who's ready to fight when the time comes," someone growled in the darkness. "Now stop crying and get across that river," the man said from behind.

---

[2] More than 24 miles.

Pinochos turned to see who'd just spoken to him. A short, stout man stared back at him with eyes that looked black in the moonlight. Seeing the silvery white hair on the man's head and beard, Pinochos turned, shook his head, and trudged off into the water.

***

Nearly fourteen hours since they'd started their journey, men guzzled their last drinks of water in preparation for the attack. Nuri could see the enemy encampment ahead of them in the darkness. The light, sun-bleached fabric of their tents seemed to glow in the moonlight. It gleamed in the darkness off of Ammonite shields and spears. Good thing we don't have that problem, he thought to himself. Nuri ducked back behind the small hill-crest and inspected the men closest to him.

"Check the men nearest to you," he whispered, "make sure they are completely covered."

All down the line, men dipped their hands into jars of black ashen clay and smeared it onto the faces, necks, shoulders, arms, hands, and legs of their comrades. They were nearly solid black, covered in clay made from soot. The whites of their eyes seemed to glow in their sockets. Weapons, clothing, hair, everything was smeared and matted with the ashen clay. The wind continued to howl as they positioned themselves to cross the last space that separated them from the enemy they'd been marching towards for the past fourteen hours.

The men waited for Nuri's signal. Nuri watched the stars as they sunk below the western horizon. When the last star of the southern triangle constellation touched the horizon, the entire Israelite force would attack. He waited as Vega, then Deneb, disappeared from sight. Slowly, Altair sank until it touched the edge of the sky.

"That's it. Give the signal," he instructed. The man next to him sprinted down the back side of the short slope. At the base was another Israelite eagerly waiting next to a small makeshift structure about two cubits in height.

"We're ready, give the signal."

Tzevi reached down and pulled open the camel hide cover draped over the small structure. As he did, light poured out of the opening away from the hill. He reached in and withdrew a flaming torch, then lifted it high above his head and began waving it back and forth. Sparks flew and danced all around him. About one stadion away, the same actions were repeated by the next signaler, then again, and again down the line until tens of thousands of men jumped to their feet and charged over the hills and out of the shallow wadis that had concealed them.

Nuri had been the first to his feet. He quickly looked back as he sprinted forward and saw the light from the signal torches disappear behind the defilade of the terrain. The howl of the wind and pounding of their feet on the hard ground was the only thing that could be heard. The beat of his own heart and heaving of his lungs seemed louder still as he sprinted forward through the darkness alongside his fellow Israelites toward the unsuspecting Ammonite encampment.

From the base of the hill, Tzevi could see the faint silhouette of men disappearing over the hill-crest against the starlit sky. To the west, he could see the distant light of a fellow signaler. He smothered the flame then followed after the men, sprinting up the hill to catch them.

***

Salim awoke and emerged from his tent. He cursed the wind as he stumbled wearily a few yards away and passed his sleeping watchman. For a moment he considered kicking the man, but then, what did it matter, he thought. These pathetic Israelites would be surrendering to them in a few hours anyway. The high walls of the city were just beyond bowshot. All appeared quiet on the wall and its towers. He let the man sleep as he relieved himself with his back turned to the wind as it whipped around him from the east. He looked up and scanned the sky. The moon and stars were exceptionally bright. He lowered his eyes to the terrain before him. He started to turn when something caught his eye.

A wave of darkness seemed to be spreading across the open ground to the north of the city. His eyes strained to focus in the darkness. He looked to the sky to see if some cloud was passing overhead. There was not a cloud in sight. He looked back at the enveloping darkness and wondered momentarily if he was dreaming before the grave reality struck him. He turned and shouted to his men.

"WAKE UP! WAKE UP! WE'RE BEING ATTACKED! WAKE UP! ARM YOURSELVES!" Salim shouted as he ran for his spear and sword belt. The men around him were jumping to their feet and searching frantically for their weapons in the darkness.

Salim grabbed his spear from his tent and jammed the spike into the ground then struggled to strap the sword around his waist. He looked up as the first wave of blackened foe reached their position. Terrified, he dropped the belt and grabbed his spear.

Salim looked up just in time to see a blackened club hurdling through the darkness before it struck him in the face, smashing his nose and teeth. Salim reeled as the club's owner slammed into him, knocking him back to the ground. The only features Salim could make out of his attacker were the whites of his eyes and clenched teeth as his own spearhead was thrust into his stomach, pinning Salim to the ground. Silently and mercilessly, the blackened menace above him wrenched the spear from Salim's gut and hurried off in search of his next victim.

***

Saul and his men had reached the Ammonite encampment almost completely without detection. Many Ammonites were still sleeping when the Israelites reached their line. Even where more vigilant watchmen sounded the alarm, it was too late. The Ammonites awoke to a nightmare, engulfed by a flood of terrifying shadowy figures. All across the line, the sound of wooden weapons could be heard striking, smashing, and crushing flesh and bone. Screams of terror filled the air. The Ammonite armor and shields made little difference as it lay on the ground, its bearer caught up in the battle before any chance of donning it.

The Hebrews looked more like voids in darkness than men. Terror, chaos, and confusion crippled the Ammonite camp. Their commanders struggled momentarily to coordinate a defense before the darkness swallowed them. A hundred thousand individual battles raged.

Startled Ammonites fled into the open space between the encampment and the stone walls surrounding Jabesh. A hail of arrows and stones rained down on them from vigilant watchmen high atop the city walls. In the darkness and confusion, bewildered Ammonites continued to pour into the killing zone as more and more Gadites hurried to the towers, eager to aid their rescuers. The space became so filled with Ammonites that those atop the walls could hardly miss as they hurled stones at the men below. Those who entered the space were smashed, skewered, or trampled as each man sought to save himself from the blackened enemy soldiers on one side and raining projectiles on the other.

Nuri's division was enduring the heaviest fighting. Having penetrated the enemy's encampment all the way through to the open space, one of his three captains, called to the men, "WEST! TURN WEST!"

Nuri's other two captains turned their men eastward and the slaughter continued. As they pushed eastward, those not trapped against the city's walls took flight. Confused and terrified, trained Ammonite soldiers left spears and shields in their haste to join their fleeing comrades. The Ammonite battalions in reserve east of the city were awakened by the sound of men running through their camp in the darkness.

"THEY'RE COMING! THEY'RE COMING," the retreating men shouted above the howl of wind as they fled to safety.

As the onslaught spread through the camp, King Nahash sent instructions for his generals to form a counterattack and push the Israelites back. The messengers never returned. It was too late. The Ammonite commanders in reserve frantically attempted to rally their men, ordering them into formation, but it was no use. The mass of retreating men was more persuasive than the most composed officer. From atop their horses, King Nahash's guard could see the unimpeded attackers coming nearer to their position by the second.

"My King, you must go! It's too late! The enemy is nearly upon us."

Nahash resisted. "TURN THESE MEN AROUND," he shouted.

The captain of his guard dismounted and seized him.

"If you don't leave now, you will be killed!" The captain shouted.

Unbelievable, Nahash thought. Only minutes ago, he'd been sleeping soundly, assured that the last bastion of Hebrew resistance east of the Jordan was firmly within his grasp. Now, somehow, the clinched fist which held it had been severed completely. The battle was over before he had any opportunity to influence it. All their training. All the wealth invested in these men. This campaign. Wasted.

The captain forced the reigns into Nahash's hands and assisted him onto the horse.

"GET HIM OUT OF HERE," the captain shouted to his men. No further instruction was needed. With their shields outward, the mounted guards encircled the king.

Nahash took one last look at the disastrous melee before him. How had this happened, he wondered as he turned and fled the encampment towards Ammonite territory. The captain took a torch from its place on one of the large wooden beams and set the canvas of the command tent ablaze. He watched the flames begin to climb the tall slanted canvas, then turned and kicked his gelding hard as Israelites flooded into the adjacent tent.

The Israelites paused momentarily in the open space of the king's tent, their eyes adjusting to the well-lit interior. Light from numerous torches gleamed off of polished gold and silver accouterments. One of the Hebrews, a man of Judah from Bethlehem, was the first to hear the noise originating from a room in the southeastern corner of the tent. The Hebrew instinctively crept toward the sound as others poured through the tent in pursuit of the fleeing guards. As the man cautiously approached the sound, he heard the hushed whispers of a woman.

"Shhhh, shhhh, you're ok, ima is here. Shhhh," he heard the voice say in Hebrew. He snatched the canvas wall to one side as the occupant let out a frightened gasp, turning away from the dark and menacing intruder, she shielded two small creatures with her own body as she waited for the attacker to strike.

"You speak Hebrew?" the Hebrew asked.

The woman opened her eyes and turned to see the terrifying figure.

"Yes," she answered as tears ran down her frightened face.

Even in her terror, the Hebrew was astonished by the beauty of the young woman.

"Are you an Israelite?" he asked.

She nodded.

"What have you got there?"

The young woman moved slightly to one side as two beautiful young girls peered up at him with tear-streaked faces.

"My daughters, please do not hurt them," she pleaded.

"What are you doing here?"

Her eyes shifted to the ground. "I was taken… Nahash…."

The realization struck him. This woman belonged to King Nahash. In their haste, Nahash's guard had not bothered with evacuating her and the children. The Bethlehemite looked behind to see the flames climbing the walls and ceiling of the tent on the opposite side. He moved to the exterior wall behind the young mother and slashed a large opening with a captured Ammonite sword.

"Come on, through here," he commanded as he held the canvas open.

The woman hesitated.

"I'm not going to hurt you; we're here to save the city."

The woman lifted one of the girls and struggled to take the older of the two in her arms before the Bethlehemite moved to aid her. The frightened girl withdrew in terror at his blackened and blood-spattered appearance.

"Don't be afraid," he said. "I'm a Hebrew, like your mother, like you. I'm not going to hurt you."

"It's alright Zeruiah," her mother assured her as she pulled the girl up by the arm.

"My name is Jesse," he said in a soft voice. "Come with me Zeruiah," he said as he grabbed the girl and lifted her with his left arm, then stepped through the slashed tent wall into the open air. Most of his fellow Hebrews had continued east beyond the tents in pursuit of the fleeing Ammonites. The dead littered the ground all around. He held the canvas open as the young mother stepped through with her other child to safety as the flames rose to the apex of the large tent, illuminating the battlefield and corpses all around them.

"Come on," he shouted over the din as he led the trio to safety.

***

From atop the walls of Jabesh, watchmen shouted updates down to the mass of men which was still growing just inside the city gates. Many of them, including Shiza, had been there all night. They could hear the battle raging outside the walls. Reports of the battle from the men on the wall exhilarated them. Those on the walls and ramparts had quickly run out of rocks and other projectiles. Those at the base frantically passed ammunition up the lined stairway to those at the top.

"OPEN THE GATE!" Shiza shouted impatiently. "Will you sit here in safety while the rest of Israel fights for your freedom?"

The men around him glanced at him from the corners of their eyes. For a moment, no one responded.

"OPEN THE GATE" he shouted again, much louder this time.

Suddenly, from somewhere in the crowd, another shouted in reply, "OPEN THE GATE!"

Shiza shouted again, "OPEN THE GATE!"

Again, his call was echoed from within the crowd. Another joined in, then another. Shiza pushed his way through to the massive barred door.

"Well? What are you waiting for?" He asked the guards.

The guards themselves, moved by his fervor, turned and began to lift the large beam. Other men close at hand rushed to their aid and quickly hoisted the heavy wood from its rails. No sooner had they heaved it to one side than the others began pressing against the heavy gates. Men poured from the opening and out into the battle.

As the men from Jabesh sprinted into the fray, they had little difficulty discerning friend from foe even in the pale blue light of the moon. The enemy fled east as the fresh waves of Israelites attacked from the city.

Shiza, armed with a heavy olivewood club, sprinted toward the foe possessed by a thirst for blood and vengeance. A large Ammonite soldier turned to face him and raised his left forearm to block as Shiza's club came smashing down. The heavy weight of the club snapped the man's arm like a twig. He stumbled rearward as Shiza swung sideways towards the man's head narrowly missing him as he fell backwards to the ground. Shiza swung again only to have the club batted aside by the man's foot. He swung again and smashed the ground as the man rolled to one side. The Ammonite saw an opportunity and tried to use his good arm to scramble to his feet, but Shiza recovered quickly and swung again, this time coming down right on top of the man's back. He wailed in agony, arching rearward as Shiza swung again and struck the back of the soldier's head.

From the corner of his eye, Shiza saw a figure approaching from his right. He turned to see the oncoming Ammonite, this one armed with a sword. Shiza defensively swung the club blocking the enemy's sword. The weight of the heavy club nearly knocked the short bronze sword from his attacker's hand. He retaliated by slamming into the Israelite with his shield. Shiza recovered and struck the top of the shield with his club, but narrowly escaped the man's blade as he countered, jabbing his sword at Shiza's abdomen. Shiza swung again, sideways this time, and struck the shield on the man's left side. He cocked for another blow as the Ammonite tried to regain his position, but was too late. Shiza struck the Ammonite hard in the ribs. Shiza swung again, this time smashing the man's knee. The Ammonite crumpled into the dirt with a cry of pain before Shiza delivered the final blow.

Suddenly, Shiza was knocked to the ground from behind by a fleeing Ammonite, causing him to lose grip of the club as he tumbled over his last opponent's body. As they both struggled to their feet, Shiza saw the confused terror on the young Ammonite's face. He dove at Shiza wildly, tackling him over the body of a dead Ammonite. The man's hand went straight to Shiza's face as he attempted to gouge Shiza's eye. His left thumb sank into the empty socket as Shiza trapped the man's right hand and elbow and thrust his hips upward throwing the man off of him and face down into the dirt. Shiza was the first to his feet and kicked the man's face as he tried to stand. The Ammonite turned and tried to flee as Shiza jumped onto his back, wrapping his right arm around the man's neck and locking it in the crook of his left arm. They toppled forward to the ground as the Ammonite tried desperately to roll out of the tightening grip.

Shiza rolled to his back and dug his feet into the man's hips, instinctively arching his back as if to pull the man's head clean off. The Ammonite struggled for what seemed like an eternity among the chaos that ensued around them. Men tripped over them as they rolled and struggled in the dirt. The Ammonite clawed and pulled at Shiza's arms. Shiza squeezed with every bit of strength he had left before realizing that the enemy was no longer struggling. The man's arms dangled limp at his sides.

Shiza shoved the lifeless body off to the side and stood. Surveying the madness all around him, his eye locked on one man moving quickly towards him, armed with sword and shield. Unarmed, Shiza glanced at the ground searching for the club. The man was nearly upon him. Shiza leapt instinctively to the right, narrowly avoiding the man's sword. He seized the Ammonite's shield and spun to the left throwing his attacker off balance.

As the enemy rolled back onto his feet, Shiza snatched a sword from a dead Ammonite's scabbard when something smashed his face and nose, knocking him rearward. For a moment, all was black. A dread gripped Shiza as he prepared to feel the enemy's blade pierce his body. The smell and taste of his own blood filled his mouth and nostrils. He swung the sword wildly in a futile effort to fend off the unseen attacker while his vision returned, his nose and face throbbing. When he regained sight, he could see a blackened figure pinning his attacker to the ground at the end of a spear. The blackened man pulled Shiza to his feet, then, without a word, disappeared in search of his next victim.

As the first rays of light began to show on the horizon, the battle continued. Here and there were pockets of fighting where groups of Ammonites had managed to form small defensive circles. Even for these disciplined enemy soldiers covered in armor and armed with spear and shield, from atop the wall, they looked like islands in a sea of darkness, the rising tide steadily and methodically overtaking them.

With each passing moment, the Israelites gathered more spears, swords, and shields from the slain at their feet. The well-trained Ammonites tightened their formation until they were shoulder to shoulder, each man's shield overlapping his neighbor's. Their spears rested atop each shield like the quills of a giant sea urchin, ready to pierce any that dared come within striking distance. Alas, their valiant display merely delayed the inevitable as the barrage of arrows, spears, swords, javelins, and rocks continued to rain down on them. One by one, they fell until none remained.

There were no prisoners, no hands raised in plea for mercy, no laws of conflict which could be relied upon, no escape apart from death.

As the battle waned, Saul sent messengers to locate Mordecai, Nuri, and Tzuriel. Their reports came back quickly. Overwhelming victory.

Nuri was in the process of pulling men back from pursuing the Ammonites too far east of the city. The newly appointed generals and commanders tended to their men, seeing to the needs of the wounded as the newly liberated people of Jabesh poured out of the city, lavishing their rescuers with appreciation.

Saul surveyed the aftermath. The wind from the night before had ceased. A light morning dew had settled on the field of battle as the sky turned shades of light blue. It was in many respects, the dawn of a new day. Most of the men were ecstatic. They shouted praises to Yahweh and sang songs of Judah, Joshua, and Gideon, songs of God's power and might. Some men, overcome by their bodies' response to the battle shook violently. Others moved from one blackened body to another, calling out the name of a brother, son, or father.

Small parties had begun separating the dead, gathering the mass of Ammonite corpses away from the city. Already, the sky over the massive and growing accumulation of enemy dead swirled with birds. It would be a good day for them.

Along the city wall, a much smaller number of Israelite dead were being gathered to be cleaned, identified, and prepared for burial. Elderly women and men from the city had already begun tending to their fallen rescuers. Saul watched as they gently and lovingly caressed away the filth and grime from the faces of the venerable dead. He looked at their faces, faces of men he had called to fight.

"Come sir," Adriyel said. "There's nothing you can do for these. There are still living that must be tended to. "

Saul walked along with Adriyel close at hand, an Ammonite spear clutched in both hands. An Ammonite soldier reached to touch Saul's foot as he passed by. The man looked at Saul with pain-filled, emotionless eyes. Saul surveyed the man's injuries. His other arm was severed just above the left elbow. His entrails spilled out beside him in the dirt. Adriyel held out the Ammonite spear with an open hand.

Saul took the weapon and held the point just above the dying man's heart. As he gripped it firmly in both hands, the man nodded and closed his eyes. Saul drove the point down through the man's heart as hard and accurately as his fatigued limbs would allow. The man let out a strained grunt as the spear passed through him. He opened his eyes and stared up at Saul, his face taut with pain. Slowly, the painful expression of his face relaxed and faded to one of quiet peace. Only then did Saul wrench the spear from his body. If not remorse, Saul couldn't help but feel some respect for this man who'd accepted death so readily. He turned to give the spear back to Adriyel but noticed that the warrior had already acquired a new one.

As Saul continued through the field of battle, some stood as he passed, others knelt. Unsure of the proper custom of showing respect for a king, others simply bowed their heads. This was, after all, a new thing in Israel. He saw Israelite men here and there weeping over another blackened body. The Israelite casualties were few, however, and most of the injured would survive. Many were searching the Ammonite dead for valuables, seizing any jewelry, coins, or other valuable trinkets that could be found. Since they'd been slain amidst their tents and belongings, loot was plentiful. Several men noticed that some of the Ammonites carried small medical kits and were amassing as many of these invaluable treasures they could carry.

As they passed a wounded Israelite, Saul knelt beside him. The man's left thigh was deeply gashed and bleeding, a familiar type of injury as was not uncommon to see on a farm. Saul placed the man's hands on the wound and pressed it.

"Keep pressure on it," he instructed. As Saul looked at the soldier's face he realized the Israelite was merely a boy. Though it was difficult to discern given the youth's blackened appearance, Saul guessed he was no more than fifteen. Saul stood and looked among the Ammonite kits and materials as Adriyel joined in the search. It seemed one of every four to six of them possessed the small leather medicine bags. Saul located one and dumped its contents on the ground. There was wood gauze, a small leather belt, a jar of honey, and a jar containing a fine orange powdery substance.

Saul dabbed the substance with the tip of his finger and touched it to his tongue to confirm its identity. Taking the orange substance, gauze, and belt over to the wounded youth, Saul knelt beside him.

"Give me your water," he instructed Adriyel before gently pouring it over the wound, washing the grime and soot away as well as possible.

"I'm going to pack this into the wound and wrap the gauze around it," he said to the youth, displaying the orange-colored substance. "What's your name?"

"Ahithophel," he replied, looking wearily at the substance in the king's hand. "What is that?" he asked, trying not to grimace or writhe as his king packed the wound with the orange substance.

"Turmeric," Saul replied. "It comes from a plant root. It will help."

"At least these filthy ba…." the boy caught himself, wary of swearing in front of the king. "At least these filthy beggars are good for something," he continued. The wound burned as the spice touched his maimed flesh. "My mother always uses sugar," he said through clenched teeth.

Saul nodded as he worked on the youth's leg, wrapping the wound tightly with the gauze and leather belt, all the while considering how beneficial such items might prove in future battles. They hadn't even had swords or shields coming into this battle, much less the luxury of medicine.

The realization of the day's victory truly began to materialize as if for the first time. It was just like the stories of Moses and Joshua. It was just like Ebenezer.

"We really did it," said one of the wounded youth's companions to Adriyel. "We really crushed them, didn't we?"

"We sure did," Adriyel replied.

"God was with us today," Saul said as he finished the bandage. "Don't try to walk. We'll get something to carry you on."

"Thank you, sir," the boy said. "For this and for leading us here. I know there were men who wanted to pay off the Ammonites."

Saul nodded. He couldn't bring himself to acknowledge the thanks. He did not feel that it was due him. Saul turned to the two young men nearest him who'd been observing the encounter and appeared to be acquainted with the injured youth.

"You two, do you know this man?"

"We walked all day and night with him," one replied. "He even saved my skin once or twice during the battle."

"Ahithophel?" the other responded. "Well I've known him a full two-days or so."

"Good. I trust you will see that he is taken care of."

"I'll treat him like my own child," the second youth responded.

Saul smiled. This sarcastic and lively youth couldn't be more than sixteen.

"What's your name?"

"Hushai," he said with a bow. "Your faithful servant."

Saul looked to the third man, who stood quietly observing the interaction. Surprised, Saul realized he was not an Israelite, but a Hittite, the dark soot having hidden the youth's appearance. "And you?"

"Huzziya," said the young Hittite.

"He's a man of few words sir, but if I may say so, I didn't see anyone fight harder than this man, Israelite or not," said Hushai.

"He slew the man that did this," Ahithophel said. "I owe him my life."

"A worthy addition to our people indeed," Saul said as he placed his hand on the young man's shoulder.

"Huzziya the Hittite and Hushai and Ahithophel of Judah." Saul said confidently guessing their tribe by their accents.

"That's right," Hushai replied as the others nodded.

Given their similarity and geographic proximity, only the most discerning ear could differentiate between a Benjaminite and a man of Judah on accent alone. This was in stark contrast to their relatives to the north, whose dialect sometimes seemed an entirely different language. There had been numerous recent instances when Saul required the assistance of Adriyel to understand elders from the tribes of Asher or Naphtali.

"King Saul!" Someone shouted from behind.

The four men turned to the approaching runner.

"Nuri requests your guidance. The men of Jabesh are looting the Ammonite camp. He requests your instructions as to how the spoils should be divided. Men from the other tribes are saying that the loot belongs to ten tribes who traveled here to fight."

Saul turned back to the three young men.

"It was a pleasure," he said, then turned to accompany the runner back to Nuri.

"What does Samuel have to say," Saul asked as they walked.

"I don't know sir, no one has seen him. Would you like for me to find him?"

"First take me to Nuri. Is Abner alright?"

"He is sir," the runner said as they walked hastily towards the general's position.

Saul scanned the men for the face of his young cousin as they approached. The boy had rarely ventured far from Nuri's presence since they left Gibeah. Saul was relieved when he spotted the young man standing to Nuri's rear as the general argued fervently with a man from Jabesh.

Saul could hear a heated argument as they approached.

"Go find Samuel," Saul instructed the runner, who dashed off in search of the prophet.

"King Saul," said the man from Jabesh. "I beseech you, our people have been oppressed by the Ammonites, our cities have been razed, our hard-earned wealth stripped from us. Should we not use this bounty to restore the tribes of Reuben and Gad?"

Nuri countered, "these men have come from far and wide to liberate this city. Now you wish to take the bulk of the spoils for yourself without so much as consulting the king?" Nuri turned to Saul. "My lord, when our forefathers entered this land, God forebode them from taking certain of the enemy's possessions. When even one disobeyed, Joshua's army paid dearly. I merely suggest that we consult with the Almighty before anyone counts the enemy's wealth as our own."

"I agree," said Saul. "I've sent your runner to locate Samuel. We will do as the Lord commands."

"I thought you were King," the man from Jabesh sneered.

Saul turned to the man, he'd become rather accustomed to such disrespectful remarks and was becoming increasingly skilled at parrying them.

"I am your King, I AM is your God, and Samuel is His prophet. We will see what he has to say."

He received no retort from the man. Nuri nodded approvingly. As the three men waited for the prophet to arrive, runners were sent to the other divisions to locate Mordecai and Tzuriel.

As they waited, Nuri and the man from Jabesh showed Saul the tents of King Nahash that had not been destroyed by fire. Each wall was decorated with elaborate embroidered murals. The murals themselves bore gold and silver laced into the stitching. The mobile treasury from which King Nahash paid his soldiers was there.

"Think what Israel could do with this wealth. Think about how our people have struggled under the yoke of these Ammonites," the man of Jabesh said.

Saul nodded, then turned and walked out of the tent. Samuel had not yet arrived. Impatiently, the man from Jabesh asked, "Should we go to him? I understand he is quite old."

All around them, the young men who'd endured the long march erupted in laughter. Having returned to the city before Samuel joined the army at Bezek, the men from Jabesh had never seen Samuel. Confused, he looked to Saul.

"You will find that he is rather spry for his age," Saul replied.

Just then the two blackened men could be seen approaching purposefully. Even with his hair and beard matted in black clay, Samuel was easily identified by his gait, his long strides causing the young runner to half walk, half trot alongside him.

"What's this," Samuel asked as he reached the men.

Saul skipped the niceties, for which he knew Samuel possessed little patience.

"What would God have us do with the Ammonite riches? Should we divide them amongst the tribes? Destroy them as at Jericho? Or," Saul asked, "is there something we have not considered."

"It is good that you have asked these things. I too have sought the Eternal's guidance in this matter." Samuel shook his head. "On this, He has remained quiet. I believe God would see what you would do."

This was the last answer Saul wanted to hear and the one he'd least expected.

"You are the anointed," said Mordecai. "If I may, I suggest we look to the past to guide the decisions that lay ahead."

"Go on," Saul said.

"When Joshua brought our people over from this land, Jericho was the first battle our people faced. Much like today, the odds were against our people, but the Lord went before them and delivered the victory. No Israelite was allowed to keep anything from the spoils of the battle. They were a sacrifice, an offering that belonged to the Eternal. The first fruits of a new era for our people."

"One man disobeyed their instructions and thirty-six men paid the price for that one man's mistake. How much more if the entirety of the people take the spoils of today's victory?"

The man from Jabesh shook his head vehemently.

"This battle, these treasures are the first fruits of your Kingship. If you divide these things up among the people, certainly they will be happy, but is it not better to please the Lord in your first act as commander and king of His people?"

Saul looked to Samuel, who nodded approvingly.

"The victory belongs to God. So too the spoils. Instruct the men to gather all of the belongings of the Ammonites."

"This is ridiculous," growled the man from Jabesh.

"Burn it all. We will return as we came and if the Lord wants to prosper us in return for the sacrifice today, well then, He is able to do so."

"Wait! Wait," the man from Jabesh interjected. "You want to burn it? To burn... everything?" he asked. "The gold, the swords, the shields? We don't have any armor. What if the Ammonites return? What if they come back? How will we..."

"We didn't have any armor today. Nor shields. Nor gold. And *you* didn't win this battle. You called for help and were delivered," Saul replied forcefully. "Burn it!"

Each of Saul's generals commanded that the wealth and weapons, indeed, every possession among the Ammonites should be collected and brought to be destroyed. Samuel directed the men to build altars of wood from the Ammonite tents, wagons, and provisions. The Levite priests who'd accompanied them to the battle would assist Samuel in sacrificing the Ammonite livestock and horses, of which there were many.

The men stacked the swords, shields, helmets, gold, and silver on top of the wooden altars. Many among them grumbled about the great fortune that was about to be set ablaze, but most simply marveled at it.

When all had been prepared according to Samuel's instructions, Saul instructed the men to assemble around the altars. With the people of Jabesh watching from atop the wall, Saul addressed the army and commended the men, praising them for their faith and bravery and exalting God for their victory.

"While we celebrate a victory here today, it is not without loss or sacrifice," Saul said. "These are those who have gone to sleep. Remember their names. Tell their stories." Saul then read the list of names, their fathers and grandfathers, tribe and town. There were comparatively few casualties, but enough to provide a somber reminder for those present that even victory has its price. Those who'd known them wept amidst the crowd as Saul continued.

"Samuel once told me that God uses the weak things of this world to humble the strong. We came here armed with wood and stone against a foe armed with shield, spear, and sword. God has revealed his faithfulness, showing His strength in our weakness. Today, the Ammonites were defeated not by the sword or by the spear. Today, our enemies know that there is one true God, the God of our people, that the great I AM is not dead, nor does He sleep! Today, they know that we are His people!"

The army erupted with a loud and joyous cry that was echoed along the wall of Jabesh Gilead. Then, slowly, the shouts and cries receded into a chant, "LONG LIVE THE KING! LONG LIVE THE KING!"

Saul motioned for the men to be still and quiet down. The chant subsided.

"I'm going to ask Samuel to pray and then we will offer the wealth of the Ammonites to the Eternal as our ancestors did at Jericho. Once we have done so, the people of Jabesh have expressed their desire to show their thanks and have asked that you join them inside the city for a celebration."

This was followed by more shouts and praises as Samuel took Saul's place before the army.

"All praise, honor, and glory be to the Eternal God who saves. We thank you for this victory. We offer this, the wealth of the Ammonites in thanks and recognition that you are our provider and our strength."

Samuel lit the torch, then with it, lit Saul's, who passed the fire to Nuri, Tzuriel, and Mordecai. The men walked from altar to altar setting each ablaze, accompanied by more shouts of praise and victory from the men, though there were many who seemed less enthusiastic.

The people of Jabesh had come outside of the city to witness the spectacle and welcome the army into their city and homes.

Despite the allure of the festivities, many of the married men, those without sons old enough to look after their families, had gathered into small bands to begin the long trek home through the darkness. Gadites from the city brought provisions, fresh water, and cloaks. Those who'd marched and fought alongside each other exchanged solemn good-byes. Larger groups were formed for those escorting litters bearing their fallen comrades, which had been cleaned, anointed, and wrapped for burial by grateful people of the city. They departed almost without notice amidst the music, dancing and singing.

The celebration was everywhere. Families crowded around to hear stories of the day's battle. Men joked and chided each other about the follies and miseries they'd endured together during the march to Jabesh and the ensuing battle.

The men were welcomed into the homes of Jabesh Gilead where warm baths, food, clean clothing and wine awaited them. The wounded were tended with special care and attention. Despite their weariness and fatigue, most of the men celebrated and feasted till late in the night. It had been well over thirty hours since any of them had slept, but they were heroes and enjoyed their temporary status as celebrities among the people who'd witnessed their acts firsthand.

Saul, Adriyel, and the generals retired to Manasses' home along with Samuel and Nathan, leaving the men to enjoy themselves in the absence of their commanders. Abner accompanied the elder men despite the jeers and pleadings of those his own age.

In the relative quiet of Manasses' home, the generals spoke of prior battles, of friends lost and victories won. They spoke of their homes and families. Abner and Nathan listened intently to these old warriors, soaking in every detail of the collective knowledge these wise men possessed. Hours and many cups of wine later, Saul and each of the generals, save Nuri, eventually gave in to their body's need for rest and retired for the night. Nathan slept soundly, face down between his crossed arms on the table. Samuel had somehow disappeared hours earlier, though to where, no one knew.

Nuri, seeing that he and Abner were the only ones still awake, straightened.

"Come, I want to show you something," he said to Abner, as he stood and proceeded to the door.

Passing the royal guards who stood watch outside Manassas' home, they walked through the streets of Jabesh Gilead to the city wall. They could still hear the sounds of the celebration going on in various houses; a poorly played flute, muffled singing, and loud laughter.

They were both still mostly covered with the black soot from the night before and approached the guards without notice. Reaching the wall, Nuri woke the two city guards manning the entrance to a stairway leading up to one of the many ramparts along the wall.

"Good morning," he said as the two men straightened. "Look lively men, if any of our enemies are students of warfare, they would know to attack us while we're basking in the glory of today's victory."

One guard pulled a cord which hung from the rampart, alerting the guards above. Abner looked up to see a guard poke his head over the edge of the wall looking down at them. One of the men on the ground had difficulty maintaining his posture. Abner could smell the strong odor of wine about him.

"Hey old friend," said the general, "You're lucky it's just us that found you in this state. If your captain or a city official had found you like this, they might have your head. Who would support your family then? You're the first line of defense for the city, not to mention the only defense for your brothers above you. You wouldn't want someone slipping in and giving them the surprise now would you?"

The man shook his head, "No sir." The surprise visit had caused him to sober up a bit.

"Well, let's keep this between us. I trust you'll not let this happen again."

"Never!" He said emphatically. "Th-thank you," he stammered, clearly moved by the grace bestowed on him by the old soldier.

"Here," Nuri said, handing the man the cup of tea he'd been sipping. "Drink this and get your wits about you."

The man thanked him again as the two proceeded up the staircase to the ramparts above. Reaching the top, Nuri spoke to the two guards, instantly putting the men at ease. As he and Abner stared out beyond the wall, he pointed out the fires below. All around the glow of fires, shadows of wild dogs and hyenas danced in the darkness as they searched the ground for any unburied dead, licking up blood wherever it could be found. Snarls could be heard as the animals fought over pieces of flesh or blood-soaked cloth.

Nuri and Abner leaned against the walls watching the feeding frenzy below.

"Wow," Abner remarked. "I've never seen so many of them."

Nuri nodded.

"A similar scene is playing out among the Ammonites right now," Nuri explained. "Opportunists will flock to King Nahash's side to replace the fallen captains. One or more of his generals might even try to depose him. Their cousins, the Moabites to the South, or the Assyrians to the North may try to take advantage of their weakened state to gain more territory for themselves." The old general paused momentarily. "But in the end," he said stoically, "their hatred will return to that which they despise the most."

"Us," Abner said.

The old soldier nodded as he turned to his young pupil.

"Never lower your guard. In victory or defeat."

***

The next day Saul and his generals discussed further care and treatment of the wounded until they could be moved to their homes safely across the Jordan. The rest of the army was given another day of rest before they would return to Benjamin.

Elated by their victory, the people's faith in their new King reached new heights. Samuel seized the opportunity to reaffirm Saul's Kingship. While gathered at Jabesh Gilead, Samuel addressed the people.

"Some of you have come to me and expressed your enthusiasm for your new King. This is good and pleasing to God." Samuel said. "Some of you have even expressed your desire to avenge your king for those who have dishonored him since he was chosen at Mizpah. Indeed, there are many here now who questioned his leadership. But God has given your king great wisdom in saying that "not a man shall be put to death this day, for today the Lord has accomplished salvation in Israel." It is not his desire that Israel should be divided against itself. Forgive your brethren as your king has chosen to do. If you would do anything to show your approval for your new king, come, let us go to Gilgal and renew the kingdom there."

Still basking in their triumph over the Ammonites, the people were quick to agree. They assembled by tribes and returned to their lands in order to gather their families, provisions, and offerings to be presented at Gilgal the following week.

Word of their victory had spread throughout Israel and the returning volunteers were welcomed and praised in every village and hamlet they passed through as they returned to their homes. Saul and the men who accompanied him were greeted along the way by Israelites and travelers from various peoples and tribes who'd come to see this new King of Israel.

When he finally reached his home in Gibeah, Ahinoam was waiting to receive him outside their home accompanied by a crowd of family and guests. The women in her service had taken great care in preparing the Queen for Saul's return. He almost didn't recognize her in the regal clothing and makeup that she now wore. Though attractive as a working-class farm girl, Saul had never seen Ahinoam so beautiful as she appeared now. Seeing his proud Queen, Saul realized that for the first time, he was beginning to feel like a King.

INAUGURATION

1095 BC, Gilgal, Benjamin, Israel

*Then Samuel said to the people, "Come, let us go to Gilgal
and there renew the kingdom." So all the people went to Gilgal,
and there they made Saul king before the Lord in Gilgal.*
I Samuel 11:14-15

As the people prepared for Saul's inauguration at Gilgal, men
were chosen among the numbers that now accompanied him
to fill positions as scribes, tax collectors, and the full array of
other services that would be required of the newly formed government.
Valiant men who'd performed many feats at the battle of Jabesh pledged
their lives in service to him.

At Mizpah, the crowd had dwindled to mostly Benjaminites, local
Ephraimites, and some Judahites by the time Saul was selected by lot
and anointed King. At Gilgal, the city swelled beyond the walls as all
twelve tribes gathered to praise and celebrate their new victorious
deliverer. Oxen, sheep, and goats in great numbers were brought to be
sacrificed to the Lord. As at Mizpah, Samuel reiterated the rights and
privileges of the king, along with the expectations placed upon him.
By the time Samuel finished the ceremonies, the people's hearts were
full of excitement and rejoicing. Saul and Ahinoam were seated behind
him as he addressed the people.

"The Lord has done a great thing for Israel," Samuel shouted above
the crowd. The people roared with cheers. "You rejected His divine
leadership and still, he wrought victory on your behalf." The noise of
the people began to fade as he spoke. "It seems His patience is as bound-
less and unending as your propensity for unfaithfulness. Now, behold,

I have obeyed your voice in all that you have said to me and have made a king over you. And now, behold, the king walks before you, and I am old and gray; and behold my sons are with you. I have walked before you from my youth until this day. Here I am; testify against me before the Lord and before his anointed. Whose ox have I taken?" Samuel asked, pausing for any to respond.

The crowd was silent.

"Or whose donkey have I taken?"

Again the awkward pause.

"Or whom have I defrauded?"

Still no one answered.

"Whom have I oppressed?"

The unexpected turn in the ceremony caused Saul's face to redden. He sat quietly while the prophet delivered his stinging rebuke.

"Or from whose hand have I taken a bribe to blind my eyes with it? Testify against me and I will restore it to you!" Samuel demanded of the people.

His countenance was that of an angry father. All was silent for a moment. A solitary elder, older than Samuel, stepped forward.

"You have not defrauded us or oppressed us or taken anything from any man's hand," the elder shouted.

Another ancient-looking man shouted. "Never!"

"Never," replied another.

"Not once have you defrauded," said another.

"The Lord is witness against you, and his anointed is witness this day that you have not found anything in my hand," shouted Samuel as he turned and held his arm towards Saul.

"He is witness!" Shouted the first elder.

The others repeated the same.

"The Lord is witness who appointed Moses and Aaron and brought your fathers up out of the land of Egypt." Samuel shouted. "Now therefore stand still that I may plead with you before the Lord concerning all the righteous deeds of the Lord that he performed for you and for your fathers. When Jacob went into Egypt, and the

Egyptians oppressed them, then your fathers cried out to the Lord and the Lord sent Moses and Aaron, who brought your fathers out of Egypt and made them dwell in this place. But they forgot the Lord their God! And he sold them into the hand of Sisera, commander of the army of Hazor, and into the hand of the Philistines, and into the hand of the King of Moab. And they fought against them. And they cried out to the Lord and said, 'We have sinned, because we have forsaken the Lord and have served the Baals and the Ashtaroth. But now deliver us out of the hand of our enemies, that we may serve you.' And the Lord sent Jerubbaal and Barak and Jephthah and Samuel and delivered you out of the hand of your enemies on every side, and you lived in safety. And when you saw that Nahash the king of the Ammonites came against you, you said to me, 'No, but a king shall reign over us,' when the Lord your God was your king. And now behold the king whom you have chosen, for whom you have asked; behold, the Lord has set a king over you!"

"Long live the king! Long live the king!" the people shouted in unison. The men thrust their fists to the sky as they chanted.

Samuel silenced the crowd.

"If you will fear the Lord and serve him and obey his voice and not rebel against the commandment of the Lord, and if both you and the king who reigns over you will follow the Lord your God, it will be well," he shouted. Then Samuel spoke slow and deliberately, "but if you will not obey the voice of the Lord, but rebel against the commandment of the Lord, then the hand of the Lord will be against you and your king!" He shouted, pointing towards Saul.

He could see the people begin to murmur amongst themselves. Several looked at him questioningly.

"What's he getting at?" One man whispered to another.

"Same spiel he does every time…" the second whispered in reply.

"Now, therefore, stand still and see this great thing that the Lord will do before your eyes," Samuel shouted as he lifted his hands to the sky.

The crowd looked above them as many realized, to their amazement, that the sky had begun to darken with thick clouds overhead.

"Is it not wheat harvest today?" Samuel asked, allowing the question to sink in. "I will call upon the Lord, that he may send thunder and rain. And you shall know and see that your wickedness is great, which you have done in the sight of the Lord, in asking for yourselves a king." Samuel raised his eyes to the darkened sky. "Lord, send a devastating rain that these rebellious people would remember this day!"

The people began to murmur as the clouds rolled overhead. Suddenly, lightning flashed, and a deafening thunder cracked. The massive crowd shuddered at the sound as the rain began to pour. Many dispersed into the nearby homes and businesses. Travelers gathered under whatever cover could be found as the downpour increased. Lightning flashed and thunder boomed all around. A crack of thunder sounded from within the city, sending the remaining crowd scattering for shelter. Saul and Ahinoam were ushered into a nearby dwelling along with those who'd recently pledged their allegiance. Samuel stood unmoved, still praying with his face to heaven, his arms outstretched with his palms towards the sky.

The people watched as Samuel prayed and the rain thickened until he could barely be seen from the windows and doors of the city. The tribal elders sent their sons to plead with him that he would pray for the people and ask the Lord to bring an end to the downpour.

Samuel continued to pray for the storm.

One by one, the elders emerged from their hiding places and approached the prophet. "Please!" the old men shouted over the storm. "Please pray for your servants to the Lord your God, that we may not die, for we have added to all our sins this evil, to ask for ourselves a king."

"We were wrong," another elder shouted. "Forgive us!"

Saul left the shelter of the home where they'd fled and joined the elders in their pleading. Others left the refuge of their shelters and joined Saul and the elders in the pouring rain, pleading for mercy. Samuel was again surrounded by people, now shivering and drenched to the bone.

Finally, the prophet lowered his head and opened his eyes.

"Do not be afraid!" he shouted to them. "You have done all this evil. Yet do not turn aside from following the Lord, but serve the Lord with all your heart. And do not turn aside after empty things that cannot profit or deliver, for they are empty. For the Lord will not forsake his people, for his great name's sake, because it has pleased the Lord to make you a people for himself. Moreover, as for me, far be it from me that I should sin against the Lord by ceasing to pray for you, and I will instruct you in the good and the right way. Only fear the Lord and serve him faithfully with all your heart. For consider what great things he has done for you. But if you still do wickedly, you shall be swept away, both you and your king!"

The listeners had gathered close, straining to hear the prophet above the rain. Once again, they were shoulder-to-shoulder around him. Some prayed, and many swore oaths of their future faithfulness.

The rain began to subside. The downpour lightened slowly until nothing but the thick humid air remained. Then, quite unceremoniously, the prophet began making his way through the crowd to the open street and out of the city. The young apprentice pushed his way through the people into the open and sprinted down the street to catch up.

From within an adjacent inn, the innkeeper's wife watched intently and craned her head out of the window looking up towards the sky. "Amazing!" She said aloud.

"Ah! You could see the rain was coming before he started," her husband replied. "Everyone knows it never rains that hard for long."

"That's just the kind of thinking that Samuel just warned about!"

The innkeeper scoffed and waved off the comment as he watched the new king and his entourage enter to dry off and prepare for their journey back to Gibeah.

Putting on an entirely different demeanor, the innkeeper welcomed them.

As Saul dried himself by the fire, he thought on Samuel's words. Each time Samuel had warned the people of transgressing, he'd specifically addressed them with the words 'and your king.' It was a somber reminder of the weight he now bore. As his pulse hastened and his chest tightened, Saul tried not to let the dread of it overcome him. He closed his eyes and focused on the warmth of the fire. Slowly, the anxiety dissipated as Ahinoam leaned against him. She clasped his hand in her own and prayed a silent prayer for his peace of mind and wisdom for the task that lay before him.

PRODIGAL SON

1095 BC, Ramah, Benjamin, Israel

B y the time Samuel arrived at his home in Ramah, several weeks had passed since Saul's inauguration at Gilgal. The time alone was desperately needed. In the solitude of the long trek, he'd poured out his heart to God, pleading for intercession in the lives of his sons. He remained hopeful that the recent turn of events had sufficiently softened their, as yet, impenetrable hearts. Nathan came out to greet him as he approached.

"They're here as you requested," he said.

"How much did you have to pay them?"

"Less than you set aside, but even now, they're nearly as drunk as they were when I found them. Joel insisted on bringing several of his harem with him. They seem to think there is something to gain by their presence here. I apologize, but it did make the task of persuading him a bit easier," the servant explained.

Samuel shook his head as he walked toward the dwelling. He could hear his sons' drunken laughter before he entered. It fell silent as soon as the door swung open and Samuel stepped inside. Joel pushed the young prostitute off of him and stood as Samuel entered the room. Abijah merely returned a cockeyed gaze as Samuel glared at him in disappointment.

"Leave us!" Samuel instructed the two young women clinging to his son. They looked up at Joel who nodded to them, indicating they should obey the old man.

"Leave us!" Samuel shouted again as the two scurried out the door. Samuel walked to the hearth and placed his hands upon the mantle, looking down to the earthen floor.

"Do you know where I've come from?" Samuel asked them.

"You've come from," Abijah started to say, pausing to collect his drunken mind, "anointing your new heir."

Samuel turned to look at his son. "Heir? No. I've come from anointing God's chosen King. Your King." Samuel paused to gauge the reaction of his sons.

"Well then, I guess we're all out of work then, eh?" Abijah said with a smile.

"You will no longer judge God's people. They have rejected you. They have rejected me. King Saul and his heirs will now judge Israel. You two will have to find some honest work. You will have to work with your hands and by the sweat of your brow, do you understand?"

"Are we not entitled to a seat in the king's court? Perhaps as his spiritual or legal advisors?" asked Joel.

"I've instructed Saul that you are to have no part in his house. That he give you nothing."

"You would have us become beggars? You would have us reduced to nothing?" Joel pleaded.

"He would have us beg *him!*" Abijah shouted. "Our all knowing abba!" Abijah smirked.

"I would have you become honest men," Samuel replied. "I have failed you and as a result, I have failed God and His people. You will remain here with me and not return to Dan or Beersheba."

Abijah huffed. "Why should I stay here? I have my own possessions, my own home. I'm no child for you to command anymore."

"If you should return to Beersheba, you return to a people who no longer believe you are a servant of the Lord, a people who despise you and deservedly so. A people whom you have robbed and over whom you no longer have any sway. How long do you think your possessions will sustain you there?" Samuel allowed his words to sink in.

"Even now, I imagine your possessions are being reclaimed by their true owners," Samuel said calmly. "I doubt very much that you will have anything to return to my son."

"You've conspired against us!" Abijah shouted as he jumped to his feet. "You... you old wind-bag! You expect me to just come back here and be your servant? King or no king, it makes no difference to me. I can go and do as I please," he shouted at the old man raising his fist. He hesitated and turned to the door where he knew Nathan waited on the other side, then lowered his arm. "I don't need you," he said before turning to leave.

"Abijah," Samuel called after him, "if you leave, I cannot protect you."

"Abijah, please!" Joel said, attempting to calm his younger brother and mediate the escalating situation.

"I'm a grown man! I don't need your protection," he shouted as he stepped out.

Samuel looked to his remaining son, standing at the threshold and watching Abijah leave, taking the prostitutes with him.

"It seems your companions have abandoned you," Samuel said.

Joel dropped his head. He'd been so foolish to allow them to follow him here. How disrespectful it was to bring those women into his father's house. He deserved to be embarrassed by them.

"I have wronged you and I have wronged the people, father. But what can I do now that I have made an enemy of God? What hope is there for me now having corrupted His law?"

"I do not know what God has planned for you my son, but if you repent and turn from your ways, He is steadfast in His love and forgiveness. If you truly humble yourself, there may be hope for you yet."

Joel dropped to his knees at his father's feet and bowed his head.

"If you will allow me Father, I will stay here and serve you. I will do whatever you ask of me."

ABOMINATIONS

1094 BC, Gath, Philistia
(modern-day Israel, approximately 15 miles inland
from the Mediterranean Coast)

There were giants in the earth in those days; and also after
that, when the sons of God came in unto the daughters
of men, and they bare children to them, the same became
mighty men which were of old, men of renown.
Genesis 6:4

T he nursemaid cradled the huge child in her arms and carried him over to the physician for inspection. He unceremoniously took the child over to the table where numerous lamps burned. Laying the child down gently, he began a thorough inspection, as several others looked on.

The nurse watched hesitantly.

"Hmm, it is better than some of the others," the physician said as he turned the child over. He measured every inch, reading the numbers aloud to the aid at his side. He counted each finger and toe and noted every possible observation, including skin tone, eye color, and head circumference.

One of the priests turned to see the several women preparing the child's mother for burial. He walked over and looked down at the face of the poor soul who'd given her life in service to her people, though, not willingly of course. Nevertheless, her sacrifice, along with others like her, would serve their people well in the years to come.

"How much does this one weigh," asked the chief priest as he watched the physician.

"Just over eleven mina."

"Dagon be praised," the chief priest exclaimed. "My largest son was only six mina at birth."

"Not the biggest one yet," replied the physician, "but no malignant abnormalities with this one," he stated coldly. "I would say it was a success. He is certainly worth keeping... for now anyways."

"What do you mean? What *is* wrong with him?"

The physician held up one of the infants hands and indicated the extra digit.

"Six," the priest said as his face contorted with disgust.

"On both hands and both feet," the physician confirmed. "Like I said, it is nothing malignant, and it's not as if you bred them for their looks is it," the physician asked rhetorically as he looked over to the large woman being prepared for burial. "Besides, I believe this particular defect is not uncommon with them. I don't see anything that would keep him from serving his intended purpose in the years to come. It's possible some malady could manifest itself later, but for now, from a statistical standpoint, I believe it is worth seeing how he turns out."

"Hmm," the priest grunted. "Very well then. See to it. How many are left?"

"She was the last," the physician replied stoically. "This one makes five viable specimens. The others are doing well. Their progress is promising. You should stop in and see them before you leave. The two oldest are developing as hoped; much larger than any normal child of course."

"Very well," the priest replied as he turned to leave. He stopped at the door. "Send me your bill and expenses. I will be checking in from time to time."

TRAPPINGS

1094 BC, Gibeah, Benjamin, Israel

It had been months since the deliverance of Jabesh Gilead. Saul stood watching, as what would become his palace began to take shape. Teams of men cut and placed stone and erected wooden frames that would be used by the masons to lay the rock archways into the hall where he would hold court and resolve disputes among his people. How different life has been in the past months from what it had been prior to the battle. Servants, gifts, and materials were in no short supply. The very thought that the project being constructed before him was meant to be his future dwelling was surreal.

"It all seems too much," Saul said.

"Nonsense," Nuri responded. "You are God's anointed. Who else can claim such title?"

Saul shook his head. He didn't feel any different. What he had done, what he had said leading up to the battle had been so quick, so rash and unplanned. It had seemed easy compared to what awaited him now. Years of thoughtful planning and contemplation, which would be scrutinized by thousands upon thousands, now awaited him.

Nuri turned to see the caravan approaching from the east before Saul noticed it.

"What have we here?" Nuri asked.

Saul turned to see the new arrivals climbing the hill towards them.

"Indeed," Saul replied.

They watched as the caravan grew closer to the construction site and ascended the hill of Gibeah towards them.

The leading elders from the city of Jabesh Gilead presented themselves with bows to their new king. Saul recognized some of them as the same men who met him on his return from the fields several months ago, though the one-eyed Reubenite was not among them as before. Several of the more elderly men among them were assisted off of their donkeys as Saul welcomed them and exchanged embraces. Each of them knelt and kissed his hands in displays of respect and heartfelt appreciation.

"My king," one of the men spoke. "We and our tribe owe you a great debt," he said as his face contorted with emotion. "You purchased our very lives, the lives of our children and grandchildren, the lives of our wives and servants. With all that occurred before and after the battle, we were unable to sufficiently demonstrate our appreciation for the mighty blow that you dealt our enemies. To show our appreciation, the people of our city and tribe gave an offering and our most skilled craftsmen have labored to create a gift suitable for the first and only king anointed by the Eternal God of our people."

The old man turned and motioned for a large younger man who bore a strong resemblance. The younger man stepped forward holding a beautifully decorated acacia box with gold trim, hinges, and latch, inlaid with silver artwork. Holding the box with one hand underneath, he opened the latch and lifted the top, slowly revealing the contents.

Within the box was a crown flanked on either side by thick armlets. The elder carefully lifted the crown with both hands from the purple cushion on which it sat. It was made of finely polished gold with stones set into it at intervals like the markings of a sundial: ruby, topaz, emerald, turquoise, sapphire, diamond, jacinth, agate, amethyst, beryl, onyx, and jasper, twelve of them in all. Saul recognized them immediately as the same stones born upon the priestly vest, each representing one of the tribes of Israel.

The old man turned the crown to display an inscription engraved on the interior of the crown, near the forepart.

"You shall love the Lord your God with all your heart and with all your soul and with all your might," the elder read. "The same is written on the armlets."

Saul accepted the crown and turned it in his hands, examining the fine craftsmanship and engraving.

"I have not seen finer craftsmanship," Saul replied with sincere appreciation. "I do not know what to say," Saul said as he lifted his eyes to the men before him.

The men smiled, pleased with the king's response.

"May I?" the elder asked as he reached towards the crown. Saul extended the crown as the old man took it and lifted it up. Saul lowered his head and allowed the elder to place the heavy crown upon his head.

It fit perfectly. Somehow, the craftsmen had known his exact measurements. Saul recalled that months ago, Nuri had carefully obtained measurements for what Saul believed would be used for his armor. Saul turned to Nuri.

"A perfect fit," Saul said.

Nuri smiled.

The elder then removed one of the armlets from the box. It was about half the length of Saul's forearm and, in addition to the inscription, bore a round, flat onyx stone, much larger than the ones inlaid into the crown. On the stone were engraved the names of the twelve tribes. He opened the armlet and held it towards the king as Saul held his arm out and allowed the elder to clasp it around his wrist. He repeated the gesture with the second armlet which was like the first.

"These are beautiful," Saul said, dumbfounded. "Truly marvelous."

The elder nodded as he looked at his compatriots.

"One last thing," the elder said as another man produced a neatly folded garment from a new leather bag.

With the assistance of a second man, they carefully unfolded a robe of blue, purple, and scarlet. An embroidered cherubim with outstretched wings reached the entire length of the garment, a beautiful tribute to the trappings of the Holy Tabernacle. The men displayed the robe to Saul before moving to him and fastening it over his broad shoulders with a heavy clasp that rested upon his chest.

Saul held out his arms and examined his new adornments as the men looked on with delight.

"Now you look like a king," Nuri announced.

"I'll say," Saul affirmed with a smile. "Never has a king been dressed with finer raiment, I am certain."

"We are happy that you are pleased," the elder declared. "What more can we do for you, my king? We are all your faithful servants."

"Come, let me show you our new capital while you are here," Saul said as he stretched out his arm and took the elder to his side. "Come, all of you. Welcome to Gibeah."

INTERLUDE

1085 BC, Gibeah, Benjamin, Israel

*Now there was no blacksmith to be found through-
out all the land of Israel, for the Philistines said, "Lest
the Hebrews make themselves swords or spears."*
I Samuel 13:19

"To ón-o-má mu íne," the instructor annunciated in perfect Greek.

"To ón-o-má mu íne," the student repeated.

"To ónomá mu íne Jonathan."

Again, the student repeated the phrase.

"Now in Egyptian and Ugaritic."

Jonathan hesitated momentarily, then responded in both languages.

"Very good young man," the instructor praised in his native Egyptian.

"Thank you," the boy responded in Egyptian. "Shall I put my sword on now?"

The instructor acted as if he hadn't heard the boy.

Jonathan sighed, impatiently, then repeated the question in Egyptian.

"If you're ready," the Egyptian responded.

Prince Jonathan hurried over to a hook on the wall and took the leather scabbard and belt and fastened it around his waist. Drawing the wooden sword, the young man squared off to his instructor. "On guard!" He said in Egyptian.

The instructor quickly seized his right wrist and bending Jonathan's sword arm at the elbow, put the boy's own blade towards his throat.

"Never advertise your attacks. I have taught you nothing if not this," the Egyptian said before releasing him. Drawing his own wooden training sword, the Egyptian squared off from his pupil.

Attempt after failed attempt, the boy struck at the dark-skinned man before him, each time being parried and struck in return, then corrected. The instruction continued on in this way until the boy finally relented, too tired and sore to continue.

"I can't even graze you," he complained.

"I should hardly think myself worthy to be your instructor if you could," the Egyptian responded. "You are a prince. You must learn tactics and how to maneuver armies if your people are to survive. You alone cannot preserve this nation of yours."

"But I want to be a warrior and why would they follow me if I don't know how to fight?"

"A kingdom requires many warriors. Do you think you can fight all your nation's battles by yourself?"

"What do you mean," the prince asked as he attempted another attack.

Blocking the pupil's sword, he responded, "it means you should learn to be what God made you to be before you pursue your own desires. Most men struggle with this their entire lives, pursuing the desire of their hearts. They never ask themselves who or what God intended them to be. You are fortunate, young prince. You already know what God intends you to be. He made your father King, and so you are a prince by your very birthright." The instructor launched an attack, swinging the wooden blade at the boy's head.

Jonathan ducked underneath. "But God chose my father to be King, what if he chooses someone else to be the next King?"

"That is not the way Kingships work," the Egyptian responded as the two circled each other. "You will be King when your father passes."

"Just because my father is King? That hardly seems like a good reason."

The instructor swung the sword in a downward motion towards Jonathan's head. When Jonathan moved to block it, he was swept off his feet, landing flat on his back with the tip of the Egyptian's wooden sword pressed against his neck.

"It is reason enough," the Egyptian said sternly. "There are plenty of men who will be happy to spill your guts and take the crown from you."

"All the more reason to focus on swordsmanship," Jonathan said as he stood to his feet and took an offensive posture.

"And what if those men have an army? What if those men are better trained, stronger, and more experienced than yourself," the instructor asked as he parried the boy's attack. "One day, if God allows you to grow old, you may even be challenged by someone younger than yourself. Will you rely on your own strength in each of these scenarios?"

"So I'm just supposed to let someone else do the fighting for me?"

No sooner than the question had left the boy's mouth had the instructor disarmed him and brought his wooden blade down before stopping abruptly no more than a hand's breadth from the boy's skull.

"In a sense, yes. There is a time when a king should fight, but if a king subjects himself to constant dangers on the front line, instead of leading his men, he will do them more harm than good," the Egyptian explained. "How will you maneuver your forces with any skill, when your entire focus is trained on the man directly to your front trying to kill you?"

He picked up the prince's sword and handed it to him, further illustrating his point.

"But why should anyone else risk his life or die for me?"

"You are the only one who can answer that question. By your conduct, you give value to their service. If you are a poor king, the men who die defending you do so in vain. If you are a great king, well, then there is no better death for a soldier than to give up his life for a noble and worthy cause greater than himself. And so you should learn to lead in a way that merits the devotion and fidelity of your men and subjects."

Jonathan looked at the sword extended in front of him. He reached out his hand and accepted it.

"How could I possibly live up to that," the boy asked, clearly disheartened.

"I do not claim to have all of the answers my boy," said his instructor, "but you're asking the right questions."

Jonathan was startled by a low voice from behind him. Turning, he saw the white beard and silhouette of a familiar bald-headed man sitting in the shadows.

"I might have some guidance to offer in this regard, if there were such a man willing to hear it and put it to good use," said the old prophet.

"Samuel! I didn't know you were coming," Jonathan exclaimed, momentarily forgetting the weight of his birthright.

"You shouldn't trouble yourself too much with that. I rarely know whether I'm coming or going. How should anyone else?"

The young prince embraced the prophet, who returned the gesture of affection. Stepping back he looked at the budding young prince.

"My, you have grown. I must make a point of visiting more often." Turning to the instructor, Samuel asked, "may I borrow your pupil for a while?"

"Certainly, your timing is perfect. We were just finishing up for the day."

"Ah," Samuel said with a nod. "I've never been accused of being prompt, but I suppose there is a first time for everything."

***

Jeribai's sweat poured out in the mid-day sun as he drove the mattock down again. It clanged and jolted his hands upon striking the earth.

"AH!" he shouted. "Another rock!"

His younger brother, Joshaviah, began working the shovel around it throwing earth up and out of the hole they'd been digging.

"It's a big one," Joshaviah said as he scrapped the dirt away. "Your hands ok?"

Jeribai shook his hands in an effort to make the throbbing go away. "They will be when they stop hurting."

Once the rock was sufficiently uncovered, they knelt down and grasped it. "On three," Jeribai instructed, "one, two, three!" The boys heaved the stone up and out of the hole. They watched as it landed with a thud on the outside, making sure that it didn't roll back in and onto their feet.

"Here," Joshaviah said, handing his brother the shovel and taking the mattock, "let's switch for a little while."

"Thanks," the older brother replied looking at his hands. A callous had torn loose when he'd struck the last rock, revealing a small circular patch of bright red flesh underneath. He put his hand to his mouth and bit the flap of skin off to prevent it from pulling more skin away as he continued working, then spat the chunk of hard thick skin to the side.

"Yum!" Joshaviah said as he swung the mattock.

"How's it coming down there?" They heard from above as a shadow cast over them from outside of the hole.

"More rocks." They replied simultaneously.

The two boys stood in a 4 by 4 cubit square hole about 4 cubits deep. Their father handed down two thin copper rods, each about one cubit in length with a ninety-degree bend at one end. Jeribai, took one in each hand and held them parallel to each other and the ground. He walked around the inside edge of the hole then turned towards the center. As he did, the two rods turned inward, crossing each other.

"Dead center! Great job men!" Their father exclaimed.

The two boys smiled, thankful that they wouldn't have to recenter the hole and hopeful that they'd strike water sooner than later.

"This is going to be a good spot!" their father said enthusiastically. "They're fortunate it's so close to where they'd like to build. They won't have to change the location at all, it will be right inside their perimeter wall."

The two boys had been digging wells with their father long enough to know how seldom this occurred. If you could afford to build a new home, seldom did it occur that the chosen location would have its own water source so close by.

Elnaam reached down and took Joshaviah's hand as Jeribai assisted him out of the hole. They both reached down and took Jeribai's arms and hauled him out. They walked to the shade of a nearby terebinth tree and sat on the ground to eat the bread and honey Elnaam had obtained for them from the market in Gibeah while he climbed down into the hole and began breaking up the ground in the bottom of the pit.

The boys chewed the bread lazily, enjoying their brief reprieve as they listened to their father swing the mattock. Their enjoyment was interrupted by the sound of a loud clang, only this time, it had the distinct sound of cracked iron.

"Someone is about to be dipped," Jeribai said in a low voice as they heard their father shout from the bottom of the pit.

"Well I'll be dipped!"

Joshaviah nearly choked on his bread as he tried not to laugh at their father's misfortune. They both stood and walked to the edge of the hole. Peering in, they could see their father crouched at the bottom.

"Did it break?" Jeribai asked.

"Yes," Elnaam replied as he stood and lifted the handle and broken chisel up to his eldest son.

Jeribai took and examined it. The chisel had completely broken free from the eye where the metal head attached to the wooden handle.

The boys didn't have to ask what this meant. It was their last functional mattock and without one, there would be no more digging in this hard and rocky soil.

Their father reached up with both arms and the boys hauled him out of the hole.

"Let's get a fence put up so no one falls in. I'll have to go to Ekron or Gath and trade some of our broken ones just to get them to fix one," Elnaam said, fuming with anger. "Those…" He stopped himself, struggling to control his frustration. "They won't take gold or silver for iron anymore. They have strict laws against it! They rob us of iron today so that they can conquer us tomorrow."

"What about the blacksmith near Geba? Can't we go to him?" Jeribai asked.

Joshaviah wondered if his brother could really be asking this. While he knew that the broken implement had to be repaired, he was inwardly thankful that their work for the day could not continue.

Elnaam looked at his sons without speaking for a moment.

"No one has seen him for more than two months now. I went to see him a while back and found his shop had been burned to the ground. His neighbors say it happened in the night. No one saw who did it."

"There's got to be another Israelite blacksmith somewhere," Jeribai protested.

"Enoch was the last one that I know of. It is not something you can just pick up. His fathers have been blacksmiths for centuries."

The boys stood waiting for their father's instruction.

"Let's pack up and head home. I'll need to get the other tools that need fixed to use as payment."

"Does that mean we can go with you?"

"I will go to Ekron by myself. You two will go stay with your cousin Jehu in Anathoth till I return."

"Father, I'm a grown man." Jeribai pleaded. "You will need help. I want to go with you. If some good-for-nothings see you by yourself, you might get robbed or beaten. Let me go with you."

"Me too Father!" Joshaviah pled. "I can help. The more of us there are, the better."

"Ha! Grown are you? Cause I don't see hair on your faces!" Elnaam retorted. "You're barely adolescents."

"Father, you told us not to go near the Philistines alone. You must take someone with you, even if it's not one of us."

"I'll think about it, but not another word!" Elnaam said as he stuffed the shovel and broken mattock into the leather sacks hanging on either side of their donkey. "Now, you know the way to Anathoth?"

With resignation, Jeribai nodded his affirmation.

"You're sure you can get there without me, yes?"

"Yes, Father."

"Which way is it?" he asked.

Jeribai raised a hand, pointing in the direction of the city. "That way. About sixteen stadia."

"Ok," their father replied. "Ok," he repeated, sensing their apprehension. "You're nearly men, I didn't mean to say that you boys aren't

163

brave or strong. It would just be a waste of your time for you to come with me. It's a long way and you'd be very bored. Make yourselves useful at your cousin's. It would make your mother happy. I'll come and get you tomorrow and we'll get back to work. Now go ahead and I'll see you early tomorrow."

Though not wholly naive to the gravity of the situation, neither wanted to cause their father any more grief than life had already dealt him. The two boys quietly obeyed as their father departed for the Philistine city of Ekron.

***

"I'm glad you're here," the prince said, nearly jogging to keep up with the old prophet.

"Why is that?"

"I've been studying like you said. I get up early, I study the law, the scriptures. I'm learning Egyptian, Ammonite, and now Greek. I'm learning the tactics and strategies of the Pharaohs, Assyrians, and Philistines."

"That's great young man, but what is it that troubles you," Samuel asked.

"I want to be a fighter, a warrior, not just someone who sends others into the battle."

"Ah! I see. And you enjoy your physical training more than your studies I suppose?"

"Well, yeah," Jonathan exclaimed.

"Sparring is more agreeable to you than the law?"

"Yes! I knew you'd understand!" The young prince said.

"I suppose I could find someone else to lead our people when your father is gone, perhaps someone more erudite and less energetic."

The youth huffed. "I know I need to learn it, but I'm better at sparring than I am at reading and memorizing laws," he insisted. "Sure Hodavyahu beats me every now and then, but against most of my training partners, I usually win. None of them have to learn all this... this... other stuff."

"Sounds like maybe you need some new training partners," Samuel suggested. "And how many of them will take your father's place as King?"

Jonathan dropped his head as they walked. "Well, *you* said God should be our King."

Samuel stopped to face the boy.

"Look, you're a smart young man," he said. Examining the boy's eyes, Samuel considered how to address the question. "I said that before the Lord anointed your father and it *was* true then. It remains true now and Yahweh should be our Lord and King. Your father should look to God's leading to instruct his own decisions, as should you when you become king. As His anointed, it is the king's responsibility to lead in a way that pleases God. Not everyone agrees on the way we should go as a people. That's where your father comes in. He bears the weight of leadership so that the people may have a common direction."

"No skill is honed or developed, but by discipline. I know your training is painful, boring at times, but you are planting seeds of discipline. If you persevere through the difficulty and drudgery, those seeds will produce righteousness. The fruit of a righteous king is peace. Peace for our people."

"I know that you would lay down your life for our people, but this is why you must be prepared to lead. Not every man who would lead cares for our people as you do Jonathan. Do you understand? You must lead in order to preserve the lives of your people. Sometimes this will require the blood of valiant men. You should bear this with a heavy heart," Samuel said, stopping to look the young man in the eye. "It is good that this concerns you, but remember too that one day your life may indeed be required. I would encourage you to go and do as you feel the Lord directs you. Trust His leading, even if you do not understand it."

The prophet began walking again as the young prince hurried to keep up.

"You mean like when Joshua led our people to march around Jericho?"

"Explain," the old prophet replied.

"Well, it goes against everything I'm being taught about military strategy and tactics. Why would the army announce to the enemy that the attack was coming? Why would they show themselves in broad daylight and give up all hope of surprise if God had not led them to do so?"

"Good question. Why did they?"

"Well, they trusted and obeyed, even though it didn't make much sense," Jonathan said. "I think it was a test."

"You think right young man," Samuel affirmed. "And someday, God may test you. To outsiders, His instructions may seem foolish or reckless even. I won't always be around to inquire of the Lord, but I'll tell you something," Samuel said as he stopped walking and turned to Jonathan. "God speaks to all of us, not just me. He speaks to us primarily through His word, which is why it's so important that you know it."

"I'm nearly finished writing my own copy of the law," Jonathan said.

"Very good, and when you're done you must study it and study it some more. The King of Israel must know the law better than anyone if he is to discern the will of God. You can't obey it if you don't know it. You mustn't just know the law verbatim. You must know the *spirit* of the law. But God speaks to us in other ways as well my boy. He speaks just loud enough for you to hear Him. If you aren't close to Him, you may not hear Him. Most people put too much distance, too many things or people between God and themselves to hear His voice above all the noise. Do you understand?"

"I think so."

"Good," the old prophet replied.

As they continued walking along the perimeter walls of the king's palace, the prophet could tell that something still troubled the boy.

"What else do you want to ask me?" Samuel inquired.

"I've heard rumors, rumors of war with the Philistines."

"Our people have enjoyed a brief period of peace since the battle with the Ammonites at Jabesh Gilead. You've been fortunate to come up during this time, but yes, a fight with the Philistines is on the horizon. They are preparing a way to subdue us. All over Israel, metal suitable for weaponry is becoming more and more scarce among our people. I can assure you that this is by design. Any Israelite who so much as dabbles in the art of blacksmithing has a price on his head." Samuel thought for a moment about the stories he'd heard all across Israel. He decided to spare the details.

"You know that they are a formidable enemy," Samuel continued. "Comparatively, they are much like us in many ways. They had to fight to get here, to carve out what land they now possess, but they do not fear Yahweh. They worship fish-headed idols, things made of their own hands. Their practices are abhorrent to the Lord. You should study them. Try to understand them, but do not be afraid of them."

"No, no, it's not that. I'm not afraid, I just," he paused, trying not to sound too prideful. "I just worry that Father will not allow me to fight. That I may be too young to lead men in battle."

The prophet laughed.

"I should have known. Our people have rarely known any peace that lasted long enough for one man to be born and die without some war or battle to fight. You will get your chance. Just make sure that you are ready when the time comes."

"He will be," said a familiar voice from behind them.

"Uncle Abner" the prince exclaimed.

"Jonathan," Abner said as he embraced his young nephew, then turned to the prophet. "Samuel, how are you?"

"Well. I've come to pay my condolences. Your mentor was a courageous warrior and a man of God. I hear that he has trained you well."

"He was a blessing to us all, myself especially."

"Tell me," Samuel said, "what will be your first act as commander of the army?"

"Army?" Abner laughed. "I aim to create an army. What we have is a makeshift militia of poorly trained and ill-equipped volunteers. My first goal is to create a professional fighting force, a real army."

"And how do you intend to do that?"

"Training. Tough, realistic training. Under Nuri, we trained volunteers from the tribes twice a year. We assemble only when a threat is imminent. We're not capable of defending at a moment's notice, much less performing any sort of offensive strike. Already the Philistines are preparing the way to annihilate us. Nearly every last weapon gained from prior victories has been stolen, pilfered, or traded. We must begin to rearm ourselves and prepare to fight back. Do you not agree?"

"I believe God rewards diligence. There are many in Israel who profit from peace with our enemies and will oppose your plans."

"Indeed there are those who prefer and profit from our current predicament, but no one makes peace with the weak. When we are strong, then the Philistines, the Amalekites, the Amorites, Moabites, Ammonites, and the like will come to us with offers of peace. They desire our annihilation. Only when they respect us will they present favorable terms. Only when they fear reprisal will their raids come to an end. They do not recognize our inheritance of this land and why should they?" He asked rhetorically. "The truth is, we have no alternative."

Samuel had always been fond of Abner. Much like himself, he was never one to mince words.

"You have a worthy, but difficult task ahead of you," Samuel responded. "No one likes taxes and armies are expensive. It will be difficult."

"Yes. We've already met much resistance," Abner responded. "If you could show your support for our efforts, it may help things along."

"I will pray and do as the Lord instructs, but do not think that the people will fall in line simply by a word from me. If that were true, we would not be having this conversation."

Abner smiled. "Indeed."

YUVAL

1083 BC, Benjamin, Israel

Yuval was at the brink of death the first time he saw the prince. Abandoned by his father and caring for a growing child, his mother had resorted to the only work she could find, an ancient occupation. She spared Yuval as much as she could, but there was no hiding the unsavory business. She would instruct Yuval to go play outside or send him on errands to the market as men came and went from their home, leaving their meager tribute that kept Yuval and his mother scratching for food each day. It had been this way for years. Yuval struggled to find work of his own, anything to earn money so that he could help his mother.

At only 12 years old and scrawny, he resembled a skeleton more than a young man. When his mother began showing signs of illness, Yuval resorted to begging. When his begging did not work, he resorted to stealing. He would steal food from the market and coins from unsuspecting vendors, merchants, and customers—anything to sustain them. It was no use however. The disease worked quickly and mercilessly.

One evening when he returned from the market with some stolen fruit, he found her unresponsive. He'd tried unsuccessfully to wake her, shaking her and shouting her name. He thought for a moment whether he should go for help but realized it was no use. She was cold to the touch and no one, not even Samuel the prophet, could bring her back now. He crumbled to his knees and slumped over her lifeless body. Placing her cold hands on his face, the boy wept for hours until fatigue finally overcame him.

He awoke on the floor beside her mat. Still clutching her hand, he heard the noise that had roused him. A customer had come to call upon her and was rapping on the door frame. When no one answered, the man entered. The mourning adolescent was appalled and enraged at the intrusion. The nerve of this man, he thought. Did he think he owned the place? Did he think he owned her?

Yuval was on his feet before he knew it. The man looked silently about the room as his eyes adjusted to the darkness, calling his mother's name. As Yuval watched the man, years of built-up rage took hold. Grabbing a broom handle leaning against the wall near him, Yuval swung it at the man's head, striking him so hard that it splintered the shaft with a loud crack. The man fell to the ground. Yuval struck him again and again. The man's arms were streaked with blood as he raised them to protect himself. Striking the man's head again, his body went limp and his arms fell to his side as he lay on the dirt floor. Yuval relented suddenly as his mind returned. Looking at the splintered broom handle now covered with the man's blood, a wave of fear and dread washed over him. He dropped the shaft and ran from the dwelling.

He never returned. The fate of his mother's body or the man had to this day remained a mystery to him. He moved from town to town until at last he arrived at Gibeah, where he lurked in the shadows, living off of whatever refuse he could find to sustain himself. He knew that King Saul lived here. There would be wealth and with wealth, there would be surplus and waste. The boy was shrewd and reasoned that if one must live off of the discards of another, it was better to be near those who lived in excess. As the months passed, creeping about the palace's outer wall, Yuval noticed the coming and going of the young princes. Prince Jonathan, the eldest, came and went the most and Yuval saw him with enough frequency to realize they were about the same age, though Jonathan was clearly in far better condition.

One day when the prince passed, escorted by several of the royal guards, the young prince's gaze had fallen upon the urchin boy. Yuval met Jonathan's gaze and refused to look away. There did not appear disdain or pride in the young prince's eyes. It was different from the looks Yuval was used to. Yuval stretched out his hands, as the other urchins did at the Prince's passing. To his surprise, the prince placed a large silver coin in his outstretched hand. He instantly clinched it, drawing it close to his body and fled the mob of other beggars.

Stirred by something in the young man's face, the prince watched as the boy fled with the precious silver.

Yuval retreated to his only place of solitude, an olive tree located in the middle of a vast cemetery near the edge of town. He examined the coin. No one apart from his mother had ever given him anything before. He'd worked for money in the past, but never had he been given anything of significant value, much less a coin of this size and quality. As he gazed at the shiny coin, he heard the sound of someone approaching. Quickly he spun around and peeked over the rock he'd been crouching behind. Some of the other local beggars were approaching. Two grown men had followed him. He knew instantly their intent. He stood and began to flee in the opposite direction but was caught by the nape of his neck. He'd not seen one of the beggars sneak around to cut him off. The grown man thrust him to the ground.

"Give it up boy and we won't have to kill you."

Yuval grabbed for anything he could find. His hand searched the ground as he watched his attacker. His hand came to rest upon a fist-sized rock and slung it at the man's face as he turned to run, only to be caught once again by one of the other men he'd seen approaching. The man held his left arm as the other seized his right. The original attacker walked slowly around to his front.

"You see? There is no use." The man bent down and picked up a rock. "Like throwing stones, do you?" he said before smashing the stone against Yuval's face.

The boy's eyes and nose burned with searing pain. The man reared back again and punched him in the gut. Yuval doubled over, still held up by the other two attackers. The third man searched his ragged and tattered clothing. Finding nothing the man punched his already broken nose.

"Where is it?" he shouted.

The other two men shoved him to the ground.

"He was over here," one of them said as two of them searched the ground where Yuval had been. Turning over the rock where Yuval had hidden the coin, one of the men shouted with elation, "I've got it! I found it!"

The third man leaned over and patted Yuval on the cheek.

"That'll be all then."

Yuval watched the blood pour from his face into the dirt. It trickled onto a sharp rock, roughly shaped like a pyramid.

As the third man joined his mates, Yuval grabbed the rock and stood. The men paid him no attention as they examined the coin. He threw the rock as hard as he could at the third man's head, striking him directly in the temple. The man stumbled, then fell to the ground. The others looked down at him, then back at Yuval. He turned and sprinted away as they lunged after him.

The men were close behind him as he ran. His lungs burned with the dry air. The blood from his face sputtered as he gasped for breath. As they made their way through the cemetery and back alleys of Gibeah, the thugs would not relent in their chase. Yuval realized he was headed towards the palace. It occurred to him that if he could make it to the gates, the guards might intervene before these men could kill him.

As he closed the distance to the palace gates, his legs nearly gave out. He stumbled and fell just before reaching them, then crawled towards the gate. Looking behind he saw the men were nearly upon him. A crowd of bystanders near the gate cleared the area, seeing that some violence was afoot. Yuval threw his body upon the gate and banged on the door just as the vagrants reached him and snatched him down into the dirt. They began kicking him as one of the palace guards shouted from the rampart overlooking the gate.

"Halt! Stop that!" Yuval heard the guard shouting.

The men kept kicking him. One of the hoodlums drove his heal down into Yuval's already smashed face. Then, as quickly as it had started, the kicking stopped. Yuval opened his eyes to see his attackers restrained by the royal guards. An officer addressed them.

"What's going on here? Why are you beating this boy?"

"He assaulted our friend!" exclaimed one.

"He killed him," said the other. "Just go look in the cemetery, you'll see he smashed our friend's head in with a rock!"

Yuval struggled to his feet as the officer dispatched four of his men to go to the cemetery and investigate.

"What do you say?" He asked Yuval.

His head was still spinning. His face seared with pain. He tried to speak as blood poured from his mouth. He looked up to see that the prince, hearing the commotion outside the gate had come to see what it was about. Their eyes met and Yuval hoped that Jonathan recognized him.

"These men stole from me. Their friend smashed my face and took the coin the prince gave me. Yes, I threw a rock at him, but only to recover what was mine."

Jonathan listened to the battered boy. He considered the blunder he'd committed in giving such a grand prize to him in front of the others this morning. His own careless actions had brought this pain upon the boy.

"Yes, I recognize him. I gave him a coin just a little while ago," Jonathan said.

A wave of relief washed over Yuval along with a strange feeling he was not accustomed to. Yuval nodded as he tried to compose himself.

"Do you still have it?"

Yuval shook his head and pointed to the two men. One of the guards searched them and located a single coin in one of the men's garments. The guard handed it to the Prince.

Jonathan examined it. "He's telling the truth," said the prince.

The officer ordered the two thugs taken to jail to await trial before turning to Yuval.

"Where is your home," the officer asked.

Yuval was bent over, holding his crushed nose, and trying to stop the bleeding. Composing himself he straightened and responded.

"I have no home."

"Then where might I find you when these men are tried?"

Uncertain, Yuval stood silent for a moment.

"We'll deal with that later," said Jonathan. "Come, let's see you get fixed up," Jonathan said waving Yuval to follow him into the palace grounds. Yuval looked at the guard and back at the prince. Jonathan stood waiting for him. Yuval looked at the officer who motioned for him to follow. The three proceeded through the gate, followed by several other guards.

Jonathan ushered the boy to a hall and had him sit as one of the guards was sent to locate the royal physician.

"Tell me exactly what happened," the officer instructed.

Yuval told the story of what had transpired in the cemetery. He assumed he had killed the third man he'd struck with the rock in the cemetery.

The physician arrived and began attending to the boy's shattered nose while the officer spoke separately with the prince.

"Thief or not, the boy would not be justified in killing the man. I'm afraid the boy may be guilty of the more egregious offense."

One of the guards entered the hall upon return from the cemetery.

"We found no one sir. There was some blood on the ground in several places, but no body. Looks like the thief must have taken a good knock, but he isn't dead. Shall we attempt to identify the man or locate him?"

The officer turned back to Jonathan. "I stand corrected," he said. Turning to Yuval, the officer asked, "What say you? Shall we look for him?"

Yuval shook his head. He would rather administer his own punishment if the opportunity later presented itself.

"Tend to the others as you see fit," Jonathan instructed, then walked back over to where Yuval was being treated.

"What is your name?"

"Yuval."

"Who is your father?"

"I have no father."

"And your mother?

"She died."

"Do you have any family? Someone who looks after you? Anyone," the prince asked.

"I get by on my own," Yuval responded coldly.

The surgeon pretended not to pay attention to the conversation as he worked, but Jonathan could see the strain of emotion in the man's eyes. He knew the old man had a soft spot for the less fortunate and carried substantial sway with his father, the king.

"Well then, it seems that you answer to no one," Jonathan said.

Yuval was quiet. The surgeon continued cleaning and bandaging his nose.

"That being the case, I hope you would consider a proposal," said the prince. "You see… as you know, I am Israel's first prince. I'm the eldest of my brothers and constantly find myself in short supply of someone to train with. I hope you would consider becoming my training companion. You would be trained as I am trained. You would eat as I eat, study as I do, go where I go."

Yuval was silent. He contemplated whether he could possibly have heard correctly.

"Well, what do you say? You are the perfect match. We're practically the same size. I bet we're the same age. Are you thirteen?"

"Almost, I think."

"See? What do you say? Will you train with me? We'll fight together, but only to make each other better, not to injure and not until you're healed."

"I will get to go where you go and eat what you have left?"

"No! No! You get to eat what I eat, not my leftovers. You won't be much of a training companion if you aren't healthy."

"He's pretty healthy considering," said the surgeon, examining Yuval. "But I imagine on the right diet he'll add weight quickly." Finished working, he took Yuval's arm in one hand, grasped behind his neck with the other and sat the boy up.

Now face to face, Yuval looked at the first prince of Israel, then to the royal surgeon. They both stared at him eagerly awaiting his answer. Still somewhat in disbelief, Yuval knew that even to be treated poorly by a prince would be far better than the life he'd been living.

"When do we start?"

SUCCOTH

1082 BC, Jordan River Valley, Israel

A mob of fallow deer chewed clover in a lush green field as the sky began to turn hues of pink and orange. It was a beautiful setting for an early morning hunt. Three hunters watched as they lay prone, peaking over the rise of a small hill that concealed their approach.

"What's the plan?" asked Hammurabi.

Reading the terrain and feeling the breeze against his face, Bani laid out the plan of attack. Zelek listened intently to his uncle and the man he called father. Hammurabi nodded his approval and the three moved to the positions Bani selected for them.

"You good?" Bani asked his young nephew.

Zelek nodded. Though only twelve years old, this was far from being his first hunt after all.

Bani turned and disappeared down the wadi to flank the group of unsuspecting animals. A short while later Zelek could see the animals raise their heads one by one as they sniffed at the air. Though Zelek could not see him, he knew Bani was now upwind from them and opposite the small field from his own position with the animals in between. The deer were becoming agitated now. Their eyes all oriented in the direction of where Zelek knew his uncle was concealed. Zelek saw his uncle stand and quickly loose an arrow at one of the does.

Another arrow struck one of them from the north as Hammurabi sprung his attack and the other does sprinted off towards Zelek, who was now positioned at the most likely avenue of escape opposite from his uncle. He crouched and drew the bow as the animals sprinted towards him. His heart pounded in his chest. He focused his eye on the top edge of the arrowhead centering it between the edges of the shaft, selecting one of the animals as they sprinted past him, its image a blur behind the projectile. He let out a breath and steadied his arm as his upper body tracked the fleeing deer as it ran past. He slowly uncurled the tips of his index and middle fingers. The dried sinew of the bow string sprung forward sending the arrow to its mark, striking the doe just behind its shoulder and sending it toppling into the dirt. Zelek sprinted to the animal and drew his knife.

Zelek paused momentarily avoiding the doe's sharp hooves as she spun and kicked in the dirt. Seizing an ear with his left hand, he sank the stone blade into the animal's neck and pressed forward mercifully draining the wounded animal's life from her body. Her writhing slowed as the blood poured into the dirt.

Hammurabi was by his side now. The boy looked up, panting excitedly. Hammurabi smiled approvingly at the young boy. Bani soon joined them and lowered a doe from his shoulders next to Zelek's kill, then nodded approvingly with an expression only Zelek, Hannah, and Hammurabi would recognize as contentment. To the youth, this was the utmost affirmation from his uncle, the most stoic of men.

Without a word, Hammurabi and Zelek went to work quartering the animals, removing the muscles of the back and neck, along with the edible organs as Bani went back to track the third that Hammurabi had shot. They were finishing with the second when Bani returned a short while later with Hammurabi's kill. When they'd finished harvesting the meat from the three does, they buried the remains, which were few.

The two men and youth wrapped meat in the leather it had been laid upon and tied it firmly, then shouldered the heavy loads. Hammurabi looked approvingly at the young man. Zelek smiled in return.

"You did well today son. Now I can let you two do all the hard work."

The young man beamed. Still excited from the hunt, he couldn't wait to share the story of today's events with anyone who would listen.

The three set out for the hike several miles to the market at Succoth where they sold wild game to the local butcher. Unlike most places, they were welcome by the butcher and his wife with whom they'd established a longstanding relationship and it was conveniently located in the market outside of the city's western gate to accommodate travelers who didn't want to trouble themselves with local authorities by entering any of the city's various gates. Since the time of Nahash's campaign twelve years earlier, coming in and going out of the city was tightly controlled.

Led by Bani, the only one among them bearing the appearance of an Israelite, Hammurabi and Zelek donned their usual slave attire as they approached the city. They navigated the back alleyways to the butcher shop and rapped upon the door at the rear of the establishment. Zelek heard the butcher's wife from within.

"Who is it?"

"Bani. We have fresh game for you," he said.

A moment later, the door was opened and an elderly woman welcomed the men in through the back of the home that doubled as their storefront. It was still early in the morning and prior to the market's peak hours. The butcher's wife, a kind and gentle Hebrew poured the men some tea and began preparing some of the meat for the three hunters to eat, as had become their custom during these visits. While the meat cooked, she summoned her husband from the front of the small building. A moment later he entered with a warm greeting for his guests.

"Three does! Did you really kill three does this morning?" he asked joyfully as he embraced Hammurabi, squeezing and shaking him to the point of discomfort.

When the butcher released him, Hammurabi nodded and smiled.

"These men are turning out to be quite the hunters."

"Well, they have a good teacher," said the butcher.

The warmth and sincerity of this large Israelite stirred Zelek's curiosity. He had not been permitted to accompany his uncle and Hammurabi on many of these trips and he had little interaction with anyone outside of their small family. He examined the old butcher's face, his scarred right eye socket and the marred leathery skin around it. His hands were huge and cracked like the mud when it dries. His arms were at least as thick as Hammurabi's thighs. His belly stuck out slightly, but no further than his barrel chest. His skin had a reddish hue. The man reminded

Zelek of a bear he'd once seen in the hill country, standing upright. He wondered if the man's size and formidable strength were perhaps a result of the constant supply of meat in his diet.

Zelek's eyes passed to Hammurabi and Bani as they talked. Their arms were lean and defined. Their legs and calves the same. He wondered momentarily if the difference in body types was due to their way of living, hunting and running, living off of the land, or simply by virtue of their birth. Zelek wondered if he would look like Hammurabi when he was grown. There were very distinct differences in the appearance of his father and uncle, and Zelek clearly favored his Ammonite father more than his Hebrew mother.

His uncle was only six years older, but seemed much more. He always had. Zelek had pieced together only some of the grim story as to how his maternal grandparents had died and how Hammurabi had come into their lives. He'd been witness to the occasional nighttime terrors his young uncle still suffered as he slept. It gave Zelek an eerie feeling to think of what could cause such a man so much fear and turmoil these many years later. Still, he was old enough to do the math now and knew the story he'd been given didn't add up. He knew better than to ask his mother or Bani about the event and he loved his father, if that's what he was, too much to dwell long on the matter.

"King Saul is recruiting an army to fight the Philistines. He's already raised taxes for just such a purpose. Or so we are told," said the butcher. "You know soldiering. You would be a valuable addition to King Saul's army."

Hammurabi laughed.

"I'm sure an Ammonite would be as welcome in Saul's army as a leper."

"You might as well be an Israelite. You wouldn't be the first outsider welcomed into our fold. You have an Israelite wife and brother-in-law. Your son is half Gadite. People are less prejudiced in the hill country - the land of two-eyed Israelites," the butcher chided.

"From what I hear of King Saul, he is not very welcoming of Gentiles."

Zelek winced. He hated the term the Hebrews used for the outsiders.

He hated it even more when his father used the term to refer to themselves. As much as he hated it, the sting was lessened by the fact that Hammurabi too was an Ammonite.

"If only the rest of the world were as welcoming as you gentle souls," said Hammurabi.

"They'll take gentiles as armor bearers for Israelite officers. Bani, you're an Israelite, Zelek could be your armor bearer. Why, as skilled as you men are, they'd be foolish not to take you. Anytime Saul has found someone worth his salt, he's been quick to add them to his ranks. Hammurabi, I'm sure you could…"

"And who would bring you fresh venison and take care of me?" Asked Naomi, sensing the discomfort of her young guests.

"I'm just saying my love, Yahweh is generous and merciful, he welcomes all who wish to follow his ways," he said. Turning to Hammurabi, "You are already living by His laws my friend. Why not become a follower of the One True God? Become like one of us?"

Zelek looked hopefully to his father, trying not to let his expression betray his feelings.

"No, I've heard of the ritual you all insist upon for one who becomes a follower of Yahweh. Your priests are the real butchers," he said with a smile.

Naomi nearly burst into laughter.

"She laughs!" said the butcher who began to chuckle as well. "Yes, I suppose it's a much easier decision for female converts."

"I have no doubt that it is. Besides," said Hammurabi, "my days of fighting are over. My body is not what it used to be, Hanna has made me too comfortable," he said sarcastically as he patted his flat stomach.

"My friend, behold!" he said stretching his arms out. "This is a man past his prime," he said as he grasped his belly and shook it. "You, on the other hand, are in better condition than any Israelite I know and these young men look as if they were the firstborn of Adam. Whether you serve the army or serve the One True God are two separate issues. What could be more important than the fate of your soul?"

"The fate of others I suppose," Hammurabi answered.

"Quite right, but you are the man of your home. As you go, so goes your household," the butcher responded.

Hammurabi nodded.

Not wanting to press the matter and risk offending his guests, the butcher dropped the matter. He'd weighed the venison as they talked and was just finishing counting out the pieces of silver for their payment. He counted off the pieces a second time as he dropped them into Hammurabi's small leather satchel.

"I know you like to keep your visits brief. Is there anything else we can do for you men before you leave?" asked the butcher.

"Oh, oh," said Naomi before she turned and disappeared in the rear of the dwelling. A moment later she emerged with something wrapped in a small woolen sheet. "This is for your lovely wife and soon-to-be," she said as he handed it to Hammurabi.

"Ah! You nearly forgot," exclaimed the butcher.

"Well, you were no help," she replied as she clapped him on the back.

"Thank you," said Hammurabi. "You two are very kind."

"How is she coming along?" the elderly woman asked in a motherly tone.

"She's doing well. Nearly about to pop. The baby shouldn't be long now, which reminds me that we'd better get going."

"Yes yes! You'd better get back," said the butcher as he embraced Hammurabi in his immense arms. One by one he squeezed each of his guests with a bearlike hug before they departed for the long trek home. Zelek hated leaving the couple. They felt like family. He had so many questions about this "Yahweh." He wanted to belong to somewhere, something, to have a people, a nation, but his questions would have to wait.

Hammurabi and Zelek donned their hoods and followed as Bani led them through the back-alley streets away from the city. After withdrawing a sufficient distance from the town, they removed the covers from their heads and walked abreast of each other. Zelek was now eager to get home to his mother, who'd be waiting anxiously for their return. He knew she hated being alone and he detested leaving her that way for long. They all did, but this was the only life Zelek had ever known, a life hidden from view and devoid of human interaction apart from their small family and the kind butcher and his wife.

As isolated as his life was, hers was more so. His mother was a beautiful Hebrew woman, his father an Ammonite. Town people already looked upon his father with scorn, but to see a beautiful Hebrew woman with him would be too much. It raised too many questions and it was too risky. As the wife of an Ammonite, she had no place among her people. As Ammonites, he and his father had no place among them either. Bani alone was left with the choice of whether to stay or go and he seemed reluctant to do so. Though neither had a frame of reference, separated by only six years as they were, their relationship was more like that of two brothers than uncle and nephew.

As they jogged along toward their secluded home, Zelek couldn't help but wonder what made Bani stay. Why did he feel such allegiance to Hammurabi? Despite their isolation, Zelek had heard enough stories and read enough to know that brother-in-laws owed no special duty to one another. Regardless, Zelek was thankful that he stayed.

INCEPTION

1081 BC, Bethlehem, Judah, Israel

*Caleb said, "So now give me this hill country of which the Lord
spoke on that day, for you heard on that day how the Anakim
were there, with great fortified cities. It may be that the Lord will
be with me, and I shall drive them out just as the Lord said."*
Joshua 14:12

The young priest shouted his Passover message so that all present could hear in the small Judahite village. Quoting from the scrolls he'd studied nearly his entire life, he told of how the great "I Am" sent plague upon plague against the Egyptians. How the men of Israel covered their doorframes with the blood of the lamb. How the angel of death passed through Egypt, taking the lives of every firstborn, save those whose homes bore the blood.

He told of how the Israelites had left and become trapped at the sea with the Egyptian army hot on their heels. How Yahweh parted the waters and delivered their people on dry ground to safety while decimating the forces that pursued them. How they'd come to the edge of the promised land their forefathers had inhabited, the land given to Abraham, Isaac, and Jacob.

"'Yet you would not go up, but rebelled against the command of the Lord your God. And you murmured in your tents and said, 'Because the Lord hated us he has brought us out of the land of Egypt, to give us into the hand of the Amorites, to destroy us.' Where are we going up? Our brothers have made our hearts melt, saying, 'The people are greater and taller than we. The cities are great and fortified up to heaven. And besides, we have seen the sons of the Anakim there.'"

A young, red-haired boy sat in the crowd under his grandfather's arm. He tilted his head back and whispered.

"Saba."

The old man inclined his ear.

"What's an Anakim?" asked the little boy.

Obed turned his head slightly towards the boy. "The elders say they were giants," he whispered. "My grandfather used to tell me they were twice as tall as any man. They say they are the descendants of angels who took mortal women for wives."

"Have you ever seen one?" the boy asked. Eagerly awaiting his grandfather's answer, he felt a painful thump on the back of his head. The boy winced and turned to see his father giving a disapproving scowl.

"No, he's never seen one. Now pay attention," said his father in a stern but quiet voice.

The old man pulled his youngest grandchild closer to comfort and shield him from any further scolding.

The Rabbi continued, "Moses told them not to be scared. 'Don't be afraid of them! The Eternal your God who goes ahead of you, will fight for you just as He did in Egypt – you saw Him do it!' But they did not believe Moses. They did not trust God who had brought them so far and done so much before their very eyes. But Joshua and Caleb were not afraid! They insisted that God would go before them. They'd seen him part the sea. They'd seen his provision in the wilderness and they knew that if God could bring them out of slavery, if he would destroy the entire army that pursued them, then he would help them face any adversity."

The boy's mind swirled with the thought. Caleb and Joshua wanted to fight the giants when no one else would. How would they do it, he thought. The boy listened intently hoping to hear how these two legendary men of Israel fought and killed giants. To his dismay, the Rabbi had reached the end of his story.

"Those unfaithful and doubtful people never got to enter the land. For forty more years, our people waited, while those who grumbled died off in the wilderness. Joshua and Caleb alone were able to see it because of their faithfulness. In these trying times, I urge you not to lose hope as our forefathers did. Yes, our enemies have great power. They are mighty, but our God is mightier! We do not fight with sword and spear! The Lord, the God of Israel, the Great 'I Am' fights for us," the priest proclaimed with great enthusiasm. The priest lowered his voice, drawing his listeners in.

"And given my current audience, I might also add - never forget that it was your forefather, Caleb, who took the land inhabited by giants, the land you now possess! The tribe of Judah inherited the land of the Anakim and slew them. You are a tribe of giant slayers!"

The boy was ecstatic, "Caleb was from the tribe of Judah?" he excitedly asked his grandfather, having forgotten his father's last painful correction. He was saved by the conclusion of the rabbi's message.

With a smile, Obed ruffled the boy's thick hair. "Yes David. You might say he married into it, but yes." The crowd was dispersing now and the old man stood, taking the boy by the hand. "You know what else?" he asked rhetorically. "Our people were great shepherds back then. Just like you and I. Just like my mother's people."

The boy's father gave an audible sigh. "Raising sheep might have made sense for wandering nomads who lived on manna from heaven, but we have a home, we have land, we have taxes to pay," Jesse said. "Your great-grandfather knew this," he said to the boy as if his father weren't standing there beside him. "You'd be better off getting the shepherding out of your system now son. Your great-grandfather Boaz was a wealthy man. He knew how to tend the land. All sheep and goats are good for is eating and defecating."

The old man ignored the remarks. He was used to his son's disrespectful attitude towards shepherding and his Moabite ancestry. Jesse's distaste for shepherding and sheep ran deep. He'd come to resent anything remotely associated with his Moabite heritage. What remained of their flock was maintained by Obed himself. Now that Jesse had taken over the land, he spent only what was absolutely necessary to maintain the flock and appease his father, who was by now far too old and feeble to make it a profitable endeavor. Obed's failed investments and attempts to maintain, much less grow, his father's wealth were a source of constant criticism by his son. The land Jesse had inherited was far smaller than what Obed had started out with, since much of it had been sold or leased to others in order to make ends meet.

"It's easy for you to criticize me when you have eight sons to tend your fields," said Obed.

"Always the same excuse," he said indignantly. No son of his was going to end up a wandering shepherd. At least not if he wanted any share in the family business that Jesse had managed to restore. "The truth is, your grandfather has too much Moabite in his blood. He can't help but want to spend time with the sheep. Just like his singing, dancing, and music playing," Jesse said loud enough for his father to hear.

Sensing the tension, the boy thought again of the rabbi's story. "Father, have you ever seen a giant?"

"No," he replied curtly.

"How could a normal man fight a giant?" the boy asked.

Jesse was growing increasingly impatient with his father's pace. "Why don't you ask your grandfather?" he replied before walking on ahead of them to catch his eldest son. Placing his arm around Eliab, he leaned and spoke into his ear.

David continued walking alongside his grandfather and took him by the hand as they plodded along after the others. David pulled at the man's leathery hand.

"Saba?"

"What is it my boy?" Obed asked.

"What's a Moabite?" he asked.

The old man grinned and lightly squeezed the boy's hand.

"They are people. Just like you and me."

***

1081 BC, Gibeah, Benjamin, Israel

"Prince Jonathan," the guard whispered. "It's time."

"Thank you," he heard from within the prince's chamber.

Jonathan arose from his bed and exited his room, accepting the lamp from the guard standing just outside of his doorway.

"Thank you," he said again.

"My pleasure," the guard replied.

Taking the lamp, Jonathan returned to his room. He walked over to a basin and splashed water on his face, then dried himself. He stretched and shook off the chill of the early morning, then proceeded to a table on the opposite side of his chamber where a long scroll was partly unrolled and weighted with polished round stones.

It was written in the prince's own hand, his own personal copy of the law received by Moses and given to the people of Israel at Sinai. He looked over the words and removed the small stone that marked the place where he'd stopped reading the day prior. He positioned the lamp and adjusted the wick slightly, then read the words.

If you walk in my statutes and observe my commandments and do them, then I will give you your rains in their season, and the land shall yield its increase, and the trees of the field shall yield their fruit. Your threshing shall last to the time of the grape harvest, and the grape harvest shall last to the time for sowing. And you shall eat your bread to the full and dwell in your land securely. I will give peace in the land and you shall lie down, and none shall make you afraid. And I will remove harmful beasts from the land, and the sword shall not go through your land. You shall chase your enemies, and they shall fall before you by the sword.

Five of you shall chase a hundred, and a hundred of you shall chase ten thousand, and your enemies shall fall before you by the sword.[3]

Jonathan gazed at the last sentences, then read them again aloud.

"'You shall chase your enemies, and they shall fall before you by the sword. Five of you shall chase a hundred,'" he paused. "Twenty to one," he said to himself. "'And a hundred of you shall chase ten thousand, and your enemies shall fall before you by the sword,'" he read aloud. "I like those odds."

He rewrote the lines on a separate, smaller scroll he used to record certain promises and scriptures he especially liked. He finished reading to the bottom of the exposed portion of the scroll. The prince then carefully rolled the top of the scroll down to where he'd finished and repositioned it at the top of the table. Replacing the weights, he unrolled the lower portion of the precious document and reset the lower weights to prevent it from unraveling any further. He could see the morning sky already beginning to lighten outside his window.

The prince secured the leather belt that held his scabbard and sword to his left hip, then took the shield and spear from their stand and hurried out of the room. Exiting the room, he proceeded down the hall to the stairway that led down to the palace courtyard, where Yuval faithfully awaited his arrival. It was cooler outside as the temperature dropped slightly before sunrise.

"Sleep in this morning?" Yuval asked as the prince entered the yard.

"Ha!" Jonathan responded. "I found a verse I wanted to remember."

"Spare me. Are you ready at least?"

The prince smiled.

Yuval took off at a sprint with the prince in close pursuit.

They reached the training grounds breathing hard and already sweating profusely. They entered the arena and looked around.

"Looks like we're early," Yuval said.

---

[3] Leviticus 26

"Not a chance," said a voice from behind. The youths turned to see their instructor perched on a bench several rows up from the ground. "I hope you saved some of that youthful energy for today's instruction. Get your knuckle-splitters and take your positions. We have a lot to cover today."

The two went over to the rack of wasters or "sticks" as they were most commonly referred to and selected two of the least splintered options.

The two squared off in the arena and began methodically and slowly moving through the standard drills, trading roles as attacker and defender. The instructor spoke seldom and only when necessary to make adjustments to each man's form.

The crack of the wooden swords colliding and heavy breathing was the only sound in the uncharacteristically vacant arena. The speed of their movements increased slowly as the day progressed through the series of movements which varied only slightly from one drill to the next.

"Mastery of the basics will triumph over fancy swordsmanship every time," the instructor reminded them. "You will be fighting with men to your right and left. You're no good to Israel till you can fight as a team. You can't fight as a team until you master these basic maneuvers."

Whenever one of them swung wildly or even slightly outside of the imaginary box that encompassed the area directly to his front, they received a stripe across their shoulder or triceps with the quick flick of their instructor's switch. By now, the prince had far more stripes across his upper arm and shoulder than Yuval, who was arguably the better swordsman.

Yuval's waster struck the prince's, sending the tip of the wooden blade off to the right.

THWACK! Another stripe formed on the prince's arm as blood rushed to the surface where he'd been struck.

"You just severed the man's bicep to your right. How does it feel knowing he'll never be able to use his left arm again?"

Apart from the painful reminder on his arm, it was a sobering thought. "Not good," the prince answered.

"Your enemy is in front of you. Keep your weapon pointed in that direction and you'll be a lot less likely to sever the arm or an artery of the man to your right or left. Take your friend here," the instructor said, seizing Yuval's arm. "What happens to him, Prince, if he severs your forearm in the heat of battle? Will King Saul forgive him?"

"Not likely," Jonathan conceded.

"No, not likely," the instructor assured him. "Yet if you pay him the same favor, his wife and children die of hunger. Continue."

The rest of the day progressed without incident as the prince became increasingly mindful of maintaining control of his wooden blade.

A long day of training concluded, the prince was silent as they walked back to the palace and guard barracks.

"You know, we're still a long way off from being old enough to serve? We've got plenty of time to get better," Yuval said.

"I know that," Jonathan said, "but I have to set the standard. Everyone will look to me as the prince. If I slack off, it will give everyone else an excuse."

Yuval stopped. The prince turned to see him looking very irritated.

"What?"

"You're the prince! You can just order everyone to do the fighting for you."

"That might work for other peoples. That has never been the case for our people. Maybe if you read the scriptures you would understand that. A leader of Israel must always lead by example. We do not sit on the sidelines. Our people do not go to battle without a leader at the front. Joshua, Caleb, Gideon, Ehud, my father. I must push myself harder than anyone else."

"I'll take your word for it," Yuval responded as they began walking again. "Hey, look at the bright side. By the time we're old enough to fight, we're going to be way better than anyone else. No one else gets this level of training at our age."

BRED FOR WAR

1081 BC, Gath, Philistia
(modern day Israel, approximately 15 miles inland
from the Mediterranean Coast)

"FIGHT," the instructor shouted.

The two massive adolescents charged at each other. The larger of the two struck with such force that he knocked the other clean off of his feet. The smaller boy fell to the ground with a thud as the large boy pounced on top and began to pummel him with his fists, as he was compelled to do by his onlookers.

"Enough!" The instructor shouted finally. The boys quickly got to their feet. They were barely teens and already larger than the man shouting at them and peppering them with insults. The trainer, who would be an imposing figure to most ordinary men, turned his attention to the smaller boy.

"You think that will do against the same people that produced Samson? He was no bigger than I and he'd have ripped your head clean off your body for the sheer pleasure of it." Turning to the larger boy he shouted, "You think you can take it easy because you're a big, strong freak?" the man asked.

The boy's face wrinkled.

"SAY!" the instructor demanded.

The boy tried to hide any emotion from his tormenter.

"What is it? Are you as stupid as you look, or do you think you can take me you dumb ox?"

Before the large boy could answer, he was struck by the man's open palm across his jaw.

"The next time I ask you a question, you'd better give me an answer," demanded the instructor. "Now," he said, taking a wide stance to demonstrate, "a smaller opponent can topple a larger one by lowering his center, his weight, and driving upward," he said as he demonstrated. "You must put your weight under the opponent. Your strength is tied to the ground. You must explode upward," he said springing upward from a squatted position.

"Goliath, charge me," he shouted to the larger boy.

The boy lurched toward him as the instructor quickly squatted and caught the boy under the ribs. Driving his heels in the dirt, he lifted upward pushing the boy off his feet and flat onto his back in the hard dirt, knocking the wind out of him. The huge boy gasped for breath.

"Do you see Ishbi," asked the instructor looking incredulously at the smaller of the two boys.

Ishbi nodded, feeling sorry for his sparring partner, but not daring to show it. Goliath quickly regained his breath and returned to his feet and the grueling training commenced yet again.

In a tower high above the training ground a gray-haired man watched intently.

"You were foolish to think you could raise them in this way," the general said. "They are more likely to bear hatred towards you than devotion," he remarked.

King Maoch paced the floor.

"Much thought went into this," he replied. "We have poured resources into their training, their accommodations, their food. Do you know how much they eat," Maoch asked rhetorically. "Gorgo was said to be the best there is! His name is known throughout Philistia, through-out the Mediterranean and the Aegean!"

"Gorgo is a mercenary and prizefighter. A general and devotee of the pentapolis, he is not. What allegiance does he have to Philistia?"

Maoch removed the heavy crown and rubbed his forehead. "How could I have been so foolish? What can we do now?"

"Why do you love Philistia?" the general asked.

"It is my home. These are my people," Maoch responded.

"You enjoy the comforts, the sights, the smells, the people of your home?"

"Of course!" Maoch replied.

"And they," the general pointed down to the training grounds below, "do you think they feel the same positive feelings associated with this place?"

Maoch looked down as Gorgo launched into another tirade, scolding and slapping one of the youth.

No answer was required.

"It is highly likely that the only devotion any of them have is for one another, which is something I suppose," the general added. "The point is, one cannot just be told to love Philistia. They must be shown that mother Philistia loves them, that Dagon their father loves them. We must show them that the people of Philistia deserve their devotion, their very lives."

"And how do you propose we do that?" Maoch asked. "They have been indoctrinated since birth. They know what we have told them and believe because they know nothing else."

"Yes. You have made fools of them by withholding a proper upbringing. Their ancestors were kings, not mere soldiers, they were men of renown. I dare say that they are not as dimwitted as you might think."

"What would you have done?" Maoch asked, irritated. "They were bred for this, like a prize horse, it's not as if their father would have brought them up and not one of their mothers survived giving birth to them."

The general nodded. "They present an interesting dilemma, I give you that." The general paused, considering the problem. "Our men fight for Philistia because they believe Philistia will fight for them. When the Hebrews along the border look to expand their territory, or Egypt seeks again to impose her will, our people trust in the strength of Philistia to preserve that which they hold dear. They know that they have much to gain by fighting because their interests and those of Philistia are aligned. These boys, if that's what you can call them, have no interests. You have withheld women from them. You have withheld freedom, wealth, and privilege from them. They train to avoid correction and punishment." The general paused again, his shrewd mind turning over the problem. "You want to produce more of them. You want them to fight for Philistia. There may be a way to accomplish both."

"Go on," Maoch responded, eager to hear the general's suggestions.

"Are you familiar with the story of the ancient King Gilgamesh?"

ZELEK

1081 BC, Jordan River Valley, Israel

Zelek peered through the open door to his mother, lying upon her bed, beads of sweat collecting on her forehead and cheeks. Hammurabi wiped Hanna's head with a cloth and brushed the hair from her face then gently cradled her head and ladled some water to her mouth.

"Drink," he said, "you must drink" he pleaded in Ammonite accented Hebrew.

Zelek watched as his mother weakly sipped at the water from the ladle and his father laid her head back on the pillow.

Hammurabi stood and walked to the doorway where Zelek watched his mother anxiously. He placed the hand behind the youth's head.

"Your mother needs medicine. I need the two of you to go to see the butcher."

His father began writing out a list of ingredients. Bani sat with his back against the wall near the fireplace.

"I'd best go by myself. Zelek can't help me there and we'll only risk trouble if he comes."

Bani's points were valid, but there was nothing the youth could do here but fret over his mother's fate.

"It's better you don't go alone. I don't want you running into trouble along the way; I'd like him to go with you. You may need help and I can't leave your sister," Hammurabi said. "You've been to the butcher enough to know what to do. Both of you go and give him this," he said handing off the parchment. "Let them do the shopping and pay them extra above whatever they ask. Get back here as soon as you can," he said handing Bani a leather purse of silver.

Zelek kissed his mother's forehead and promised to return as quickly as possible.

Bani touched his sister's hand as he looked down at her in her fragile state. She looked up at him and placed her other hand on top of his. His eyes drifted down to her pregnant belly then back up to her glassy eyes. He stepped away without a word as his hand slipped from hers.

***

Zelek waited impatiently for the butcher and his wife to return from the market with the items from his father's list. He stared out the small window of the butcher's shop watching Hebrews of the city pass by with impunity. His head still covered, he watched with envy as they went about their business. Even the slaves among them needn't cover their faces. He longed to be one of them, one of something. He'd hoped their anger had cooled over these many years since the war with the Ammonites. Perhaps, one day he could take part in society as others did. Certainly if they knew he was only half Ammonite and wasn't even old enough to have been alive during their war, much less participate in it, he might not have to hide.

Suddenly a pedestrian caught Zelek's eye. He stared for a moment at the beautiful creature that had passed only feet from him. He looked around the room, Bani had still not returned from going to relieve himself. With no one to stop him, Zelek stepped out the door and into the alley. He walked down the alley to the street and peered around the corner in the direction the girl had gone. There she was, though she was joined now by several boys slightly older than Zelek.

As they walked alongside her, one of them stepped to her front and began walking backwards as she tried to move around him and continue about her business. It was plain to see that she was annoyed with the boy. She continued walking with her head held high, seemingly indifferent to the adolescent males until one of the youths grabbed her hand. Without realizing what he was doing, Zelek stepped out from the concealment of the alley as the girl snatched her arm away from the young man. The single youth who'd grabbed the girl's hand looked up to see Zelek standing in the otherwise vacant street. As he peered around the girl, Zelek noticed for the first time that the boy bore a patch over one eye. The boy gazed menacingly at Zelek with his one eye. .

The other two youths noticed his reaction and turned to see Zelek. "What do we have here?" One of them said. The girl glanced at Zelek, then turned and walked hurriedly away in the opposite direction, seizing her opportunity to be free of the three boys.

"Looks like he wants to say something to you," said one of the smaller youths.

"He *looks* like an Ammonite," said the boy with the eye patch. He was clearly the oldest among them, though Zelek guessed he was roughly the same age as Bani.

"He sure does," said the third boy. Zelek noticed he had a distinctly crooked nose as they walked towards Zelek. Suddenly he deeply regretted leaving the butcher's shop. Still, he refused to cower as the youths approached him.

"Where'd you come from boy?" asked the one-eyed leader of the trio.

"I've come to buy some things," Zelek replied.

"Ah, and you thought you'd spy on us, huh? You nosey Ammonite!"

"I wasn't eavesdropping, I just…"

"What's your name boy?" one of them asked as he shoved Zelek.

Zelek had had enough. He shoved the youth back, taking him by surprise and knocking him onto his back. Embarrassed, the boy got to his feet and sprang to tackle Zelek. Zelek instantly shoved the boy's head and shoulders to the ground sending him face-first into the dirt at Zelek's feet. One of the others punched Zelek across the right side of his jaw, taking him by surprise. The other swung and hit him a second time. By now, the third boy had gotten to his feet.

Stunned, Zelek swung wildly at the boy with the crooked nose, but was caught from behind by the one-eyed attacker. The older boy held his arms as the others punched and kicked Zelek's abdomen until he doubled over and was shoved to the ground. Balled up with his hands over his head, the three boys began kicking and stomping him. Zelek rolled over to his back and caught one of their feet and held it as the boy hopped on one foot. Zelek cocked his right foot and kicked his heel upward into the boy's crotch. The youth let out a cry of pain and fell to the ground cupping both hands between his legs.

Another of the boys drove his foot down onto Zelek's nose. His vision blurred and for a moment, all he could feel was stunning pain around his face and eyes. He covered his head again, curling up into the fetal position as the two others continued kicking him. He tried again in vain to grab one of their feet.

"What's going on here?" he heard a voice shout. The kicking stopped as the youths saw two adults approaching.

"This Ammonite just attacked us!" one of the boys shouted.

"He was spying on us from over near the butcher's shop. When we asked who he was he attacked us," another one shouted.

"He's an Ammonite for sure! Just look at him," said the one-eyed boy.

The adult grabbed Zelek and pulled him to his feet, pinioning his arms to his side. He looked at the boys' faces as Zelek tried to gain his composure.

"Who are you? What are you doing here?" the man asked, glaring at him with a single eye.

Zelek looked at the face of his interrogator. The flesh around the man's right eye was marred and there was nothing but a ghastly fleshy impression where the man's eye should have been.

"I, I..." Zelek shuddered. He thought about how they had always been to see the butcher covertly, how his father had always been respectful of the man and his wife by always going to the rear entrance. He knew that telling the truth would ruin the man's livelihood.

"Don't think, just tell me where you've come from," the one-eyed man demanded. "What are you doing here?"

"Ju-just visiting the market," Zelek stammered.

"Visiting who?" the other man shouted as Zelek realized that he too had the same scarred indention where his right eye should be.

"The town. For provisions, we didn't mean any harm…" his sentence was cut off.

"We? There are more of you? Where's the rest of your party?"

"No, just… they're…"

"He's a spy" one of the boys shouted.

"Who sent you?" the other adult asked.

"No! We just…" Zelek started to say, but his words were interrupted by a familiar voice.

"LET HIM GO," the voice exclaimed.

The two men turned to see Bani standing behind them. "Who are you? You know this gentile?"

"He's my nephew. Now let him go!" Bani demanded.

The adult who'd been holding Zelek's arms loosened his grip but held tightly to one of Zelek's wrists as he turned to address Bani. The men looked at each other with the same disgusted expression.

"I think we need to take you two to the magistrate before we can let you leave. I've never seen you here before."

"We were just getting provisions and now we're going to be on our way. You need to let him go," said Bani stepping towards the men.

They both stepped back simultaneously, pulling Zelek with them. All three youths were back on their feet now. One of the men instructed the youth opposite him to go alert the authorities. The boy, now recovered from Zelek's kick to his groin seemed to welcome the opportunity to extract himself from the escalating situation because he turned and sprinted away instantly.

A moment later Bani took another step towards the man still grasping Zelek's wrist. The other adult stepped towards Bani and was struck before his foot touched the ground. He landed on his back in the dirt and didn't move. Zelek's captor released him and tried to seize Bani before he was struck with Bani's left, then right fist. He lay sprawled out on the ground next to his colleague. The remaining youths turned and fled as Bani seized Zelek's wrist and pulled him hurriedly back towards the alley near the butcher's shop.

Without speaking, they continued running until they reached the edge of the market, scanned the area, then sprinted from the cover of the buildings to a small wadi and ran as fast as they could away from the city. As they reached the Jordan, they hurriedly waded across, instinctively putting a barrier between themselves and any pursuers. Not a word had been spoken among them since they left Succoth. Their lungs burning, both knelt next to the river and cupped handfuls of water to their parched mouths.

Bani shook his head, "You know better than to wander off! What were you thinking?"

Tears started to stream down Zelek's face. "I don't know, I'm sorry. There was a girl, I… I just…."

"A girl?" Bani shook his head again, still panting from the run. He cursed. "I didn't get the medicine!"

Zelek's heart sank. Now, because of his carelessness, his mother was in jeopardy.

"We have to go back," Zelek said as he turned and headed back into the water towards the eastern bank.

Bani seized his shoulder. "Are you crazy? They'll kill us for sure!"

"But we didn't do anything! We'll just get the butcher to explain. They'll vouch for us."

"The butcher is not from there. You ever notice that he has both eyes? You ever notice that they always keep us hidden?"

When Zelek didn't respond, Bani continued, "They'll think he's a traitor just for helping us. They'll treat him just like they'll treat us," Bani shook his head. "We, our family, is an abomination to these people."

Zelek remembered the disgusted look on the other youths' faces and how the men had instantly treated him. Bani was right.

"What do we do?" Zelek exclaimed worriedly.

"There's another village, Aenon. It's north of here just on the western side of the river. It's been years, but Hammurabi and I have been there before. They may have what we need. I can go into the town and get the medicine while you wait nearby. If we hurry, we'll make it there before anyone from Succoth. They'll be looking for the two of us. If I go by myself, I won't stand out."

Zelek nodded vehemently and the two started off.

"Wait!" Bani shouted. "If they track us here, they may be able to follow us. Let's walk up the river a ways to throw them off before we head to Aenon."

The two ran upstream in the shallow waters at the edge of the Jordan for several stadia before setting foot back on dry ground. Bani knew it was another two-hour trek to Aenon if they ran. He wondered if his nephew was prepared for a journey that would take a minimum of four hours of hard running. He slowed his pace and stopped. Zelek paused behind him.

"What's the matter?"

"Look, I know you're strong for your age, but we have a very long way to go and you can't go near the city anyway. I'm going to need you to hide out here while I make the trip into Aenon. I'll get back faster if you're not with me."

"What?" Zelek exclaimed. "You want me to wait here by myself?"

"Get it together!" Bani said sternly. "You have to. I'm sure we've lost them or I wouldn't be asking you to."

"What if they have dogs?"

Bani shook his head. Zelek was right. He'd not considered this possibility. They knew what a well-trained animal was capable of since they'd often hunted with two dogs Hammurabi had found as puppies on a prior trip to Succoth.

"Alright! You can go with me for a while longer, but once we get some more distance between us and them, you'll have to wait. We have to get back as soon as possible and you'll just slow me down."

Zelek nodded and the two went back to the river, searching southward before leaving the concealment offered by the vegetation. Fortunately, the great variation in depth and width of the river during the dry and rainy seasons left the river bank, during its lowest, mostly vacant. During wetter periods of the year, the bank grew substantially and there were many homes and settlements further uphill where the floodwaters would rise. Now, during the dry season, they could move relatively undetected.

They ran as fast as Zelek could keep up, moving from the shallow water on the river bank to the firmer ground periodically to ensure they were not followed. Approximately ten stadia south of Aenon, Bani concealed Zelek in a patch of vegetation and placed a conspicuous-looking rock near the path to mark the location of the hideout on his return from Aenon. As he departed, Zelek was amazed by Bani's speed after they'd already covered so much ground.

He lay there in the sandy dirt watching in the direction Bani had left, waiting for his return and listening for any sign of man or animal approaching from the south. Though he was shielded from much of the sun's rays, the heat of the day weighed down on him. He grew weary and his eyes became heavy. Before long, Zelek slipped off to sleep, lying prone in the shade of the vegetation near the river bank.

When he was shaken awake, he whirled and lashed at his attacker. Suddenly, he was pinned to the ground, straddled by the intruder, his mouth covered.

"Zelek! Stop fighting!"

Zelek recognized the voice instantly and stopped struggling, though still blinded by the sunlight. He squinted, trying to see.

Relieved, Bani helped him to his feet.

"I got what we need. Now let's get back home as fast as we can. We need to cut straight through the hills so we don't run into anyone."

They stepped out of the vegetation to the bank of the river.

"Have you had anything to drink?" Bani asked. "How long have you been asleep?"

Zelek examined the sun. It was nearly evening. He'd been asleep for hours since Bani left him. Ashamed, he confessed he was not sure. Realizing for the first time how parched his mouth was, he guzzled the water. Bani took the skin and walked down to the water to refill it. When he returned, Zelek took another long drink.

"You good?" Bani asked.

Zelek nodded, still ashamed for falling asleep under these conditions.

"Alright, let's get a move on. Try to keep up will you?"

They found a trail through the thick brush that lined either side of the river and traveled west away from the Jordan and towards the hill country, then south along a path Zelek found vaguely familiar. Before long, the sun began to set. Darkness fell quickly on the Eastern ridge trail, but reaching the crest of a hill, Zelek thought he recognized the last stretch of land before them. In the distance, even in the failing light of day, he could see a single pillar of smoke rising from the forested hills ahead of them. Encouraged, he quickened his pace.

As the two drew closer, the smell of smoke was thick in the air, more so than any standard fire they were used to. Zelek expected the bark or whine of the dogs as they approached, but none came. Bani stopped suddenly on the trail in front of him and turned to halt Zelek.

"Shhh," Bani whispered with his index finger over his mouth.

The hairs on the back of his neck stood on end.

"Something's not right," he heard Bani say.

Suddenly the overwhelming sense of urgency for his mother gripped him. Zelek jerked away and sprinted forward through the darkness down the path to their secluded home. Breaking from the vegetation to the small clearing around the home he expected to see, his mind struggled to comprehend what his senses perceived.

The smoldering ruins of the only place he'd ever called home made it difficult to breathe. He tripped over something soft in the darkness and fell to his knees. Eyes burning from the smoke, he groped the ground until his hands fell upon the limp body of the female cur. He felt the moist, blood-soaked fur around the arrow in her ribcage.

"Bani!" Zelek cried out. "Bani help!" he shouted. The only other sound was the crackling of embers in the smoky hollow of the forest. "Bani!" Zelek shouted again.

Suddenly Bani's hand clasped over his mouth. "Shhhhh!"

Zelek tried hard to regain his breath, struggling to breathe from the smoke and the knot welling within his dry throat. Bani pulled him up and away from the smoke into the wood line.

"Bani, she's dead. They killed her," Zelek whimpered.

"Shut up, that old dog is the least of our worries right now."

"Where is Father? Where is Mother?"

"I don't know. Just keep it down while I look around. We don't know if there is anyone still here. You've got to keep quiet."

"Don't leave me," Zelek pleaded.

"Just stay close behind me. Keep quiet, you got it?"

Zelek nodded and Bani turned and began quietly, stealthily, circling the treelined perimeter of the smoldering ruins. Their eyes scanned the darkness for any sign of movement. Coming back to their original starting point, Bani was satisfied the arsons had departed. Taking some dried limbs from the ground, he bundled them into a small torch. Moving to some flickering embers, he blew softly till sparks lit the dry wood, illuminating the ashen heap before them. Nearly everything had been consumed by the fire. Bani stepped over the rubble into what used to be their home and held the small torch low, scanning the ground.

Zelek watched from just outside of the rubble when he saw Bani suddenly stop, frozen as he peered at the ground. He knelt and placed the torch on the ground as his shoulders began to quake and heave.

"Bani?" Zelek whispered. "Bani? What is it?"

When his uncle did not respond, Zelek stumbled over the ruins and stood next to him. He struggled for a moment to make out the charred black objects that lay before his uncle. As he followed the contour of the shape, he could see the unmistakable outline of two human bodies.

***

The youths hurriedly made their way back to Succoth, pulled faster by their hounds. They hadn't spoken since leaving the scene of their crimes.

One of the youths, overcome by dread, finally wailed, "Why'd you have to do that back there? It wasn't the Ammonite kid or the other guy!"

"Shut up you! Didn't you see that he was an Ammonite? He must have killed that Israelite woman right before we got there. He deserved it!"

"You don't know that! He looked like he was mourning."

"So what if he felt bad about it? He and that other Ammonite were spies. What's he doing on Israelite land anyway? Huh?" he questioned without giving time for the boy to respond. "They were spies for sure. You kids are too young to remember when they came. You should be thankful! I should get a reward for what I did."

The younger boy stopped.

"Then why'd you try to cover it up? Why'd you set the place on fire? You wanted to cover it up!"

"Shut up!" shouted the one-eyed youth as he struck the younger boy, knocking him to the ground. He pulled his father's sword from its sheath and pointed the tip toward the boy on the ground. "You say another word and I'll cut your throat!"

The boy tried to restrain his tears as he gazed from the ground back up at the menacing older boy's face. The third boy with the crooked nose stood looking down at him indifferently.

"You're just as responsible as I am. You were just too scared to do anything. And don't forget that you set the place on fire too! Didn't he Elizur?"

"Sure did," Elizur responded.

"We all did. If I get in trouble for anything, so will you. So you'd best keep your mouth shut you sissy."

The boy sniffled and clenched his teeth.

"Say it! Give me your word you're gonna keep your mouth shut!" Shouted the one-eyed adolescent.

The boy nodded.

The older boys turned and proceeded toward Succoth as he stood and followed after them in the moonlight.

***

The next morning Zelek awoke to the sound of clacking of rocks. He wasn't sure whether he'd really slept at all. He'd hoped it was all a dream or nightmare. The terrible reality set in as consciousness returned to his tired, cold, and damp body. Exhausted and nearly blinded from the smoke and tears, his body had apparently given in to sleep at some point during the early morning hours. He arose and went towards the sound of the rocks.

Bani knelt next to a pile of rocks he'd already gathered near his sister and Hammurabi's bodies that now lay in a shallow grave. He'd covered them with whatever charred blankets he could find among the remains of the dwelling. Her lower half was already covered with stones. Lines from his tears streaked his darkened face, the only indicator of the internal turmoil that lay beneath his stoic façade.

Zelek began to feel the tears well up again and tried to push them down, letting out a muffled whimper.

"Pull yourself together," Bani snapped. "I was younger than you when I lost my parents," his voice cracking as he continued gently stacking the rocks one at a time. "You have to focus on something else. For now, focus on the task of burying your mother and father, then focus on something else. Be happy that we have the opportunity to bury them. Your mother and I didn't have that luxury."

Zelek knelt down next to Bani and stared at the covered face of his mother. He tried to force the image of her charred remains from his mind, past the feverish, sweat-soaked face he'd seen just yesterday and to an earlier time, when she was happy, healthy, and vibrant.

"We don't know where our next meal will come from. Focus on that. If you can't focus on anything else, focus on killing the ones that did this. Don't let your mind come back here, back to this place. When we leave here today, you have to put a wall around this place in your mind. Do you understand?"

Zelek momentarily felt the sorrow subside as he focused on the faces of the boys he'd encountered the previous morning. Bani was right. He'd been through this before and look at him. Zelek had always looked up to his uncle and now they were all each other had.

"I'll kill them. I'll kill those…"

"Not yet! That time will come. They'll be expecting us. Do you remember the story Hammurabi used to tell us? How his father waited years to take vengeance on his enemies? It will be best if we wait. In the meantime, use it. Use your hatred to distract you when your mind comes back to this place. Hate is more useful than sorrow."

Zelek began stacking the stones neatly around his mother's covered body.

ADINA

1080 BC, Bezer, Reuben, Israel (modern-day Jordan)

Shiza could hear the cracking of wooden swords outside as he stretched his aching muscles. A new ache for the new day, he thought to himself. His joints popped as he rose from the rug where he conducted his daily prayer, then warming his muscles through a series of calisthenic exercises. He spread his arms wide and moved them in a circular motion over his head, then back down to the rug at his feet. His young children had rushed through their own exercises and already begun to train. Shiza had learned to take things slow during these first few minutes of the morning, the days of training without a proper warmup had passed long ago.

Completing his routine, he exited the home where his wife and eldest daughter were already preparing the day's meals. In the yard, Adina and Abby, the youngest of Shiza's daughters, squared off with their training shields and wooden swords. Adina attacked as Abby blocked the blow with her shield. Squaring off again, Adina attacked, modifying the maneuver only slightly. Abby blocked it again.

"Good!" Shiza shouted.

Adina continued striking at his young sister, varying the drills with each successive attack. Abby defended, blocking the blow each time. Satisfied, Adina instructed his sibling in how to counterstrike the opponent, thrusting the wooden sword forward in a stabbing motion.

"Now you do it," he instructed.

Abby executed the maneuver perfectly, blocking, then thrusting her wooden sword at the imaginary opponent's belly, groin, or inner thighs.

"Excellent!" Shiza praised.

Adina took his position facing her and began striking at her again. Slow at first, then gradually increasing the speed of his attack as she defended, then thrust the dull point of her wooden sword at him, often striking him. The jab was absorbed mostly by the thick leather cover he wore over his abdomen and lower body.

Everyone had been up for hours already. Shiza knew his home was run more like a military outpost than a loving family, but they were happy. He was pleased with the progress they'd made over the years. It was easy to see when he watched other youths play and interact. They were less aware, less alert. His children carried themselves differently. His daughters especially stood out among girls their age; they seemed so much older and mature. They stood tall. Their faces, while content, were more resolute. Their eyes met those of strangers and held their gaze instead of immediately looking down as others invariably did. They were vigilant and they were confident despite the scars of their past.

Other intrigued children often came to watch them train. While all were welcome, few stuck with the family's strict regimen for long, eventually falling off. It happened on occasion that Adina would be challenged by young men of the city, seeking to sort out the pecking order as young men are apt to do. Rumors had spread about Adina. His fame had become a challenge to their sense of pride, especially among older boys. So, on occasion, his training would be put to the test. Once in the market, an older, larger boy accompanied by two others had challenged Adina, shoving him into a narrow alley away from prying eyes. Shiza pretended not to pay attention while the boys harassed his son.

Adina initially attempted to avoid the confrontation and made several attempts to walk past the youth, only to be stopped each time. Shiza turned his head inconspicuously to meet his son's eye without alerting the other boys. Adina stood calm, his face displaying no emotion despite the threats of the older boy towering over him. Spurred on by the other two, the large boy escalated his barrage of insults and slapped Adina hard, turning his cheek a bright red. Shiza finally gave the gesture his son was waiting for. A slight nod of his father's head was all Adina needed.

Adina struck the bully with such force and speed, that he hardly knew where the strike had come from, much less the two that followed. His nose smashed and eyes blurred, he backed away in terror with his hands stretched out defensively while his two companions sprinted out of the alleyway, passing Shiza as they went. Adina allowed the wounded boy to leave without further injury before he rejoined his family in the crowded market. The boy never challenged Adina again and his nose never looked the same.

Shiza sensed the day was approaching when his son would become restless and begin to seek out his place in the world. Despite the rising threat in the West, Adina dreamt of repaying their neighbors to the East for the deeds done to his family and for his missing right eye. They knew that service to King Saul meant fighting Israel's current battles, not reliving past ones, and the Ammonites had not posed any real threat since their defeat at Jabesh. Shiza understood his son's reservations. They were far east of Israel's heartland. If not for Bezer's status as a city of refuge, it would have been all but forgotten by the rest of the tribes. Given its status, however, it enjoyed an exceptionally high number of alleged murderers, thieves, and adulterers.

Shiza, in his role as keeper of the peace, was often summoned to settle disputes and when necessary, to arrest unruly refugees. There was certainly no small amount of vindication that Shiza felt when the same cowardly elders who'd betrayed him fourteen years earlier called upon him to assist in such matters. It was hardly a job for one man, but it suited him and it paid well. He hoped for something better for Adina, but the young man seemed content to follow in his father's footsteps. One could hardly blame him given the events of his childhood. Adina's intense devotion to the family was a point of pride for his father. Regardless, he relished this time with his family and Shiza was in no hurry to see any part of it dispersed.

ARMOR BEARER

1079 BC, Negev, Simeon, Israel

The two young men spoke quietly as they crouched low to the ground. Jonathan examined the footprint of their prey.

"It's fresh," the prince whispered, restraining his excitement.

Despite the prince's demeanor, Yuval's heart pounded at the sight of it. "You know this is idiotic right?" Yuval whispered.

"I've always wanted to kill a lion and I'm not going to miss the opportunity now," Jonathan shot back. Looking down, his eyes followed the tracks from the path into the sparse, yellow grass.

Thinking back on the day of his deliverance, Yuval realized that he'd had no idea of what he was getting into. Still, he wouldn't have traded it for anything. The prince had proven to be the most devoted of friends. Theirs was not a master-servant relationship as these terms were most often used. The young men pushed each other. An outsider might have thought them brothers. Yuval, too stubborn to be outdone, and Jonathan, too fine a prince to give anything less than his all.

It seemed everyone loved the prince and his ever-present training partner was no different. Jonathan shared everything with him and if not for the king, Yuval would have lived in the palace.

Getting his father's approval to take in Yuval had been a difficult matter, even with the aid of the surgeon. However, after the prince's instructors insisted upon it, Saul observed the benefits firsthand. Jonathan's equal in stature, strength, and drive, Yuval had been a Godsend. Saul was no longer pestered by the whining of his younger sons whenever Jonathan became bored or restless, inevitably turning his attention to his brothers who'd been unable to compete. With Yuval around, the younger princes were free to sort out their own pecking order, though each of the four brothers, save Ishbosheth were separated by less than two years.

Yuval never spoke of his prior life, and though curious, Jonathan never inquired out of respect for the boundaries his friend had erected. Yuval worked twice as hard as could be expected of him, further depriving the king of any justification to question his presence. For his part, the prince used any opportunity to elevate his young companion.

So it was that while Yuval questioned the young prince when he snuck away from camp and the protection of the royal guard, allowing him to go alone never crossed Yuval's mind. Now, however, he was beginning to question his decision not to at least alert someone, though he knew it would have destroyed the trust he alone shared with the prince.

Yuval cursed and followed Jonathan into the tall grass.

The lion's path was clear. The morning dew made his tracks easy to follow through the dry grass and patches of bare earth and soon they arrived at a thicket along an intermittent creek bed in a deep canyon. The trail led right to a dark void in the thick underbrush.

"Ok, that's as far as we can go. You'd be a damned fool to go in there with just a bow. I get it out here, but in there we've got no chance," Yuval cautioned.

"That's why you're here," Jonathan replied and nodded to the spear Yuval clutched firmly in his hands.

Yuval gritted his teeth and shook his head. He wondered if Jonathan could hear his heart pounding in his chest. Sweat gathered on his forehead. He tried desperately to control his breathing as they'd been taught. He reached to grab Jonathan's arm, but too late. Jonathan moved from the grass across the short distance to the thicket and waited for his eyes to adjust as he peered in, with his left hand extending the bow, he held the arrow cocked and ready with the right.

Yuval watched him creep slowly into the brush. He cursed again and bounded across the space to his friend. They crept silently, careful not to step on anything that might alert their prey. A twig snagged Jonathan's ezor without his notice. Before Yuval could reach out to stop it from snapping, it broke free with a loud snap. To their heightened senses, it sounded like thunder in the underbrush. Both of them froze instantly. Suddenly a low rumble started to their right. Their heads jerked to see the source of the noise. The low rumbling growl grew louder. Brush obstructed their view of the predator, though they could make out some of the details of its face through the vegetation. The growl morphed into a menacing snarl as he bared his large fangs. He was crouched low, ready to attack.

Jonathan whirled and released his arrow as the lion lurched through the underbrush. In an instant, it had knocked him to the ground and was on him. Yuval drove the spear into the animal's ribs as it landed on top of the prince. Reacting as he had been trained, he wrenched the spear out and plunged it again as the lion turned its attention to Yuval and snarled in agony. As it tried to retaliate, Yuval pushed harder against the spear keeping the lion's deadly claws just out of reach. He pressed the spear deeper as the lion let out a loud cry. It rolled on its side and clawed at the spear shaft. Jonathan scrambled back to his feet and joined Yuval, pushing down on the spear and driving it further into the beast, holding it to the ground. Neither dared let go of the spear, the only thing separating them from its massive sharp claws. It tried to bite at the shaft of the spear and gouged deep marks into the wood as it fought.

Finally, the lion's writhing limbs began to slow and weaken. Its body began to relax and its head drifted to the earth. The young men stood silently holding the spear shaft. Moments passed without a sound other than the heavy breathing of the two youths. Jonathan lowered his arms from the spear. It stayed in place, suspended by Yuval's grip, still firm on the shaft. Jonathan retrieved his bow from the dirt and poked at the beast's eye with the point of an arrow. The animal lay still. Jonathan knelt and tried to wrench the arrow from its chest when Yuval noticed his wounds for the first time. The sides of his back and rear of his right shoulder were streaked with four deep, jagged gashes over a handbreadth in length on either side. Blood was steadily running from them down the prince's back.

"Your back!" Yuval shouted. "You're all cut up."

Jonathan, unable to see the wounds, reached behind his lateral muscle. His fingers touched the gashes on one side, then examined his blood-soaked fingertips. Yuval could see an instant change in Jonathan's demeanor. Still seething with adrenaline, he'd not felt the deep cuts up until this moment. Now that the danger was gone and feeling the extent of the injuries with his fingertips, the wounds began to burn intensely.

"Get down so I can bandage it," Yuval instructed, dropping the spear. He fumbled for the pouch tied about his waste and dumped the contents on the ground. Seizing the turmeric as Jonathan lowered to the ground, Yuval popped the cork lid off the top of the bottle and began sprinkling the contents onto the Prince's wounds. In that moment he was glad the prince was not able to see his hands trembling as they were. Jonathan's back tensed as the wounds burned with the natural antiseptic.

Yuval grabbed the roll of linen cloth from the dirt and began wrapping it tightly around the prince's torso and shoulder. The effort seemed futile given the severity of the gashes and soon they were soaked in crimson blood. He pulled Jonathan's pouch from his waist and took the dressings from within, tying it as tightly as he could.

"That's it. We've got to get back to the doc!" Yuval said excitedly as he pulled Jonathan up.

The prince stood and winced at the pain. Yuval went ahead pushing the brush of the thicket out of the prince's path as they proceeded towards the open field. The boys hastened their pace when they reached the tall grass. Once in sight of the camp, Yuval sprinted off to alert the physician. Before Jonathan could reach camp, two guards had joined his side. They proceeded to the king's tent as the physician prepared an operating table and instructed Yuval to boil some water.

The physician cut the bandages between Jonathan's shoulder blades and removed the cloth. He touched the turmeric and gave Yuval an approving nod. A moment later, King Saul rushed into the tent accompanied by General Abner. His eyes fell upon the wounded prince.

"What happened?" the king inquired of Yuval.

"A lion attacked him." The boy responded.

"A lion? Here in camp?"

"No, Father," Jonathan interrupted. "I went after a lion. We hunted it."

"Where were you?" the king asked Yuval incredulously.

The young servant stood in silence fumbling for an answer that would not betray his friend or cost his own position, perhaps even his life.

"He had no choice but to follow me Father," Jonathan spoke up again. "If it were not for Yuval, it would have killed me for sure," he said through gritted teeth as tears of sheer pain dripped from his face into the dirt.

"You foolish children!" Saul shouted. "How bad is it?" He asked the physician.

Still cleaning the wounds, the doctor simply shook his head. "I don't know yet."

"Jonathan!" Malkishua shouted as he, Abinadab, and Ishvi came running into the tent. Seeing his brother was in too much pain to answer, he turned to Yuval. "What happened?"

Again, Yuval was unsure what to say. "A lion," was all he could say before he was graciously interrupted by the physician.

"Bring me some boiled water and turmeric," he demanded. "I have to make sure these are clean before I can stitch them up!"

One of the guards disappeared from the tent and returned moments later, handing the water to the physician's assistant.

The two men washed the dried blood and dirt from Jonathan's back and arms. The assistant applied clean gauze to the bleeding wounds as the physician examined them.

"It's bad," the doctor said finally, "but as long as it doesn't get infected, I think he'll be ok. I'll have to clean them and rebandage them daily. He turned to Yuval, "Good job young man."

"Thank you God!" Saul said looking upward.

Some of Yuval's tension faded for the moment.

"How did you survive?" Saul asked.

"We killed it," Yuval responded.

"Where is it?"

"I'll show you. It's that way, not far."

"Ribai, Dodo!" Saul called. "Go with him and bring the carcass here," Saul instructed two of his personal guards.

"Can I go?" Malkishua asked.

Saul thought for a moment, looking at the two guards he'd selected, some of the most skilled men in his army.

"Yes," he said, then turned to another of his guards. "You go with them as well."

"Me as well Father?" asked Abinadab.

"Yes, yes. Go."

Ishvi stayed by his brother's side helping the physician tend to the wounds.

A short while later, the six returned with the beast strung from his legs below the shaft of a spear. With one end of the spear resting upon Yuval's shoulders and the other upon Dodo's, the lion dangled between them, its head nearly dragging as they went. It had a thick red mane. Its mouth hung open, revealing four huge fangs. It was the largest lion any of them had ever seen.

Jonathan summoned his strength and lifted his head from the table to see the lion as they carried it in. Realizing now how large the animal was, he grasped the foolishness of his endeavor. His eyes passed from the beast to meet Yuval.

"Nice work Yuval!" Jonathan said. "I'd have been breakfast for sure if you'd not been there."

"Reckless fools!" Saul said as he stared down at the lion. "You ought to be dead and you're both smiling like drunken idiots!" he shouted at Jonathan. "And don't you two get any ideas!" Saul said to Abinadab and Malkishua as they examined the lion's huge paws. "Is Ishvi the only one of you who has any sense?"

Saul shook his head as he stormed out of the tent.

Abner stood over and examined the creature. He crouched and took one of the lion's enormous paws in his hand, then pressed the tip of the toe causing the razor-sharp claw to extend as Yuval and Jonathan watched. Looking at its head, he examined the teeth, its muzzle caked in dried red blood.

"I've always wanted to see one of these up close," Abner said, looking behind him as if to make sure Saul had not returned. "Truth be known. I've always wanted to hunt one myself," he said pausing to touch and feel the thick mane. Still examining the lion, he continued, "I once heard a traveler tell my father about a tribe of dark-skinned warriors south of Egypt. Their young men must each kill a lion as a rite of passage into manhood. None of them is able to take a wife until he has done so."

Abner stood and looked at Jonathan and Yuval. Seeing he had their full attention, he gave an approving nod, then turned to exit the tent, pausing at the opening. "Such an impressive animal shouldn't go to waste," he said. "I'll make sure it's put to good use."

HITTITE

1079 BC, Highlands of Ephraim, Israel

A hithophel and his young son loaded two donkeys with sacks of bread, cheese, fruits, and dried meats. The boy, Eliam, was excited to be leaving. It had been years since they'd seen his father's Hittite friend. Everything about the man, from his accent and mannerisms to the food he ate and the stories he told, inspired a sense of curious wonder in the youth. Once the small beasts were loaded, his mother emerged from the home and the three departed Giloh of Judah for the hills of Ephraim. It was a full day's journey before they reached the Hittite's humble abode among a thick stand of cedar and oak trees.

For Eliam, the place had a magical feeling to it. It was so much different from their home in Giloh, the small village north of Hebron. It was shaded and always cooler than their farm in the valley.

As they walked, the youth's mind wondered about the man they were visiting.

"Father, you always spoke of how great he was in battle, but how did he learn to fight?"

"His people were once a great nation, but like us, they have always had to fight to maintain their place in the world. His grandfather was a leader among their people and trained the men and boys to fight from their youth, including Huzziya. He attributes his family's survival to this training. Huzziya's grandfather and father refused to leave their home despite the constant conflict over their land. They were men of honor and felt it would be better to die bravely than flee and live as cowards, Huzziya would say." Ahithophel explained.

"When did you meet him for the first time?"

"We met on the road to Jabesh Gilead. I heard some young men giving him a hard time, referring to him as a Canaanite. I remember thinking that anyone who'd cover that amount of ground to go and fight with us ought to be shown some appreciation and respect, so I listened in. He just took it in stride. None of their yapping seemed to bother him. I watched him closely and became impressed with him. It was a long march so I began to talk with him and quickly took to him. It didn't take long to figure out that there was a great deal to be learned from the man. Finally, I got around to asking him why he was there to help us. He said his forefathers and ours had been friends. His people told stories of a man from Ur named Abraham that had once settled among them and purchased a great deal of land from their ancestors," Ahithophel said as he turned and winked to his son.

"Abraham was highly revered among them and they believed that God was with him. So when our people returned to the land, his grandfather and father considered the matter and all they had heard of Yahweh and how He'd rescued us from the hands of the Egyptians. They'd considered the ways of the Ammonites, the Philistines, and other Canaanite people and found our ways preferable to theirs. So, while most of his people joined the coalition to oppose us, they chose not to. Their already dwindling numbers were further reduced in the wars with Joshua and Caleb, but his tribe survived," Ahithophel explained.

"I became so intrigued with him, we spoke nearly the entire journey it seemed. It was interesting to hear our people's history from an outside perspective."

Eliam did not find it difficult to imagine his inquisitive father questioning the man during the entire trek to Jabesh Gilead. Having met the reserved Hittite before, it probably felt more like an interrogation.

Eliam listened as his father recounted every detail about the battle, how the Hittite had saved his life, and how they'd become life-long friends. He knew from prior visits that the Hittite lived in the rocky and wooded hill country, where neither Israelites nor Philistines would contest his presence. He'd been accepted as a convert to the children of Israel, but lacking any tribal affiliation or substantial means, it was easier to exist where there was neither suitable land for cattle or farming. He and his Hittite wife lived simply and possessed very little.

"I am so happy for them," his father continued, smiling from ear to ear. "They have tried for years and finally, a son! He will be like family to you. Like a brother, as Huzziya has been to me."

"A brother," Eliam said to himself. Truly Huzziya had been the closest thing he had to an uncle. He loved the man like family and thoroughly enjoyed their visits. Since his youth, Eliam had always called the Hittite his "Uncle Bear" or "Dov" in Hebrew. Given the man's stature, hairy appearance, and the location of his home, the name could not be more fitting. Through his father's stories, the Hittite had attained the status of a legend in the young man's mind. Despite the fact that the child would be 17 years younger and not of his own blood, the thought appealed to Eliam and immediately took hold.

As they drew close to their destination, they could hear someone chopping wood before they could see the small wooden structure. Huzziya's two large dogs alerted him of their approach, barking menacingly before either of the visitors could see them. Eliam paused in his tracks and the two huge animals appeared on the trail in front of them. Ahithophel called to them by name, and the two ferocious-looking animals' demeanor melted into excitement. They wagged their tails and curled their bodies as they excitedly approached the two men. Eliam petted them as they jockeyed for his father's affection.

As they drew closer, Huzziya rounded the back of the small home wiping sweat from his brow. He was clothed in an ephod and drenched in sweat. The youth couldn't help but admire the much older man's impressive fitness. A large ax hung from one of Huzziya's arms. His shoulders were still pumped and vascular from physical exertion. Veins covered his arms, shoulders, and upper chest like a spider's web. Every single one of the man's abdominal and rib muscles could be counted despite the black and graying hair of his body. Eliam was reminded of the term his mother used to describe him - "the mountain man."

A broad smile spread across Ahithophel's sun-beaten face as they approached.

Huzziya, ever stoic, swung the ax with one hand, planting it firmly in a thick cedar log. He wiped himself clean with a small towel draped on a drying rack as he approached his visitors.

Eliam watched as the two men embraced each other. Gripping each other's shoulders the Hittite looked at him.

"It's good to see you my friend," he said in a low growly voice. The man's expression still had not changed from the moment he came into view.

Turning to Eliam he greeted the youth with an embrace, then helped his mother off of the donkey she'd been riding for the past several hours since they'd reached the more difficult mountainous trails of southern Ephraim. The two exchanged a warm embrace.

"Congratulations on your new addition."

"Thank you. And thank you for making the journey. Hebat will be so happy to have another woman around for a change."

The Hittite placed his arm around the two men as he led them to the cabin.

"You've grown into a man since I last saw you," he said to Eliam as they walked.

The boy beamed at the compliment from such an impressive symbol of masculinity.

As they entered the dwelling, they were greeted by Huzziya's wife, Hebat. Holding the sleeping child, she greeted each visitor with a kiss. The men stood staring at the baby while their mother caressed the child's black hair.

"He's beautiful," Naomi said admiringly.

"That is a handsome cub you have there," Ahithophel added.

"Do you want to hold him?" Hebat asked.

Naomi immediately accepted the child and walked him around the room while the two men talked and made up for lost time. Hebat went to work on preparing something for their guests to eat.

Eliam watched his mother as she fawned over the infant. She always looked so content holding a baby. It was a shame that they'd never been able to have any additional children following Eliam's birth.

"Look at him Eliam. Isn't he something?" Naomi asked. "Here, why don't you take him while I help Hebat," his mother said, carefully passing the infant to him.

Eliam, as an only child, had always loved small children, but had little experience with babies. The infant seemed so tiny and fragile, he was apprehensive, but his mother persisted. Instructing the youth how to cradle the infant's head and body, she left him to assist their host.

He looked down at the child in his arms. "He's so small and defenseless," Eliam said. Eliam found himself uncomfortably vulnerable with the baby in his arms.

"Not defenseless," Ahithophel said, "he has us."

"What is his name?" Eliam asked.

"Uriah," Hebat replied.

"Uriah the baby bear," Eliam said.

Hebat laughed as she and the two men nodded approvingly.

"Yes, he is our little bear," she replied. "You can take him outside if you like. He just ate so he will probably sleep a while."

"Thank you my love," Huzziya said and kissed his wife before the men stepped outside, leaving the two women to catch up and prepare their dinner.

Eliam walked around the yard with the child as his father and Huzziya talked. The baby yawned in his sleep and nuzzled his face into Eliam's warm chest. The young man was surprised by the affection he instantly felt for the child in his arms.

"Little Dov," he said. A suitable nickname for a young warrior to be. "So long as I live, I'll never let anyone hurt you," Eliam said to the sleeping child.

OUTCAST

1076, Outskirts of Bethlehem, Judah, Israel

The sun had not yet risen as the young boy and his grandfather walked the field of dewy wet grass counting as they went. David knelt upon reaching the newest pair of twin lambs resting soundly against the warmth of their mother. He picked one up as the mother raised her head to look at him.

If she were not already so accustomed to this, she may have bleated in protest or stood, waking the other lamb. Instead, she simply laid her head atop the other lamb's rump and resumed her rest.

The lamb baa'ed softly as the young boy stroked its soft wool. As it began to grow louder, David set it down at its mother's side. The lamb nuzzled around her belly until it found what it was looking for and began feeding. The mother continued her attempts to sleep as her lamb fed hungrily.

David knelt again and stroked her ears and the soft hair on her forehead. He and his grandfather spent so much time with the herd that he knew each and every animal's eccentricities, what they liked, what calmed them, and what made them nervous. He knew which mothers could successfully raise twins and even triplets as well as those who could barely keep one lamb fed and healthy. This one was his personal favorite.

"David," he heard his grandfather call. Standing and moving towards the sound of his grandfather's voice, David found the old man perched upon a rock, overlooking the flock.

"You know what must be done," Obed said as his favorite grandson strode up to the base of his perch. "It's time for an offering and I'm leaving it up to you to choose which two we bring." Obed raised his hand to silence the boy as he began to protest. "You're ready; you know which two it has to be. Remember who it's for young man."

David thought for a moment. He'd been prepared for his favorite young lamb to be offered for the sacrifice, but he hadn't been prepared to be the one doing the sentencing.

"You said two?"

"That's right."

"But only one is required," he pleaded. "Why both?"

"You will see," Obed replied. "Now go and get them."

The boy did as instructed and prepared the two lambs for dedication, ensuring that they were clean and fit for presentation as a sacrifice by the priests at Bethlehem. The sun had begun to rise and turned the sky shades of pink, red, and orange.

"Do you see that David?" Obed asked pointing to the sky.

"The sky?"

"Yes, all the colors and brilliance of it?"

"Yes Abba. It is beautiful."

"God doesn't have to make the sky beautiful. He chooses to. He doesn't have to share it with us mortals, but I think he delights in us and wants us to enjoy its beauty and splendor. Man could never reproduce such beauty, but God has given it to us this morning to enjoy. Now, don't you think that a God who cares for us as Yahweh does deserves the best of what we have to offer?"

"Yes Abba," David replied.

"Don't forget to enjoy God's little blessings my son. This morning, our flock, the warm clothes we are wearing."

David sensed that his grandfather was trying to lift his spirits, but there was something more too. He knew his grandfather was completely sincere in his words. There was nothing he loved more than being among the flock, in the wild fields and hills. He felt it too.

"We should be joyful David, in giving back to God just a little of all that he has given us. I know these lambs are your favorites. You've cared for them every day from sun up until sundown and guarded them by night. But that's exactly why they are the ones we must give back to Him. You should never offer to the Lord that which costs you nothing."

David thought of his father and how he'd shown no interest in attending the offering of sacrifices today. A slight feeling of dread came over him when he thought of his father and brothers who were likely already working the ground, pushing plows and turning up dirt. How much more they would resent him for not being there toiling alongside them.

He'd only been allowed to come and tend the flocks with Obed when he'd injured Ozem in yet another fight. His brothers had tormented him relentlessly while working in the fields. Ozem, the worst of them and closest in age had it coming, David thought. He replayed the events that had gotten him banished to the flock.

"It's a good thing we're not planting carrots," Ozem had remarked. "We might mistake David and bury him out here with the rest," referring to the color of David's hair, which was a constant source of their ridicule. Ozem had kept on like that for hours as they worked in the hot sun.

"Carrot head," "carrot hair," carrot this, and carrot that, Ozem had repeatedly called him throughout the day. He'd eventually come up with a little song that he sung as they worked.

Planting seeds with a carrot head,
bright as the morning sun when it looks red.
He can never get it right all day long,
now I'm stuck baby-sitting while I sing this song…

And on and on it went. The annoying little ditty grew longer as the day progressed. Whenever one of their older brothers grew close enough to hear it, they'd laughed and sang along, adding more and more fuel to the fire as David grew less and less productive and his work became sloppier.

"Wow carrot head!" Ozem exclaimed, standing upright at the end of the long row he'd just planted and looking down the lane toward David. "I think this worm here could plant faster than you."

David looked around, hoping his father was near enough to at least become annoyed with the bickering. At least if Ozem got in trouble, David might get some temporary relief. Jesse was on the far end of the large field talking to his eldest brother, Eliab.

Ozem had already gone back to work planting the next row and working his way back towards David. As he drew nearer to David, he started up again with the idiotic song.

David felt his face grow hot. Out of the corner of his eye, he saw Ozem glance up and take notice of his flushed appearance. Seeing that he'd gotten the desired result, Ozem began laughing so hard, he could hardly get out the words to his song. David remained silent. Trying his best to conceal his anger, David turned and worked with his back towards Ozem as he approached closer and closer working his way in the opposite direction.

When David felt something land on the top of his head, he acted as though he hadn't noticed. Finally, Ozem seemed to give up. For a moment, he was uncharacteristically quiet. David tried to focus on the task at hand, when a small deer pellet landed near his hand. Still, he worked on. A moment later another small deer pellet grazed his ear and he heard Ozem let out a muffled chuckle. That was it, he'd had all he could stand. David turned and lunged at Ozem. Just as the elder brother looked up, David planted his fist square into Ozem's nose. They both fell into the dirt and began wrestling violently. David managed to get on top of Ozem, three years his elder, and began raining blows down on his already bloody face.

All Ozem could do was put his hands up and try to buck his younger brother off as his hands and face caught the brunt of David's blows. Ozem wailed in pain. A moment later, Shimea pulled David off of the defeated Ozem.

Shimea pinioned David's arms and held him, trying to speak some sense to him as Ozem sat up and gripped a finger on his right hand.

"My finger! You broke it, you idiot! You broke my finger!" Ozem shouted.

Finally, David relented and stopped trying to pull free from Shimea's grip. Now, breathing hard and trying to restrain his frustration, the tears began to well up in his eyes. Ozem gripped his broken finger with his uninjured hand. His face was red and flush with fresh bruises. Blood poured from his nose.

"You're going to pay for this," Ozem cried, moving his uninjured hand to his nose while still clenching the broken finger.

"You started it!" David yelled back.

Ozem, too frightened by the appearance of his finger to retaliate, ran off towards their home, but was intercepted by their father. David knew instantly that he would receive the brunt of Jesse's punishment for the fight. Still, he felt no remorse for drawing his brother's blood. It was a nominal but clear victory, which his brothers could not deny. However, the broken finger would hamper Ozem's ability to work and this, David knew, would not bode well no matter how much Ozem had deserved it.

The verbal lashing he received from his father was nothing compared to the amount of work he had to do in order to pick up the slack for his injured brother. When Ozem's finger was healed, however, David was pleasantly surprised when Jesse gave in and sent David to work with Obed in order to keep the two separated. Even they couldn't believe it when Jesse announced his punishment.

"That's like throwing a rabbit into the briar patch," Ozem had remarked. Still Jesse knew that separating his sons was the best option to avoid bloodshed or further setbacks in productivity. David couldn't have been happier.

Now, as David and his grandfather prepared for the trip to town, he thought to himself - if only I'd known that breaking Ozem's finger would get me here, I'd have done it years ago. David placed the lambs in satchels that allowed their heads to protrude and saddled them on either side of their small donkey. The two twins were identical in every way. A beautiful bright white covered their entire bodies.

When Obed's friend arrived to watch the sheep, the two set out for town. Normally, David would travel the same distance in half the time, but impeded by his grandfather's declining physical condition, they made slow progress. It seemed as if Obed knew every person they met along the way. David found himself strangely elated whenever his grandfather introduced him as his "right-hand man." With his father, he was the least of many, but with Obed, he was an apprentice and valued member of the team.

When they finally reached town, David noticed a wretched and haggard-looking man slumped against the gate and holding a clay cup extended from a wiry arm. Instead of following the crowd of people giving the man a wide berth as they passed, Obed strode directly up to him. The man glared up at Obed.

"What do you want now old man?"

"I promised last time that I would bring you something, and so I have," Obed replied.

"Eh?" the vagabond grunted and sat up a little, grabbing the long stick leaned against the wall next to him.

Obed unbuckled one of the satchels hanging alongside his donkey. He gently pulled the lamb from the pouch and cradled it.

"We've come to make an offering today. The Lord had blessed us with a great abundance this season and the lamb we brought for the sacrifice has a twin. I thought maybe you would like to take care of her," Obed said as he extended the lamb out towards the man.

The old wretch was clearly caught off guard. He looked at the lamb then back at Obed.

"You want me to take care of your sheep for you?"

"No, no, I want you to have it," Obed replied.

The man cocked his head to the side, suspicious of Obed's motivations.

"What do you want in return?"

"Nothing my friend. We need to purchase provisions today and I need the bags to carry other things. You'd be helping me to take this lamb off my hands. Now, if you don't mind, we'd better be going. If you don't want it, I suppose there's no harm in giving two offerings today." Obed said as he held the lamb out toward the man again.

The man took the lamb from Obed and cradled it in his arms.

"I'll take it," he said. "It will make a good meal when it's grown!"

"I suppose," Obed said as he returned to the path. "Take care now," he said as David followed him through the gate into the city of Bethlehem.

David looked back towards the man as they entered. He was quickly gathering up his things from the ground while still cradling the lamb in his arms. He appeared in a hurry to leave his spot beside the gate. He felt betrayed. His grandfather knew how much he loved that lamb. Giving it to God was one thing, but this…. David struggled to conceal his frustration.

"Abba, why…"

"Why did I give a homeless vagabond one of our two best lambs?" Obed finished his question.

David looked up at his grandfather. "Well, yes."

"Did you get a good look at him David? Did you see the clothes on his body, the sandals on his feet? Did you see the mat on which he sleeps or the cup in his hand?"

"Yes, I saw them."

"And how would you describe them?"

"I don't know. Ragged. Dirty."

"That's right, I don't think that man has had anything new or perfect in a long time. Everything that is given to him is second hand, worn out, unwanted, someone else's trash. God has been good to us and given us many good and perfect gifts. It was within my capacity today to do the same for that man. I could have given him money and perhaps he would have spent it on some strong drink. I could have given him one of our other lambs and perhaps he'd have sold it or eaten it, but I suspect he knows the value of the gift that was given to him today."

"But what if he doesn't? What if he doesn't take care of it? What if he just sells it and wastes the money?" David asked.

"Well that's up to him now. It is a possible outcome, but ultimately that is between him and God now. The Lord laid it on my heart to give to the man. I've done my part. I do not know to what end, but keep this in mind David. Any one of us could have been born into this man's situation. You or I may still find ourselves begging at the gates one day, feeble in mind or body. I don't know what calamities have befallen that man to bring him to where he is now, so how can I know him or judge his character?" Obed asked.

David thought for a moment.

"Father always said he is a lazy drunk."

"Maybe so, maybe so, but under different circumstances, perhaps I might be as well. We should be thankful for what we have and help those who don't when it is within our ability to do so."

"But how do you know he won't just kill it and eat it?"

"He might. It's his to use as he pleases now."

"But what if it doesn't make a difference? What if we took such good care of it and gave him one of the two best lambs we have and he just lets it starve to death?"

"And what if he loves it and cares for it? What if it gives him some purpose?" Obed stopped to let David consider the question for a moment. When the youth just stared up at him, he started walking again. "Not everything God lays on our hearts makes sense to other people David. I can't expect you to hear what God has whispered to me and me alone. There may come a time in your life when God asks you to do something others consider foolish. When that day comes, I hope you hear his voice louder than those around you."

David shook his head as he shuffled to keep up with his grandfather's stride.

"How do you know when God is speaking to you if no one else hears him?"

"It's not something audible David, at least not for me. It's more of a feeling, a nudge to do something, oftentimes something that you don't want to do. It may not even make sense to you at the time. I don't know how else to explain it to you my boy. I'm a shepherd, not a priest."

David contemplated his grandfather's words in silence all the way to the altar where they waited in line for what seemed like hours. As they watched the priest work, Obed pointed out the precision of the priest's movements. He was extremely efficient and methodical in his tasks. His cuts were precise and clean. Not once did any of the animals struggle when he made the cut that drained them of life. They simply went limp as if falling to sleep. David wondered if the lambs felt the blade at all. Somehow the priest was remarkably clean for the bloody task he'd already performed hundreds of times today. After every four or five animals, the priest would stop to wipe his hands, forearms, and knife free of any blood, feathers, or animal hair, then he would quickly and carefully sharpen the blade and move on to the next offering.

"I'd have cut my hand off moving the blade that quickly," Obed said. "But pay attention, look at how he moves it. It's the same movement every time, perfectly executed. How do you think he became so proficient at it?" Obed asked.

David knew the answer his grandfather was looking for. He'd heard it many times by now.

"Practice. Lots of practice."

"That's right David, he doesn't just do this a few times a day. He does it over and over, almost every day. If you want to hone your skills to become truly excellent, you have to be disciplined. You have to practice even when you don't want to."

David knew exactly what his grandfather was alluding to. Obed insisted that David carry his sling everywhere they went. Slinging, Obed had insisted, was essential to being a good shepherd. When David asked why he didn't use a bow, Obed had laid out a list of reasons. Bows were heavy and awkward to carry, whereas a sling could be easily tucked into one's ephod. Arrows were fragile and often lost or broken even when they hit their mark. It also took a considerable amount of time to produce arrows, whereas a skilled slinger could find ready ammunition just about anywhere, with little effort.

He wondered if the other, albeit unspoken, reason his grandfather insisted on the sling was so that he could carry the lyre everywhere he went. The lyre was his grandfather's favorite instrument. That too, he'd insisted David practice as often and for as long as time permitted. Time, David soon realized, was one thing that a shepherd had in abundance. As if Jesse didn't disdain shepherding enough, the fact that Obed enjoyed playing the lyre and singing only widened the gap between father and son.

"Best keep the music to yourself when your father is around," Obed cautioned.

David often wondered how and why his father bore such a venomous disposition towards this loving and easygoing patriarch. If he ever figured that out, he thought, he might understand why his father's love had also eluded him.

He pushed the painful thoughts from his mind and tried to focus on the priests as they worked.

Finally, their turn came. Obed offered up the beautiful lamb he and David had so painstakingly nurtured since its birth. The priest, standing on the north side of the altar, took the male lamb with its head firmly grasped in his left hand and ran the blade across its throat. Setting the blade down, the priest held a ceramic bowl below the wound and caught the blood as it poured out.

When the flow of blood stopped, he gently laid the lamb on the cutting table and with the bowl, dipped his fingers and threw the blood on the sides of the altar. The blood sizzled as it dried and was burned into tiny puffs of smoke. Next, the priest took the knife in hand and removed the head, then placed it in the center of the fire.

After this, he removed the intestines by making a small incision near the genitals and guiding the point and sharp edge of the blade upward from the belly to under the sternum, careful not to cut or damage any of the intestines which might pollute the aroma of the sacrifice. Removing the intestines, he then skillfully removed each leg, working the knife around the joints and cartilage so that his blade was not dulled against the bone. It seemed effortless. He placed the torso on the fire, which by now had all but consumed the lamb's head. Taking a pitcher from a large barrel of water next to the table, he washed the intestines and legs before placing them one by one on the fire. As the entire animal was consumed by the fire, the priest prayed a blessing on their behalf. Obed thanked him and turned to leave. David took the small amount of silver to which he'd been entrusted and placed it in a leather satchel held by an adolescent Levite apprentice, and they continued down the small hill back towards the gates of the city.

As they approached the gates, David's mind returned to the beggar and the perfect lamb they'd given him. To his surprise, the man was nowhere to be seen.

David couldn't help but think of the man as he and his grandfather walked the short distance back to their family's land outside of Bethlehem. His grandfather's words had stuck in his mind. He was surprised by the suggestion that he or anyone in their family might one day find themselves similarly situated to the beggar. David had never really thought much about the man or how he had come to be so destitute, but now his mind swirled with a variety of sad misfortunes that could have been the poor man's downfall. He was reminded of the story of Job and how his friends had even blamed him for his numerous misfortunes. In the end, God restored Job after he'd prayed for these same friends.

The boy couldn't help but feel that he, like his brothers and father, had prejudged the man. Then he thought of his own rejection by his father and brothers. Perhaps he and the beggar had more in common than he'd previously realized.

BRUTES

1076 BC, East of Gath, Philistia (modern-day Israel)

The hushed wedding had been arranged and performed according to plan with only minimal exposure to anyone outside the family. It was after midnight and concealed in the forests of the Shephelah, in what most other Philistines considered uninhabitable territory. Those in attendance were confident in their seclusion.

The happily wedded couple seemed to float as they made the short journey from the forest to the home that they would now share together among her family. They could hardly conceal their excitement and despite the fact that they would have to hide their union from outsiders, not even these circumstances could squelch their affection for one another.

Their families had been on the best of terms their entire lives and the marriage was almost inevitable. As they approached the small grouping of structures that was the family's home, the minds of the young couple turned anxiously to that which lay ahead. He turned to meet her eye. She was beautiful in the moonlight. She smiled with a look that said everything she wanted to communicate without speaking a word. She laid her head on his chest as the team of oxen pulled their small cart, led by her father, and flanked by her mother and brothers who kept a lookout for anyone they might encounter on the road.

They passed through a small gate in the wall that encompassed the family dwellings and proceeded to the home that would now belong to the young couple. Garlands of various flowers had been strewn over and around the door, commemorating the young couple's union. Despite their attempts to keep the wedding as discrete as possible, a mother could hardly resist. Her father guided the oxen near to the door and stopped the cart. The proud groom dismounted and gently aided his bride down from the cart. A chorus of praises and congratulations from family members cheered the couple as he lifted her. Both gleamed with youthful smiles as he turned and carried her across the threshold into their new home.

He swung the door closed behind him with his heel and proceeded to the bedroom as she pulled him in for a kiss. With her arms around him, she kissed his cheek and neck as he stopped abruptly at the doorway to their new room. Surprised, she looked up to see shock on her new husband's face. She turned to the bedroom to find the object of his alarm. Joy turned to terror in an instant as she lowered her feet to the ground.

There, sitting upon the bed in the candlelit room was the largest man she'd ever seen. Though he sat with his feet and arms crossed in a nonchalant manner, his presence, sent a chill down each of their spines. Even with his back against the wall, his legs covered the entire length of the bed.

"Well, well," the giant man said slowly. "You look surprised to see me." His deep voice seemed to cause the walls of the small dwelling to tremble.

"What are you doing here," the husband demanded. "This land is outside of your district."

The giant moved to stand but was bent over by the low ceilings of the modest home.

The couple drew back as the giant moved towards them, stooping and turning sideways to pass through the doorway to the bedroom.

"Really?" the giant asked almost apologetically. "I must have been mistaken. Whose district would you say this is?"

"I... I..." the husband stammered as he nearly tripped and fell backward over a table.

He was interrupted by another booming voice from an adjacent room.

"Certainly tis I of whom he speaks," said the voice as another huge man emerged from hiding.

The home, which was small by modest standards, seemed barely able to contain the two giants as they occupied the den with the frightened couple.

"I suppose we'll have to settle this between the two of us brother," said the first giant.

"Yes, I suppose so. She is a beauty, I must say. Well done, sir, well done," the second giant chided the husband.

"Well, I think we've overstayed our welcome Lahmi. It's time we take what is owed and be on our way," said the first and slightly larger of the two giants.

"Indeed brother."

They started towards the young bride. The young husband seized her by the hand and fled to the door. They'd nearly made it outside when her arm was seized by the enormous hand of the second giant as he followed them into the open courtyard. Her husband turned to strike the giant when he was slapped to the ground by the back of the giant's other hand. The giant flung the newly wedded bride over his shoulder as if she were a mere child. He stood straight as his brother emerged from the small home.

The families of the bride and groom stood stricken in awe and terror.

The larger of the two giants took hold of the husband's collar and lifted him off the ground with ease.

"I'm disappointed," he said as he dusted off the man's clothes, nearly knocking the breath out of him with each swat of his hand. "And hurt, if I'm to be honest."

He looked at the terrified faces of the family members, too frightened to move. They knew full well that any attempt to flee would be useless. They were completely at the mercy of the two brutes that stood before them.

"You live in safety because we fight your battles. We keep the enemy and the wild beasts at bay. This land, this beautiful home, your fields, your livestock," he said with the flourish of his hand, "you are able to enjoy in the secure knowledge that you are safe, all because my brothers and I make it so."

The giant paused, tilting his head slightly to examine the faces of terrified children clinging to their father's trembling legs. He knelt and ran his thumb along a trembling child's cheek.

"And this is how you repay us?" he asked as he tilted his head and leaned toward her.

The child hid her face as the giant stood. He paced in front of them as he shook his head.

"Is it too much to ask that we are given that which is owed? That which is our right by Philistine law and paid for with our own blood? A tradition as old as time, yet you would deny my brother? Nay! *Rob* him of his right to the first night."

The terrified family stood silent.

"Is it not enough that we lay down our lives," the giant shouted as the family winced. His dark face grew more terrifying as his fervor intensified. "What more would you ask of us? What else have we required from you?"

"It is true," an elderly women shouted, falling to her knees in front of the two massive figures. "But are you not gods? Have mercy on us! Have mercy on our daughter! We know the fate that comes to those who bear your seed! Please! Have mercy," the old woman pled, bowing her face to the ground before them.

"Ah!" the giant said, his demeanor and tone shifting to one of a compassionate benefactor. Kneeling next to the woman, he placed a hand upon her back. "Sweet child, are we not kind?" Goliath lifted his head. "Is there but one faithful among you? Just one?"

The rest of the family flung themselves to the ground and bowed before the two tyrants.

"MERCY," they shouted and prayed aloud. "MERCY!"

Goliath turned to his brother, still holding the sobbing bride draped over his shoulder.

Lahmi nodded.

"Very well," Goliath shouted. "Let it be known that my brother's mercy abounds. He has heard your prayers. You shall live this day in spite of your transgressions!"

The frightened family of the bride lifted their heads.

"Do not fear for the young damsel. She shall be returned to you once my brother has fulfilled his right and duty as your protector."

Lahmi started towards the gate as the young bride pleaded with her family as he passed with Goliath not far behind.

With the two giants' backs to him, the young husband sprinted to his father-in-law's home and emerged a moment later with a bow and quiver of arrows as he sprinted towards the gate. His father and brother-in-law seized him before he could round the corner of the home.

He struggled to break free and preserve some semblance of honor as more of his bride's family moved to restrain him.

He shouted and cursed them as they wrestled him to the ground.

"They will kill us all! Not just you," his cousin-in-law pled as they tried to calm the enraged groom.

Eventually, his anger turned to hopeless anguish as his strength faded, outnumbered as he was. His cursing subsided to an uncontrollable sobbing. The happiest day of his life, dashed along with his pride upon the reality of the day's events. In his mind, he knew they had saved him, but in his heart, he preferred death to the feeling that gripped him. What could men do but yield in the face of such horrific strength?

BAAL

1075 BC, Amalekite Territory, Negev Desert

F ar south of the land of Judah, a fire billowed dark gray smoke high above a desert mountain. Amalekite priests proceeded up the steep slope of the mountaintop overlooking the canyon of the dry Tzin Riverbed. There, atop the mount sat the altar to the rain god of the Amalekites, a fire roaring at its feet.

The remnants of disassembled chariots, carriages, and wagons were stacked high to one side, fuel to feed the flames throughout the night. The wind swept powder-like dust across the parched land and around the priests as they marched up the slope. It had been over a year since the rains had come. Even the raiding parties were not able to sustain their people any longer. The fire at the feet of the great statue could be seen for miles to the north across the Tzin Valley. The chanting of the people grew louder and louder as the sun began to set. The time to present the sacrifices was approaching.

It would have been a macabre scene for most onlookers, but to those present, it was a long-awaited celebration. Wine, plundered from Moabite and Edomite villages, was collected and saved for the day when they would prepare themselves for the ritual. Now, their holiday having arrived, they consecrated themselves and smoked the herbs that had been collected for the purpose of rousing visions and incantations. All this as a tribute to the god of rain.

Throughout the gathering, sacrifices were being prepared, bathed, and coddled in preparation for their final hours. Finally, as the last rays of sunlight melted below the horizon, a priest blew the horn from atop the temple platform at the base of the mountain. It was time. The priests lined up at the front of the temple, ready to accept the sacrifices.

Mothers and fathers formed a somber procession, bringing forth their infants to the priests who bowed graciously and proceeded up the mountain, cradling the children. Many of the parents, drunken to a stupor, seemed almost giddy about their gift, as if they expected some great outpouring of blessing from the act. Some, still hopeful for intervention, were less eager. Others, not sufficiently inebriated by the wine and herbs, came forward sobbing uncontrollably, unable to control their sorrow. Occasionally, a father pulled their child forcefully from the arms of its weeping mother. They walked resolutely towards the priests and thrust the small child forward, with the mother helplessly weeping in tow.

The chief priest watched from the distance. Fools, he thought to himself. As he watched another father hand over his child of about three years. The man appeared pleased with himself, a true believer, the priest thought. The next was another weeping mother. He watched as she backed away from the child sobbing, then turned and ran. Did she really believe her actions were motivated by faith and not pure self-preservation? Of course not, he thought. She wept because she was fully aware of the true nature of her actions. At least the faithful idiot before her believed in what he was doing.

As for the priest, he did not deceive himself. He'd always detested manual labor and lacked the motivation for any honest means of living. Deceit was his forte and manipulation his craft. In this, he'd risen to the role of chief priest and advisor to the King of Amalek. The current state of things necessitated this unburdening of the working class and they needed some greater purpose to relieve their wretched souls. And so, this process served the community, but mostly, it served the priest who would have his own needs met with more childless mothers to comfort.

The gruesome scene on the mountaintop was strategically hidden from view, obscured by the darkness and distance that separated the people from the sacred height. The chief priest proceeded to the hilltop where his assistant accepted the children one at a time, secluded by a dark veil that concealed his face. The minor priests were not exposed to the true horror of the event, further assuaging their guilt and accountability for their actions. They would be well paid for their actions in service to King Agag, who, along with the chief priest had orchestrated the great ritual for the purpose of "appeasing the gods" and "restoring the rain that would heal their lands."

Months later, if the rains had still not come, the people would be happy there were fewer mouths to feed. Raiding the Edomites and Moabites was no longer sufficient to sustain them. Rumors of tensions between the Philistines and Israelites carried the potential of creating an advantageous situation for any patient opportunist. It was time to start venturing north, back to the land they'd been driven from so many years ago.

INJUSTICE

1073 BC, Bethlehem, Judah, Israel

The streets of Bethlehem bustled with new arrivals from outside the city. Jesse hated going to the city even when it wasn't this crowded, and now, accompanied by his entire family, he was on edge as they waited to pass through the gates. As the head of his family, it was now Jesse's responsibility to ensure that the sacrifices were offered. It was expected that each family make a contribution and offer peace offerings for the coming Passover celebration.

Passover was to be held in each Israelite's home in recognition of the final plague in which God had broken Pharaoh's will, taking the firstborn from each home where lamb's blood had not been painted on the doorframe.

It had been years since Jesse had been required to make a visit to the city, Obed having done so right up until his death. Jesse was annoyed by the inconvenience of it all.

As they approached the gates, David anxiously searched the fields for the familiar beggar he'd seen so many times with his grandfather. David had not seen the man at the gate since his grandfather had given him the lamb over a year earlier. It was not until they passed the crowd near the gate that David finally located the man, just as he'd been all those times before.

He was seated near the gate, somehow looking even more dejected than before. Whereas the old man had often looked to the passersby and held his cup out for offerings, he did not so much as glance up at them as the crowds passed before him. The lamb, which would be grown by now, was nowhere to be seen. Disappointed, David turned his attention back towards the gate and tried to push the thought from his mind. Try as he may, his mind repeatedly returned to the old man and the lamb.

As they entered the gates, Jesse walked hurriedly on towards the long line of worshipers making their way to the altar.

"Come now!" Jesse said, rushing to the line.

David hurried to keep up with his father as he made a beeline for the ever-lengthening line of people waiting to present their offerings for inspection by the priest.

As David stood there in the line holding the lamb he'd selected for the offering, he examined the other animals. He felt pride in the quality of the offering he'd prepared. He alone had nurtured this one and he alone had tended the flock for several months since his grandfather's passing. The loss still burned in David's mind. The loneliness he felt in Obed's absence was not touched in the least bit by the presence of his family or the crowded streets around him. He pushed the thought from his mind as he scanned the animals in the line ahead of and behind them. He noted the distinct differences only a shepherd would notice, taking in the various markings and conditions of each specimen: a beautiful solid black lamb, a full-grown brown ram with a flawlessly groomed coat, and impressive curled horns.

Ahead of them in the line, David noticed one of Bethlehem's most prominent men, dressed in fine clothing along with his two sons. It was said that the man, Isaac, owned half or more of the businesses around Bethlehem. One of his sons, named Zeb, was about David's age. He was well known by the other youth around the city as a spoiled bully, though somehow Zeb and David had narrowly avoided clashes in the past. David craned his head, trying to see what fine specimen such a wealthy family might have.

There at the boy's feet was a very fine sheep. The young sheep had been well kept indeed. Its wool coat was brushed and clean. The sheep appeared agitated however, crying and turning its head back and forth, pulling against the rope around its neck. David took note of its distinct markings, when suddenly he recognized the animal.

David handed his lamb to Elihu and walked over to the boy, his brothers and father watching curiously as he went.

"Hey! Hey you!" David shouted as he marched determinedly towards them.

Zeb turned to see David approaching.

"That ewe! Where did you get it?" David asked pointedly.

"None of your business!" Zeb replied.

"You stole it from the old man didn't you!" David said loudly as he approached the boy.

Startled and irritated, Isaac rebutted him. "What are you talking about boy? You can't throw around accusations like that! We paid a good price for this animal."

"He stole it!" David retorted. "That old man would never have sold it. Not for any price!"

"What are you talking about?" Isaac asked. "What old man?"

As David went to snatch the rope from Zeb's hand, he was snatched into the air by a large set of arms.

"What are you doing?" Jesse demanded sternly as he restrained his son and spun him around.

David began to explain but was quieted by his father's hand across his face.

Jesse apologized to the wealthy man and took David by the arm back to their place in the line. His face was flush with anger and embarrassment.

Jesse swore under his breath. "This is the last time you accompany me to town. What is wrong with you boy?"

David's eyes and face burned.

"Saba gave that lamb to the old man at the gate. I know because I raised it and I was with Saba when he gave it to the old man! He's never once been at the gate since then until today. He's always been in the fields grazing that lamb. He coddled that lamb. He kept it in better condition than himself! He would never sell it, not to anyone!" David argued.

"You mean that old drunk at the gate? He probably sold it or traded it for a drink. He might have eaten it for all you know. That old man has been panhandling at the gate since before you were born," Jesse responded. "Now keep your voice down or so help me boy!"

David's eyes welled with tears as he shook with anger. If only Obed were still alive. It was more than the youth could take. His fists clenched as he stood there watching the boy tug the rope, pulling the sheep along every time the line moved. All the while, the sheep kept crying for its true owner, the old man who'd cared for it day and night for over a year.

David broke away from his father and took off in a sprint towards the gate.

Elihu looked to Jesse for instruction.

"Let him go," Jesse said, annoyed and embarrassed by the attention David had caused.

David struggled through the crowd of people entering through the small city gate and went straight to where he'd seen the old man.

"Where is your sheep?" he asked.

The old man appeared not to hear him and remained seated, as if in a daze.

"Where's the sheep my grandfather gave you? I know you loved it, where is it?" David pleaded.

When the old man raised his eyes for the first time to meet David's, he could see the black eye and busted lip. David noticed for the first time the old man's skinned and bruised knees.

"Did Isaac's sons do this to you? Did Zeb steal your sheep?"

The old man's lip quivered. "What do you want? Why did you give me that lamb anyway? Can't an old man be left in peace?" the old man sputtered. "Ever'thin I ever had of any value been taken from me. What you care anyway? Just leave me alone boy," the old man said as his eyes welled with tears and he buried his face in his arms.

"Who took it?" David demanded. "Who took your sheep?"

The old man lowered his head between crossed arms again and refused to answer.

David had his answer. He didn't need to hear it from the old man's lips. A shepherd knows his sheep. He turned and rushed back through the gate and toward the center of town where the sacrifices were being offered. As he approached the hill, he paused, looking for the culprit who'd stolen the old man's sheep.

His eyes followed the line of worshippers up to the altar in time to see Isaac and his sons coming down away from the priest.

"No," David said aloud.

Eliab tapped on his father's shoulder and pointed to David.

Jesse could see what was about to happen plain as day. "David!" he shouted. "David, don't you…"

His words fell on deaf ears as his youngest son was already in a full sprint towards the target of his wrath.

Zeb saw David just as his feet left the ground. The full weight of David's body stuck Zeb just above the pelvis, doubling him over and sending them both into the dirt. David scrambled to mount the boy and pinned his arms to the ground as he began hammering the boy's face with his fists. Isaac grabbed David by the scruff of his collar and snatched him rearward before Jesse seized David's arm and dragged him to his feet before pinning his arms to his sides.

Jesse shook David violently. "What is wrong with you boy?" Jesse shouted. "Get back to the sheep! Now!" Jesse said as he spun David around and sent him away. "Shimea, make sure he goes straight home!" Jesse commanded his son before he turned his attention back to Isaac.

"You're going to pay for this! You and that boy will be punished!" David heard Isaac shouting as he started back towards the gate.

"I am very sorry. I don't know what got into him," David heard Jesse reply. "Please, let me make this right," Jesse pleaded as he looked over Isaac's shoulder to the Priest behind him, not wanting there to be any more of a scene than David had already caused.

David paused and turned to see everyone in the long line of worshippers was staring at them as his father took the brunt of Isaac's tongue-lashing. Isaac's pride had been injured even more than his son's nose and now Jesse was paying the price as the man unleashed a tirade of threats and insults.

David felt like he was physically shrinking as he walked away, wincing at the insults he heard being hurled at his father.

Shimea caught up to him as they exited the gate. He turned to see the old man leaning against the wall with his head still buried in his arms.

Shimea struggled to think of something encouraging to say. He'd seen David upset before, but never to this extent, so he followed his young brother in silence as David sulked his way back to their family's land.

They were nearly home before David broke the silence.

"Guess I really did it this time, huh?" David asked.

"Ah," Shimea said before a long pause, trying to find the words. "I don't know David. Is there anyone else that could back your story? Maybe some of the folks around town. I'm sure there are people who have seen that sheep with the old man."

"No one is going to speak against Isaac and his sons and the old man is probably too afraid to tell anyone the truth about what happened. I was stupid to stand up for him. Now Father will be the one to pay for it. He'll despise me even more, if that's even possible," David replied. "So what does it matter?"

"Well, I was just thinking that if we could prove that Zeb took the ewe, then maybe your punishment wouldn't be so bad."

"What's Father going to do?" David asked. "Banish me to the fields? Father would have to see me to discipline me," David concluded.

"David," Shimea said empathetically, "Abba doesn't... Abba doesn't *despise* you. It's just that, well... you two are very different. Just like Abba and Saba were different. You're more like Saba. There's nothing wrong with that. I loved Saba too, but you know that he and Abba had a strained relationship. It was hard growing up with a father who was half Moabite back then."

"That's all he sees when he looks at me."

"What do you mean?"

David stopped and looked at his older brother incredulously. "You know what I mean. Eliab and the others call me the Moabite. Even you! Father looks at me and sees a dirty, smelly, lazy shepherd, everything he hated about Saba."

"We're just giving you a hard time David. You know it's just cause you're our brother. You should hear what's said in the fields, we all get ribbed in some form or another. It's just a fun way to pass the time."

"Maybe to you it is, but not Eliab. Not the others!" David could feel years of pain welling up inside him. "They all think I'm lazy because I'm not in the fields, but they never wanted me there in the first place. So what if I enjoy shepherding? You think it isn't hard? They don't want to tend sheep any more than I want to work in the field. Abel was a shepherd. Jacob was a shepherd too! They hate tending sheep like I hate planting and picking. They don't want to watch over sheep at night any more than I want to plow the dirt. The difference is that Father respects farming, but hates shepherding. He thinks it's lazy. He thinks it's a waste of time! The only reason he doesn't sell off all of the sheep now with Saba gone is so that he can keep me out of sight. Don't bother denying it!"

Shimea felt the sting of David's words. Many times, he'd joined in on the jeering and teasing by their older brothers, though he struggled now to remember why. David was an easy target around the rest of them after they'd spent a long day in the field together.

"I am sorry David. I know it gets a little out of hand sometimes. You know I don't mean anything by it," the older brother assured.

David shook his head as they walked abreast each other.

"You're right though; I shouldn't have treated you that way," Shimea said finally.

"I know *you* don't mean anything by it," David replied. "Besides, it's not like I can't take it or defend myself."

They walked on for several minutes before Shimea broke the silence.

"I know that you and Saba were close," Shimea acknowledged. "Closer than any of us. Closer even than Abba. So I can imagine how you must have felt seeing those brats with the sheep that Saba gave the old man."

Shimea noticed David peer off to the horizon away from him as they walked.

"Heck, I probably would have done the same thing," Shimea continued. "I don't blame you at all little brother."

The two walked on in silence with David peering off into the distance.

"Thanks," David finally said, as they approached their father's land.

TROUBLED

1072 BC, Outskirts of Bethlehem, Judah, Israel

Asahel woke to the sound of shouting outside of his room. Frightened, he shook his brother awake as he lay next to him. "Joab, Joab… wake up."

"What?" His brother whispered without opening his eyes.

"Father is shouting again," his younger brother needlessly reported.

"I know, just go back to sleep," Joab replied.

"Where is Abishai? He's not here."

Joab sat up and looked for his younger brother. By the glimmer of the firelight, he could see Abishai standing at the entrance to their room, watching from the doorway.

"Stay in bed," Joab commanded his youngest brother before quietly rising to his feet. He silently joined his brother at the doorway.

"He's been drinking again," Abishai said, sensing his brother's presence.

Through the cracked door, they could see their mother and father shouting in the open den of their home. Their mother was standing her ground.

"I want to help you, but you won't talk to me," their mother pleaded. "Please, will you just talk to me? Will you stop drinking and talk to me?"

"I can't listen to your nagging sober."

"I'm not nagging. This is the fourth job you've lost because of your drinking. You are a smart man, a strong man, you are more than capable of being a great man if you'd just stop the drinking."

"I've given everything to provide for you. I've done everything I can and you want me to give up the one thing that brings me some enjoyment, some… relief!"

"Enjoyment?" Zeruiah asked. "What enjoyment do you get from it? You are so angry when you drink."

"I'm only angry because you won't give me any peace! Nothing is ever good enough for you. Nothing is ever good enough for them!"

"I'm asking you to give up this one thing, just one thing. It is destroying you and our family."

"I'm not listening to any more of this. I'll be back after awhile," their father said as he walked towards the door. "I need to clear my head."

"So you're going to leave us again? You're going to leave us again unprotected and alone so that you can go and waste your money on wine? How do you even have the money to pay? We don't know where our next meal is coming from!" their mother pleaded as he exited the tiny home without another word.

They heard the rickety door swing shut behind him as he stumbled out into the street.

Their mother sank to the floor in frustration. Joab and Abishai were surprised when Asahel flung the door open and ran to her, embracing their mother as she sat there weeping on the floor.

The older boys followed and tried to comfort their mother.

"Should we bar the door Mother?" Joab suggested.

"He is your father," Zeruiah responded. "We must show him respect," she said stroking her eldest son's hair. "He is a good man at heart. He's just having a difficult time right now."

Zeruiah stood and ushered her sons back to bed.

Joab struggled with the idea that his father could be the same man that he'd heard others speak of so many times. How could this man have ever been the valiant warrior they said he was, Joab thought to himself.

He dared not ask the question to his mother who'd never spoken an ill word of their father. It seemed that no matter how bad things got, she would always come to his defense. She would always make excuses for him.

"God made him to be a soldier. It's hard to do something you weren't made for," he heard his mother say, like so many times before.

"He can't keep a job because of his drinking," Joab replied angrily. "He doesn't treat you like he should!"

"You don't know what he has been through," his mother retorted.

"Grandfather was a soldier too. You don't see him, acting this way. Father is right; it would have been better if he'd just died fighting with his friends!"

His mother's hand came across his face almost before the words left his mouth.

He'd gone too far and he knew it, but the frustration he felt by his father's constant absence and manic drunken episodes was more than the young man had the patience for. His face stinging, his eyes welled with tears as he awaited his mother's rebuke.

Zeruiah immediately regretted striking her son in this state. He'd been an anchor in his father's absence and his anger was certainly warranted.

She placed her hands on each side of his face and kissed his head.

"I'm sorry," she said as she pulled him close. "I don't know what I'd do without you Joab."

He returned her embrace. She looked up to see her middle and youngest sons staring from the doorway to the room where they all slept. She waved them in and the boys circled around and embraced their mother.

"Eema, when will Father be back?" Asahel asked looking up at his mother.

"I don't know," their mother replied. "Hopefully not till morning."

"You can sleep with us if you want," Asahel suggested.

Zeruiah laughed at her youngest son's attempt to comfort her.

"That *would* make me feel safer," she replied.

The boy smiled and squeezed his mother's waist and for a moment, she was comforted.

***

Hours later, Zeruiah awoke to banging at the door. Trying not to wake her sons, she gently removed her arm from under Asahel's head and hurried to the door to remove the bar that secured it.

The door immediately flung open and he stumbled into the dimly lit dwelling wreaking of alcohol.

"It's about time," he muttered.

"I'm going back to bed," Zeruiah stated. "I told the boys I'd sleep with them," she said as she started towards their room.

He grabbed her arm and spun her around before she was able to pass him. He pulled her close to kiss her when the foul odor of alcohol caused her reel in disgust.

Angered by her reproach, he backhanded her across the face.

"You're my wife, my only wife," he shouted. "Maybe I should take another who would return my affections."

"You won't support one wife. What makes you think another would have you," she fired back.

He struck her with his closed fist this time, knocking her to the floor. He stood over her and reached down to grab her hair when the tiny body of his youngest son struck him, knocking him over in his drunken state.

"Stop it Father, stop!" Asahel shouted as he clung to his father.

The man stood and pried the boy from his torso, then slapped him down. Abishai was the next to rush him. His father sent the boy reeling into the wall of the small den.

"Stop it! Stop it!" Zeruiah shouted as she pulled at his arm.

He flung her like a doll against the wall next to his middle son then started towards them.

Asahel rushed to his mother's side on the floor. She pulled her two younger sons to her when a loud crack against the back of their attacker's head knocked him face-first to the floor.

As he lay unconscious facedown on the floor, Asahel and Abishai looked above their father to see Joab standing triumphantly over him, still holding the thick wooden bar that was used to secure the door.

Zeruiah crawled forward and gently inspected her husband. Blood trickled from the gash in the back of his head as she placed her ear near his mouth.

"He's breathing," she announced. She looked up to her eldest son.

Breathing hard and holding back tears, Joab dropped the wooden bar on the ground and collapsed to his knees.

"It's ok, it's ok," she said, taking her son's hands in her own. "Put that next to the door," she said to Abishai as she pointed to the plank.

She stood covering her mouth as she looked down at her unconscious husband. She realized for the first time that her hands were shaking.

"Stay here," she said before opening the door and stepping outside, leaving the door open. A moment later she returned, pacing the floor. "It's only midnight," she said frantically. "We can't leave for hours."

She continued pacing the floor.

"No one will take us in... no one that knows your father," she said, though it seemed she was speaking more to herself than any of the boys as they stood watching. "Come now," she said, herding the boys into their small room, "get back in bed before he wakes up. He might not remember any of this." She returned to the kitchen and took the only knife they owned from the place where it was kept.

The boys quietly laid down as Zeruiah joined them, careful to place the knife close enough that she could easily grab it if the need should arise. She held her two youngest boys close to her sides. Seconds seemed like hours as they lay there waiting for the morning.

Joab propped his head so that he could just make out his father's form in the dim light of a single candle in the kitchen. Reflecting on what had occurred, for a moment he was sure he'd killed his own father. The fear in that moment had paralyzed him, but now he was kept awake by the fear that at any moment, his father might wake up. For hours, Joab turned over the idea in his mind. What if his father never woke up?

Hours later, his mother began to stir. She got up and went to check for signs of life from her husband's unconscious body. She must have found breath in him as she continued moving very slowly and quietly as she moved around their tiny home.

Joab was sure he hadn't actually slept at all and didn't want to now. More than anything, he wanted to be out of this place and away from the drunken heap of a man that lay on the floor. He rose and crept to the kitchen. His father lay in the same position he'd been earlier. A circle of dark, wet earth had formed beneath his father's torso, and the small room stunk of urine.

Joab was startled when his mother touched his shoulder and handed him a small bundle she'd prepared and wrapped with a blanket.

"I'm going to wake your brothers. We're going to your grandmother's this morning before your father wakes up," she whispered before creeping into their room.

Abishai and Asahel snuck into the kitchen and waited while their mother packed most of their few belongings. Asahel rubbed his eyes as he entered the candlelit room. He turned to Joab and whispered, "we're going to grandma's," with a smile.

Joab nodded. He too was just as elated by the news.

A moment later, their mother emerged from their room and opened the door to the alley outside. The four of them quickly filed out of the small house and into the still dark street. Zeruiah gently closed the door behind them, then took the lead as they hurried down the alley to the main street which led towards the city gates.

Joab looked back to make sure his father did not emerge from the alley as they fled what wrath might await them when he awoke. Reassured, he quickened his pace to that of his mother and brothers.

"How long will we stay with Grandmother?" Asahel asked their mother.

Their mother looked down and smiled. "I don't know my love."

"Will we see Uncle David? Do you think we can help with the sheep?" Abishai asked, practically skipping as they went.

"I'm sure that won't be a problem," Zeruiah responded nervously.

Joab's dread began to wane slightly at the mention of his young uncle.

"I wonder how many new baby goats and sheep he's got!" Asahel exclaimed.

Joab marveled that the thought of the small animals had already replaced his baby brother's remembrance of the previous night's events. Then again, he hadn't been the one that nearly killed their father and he certainly would not bear the brunt of the punishment for their little mutiny. That duty fell to his mother or himself almost without fail.

The tension in his young body began to loosen slightly as he allowed pleasant visions of what lay ahead to replace the thoughts of what lay behind them. Perhaps his brothers were right to be hopeful.

***

The three boys found him perched on a large rock overlooking his father's flock west of the fields where the rest of their uncles toiled bundling sheaves of wheat. The sight of him was hardly uplifting to the casual observer, but to the three boys he was a picture of independence and freedom. He sprang from the rock and ran to greet them.

His tattered shepherd's clothes were torn and his hair matted with dirt. His face was filthy.

"Joab, Abishai, Asahel!" David exclaimed. "I didn't know you were coming!"

David embraced each one of them as if he hadn't seen another human face in some time.

"What's the matter Uncle David?" Asahel asked. "Have you been mourning?"

"I guess you could say that," David replied. "I don't think I've seen you all since Saba passed."

The three boys hadn't yet taken notice of the absence of their uncle's beloved paternal grandfather and no one else they'd come into contact with this morning still bore the clothes or appearance of someone in mourning. They'd come expecting to be comforted by their young uncle and were unprepared for the condition they'd discovered him in.

"I'm sorry," Joab responded. He knew the old man was more like a father to David - at least, in the sense that most people associate with their fathers, Joab thought.

"It's alright. What brings you all?" David asked.

The two younger boys lowered their eyes. An honest retelling of the night's events reflected poorly upon their father. It would dishonor him to tell the full truth.

"Something happened back home," Joab said. "We need to be away from Father for a while."

"Oh," David replied, giving an understanding nod and knowing something of the rumors regarding their father. "Well, I sure am glad to see you. I guess I haven't bathed in…. Well, it has been awhile," he said looking down at his tattered and filthy sackcloth. "I must look a little haggard, even by shepherds' standards."

Abishai nodded.

"I suppose I should get cleaned up," David acknowledged, giving Abishai a wink. "I am glad you all are here! Will you all watch the sheep for me while I go wash up in the creek?"

"We will!" Asahel excitedly responded before his brothers could answer.

David tossed his shepherd's staff to Joab.

"From the top of that rock, you can keep an eye on all of them," David said, pointing to his perch before heading off towards the creek.

Joab quickly mounted the rock and surveyed the sheep below. Abishai and Asahel watched enviously below as their brother stood atop the rock, his right arm extended with the shepherd's staff planted firmly near his feet. The Pharaoh of Egypt could not have bestowed a greater honor in their young minds.

When David returned, he seemed revived. His hair, still wet from the creek but relatively clean, was slicked back, his eyes bright, and his face restored to its youthful and happy disposition.

"How long will you all be staying?" David asked as he joined Joab and sat on the rock at his feet while Abishai and Asahel played with two small lambs on the ground in the shade of a large cedar tree.

"Mother said we'll be here a while," Joab finally answered. "She's going back home today, but asked if we could stay with you and help with the sheep."

"That's a great idea!" David affirmed, sensing the uneasiness in his nephews. There would be time for details of their situation later. If there was one thing that shepherding afforded, it was time. "It's just me now so I could really use the help. I was just about to check on everyone and get a count? It will be a lot easier with the three of you helping. How does that sound?"

The three younger boys were elated.

Joab slid off the rock and joined Abishai and Asahel making his way around the flock. The brothers kept count as David introduced them to each individual sheep by name, calling attention to their specific characteristics as he went.

Abishai and Asahel followed along holding the young lambs as their concerned mothers followed closely behind.

Another young lamb sauntered up and began nibbling at Joab's sparse leg hair, tickling him as it licked at the perspiration on his skin. He bent over to pick it up and examined it, trying to find some unique characteristic.

As he cradled the soft lamb, it began nibbling at his earlobe. Even in his anxious state, Joab could not suppress the laughter that the young lamb evoked as it gummed and pulled at his ear.

"Looks like Joab has a new girlfriend," Abishai exclaimed.

The boys erupted with laughter, completely forgetting their count of the flock. For a moment, they found some relief for their troubled minds and the anxious concern for their mother and what wrath might lie in wait for her upon her return home.

PSALMIST

1071 BC, Judah, Israel

"**D**id you really want to be selected?" Raanan chided his new friend.

"Are you kidding? Those guys will probably get paid more in the next two weeks than I'll make in the next couple months back at our farm. There are a lot of us, remember?"

"Well, I'd do it for nothing as long as they keep me fed. I've always wanted to learn to fight," Raanan admitted. "Anyhow, I still say you're lucky to have brothers. I've only got sisters, so most of the hard stuff is left to me. You realize how much my father has to set aside for dowries with four daughters? Can you imagine plowing your father's fields by yourself?" he asked. "With brothers, you all get to work together. Man, what I would give to have some other men around. What's the saying? Many hands make light work? Well, I can tell you the opposite is true as well. Sure, you may have to split your inheritance one day, but you're the oldest anyway, you get a double portion. What have you got to worry about?"

"Ah! You sound just like my grandfather."

"Oh yeah?" Raanan replied. "Sounds like a smart man,"

"He was an only son. My great-grandfather was very wealthy and taught my grandfather and father how to farm, but then there were a few hard years with little rain and they weren't able to pay the workers, so many of them left. My grandfather took to raising sheep since it required less labor than farming. Much of the land grew wild and he sold or leased a large portion of it to other farmers who could afford laborers. My father detested everything about raising sheep and eventually got permission from my grandfather to take charge of the land. He revived what was left of it and made it profitable again. Sure, having a lot of sons helps, but that doesn't mean that everyone pulls their weight."

Raanan nodded as they walked along.

"I may get more than them when the inheritance is divided up, but I can promise you I have earned it and then some. When they weren't old enough to work, I was working by myself. When they did get old enough, I trained them. They always had help. I didn't. I did most of the plowing and hard stuff cause I'm the oldest. I don't think my youngest brother has ever touched a plow. The only thing he's ever done is watch the sheep. You know how hard it is to watch sheep?" Eliab asked.

He started up again before his friend could answer. "Half the time he's playing the lyre or making up songs. You can't play music while pushing a plow."

"Is that David? He's the youngest right?" Raanan asked, recalling some of the stories he'd heard during the past few months of training.

"Yeah," was Eliab's only response.

"He sounds scrappy at least from what I've heard you say before."

Eliab didn't respond.

"So, the lyre, eh?" Raanan asked, squinting one eye in the bright sun. "How did he learn that?"

"My grandfather taught him. His mother was a Moabite. Apparently they have a lot of spare, time to learn music and dancing out there wandering the desert. Music is a big part of Moabite culture."

"Is he any good?" Raanan asked.

"I suppose he was, but he died not long ago." Eliab replied.

"Sorry to hear that," Raanan said, "but I was asking about David. Is *he* any good?"

"Oh. Ah, I guess so. If you're into that sort of thing," Eliab said as he kicked a rock with the inside of his foot. "He should be. Like I said, that's about all he's good for."

"Well, as you can imagine, music is big around my house. It's hard to avoid with all those girls around. They are always singing and playing whatever instruments they could get their hands on. My youngest sister will make an instrument out of just about anything. I'd like to hear David play," Raanan said.

Eliab nodded as they trudged along, obviously not interested in showcasing his young brother's talents. By now, they'd been walking all day and only several hours of daylight remained.

"How much further is it?" Raanan asked.

"Not much." Eliab responded. "Our family's land starts just over this next ridge," Eliab said, nodding towards a far off crest. "We might actually be able to spot him from there. Some of the best grazing is just to the south of that hill."

"You mean David?"

"Yeah," Eliab replied. He'd talked enough about his useless younger brother for the day. "So what do you think the 3,000 are up to? There had to be a reason why we were all called up like that."

"I don't know," Raanan said with a sigh. "I appreciate the training though. It helps make our people strong I think. Who knows; maybe they'll actually do something this time. I know the Philistines aren't as bad out here, but there are some places in Israel where you can't have much of anything without having to worry those fish worshipers might take it from you. Imagine having to hide while threshing grain. Imagine having to bury your money so it doesn't get stolen. Out here, you still have metal farm tools. Out west, they're using rocks!"

"Yeah, but we still have to take them to the Philistine blacksmith at Geba to get them sharpened or fixed. I'd almost prefer rocks than having to deal with them."

"So you say! You speak as one who hasn't used stone tools before my friend. Of course," Raanan paused to flex his biceps, "it does have its benefits."

Eliab laughed, but he had to acknowledge that there must be some truth to his friend's statement. Raanan was probably the most physically fit man he'd ever seen. Eliab had always held the admiration of other young men around Bethlehem, but Raanan far surpassed his own physical prowess.

"So, you've told me about your brothers. Tell me about the rest of your family."

"What else do you want to know?" Eliab asked.

"I think I heard you mention a sister back at Michmash," Raanan said with a grin.

"Two half-sisters," Eliab said. "Zeruiah and Abigail."

The two men walked in silence for a moment.

"Are they married?" Raanan finally asked.

Eliab stopped and returned a momentary stern look before both men broke into laughter.

"No! But Zeruiah has three kids already," Eliab said condescendingly.

"Ah, the promiscuous sort eh?" Raanan asked wryly.

Eliab laughed again. "Not exactly. She's married, but her husband has issues. He fought at Jabesh and Ebenezer before that," Eliab said. "I should probably catch you up a bit on the family background to avoid any confusion. Zeruiah and Abigail were born before my father took their eema, Nitzevet, as his second wife. After my mother died, Nitzevet treated us all as her own. Father adopted and raised Zeruiah and Abigail, but Zeruiah has never really been my father's child. She's always been rebellious towards him, despite all he's done for them. Her sons are just as bad as David. They're like his little entourage, following him around like the sheep. Wherever David is, you can just about count on seeing Joab, Abishai, and Asahel close behind."

"So David is the leader?"

"They're kids," Eliab smirked.

"Well, I'm just saying, he's got these others following him, he must be a leader," said Raanan. Eliab did not respond, he was clearly becoming irritated with the conversation. "Is that why you're jealous of him?"

"Jealous? Look, if you're going to keep this up, you can go ahead and walk all the way to Efrat for all I care. He's a lazy, musical, momma's boy. There's nothing to be jealous of."

"Woah, woah, I'm just saying, you obviously resent your younger brother. I wish I had one and maybe if I did, I'd resent him too, but I'd like to think that we'd be on the same team. I'd want to support and help him. You're the oldest. You're set to inherit the lion's share of your father's possessions, but you can't stand your baby brother. Maybe he is lazy, but isn't that what everyone says about the youngest? What reason do you have to despise him so much?"

Raanan paused to give his friend an opportunity to answer.

Getting no response, he continued.

"I see it with my sisters all the time. Only thing is, they don't mind talking about it. You want to hide the fact that you're jealous. You are ashamed of it," Raanan said in a half-joking way to ease the sting of his words.

"Anyone ever tell you that you talk too much?" Eliab asked.

Raanan shrugged. "I'm just providing a little outside insight."

"Well you sound like a woman."

"What good is a friend if he can't be honest with you?" Raanan asked.

The two men walked the rest of the way in silence. Cresting a hill, Eliab pointed out the family's borders and lay of the land.

"The vineyard is just over that way. You can find David over there somewhere since you're so excited to meet him. That's the house just there, and the barn behind it" he said pointing. "Come on, I'll introduce you to the family and we can grab a bite to eat."

"Wow." Raanan said, surveying the land before him with its well-manicured fields, fences and gardens. "This place is incredible. I'd be embarrassed for you to visit me now."

Eliab laughed. "Like you said, there's only one of you. There's lots of us."

As they approached the home, the two were greeted by a beautiful, middle-aged woman. Exiting the house to meet them, she embraced Eliab and kissed him.

"You're back sooner than I expected," she said with a smile.

"They let most of us go home and kept only the best to stay behind."

"Then why are you here," she asked with a smile.

Eliab smiled slightly, but ignored the question and introduced his new friend.

"Eema, this is Raanan. Raanan, this is my eema, Nitzevet. We got to know each other pretty well during training. We were in the same team. He helped keep me going during the hard stuff and shared whatever food or treats his family prepared and sent him during training," said Eliab.

She came at Raanan with arms wide open. He bent down to return her embrace. She was a middle-aged woman in her mid-forties, short and petite, but felt strong and sturdy as she squeezed him. She leaned back and with the gentlest of touches, placed her leathery hand on his face.

"Thank you for looking after my boy."

"It was my pleasure. My sisters tend to spoil me. I'd be twice as large and a lot squishier if I didn't share."

"Well, young man, it's a pleasure to meet you," she said with the back of her wrists resting on her hips. "You two come inside and rest yourselves. I'm sure you're tired. You've had a long walk today," she said as she ushered the guest inside.

"The girls and I won't have dinner ready for a while. There's some fruit and nuts on the table if you want."

As the two men dropped their belongings and proceeded to the table where there were almonds, pistachios, figs, and dates, Zeruiah emerged from one of the rooms. She smiled and embraced her brother.

"So glad to have you home in one piece."

Raanan smiled. She was beautiful. He'd never have guessed by her appearance that she'd already birthed three children. Abigail joined them a moment later.

"Good to be back," Eliab said. "This is Raanan. He put up with me during training. His family lives near Efrat, so of course we became fast friends."

"Pleased to meet you Raanan."

"Likewise," he said.

Grabbing handfuls of the nuts and fruit, Eliab filled up two wooden bowls and handed one to Raanan and beckoned him to sit. They sat down and reclined against some cushions on the floor next to the wall. The two men rested their feet and chatted with the women as they went about busily preparing a meal for what seemed like an army. Raanan watched in amazement. Having grown sisters made light work for his mother in the kitchen, but his sisters never ate as much as he and his father. The meal these women were preparing looked three to four times the size he was used to.

Eliab was becoming tired of the rapid questions coming from his mother and sister, especially given the fact that he would likely have to recount all of the same details later when his father and brothers arrived for dinner. He stood up and stretched.

"Alright Eema, I'm going to see if we can find Abba and the others."

"They're working the southern gardens. All except David and Zeruiah's boys anyway," said his mother.

"You can probably find David over by the brook, it being so hot and all. Check on my boys, will you?" Zeruiah asked.

"Will do," Eliab said as he headed out the door with Raanan.

The two men proceeded around the dwelling to the south of the home and yards.

"You mean to tell me that she has had three kids?" Raanan asked.

"Yep," was Eliab's only reply.

As they crossed a grassy field and walked toward a strip of trees, Raanan could begin to hear the chatter of young boys and splashing. As they reached the trees, he saw a large rock next to a creek where one young boy bobbed in the water.

"Uncle Eliab!" the boy shot a hand out of the water and waved wildly.

About that time Raanan saw a streak of movement from the large rock to his right as another boy plunged about twelve feet before splashing into the water just next to the first boy. He quickly returned to the surface and spun around with a wild grin.

"Hey Uncle Eliab," shouted the boy as he treaded water.

"Abishai, Asahel, this is my friend Raanan," Eliab said as he slapped his friend on the back. "This is Abishai," pointing to the first and older of the two, "and Asahel," pointing to the second.

"That looks like a lot of fun!" Raanan said to the boys. He guessed them to be about seven and five years old.

"As you can see, everyone works very hard around here," Eliab said.

Suddenly a white and reddish ball of fur darted out from its resting place in the shadows towards Raanan. The small dog with a curved upturned tail barked and growled as it seized the leather of Raanan's sandal and began whipping its head from side to side.

"Whoa!" Raanan exclaimed with a smile and bent down to grab the puppy.

"That's Gideon!" Asahel exclaimed. "We're training him to help us watch the sheep!"

"Where did you find that?" Eliab asked.

"There was a litter near town. We coaxed him out with some dried meat and nabbed him," Abishai reported.

Raanan stroked the small dog's fur as he cradled it. The dog nipped at his fingers as he attempted to scratch its head.

Raanan held it out to Eliab.

"Cute little guy, huh?" he asked.

"Sure," Eliab replied.

"What? You don't like animals?"

"Not the unclean kind," Eliab replied. "My father would insist that you cleanse yourself after holding that thing."

"Come on! You try!" Asahel shouted. "Climb up over there on that side. You have to aim for this hole right here. If you land over there you might break your leg. It's too shallow."

Almost before Eliab could turn around, Raanan had set the small pup on the ground and was climbing the rock. The boys swam out of the way as Raanan launched himself off the precipice into the water. The creek was shallow enough for him to stand with his chest and shoulders fully above water.

"Wow that feels good," he said, enjoying the cool water.

"Where's Joab?" Eliab asked the boys.

"He's over there with David and the sheep," Abishai answered. "Did you kill any Philistines?" asked the younger boy as he tried to keep his head above water.

"No. Not this time," Raanan answered.

"What tribe are you?" asked Abishai.

"Judah."

"Like us!" shouted the younger boy.

"That's right."

"Hey, Uncle Eliab, he's bigger than you!" Asahel shouted.

As they were talking, Eliab walked a short way downstream and crossed on several exposed rocks.

"Why don't you try Uncle Eliab?" one of the boys asked.

"Yeah! Your friend did it," said the other.

"I've jumped off that rock more times than I can count. I was jumping off that rock before you boys were born," he replied. Turning to Raanan, he asked "You want to stay here at the nursery or are you coming with me?"

"Nursery?" exclaimed one of the boys.

Eliab turned his head to conceal his smile.

"Yeah, I'm coming," Raanan replied as he began walking out of the brook. "Has he always been like this?" he asked the boys.

They looked at each other and back at him, then simultaneously nodded in affirmation.

Raanan laughed.

"See you later," he said as he followed after Eliab.

As they walked further south, they crested a hill spattered with trees. As they reached the top, Raanan could see the land stretched out before him. Below them was a large field of opulent green with flourishing crops stretching eastward. To the west was a grove of olive trees on a hill. He could see five or so men working the field, picking weeds and throwing them into wheelbarrows stationed nearby. There were irrigation trenches stretching throughout the field and to the east tying into where the creek ran south from where the boys had been playing.

Raanan couldn't help but envy this beautiful and well-maintained farmland. He thought of his own home and how hard it had been for him and his father to care for what little acreage of cropland they had. He took it all in. He was enjoying his visit. As they continued walking, Raanan heard something out of the ordinary. He stopped to listen. He could faintly hear what sounded like music.

Eliab saw him from the corner of his eye and stopped, listening briefly.

"That's David. If you want to go see him I'll catch up with you later. Sounds like he's right over there," Eliab said pointing east.

"You don't want to go see your baby brother? Come on. I'm sure he'll be excited to see you," said Raanan, already walking in the direction of the music. "Besides, I'm your guest; you don't want me to get lost."

Eliab begrudgingly followed after him.

As Raanan walked hastily toward the sound of the music, he could begin to make out the tune and rhythm. It was hypnotizing, drawing him in.

"This way," Eliab shouted at him as he was headed straight through a field of lentils. Eliab led his friend around the crops to where he knew David would be. They all knew it to be one of David's favorite spots on account of the acoustics of the place. A small crescent-shaped hill created a natural amphitheater from which David would play in the center.

It was an amusing sight for someone not accustomed to it. As they approached, Raanan could see a young boy of about eleven or twelve, sitting atop a rock, playing the lyre and singing. He had auburn hair and a fair complexion. He was wiry and thin, dressed only in an animal skin ezor. His audience of sheep was scattered about the crescent-shaped hill eating. Raanan could begin to make out the words of the song.

> *The hea-vens announce our God's glo-ry,*
> *the skies testify of His hands' great work.*
> *Each day pours out more of their sto-ry,*
> *each night more to hear and to search for.*
> *In-audible words which can't be heard,*
> *cre-ation's man-ner of speak-ing.*
> *In si-lence it con-veys, all the an-swers*
> *that we're so desperately seek-ing.*
> *Their song has gone out unto all of the Earth.*

The boy stopped and repeated the words and the last chords, "has gone out unto all of the Earth...." Then again adjusted the melody of the words, "Their song has gone out unto all of the Earth... And their words to the end of the world...."

Though Raanan had never heard the song before, it was beautiful to his ears. New songs were rare in those days and he was sure he wanted to learn it and teach it to his family when he returned home.

They came to within several yards of the boy and stopped. Seeing his friend's amusement, Eliab chose not to interrupt David's playing but stood impatiently waiting for the song to end.

As soon as David finished the last word, Raanan clapped his hands.

"That was amazing! How did you learn to play like that? Where did you learn that song?" Raanan asked.

Surprised, David looked up to see his oldest brother and the new visitor. He'd been so focused on playing that he didn't notice them.

"I made it up," David responded.

"Wow! That's fantastic! Really, you must teach me! My sisters are all musicians and they would love to hear it."

"Sure," said the young boy with a smile, as he slid off of the rock onto his feet.

"You're supposed to be protecting the sheep and you didn't even see us walk up," Eliab chastised. "What if there had been a predator about? They'd have eaten their fill of the sheep without you even noticing."

"Not on my time," Eliab and Raanan heard a voice say from behind. They spun around to see another youth of about nine years old standing just behind them with a long, sharpened stick about twice as long as its bearer pointed directly at them.

"You see?" said David. "Nothing to worry about."

Raanan laughed again. He was very amused by this family of males.

"So you must be Joab."

"Who's asking?" replied the boy.

Eliab snatched the spear from the boy's hand.

"This is my guest, Raanan. You'll treat him with a bit more respect than that."

"Pleasure to meet you Raanan. I am David and this is Joab, my right-hand man," David said, placing a hand on his nephew's shoulder.

"I see that," said Raanan.

"He's visiting with us for a little while," said Eliab.

"What's the army up to?" Joab asked. "Are they going to war with the Philistines?"

"They wouldn't say," Eliab replied. "All I know is there were certain men asked to stay behind while the rest of us were released to go home. There was some talk about some of the trouble they've been having near Geba with the Philistine garrison there, but who knows. It seemed like they were intentionally keeping us in the dark."

"Why would they do that?" asked the boy.

"You never know who might be a spy for the enemy. It's best to keep your plans secret in such matters," Raanan responded.

"How many were chosen?" asked David.

The two men looked at each other, "what was it? About three thousand," suggested Eliab.

"That sounds about right," Raanan replied. "It's hard to tell."

Joab nodded. "Did you meet Saul or Jonathan? Did you see Abner?"

Eliab looked at Raanan, "We saw Saul and Abner. They came by occasionally while we were training, but Jonathan actually stopped and talked to us."

"What was he like?" David asked.

"Very smart," Raanan replied. "He's not much older than us, but you could tell he was very well-trained and educated. I heard he speaks seven different languages."

"Wow!" the boys replied in unison.

"I barely know two," said Joab.

"You should see his armor-bearer," Raanan said to the boys. "What was his name?" Raanan asked Eliab.

"Yuval," Eliab replied.

"That's right, Yuval. He's got to be the fittest guy I've ever seen," said Raanan excitedly. "He's a different kind of strong. He looks like he was chiseled from stone. He and Jonathan train together all of the time, grappling and striking. It was incredible to watch. I've never seen anyone train harder than Jonathan, and he's the prince."

"I cannot wait till I'm old enough to train and fight in the army. I would go right now if they would let me," said Joab, as he jabbed the air with his spear.

Raanan smiled. Clearly, the boy had been practicing. He wielded the makeshift spear skillfully and could see that the boy was sincere.

"Well, don't worry. That time will come. I'm sure there will be plenty of fighting left to do. We are, after all, surrounded by people who want to kill us."

"David has been teaching me to use the sling as well!" exclaimed the boy.

"He's getting pretty good," said David.

"Not as good as David though. You should see him! He killed three quail this morning for breakfast!"

"Really?" Raanan exclaimed. "With a sling?"

"That's right," said Joab. "He doesn't miss!"

"Alright, well I'm off to find Father. Do you know where he is?" Eliab asked impatiently.

"They're over there," said David. "By the orchard."

"You coming?" Eliab asked Raanan as he started toward the orchard.

"Just a moment," Raanan said, turning to David. "I want to learn that song you came up with. Will you teach me later," he asked.

"Sure," David shrugged.

"Great!" Raanan said before turning to catch up with his host, who was already walking hastily in the direction of his father and other brothers.

David smiled, unconscious of Joab curiously staring at him.

"What are you smiling about?"

"Nothing," David said. "It's just, no one outside of the family has ever heard me play or sing before. Apart from Saba, Mother, Zeruiah, and you three, no one has ever wanted to hear me play before. He comes from a family of musicians and thought that it was good."

"You said we shouldn't care what anyone else thinks, that we should only care about what God thinks," Joab said, staring up at David.

"Saba taught me not to care if others don't like what I like," he said with a pause. "I make up songs to please God, but it's good to know there are others who appreciate it. That's all."

ELEPH

1071 BC, Near Gibeah, Benjamin, Israel

Saul chose him three thousand men of Israel; whereof two
thousand were with Saul in Michmash and in mount Bethel,
and a thousand were with Jonathan in Gibeah of Benjamin:
and the rest of the people he sent every man to his tent.
I Samuel 13:2

"**A**n entire eleph, one-thousand men at my command and I have nothing to do with them?" Jonathan asked.

"You are to provide security in and around Gibeah and report Philistine reinforcements of the garrison at Geba," said Abner. "Their intentions are clear. Posting a garrison that close to Gibeah is a direct challenge to your father. They are testing him. By positioning our forces on either side of them, your father hopes they will get the message and withdraw. They've been pillaging from local crops, vineyards, and orchards in the area and stealing what metal implements the people have. If local Benjaminites leave, Philistines will move into their homes and become more entrenched. Your men will patrol from the south, we'll patrol from the north. It will help the people feel safe."

"Abner, this is an act of war! Of all the places they could set up an outpost, they come into our backyard. How long are we supposed to sit and wait for something to happen?" Jonathan asked.

"I didn't tell you to sit and wait," Abner responded patiently. "You're to actively patrol the area until your father says otherwise or until the Philistines provoke you to act."

"And what constitutes sufficient provocation?" Jonathan asked.

"Use your best judgment," Abner answered. "Why do you think I've persuaded your father to leave you in Gibeah with some of our most experienced men? Just remember you have a third of our best warriors. If you act foolishly, you could very well condemn the entire nation. You are, after all, the first prince of Israel."

Jonathan read between the lines.

"I understand. I need to set the example," Jonathan said slyly. "We won't fail."

"Ein breira," Abner responded.

"Ein breira," Jonathan replied.

Jonathan and Yuval strode from the general's tent to address the twenty or so officers awaiting further instructions, all of them older than the young prince, many of them by twenty years or more.

"Let's bring it in," Jonathan said as he approached. The officers and senior men drew near, forming a circle around the prince. "As you know, things have been heating up with the Philistines. They've gained a stronghold in Geba. They have a garrison of over a thousand men there. They're living off the local crops and livestock. They're stealing from our people on the land that God gave us and commanded us to occupy. It's our job to put a stop to it. There is no question they selected Geba to send a message. So, we're going to send them a message right back. King Saul and Abner will be positioned on the opposite side of Geba to the north at Michmash. The King's intent is to put pressure on them, so they are compelled to leave. Well, let's stack the weight shall we?" Jonathan said with an exaggerated pause. "Here's what I want to do."

"Ribai, I need you to do your thing. Find a pattern in their patrols and coordinate with Ahithophel."

"Ahithophel, I want to ambush as many of them as possible outside of the wall. They won't be expecting a force our size so if we split up we may be able to hit several patrols before they know what's happening. Now, these are your men, so you get us in there however you deem best, but I want that garrison and I want it soon," the prince concluded as the men nodded their understanding. "Anyone have any ideas on how we're going to get in there?"

The men stood quietly contemplating the problem.

"What if we take their armor?" Ahithophel suggested.

"Now we're talking," the prince said, "go on."

"We could ambush a patrol and dress ourselves in their armor, then use that to infiltrate the garrison. The infiltrators can open the gates for the rest of the eleph."

"I like it. What about the rest of you?"

The other officers nodded their approval.

"Very well, that's what we're going to go with. Obviously, this plan is subject to change depending on what we learn about the fortifications, their strength, and activities."

"Ribai you know the area better than most. I want you to take your scouts and find the best approach to the garrison that will avoid detection," said the prince.

"We need an idea of the Philistine's daily routine," Ahithophel said. "What times they're patrolling, what routes they're taking, how many men they're taking with them, weapons, everything. What's the best place to ambush a patrol that won't alert the rest of them? Also, where and how many gates are there? Are they keeping the gates closed? Are they using a challenge and password?"

"We need suitable staging points near the garrison's gates, as close as possible for us to stage as many men as possible without being detected. If you can, set up security on those positions, then report back."

"Got it," Ribai responded. "There is a giant sycamore tree on the north side of the stream that runs between here and Geba. Actually, there are two smaller streams that come to meet further east. That's the stream I'm referring to. There is a wealthy landowner near there with a large barn. He's a good man and would be happy to provide assistance. It would be a good place to assemble. I can send a runner ahead," suggested Ribai.

"We'll stage there till we determine the best time, method, and location for a coordinated ambush," Ahithophel concluded.

"Can you do this in less than three days?" Jonathan asked.

"That depends on what he is able to gather," Ahithophel said, referring to the reconnaissance captain.

"We'll get it done," Ribai responded. "Geba is about a day's walk. We've got plenty of time to get set up overnight."

"How soon can you get your men in position," the prince asked.

"After drawing rations and water, we can leave within the hour," Ribai responded. "We'll be in position tonight."

"Avoid any contact if possible. If it means taking longer, then take longer. We won't take action until we get word from you," said the prince. "Everyone else, we're moving tonight. We'll step off a half hour after sunset. The moon is waxing, but not quite half full, but should be up for most of the night. We shouldn't have too much trouble finding our way, but that also means the enemy can see us, so I want us spread out abreast each other as much as possible so we don't get caught squatting. Keep your platoons close enough to support each other if we get attacked. Any questions?"

"Is the garrison mounted?" one man asked.

"None of the reports I've heard suggests this, but I'm sure they have some horses for their messengers or captains," Jonathan responded.

The captain nodded.

"Anything else?" Jonathan asked.

"Do we have Abner and Saul's support on this?"

"We will when we take that garrison," the prince responded.

Several men laughed in response to the prince's boldness.

"Sometimes it's better to ask for forgiveness than permission," Ahithophel responded.

"Anything else?"

"Let's get it done," said one of the respected veterans in the group.

"Get your men ready. Let me know of any concerns you have before sunset," Jonathan said before leaving the men.

The commanders dispersed to brief and prepare their men.

As they walked, a young leader turned to his captain.

"So this is it. We're about to kick the hornet's nest."

"Looks that way," the captain responded.

The man thought quietly for a moment. "Good, we'll finally settle this business. If we win, the land will be ours, just ours. If we lose, well, that's not really an option is it?"

The older captain shook his head.

"Ein breira."

***

Arriving at the farm, the two companies with Jonathan settled into their bivouac with all but one out of every four men slipping into a deep and restful sleep after the night's long march.

Ridai had been right about the landowner. He was a godly man who'd been very successful. Jonathan liked him instantly as they spoke in the man's torch-lit barn.

"They've been patrolling the area in groups of about twenty. They'll sneak around and listen or watch for a servant using a metal implement, then they'll all come up at one time and offer to purchase it for almost nothing. They've caught several of my servants by themselves. They don't want to, but what choice have they got when surrounded by twenty armed men? I've instructed them not to resist. Their lives are not worth a spade or plow." The man paused, straining to hide his emotion.

"That's far from the worst of it. Those uncircumcised idol worshipers have assaulted our women and children. No one leaves or travels alone anymore, the women especially. It's like they are prisoners in their own land," he said in a distraught voice. He paused again, then said, "Whatever you need, you have my full support."

"Thank you, but I don't want you to get too mixed up in this. I want their wrath directed at the army, not our people. If there's somewhere you can take your family till this gets sorted out, it would be a good idea. We're going to need men like you when all this is over."

"God bless you and God bless King Saul for sending you to help us."

"Thank you," Jonathan replied.

"I must ask though, why did your father only send an eleph?"

"Only an eleph? Gideon only had three hundred." Jonathan replied, avoiding the question.

The man nodded. "Yes, but," the man paused. "Attacking them like this... there will be consequences. What does King Saul plan to do?"

"We're going to win of course," Jonathan replied.

The wise older man pressed him further. "Does he know your intentions?"

"More or less."

"Won't this anger him?"

"Only if we fail," Jonathan said with a smile.

The man nodded and placed his hand on Jonathan's shoulder.

"You have a heart like Joshua. God be with you."

"Thank you. Why don't you get some rest? No harm will come to you or your family so long as I have a man left standing," Jonathan assured him.

"When we received news that you were coming, my family and I wanted to prepare something for you and your men. Here," the man motioned Jonathan over to a stall, "we had to be careful. We worked all night. It is nothing much, but our resources are thin on account of the Philistines. We wanted to do so much more," he said as he uncovered a hidden door in the floor of the stall. Beneath it was a ladder leading down into a small room.

Holding a lamp, he proceeded down into the cellar. As Jonathan peered in, he saw that it was filled with containers stacked floor to ceiling. He picked one up and opened it. As he did, the most wonderful smelling aroma Jonathan's senses had ever experienced filled his nostrils.

"If there is anything my family does well, and I assure you there are many, it's these cakes. I borrowed every dish the village could spare. Nearly everyone pitched in."

Jonathan's heart was moved. This is exactly what he did not want to happen. He guessed that this small contribution cost the people of the area, and especially this man, more than they were able to spare. He knew that he could not refuse the gift, no matter how much it had cost.

"Thank you. Thank you," he said. "On behalf of myself, my men, and my father, truly, I am very grateful."

***

"Wake up," someone whispered, lightly shaking Eliam's shoulder, rousing him.

"Stand-to," the dark figure said, then moved down the line.

The call to "stand-to" hit Eliam like a load of bricks. It was no later than five in the morning and they'd only arrived and settled in barely an hour earlier he guessed. Oh well, in one more hour, the sun would be up and they would spend the day resting for the most part. In two hours he'd be able to go back to sleep since it would be his turn to stand watch after first light. Everything in his body told him to lay his head back down. To go back to sleep.

He shook his head to keep himself from falling back to sleep. Everyone else on the perimeter wanted to go back to sleep and certainly the men who'd been on watch prior to the call to stand-to. He looked to his immediate right and left. His teammates were already up and putting away their bed rolls. He turned over to his stomach and lifted himself from the earth, the camel hide that covered him crumpled into a heap on the ground as he stood. Shaking off the cold of the morning air, he picked up his wooden shield and spear, then walked over to the designated area and relieved himself along with several other grumpy, half-sleeping men.

As he walked back over to his unit, he could see movement all around in the dim glow of the moonlight. He took up his position amongst his teammates in the line of troops circling their position. Behind him were several more rows of kneeling men, ready to withstand an attack. Along the inner circle were the archers, bow in one hand, nocked bronze or stone-tipped arrow in the other.

They waited silently in the darkness as the sun's first rays began to lighten the sky, then peak over the hills that surrounded them. The sky turned to pink and orange as the sun rose on the horizon. If one had to be awake at this hour, at least the view made it worthwhile, Eliam thought to himself.

As daylight filled the sky, the men began to stir and murmur. Word came down the line that their host had prepared some sort of gift for them which they'd be receiving after stand-to.

Finally, after about an hour, the order came for them to return to their customary low-security watch, which consisted of one out of every four men, allowing the other three to catch some much needed rest. Eliam could see groups of two at a time heading up the hill towards where Eliam knew to be a barn from the previous night's march. He could see others returning from the same direction with what appeared to be covered dishes. Two by two he saw them coming and going as the rest of his team settled back into sleep.

"That must be our gift from the locals," said one of his teammates. The other two watched momentarily, then unrolled their mats and settled back in for a few more hours of sleep before it would be their turn to stand watch.

"Looks that way."

Eliam was not so much hungry as he simply enjoyed eating while on watch. He could think of no better way to pass the time when he had to be awake, while others slept. It also meant his teammates would be up for a while and so make his time on watch even more eventful. He started to ask his companion what he thought it might be, then realized the man was already asleep. He turned his attention outward and waited until it was his team's turn to partake in whatever it was they were getting or doing on down the line.

He stood, spear and shield in hand, surveying the horizon. It was a beautiful morning in a beautiful setting. The rolling hills stretched as far as he could see. The sun revealed a green and fertile landscape. To the south was a very large sycamore tree, the largest Eliam had seen by far. He scanned the land for any sign of enemy movement. The terrain was conducive to moving around without detection he thought. Good for us, but good for the enemy too. Eliam was only vaguely familiar with the land that surrounded him. He'd passed by it many years ago, but on the common road far west of their position. Being from Giloh in Judah, Eliam was not a great distance from his home, though they were close to the northernmost part of Benjaminite territory.

Finally, the team closest to him in the defensive perimeter came back with their own covered dish. Eliam's mood lifted when he smelled the sweet aroma. The four-man team devoured the cake as if they hadn't eaten in days.

"Wow! That's the best thing I've ever tasted," he heard one of them say.

"Sure beats lentils and rice for breakfast," said another man, whom Eliam knew as Baanah.

Eliam looked down at his sleeping teammates. He'd have to wake one of them before he could go and get their team's cake. He chose Ikkesh, the oldest among them, nudging him gently.

"You want to stand watch or go grab our breakfast? Looks like the villagers baked some sort of cakes for us. It smells awesome."

The man sat up and rubbed his eyes. "You go ahead. I'll stay here."

Eliam proceeded in the direction of where he'd seen the other men coming and going and saw the large barn they'd observed the night prior. Upon entering, he observed his father and Prince Jonathan, chatting like old friends. As he approached, he heard a familiar story.

"That was the first time I met your father," Ahithophel said, "I was 15 years old if you can believe it. We'd marched forty miles the night before. Every one of us black as the new moon." Lifting his ezor, he showed the Prince and other officers around him a large scar on the inside of his thigh. "Your father looked like a giant to us. Larger than life. We'd never seen him up close before this point. Now, we'd just decimated the Ammonites and here he was in the dirt with us bandaging up my leg…"

"With hands gentler than my own eema," Eliam interrupted, finishing his father's sentence.

"Ahh, hey there my boy," his father said, putting his arm around the young man. "Prince Jonathan, this is my son, Eliam."

"I take it you've heard this story a time or two," the prince suggested.

Eliam nodded. "Once or twice."

Ahithophel laughed, slapping his son on the back and pulling him into the group.

"Well, it's true. I learned a lesson on leadership that day. All of us fell in love with your father that day. It was his first act as king and he went in there and humped every mile of the trek right alongside everyone else. Not once did he get on horseback when everyone knew he could. We wouldn't have thought anything of it, but there he was, walking the entire way, just like the rest of us. We humped it day and night then killed the Ammonites right where they slept. Most of them never knew what hit them. Only way you could even tell who your father was is by his height. He was painted up and just as filthy as the rest of us."

Jonathan always felt a stir of pride within him whenever he heard these accounts of his father. He couldn't tell how many times he'd heard the various different accounts of the victory at Jabesh Gilead. Like the stories of old, he never tired of hearing them. It was perhaps because of the miraculous victory at Jabesh that he never questioned the stories of Moses and Aaron, Joshua and Caleb. He wanted that kind of faith and believed since his youth that this kind of faith is only grown out of adversity. The more Jonathan pushed the limits of his abilities, the limits of what was possible, the more he found that those "limits" had been self-imposed. It was for this reason that the king and queen considered him to be somewhat reckless.

Despite the king's early show of courage, Jonathan perceived that his father had lost his nerve somewhere along the way. He found his father was always concerning himself with the opinions of the masses. The way Jonathan saw things, the majority didn't always make the best decisions. People, he observed, often do what is more comfortable, what is easiest. It was, in fact, the majority opinion that caused their ancestors to not enter the promised land when they first arrived so many years ago. It was for this same reason that they wandered the wilderness for an additional 40 years before they were able to enter it again. In Jonathan's mind, it seemed more reckless to live cautiously without faith than to live dangerously with it.

"Jonathan is following in his father's footsteps. He's going to make a great king one day," Ahithophel said to his son. "Tomorrow, he's coming with us. We're the main effort."

Eliam was ecstatic, though no one could tell but his father. Outwardly, he merely smiled.

"Good. It will be good to have you with us," he said to Jonathan.

"It's your meh-ah[4] Ahithophel. I'm just coming along. If I step out of line, you let me know," said the prince.

Ahithophel laughed. "I'm just happy to have another soldier of your caliber along for the hike. Not to mention another bowman."

"Well, I wasn't planning on taking my bow. I think we're going to need more pig stickers for this one," said the Prince, referring to their spears. "But don't worry, as soon as we're inside the wall, if I see an opportunity…"

"Yes, we'll need to take out the watchmen."

"It will be my first priority." Jonathan turned to Eliam. "I hear you're quite the grappler."

"I had a good trainer," said Eliam.

"Well, there's no doubt about that. Where is that old Hittite anyway?"

"Closer than you think," said Ahithophel nodding in Jonathan's direction.

Jonathan was startled by a hand on his shoulder.

"My ears were tingling," said Huzziya from behind.

Jonathan feigned surprise by the voice, then laughed heartily.

"Father told me you two were tight."

"Well… someone has to teach you all to fight," said Huzziya. "This one," he said pointing to Eliam, "this one required very little instruction though. He's my best student, a natural."

"I'm your only student," said Eliam.

Huzziya smiled.

"Well, I'm liking our chances more and more," said Jonathan.

---

[4] Hebrew for one-hundred or unit of roughly one-hundred men.

The men around him nodded. They agreed. Each man among them was thoroughly respected by the others. Though many of them were untested, they felt theirs was the best group of warriors that had ever been assembled and there were plenty among them apart from Ahithophel and Huzziya who had fought and killed before.

"Well, I'm going to get some sleep, good night men," Jonathan said, before catching his mistake. "Correction, good day!"

Eliam watched Jonathan depart along with his ever-present armor bearer.

"You'd better do the same," said Ahithophel. "We need to work out the details of tomorrow's attack. I'll see you this afternoon son."

"Sounds good," Eliam replied and departed with his team's breakfast, leaving his father and the others to do their officer work.

GEBA

1071 BC, Northern Benjamin, Israel

*And Jonathan smote the garrison of the Philistines that
was in Geba, and the Philistines heard of it.*
I Samuel 13:3

The leaders crowded around a crude diagram of the Philistine fortress made of rocks and sticks. Information about the interior had been gained from local Hivite merchants and traders who had done business with the Philistines in the previous weeks. Outside of the miniature fortress, dirt and sand was mounded and shaped to mimic the hills, draws, and creeks surrounding the fortress. Grass and leaves had been sprinkled here and there to indicate patches of vegetation.

Ribai pointed to parts of the diagram with an arrow as he hunched over it.

"The Philistine raiding parties generally go out in groups of forty to sixty. They were smaller, about twenty or so, a couple of days ago. I suspect they've increased their presence on account of us, but for the most part, I don't think we've been detected."

He traced the arrow along a path as he spoke.

"They generally leave the fortress through the western gate. If it's a short morning patrol, they come back through the eastern side. If they're out all day, they come through the western gate, keeping the sun at their backs. They are covering a lot of ground. They stop and take what they want from the fields, herds, and orchards they pass along the way. My men have identified two specific choke points here and here," Ribai said tapping the diagram with the tip of the arrow. "They're avoidable, but like I said, they are covering a lot of ground. They come through these two gaps almost daily and always with the sun at their backs. I will not lie to you; they are disciplined. Their captains have got their house in order."

"Good," said Ahithophel. "We wouldn't want it to be too easy."

"Now, from this point they generally return along this route," he said indicating a path from the choke point back to the fortress. "From this one, they generally proceed thus," again tracing a route from the key terrain back to the fortress. "As you can see from the diagram here, they have observation of the approaching patrol for nearly four stadia. That's a lot of time for them to observe you guys and we haven't seen them run once. If you try to cover that ground quickly, they're going to know something's up," Ribai said as he stood from the terrain model.

Jonathan nodded, "Thank you Ribai."

"Another thing. One of their captains is enormous. There is no way any of us is going to be confused with that behemoth. If we're going to pull this off, we'll have to make sure the patrol we ambush isn't his."

Ahithophel nodded.

"The closest points that offer any concealment are here and here," Ribai said pointing the arrow to a pile of leaves near the stick fortress and a hill just next to it. "I'd say we can stage about eighty men here and the rest of us can come in from behind this hill just prior to the attack."

Ahithophel stepped forward and knelt next to the model.

"I want to take some archers with me. It will help us with the element of surprise and reduce their numbers before we get down to the more intimate stuff."

"Right, how many do you need?" asked Dodo.

"Four."

"You got it," said Dodo and instructed his sergeant to go summon their four best swordsmen from his century of archers. The man sprinted off to where the archers were training.

"Sure you don't need more?"

Ahithophel rubbed his brow considering the question. "I'd love to, but we need to keep it lean and whoever comes with us is going to end up infiltrating with us. I need more swords than bows once we're inside the gates."

"Then you won't be disappointed with the guys I'm sending with you."

"Thank you."

Turning back to the diagram, Ahithophel looked closely at the points Ribai had identified. "You said that is four stadia to the gate?"

"It's a fair estimate, but at least three and a half," Ribai responded.

"That does give them a long time to watch us stroll on up to the gate," said Ahithophel.

"They don't seem to pay a whole lot of attention to the returning patrols. There's maybe two guards on the wall, but if you men get up there and they don't open the gate, you're going to be in a world of hurt."

"How about this," said Ahithophel. "They can't see us till this point here," he said, pointing to the spot on the trail where the returning patrols could be seen from the fortress. "What if we stage an ambush or attack to make it look like we're being chased into the fortress? The guards would be less likely to require a password and we'd cover the ground a lot faster without raising suspicions about who we are."

"You're saying, you want us to chase you up to the fortress? That might get you men in, but it's going to get us shot to Sheol," said Hushai.

"I'm not saying you come within bow shot. You don't have to chase us all the way, just enough to sell the ruse, make it look believable. Maybe even fire some arrows in our direction to add to the deception. Your men could chase us up to about here, then go shields up. Launch a few missiles our way and hold until we get the gate open. Then there is the added bonus of having you men that much closer behind us. Let's say they don't open the gate, you can help cover us while we extract. On the other hand, if we do get the gate open, your guys will be the first in behind us."

Hushai stood silent for a moment.

"So we all stage here. You ambush the patrol and get suited up, back here at the choke point. When your patrol gets to this point, we spring a fake ambush and rush your patrol into the fortress?"

"Exactly," responded Ahithophel. "They see what looks like their own patrol running to safety and fling the gates open to receive us. We take out the archers and gate-men, then you come in right behind us."

"You know, that just might work," Hushai responded.

The men looked to the young prince. He stood over the model in the dirt, examining it.

"What do you all think?" the prince asked.

"It is bold, I will give you that," Ribai responded. "How's your Greek?" he asked Ahithophel.

"Not bad. Good enough to sound like a man running for his life," Ahithophel responded.

The other captains voiced their approval.

"I can't think of any better way," one responded. "It does require the least commitment. If it fails, well, they still don't know the full extent of our forces and we haven't exposed the main body."

Several others agreed.

"I like it," Jonathan finally added, seeing it carried the support of the men who'd actually be putting their necks on the line. "Well done! Everyone in agreement?" The captains all nodded. "Good, Hushai, I want you to take your men and stage behind the hill there. Ribai, you know what to do. Dodo, I want your men staged in the brush just there. Anything else we need to sort out?"

"Yes," replied Ahithophel, "does anyone have a razor?" he asked stroking his impressively well kept beard.

The rest of the men laughed.

"I'm sure the owner has some shears we could use," Jonathan suggested. "I must admit, I'm not looking forward to that aspect of it, but, ein breira…."

"I have a question," said Ribai. "If you ladies are going to be clean shaven and wearing Philistine armor, how are we supposed to tell your men from the Philistines once we all get inside the fort?"

Somehow this had not occurred to anyone else until this point. Ahithophel considered the problem for a moment.

"You all will be in the gate right behind us. We'll be focused on taking the ramparts first thing. Once we have the gate under control, I'll have my men shed the Philistine armor. It'll take a minute, so just make sure your guys know that if they see someone getting undressed in the middle of the fight not to kill him. It's going to be hairy for a minute, but I don't see much else that can be done."

"What are the chances they'd be suited up inside the fort anyhow," asked another captain.

"No way to know. They might sound the alarm when they see us approaching. For all we know, the entire garrison might be in full battle rattle by the time we come through the gate."

"Look, if we don't keep this very simple, it's going to get very ugly, very quick. Anyone have any other ideas?" asked Jonathan.

"If I may suggest something," said Ribai, "it is an easily defended position. I doubt that they'd be in much of a hurry to suit up as long as they think they're safe behind the walls. Either way, I think that once the imposters get through the gate, assuming they do get through the gate, they need to be focused on holding and keeping the gate open for the reinforcements. If they let that gate get shut behind them, they're dead men. I don't think they need to be worried about charging in and fighting so much as just keeping that gate open. The folks coming in behind them need to be told not to attack anyone holding the gate open, which seems obvious enough. Once the reinforcements are in, it should be relatively safe for the imposters to shed their costumes and join the fight."

The others nodded in agreement.

"Is everyone in accord?" Jonathan asked looking at each of the captains.

Ahithophel nodded.

"It's a good plan. Audacious, but simple. Worst case scenario, they don't open the gate. If that happens, the men withdraw as fast as possible under cover of our archers."

Hushai nodded. "I agree with the plan," he added, "but I think the worst-case scenario is them not being able to keep the gate open like Ribai said."

Ahithophel's expression conveyed that he agreed.

"Right. Let's make sure that doesn't happen. We'll use the spears, shields, helmets… whatever we have on hand to brace the gates open. If anyone else has any other ideas, I'm open to suggestions."

The plan agreed upon, they discussed preparations and reconnaissance of the proposed ambush sites as well as the identification and tracking of the targeted enemy patrol. Finally, just prior to sunrise, the exhausted leaders dispersed to join their men and rest before the fight that lay ahead of them.

***

Hidden among the rocky crags which lined the path to Geba, Eliam and Ahithophel looked down the line of clean-shaven Israelites, each poised and ready to spring the attack.

"You look like an ugly woman," Eliam heard the man to his left whisper to his comrade.

Eliam turned in time to see the other man respond with his best impression of an effeminate smile while batting his eyelashes. Eliam shook his head slightly and turned his attention back to the trail below.

None of them had shaved their faces in years and it had been an abundant source of banter among the men as they departed that morning from the rest of the division to the sound of whistles and cat calls from the other, still bearded men.

Eliam listened intently for any sign of the enemy patrol. It was already extremely hot and though their positions were concealed from the path below, there was nothing on the rocky slope to hide them from the blistering sun above. There was nothing to do but wait.

They could hear the Philistines' footsteps as they proceeded down the path, their shields and spears clanking against their armor. The three Philistines in the front of the column passed only cubits away. The patrol was now fully engulfed within the kill zone.

An archer sprang up beside Eliam and another further down the line and released their arrows at opposite ends of the column. Eliam heard their two arrows hit their marks almost simultaneously, making a loud thwack! Their targets stumbled out of the column as the others turned right to address the threat. Their leader lay on the ground with an arrow protruding from the front right side of his neck. Coughing and grasping at the shaft, he struggled for his last breaths as his men braced for the attack they knew was imminent.

Two more arrows were released, this time from the opposite side of the narrow pass. Screams of pain could be heard over the rocks that concealed the Israelites, still waiting for the signal to attack.

The archer beside Eliam cocked his arrow and stood, launching the missile at the Philistine closest to those who'd been leading the starboard column. The arrow struck just between the Philistine's armor and the base of the man's helmet. He crumpled instantly. The Philistine next to him in the middle column spun around in time to be struck by an arrow from across the trail. It sliced his shoulder and made a loud clang as it struck the inside of his breastplate.

In the chaos of the ambush, as their leader lay dying on the ground, the Philistines attempted to form a hasty defensive circle in the middle of the kill zone. Eliam and nearly fifty other Israelites sprang into action from behind the rocks that concealed them, sending a volley of javelins and rocks flying towards the bewildered Philistines, then ducked back behind the safety of the rocks as Philistine archers answered back. Arrows went singing past them and shattered on the rocks to their rear. Eliam could hear the next wave of Israelite projectiles from across the way striking the metal of the enemy shields and armor. That's our signal, he thought, as the rest of his unit sprang to their feet and hurdled down the steep embankment towards what remained of the enemy patrol.

Eliam set his eyes on the Philistine closest to him. The man lifted his shield and thrust his spear at Eliam simultaneously. He dodged to the left simultaneously deflecting the spear with his shield. He then thrust his spear at the man's face, narrowly missing the man's right eye. By now he was too close to attempt another strike. He slammed into the man with his shield, sending him rearward into the man behind him.

Eliam drove the spear down into the man's groin, then momentarily glanced to his right in time to see his teammate struggling to withdraw his spear from a Philistine's neck. The enemy next to him seized the opportunity and lurched towards the occupied man. Eliam dropped his own spear and shoved his friend out of the attacker's path just before the Philistine plowed into his shield, knocking the young Hebrew flat on his back. As the attacker came for him, Eliam saw his fellow Hebrew smash the base of the man's helmet with a stone hatchet. The man fell limp on the ground as Eliam regained his footing.

Eliam could see the other half of his platoon emerge from their hidden positions on the opposite side of the path. As Eliam braced himself for a counterattack, a Philistine sprinted past him. Remembering his orders, he stepped in front of the next fleeing Philistine and was again knocked off of his feet. The large Philistine stumbled momentary, then picked up speed sprinting after the first, throwing his shield and spear aside as he ran.

Eliam looked back towards the fray and saw that the entire century was now engaged in the fight. He stood and sprinted after the two fleeing Philistines. As he ran after them, Eliam realized he was not holding a weapon as his spear had been knocked from his grasp. He reached for the small axe tucked in his belt and cocked to throw it just as arrows struck the two fleeing men. They tumbled forward into the dirt, sending the closest man's helmet skidding down the rocky path. Eliam hammered the back of the man's exposed head as he sprinted past. The Philistine ahead of him rolled to his side and began to plead with Eliam as he approached. Before he could reach the wounded Philistine, another arrow struck the man, silencing pleas for mercy.

Eliam turned back to the ambush site and saw that the battle was over. None but his fellow Israelites remained. Amazingly, not a single Israelite had been injured. An overwhelming sensation filled him as he saw his father standing triumphantly among the victors. The battle had been exhilarating and already he wanted to experience it again. He'd tasted adrenaline of battle and was intoxicated by it. He began walking towards the ambush site and looked to either side of the pass in an effort to identify the bowmen who'd assisted him with the fleeing men.

"Well done men," he heard Jonathan say.

Eliam turned and saw the prince in the midst of the platoon.

"Let's get this armor off them before it gets too soaked. Just make sure the man is dead before you try to remove his armor."

The prince bent down next to a Philistine corpse. With a hammer raised in his right hand, he reached and touched the Philistine's eye with his left. When the man didn't flinch, Jonathan began loosing the Philistine's armor. He removed the breastplate and rolled the lifeless body off of the rear plate. The man had been struck under the left arm and there was a large amount of blood pooled in the armor. Jonathan lifted it and poured the blood onto the ground. He looked at the men around him, who'd been staring silently as he performed the macabre task. As if coming to their senses, they all went to work, checking the dead Philistines and removing their armor.

Eliam turned back to the two men who'd tried to escape. The two bowmen stood over one man with an arrow protruding from his face. As Eliam approached, he could hear them arguing over which one had made the better shot.

One of the archers knelt down beside the man.

"Make sure he's dead," said the second as he looked over the kneeling man's shoulder.

The first turned and looked contemptuously up at his fellow bowman.

"He's got an arrow in his face," the archer responded matter of factly.

"I'm just saying," the man responded.

As the kneeling man went to loosen the Philistine's armor, his fellow reached down and grabbed him, shouting simultaneously. Surprised, the kneeling bowman lurched rearward landing flat on his back and kicking at the dead Philistine. The prankster erupted in laughter as Eliam and the terrified bowman looked at him in astonishment.

"What the hell is the matter with you," shouted the startled man as he sprung to his feet and shoved him. "You idiot," he exclaimed.

This only seemed to make matters worse by adding to the prankster's sense of accomplishment. He was bent over in laughter. Trying hard to keep quiet and not arouse suspicion from Ahithophel or the prince, the man was shaking with laughter and seemed hardly able to breathe.

His fellow bowman looked at Eliam. They both stared at the prankster as he sank to the ground, convulsing with laughter.

"I'm Ira," said the standing bowman. "This piece of work here is Gareb, but most of us call him Joker. I'm sure that requires no explanation."

Eliam thought he could see a resemblance between the two men.

"You two related?" he asked.

Ira sighed. "There is a distinct possibility."

At this, Gareb's laughter only intensified. He crumpled over into the dirt, holding his side.

"Look you idiot, get your act together before Jonathan or Ahithophel come over here and want to know what's going on. If you can't keep your composure now, how you gonna do it when you go tromping up to Geba in this dude's underwear?"

Gareb tried to gain control over himself. Finally, he stopped laughing and stood to his feet.

"You're right," he said between restrained laughter. "I think this one really is dead."

Ira and Gareb turned to Eliam.

"Eliam," he said, realizing he'd not yet introduced himself.

They nodded, then a sheepish look came over the prankster's face.

"As in Ahithophel's son, Eliam?" Gareb asked, his voice rising in pitch.

"Yes," Eliam responded. Gareb nodded and quickly looked back down at the Philistine.

"Good shot," Eliam said, then turned and walked back to the rest of the platoon.

Ira slapped his friend on the shoulder.

"Nice job jackass," Ira exclaimed in a hushed voice.

As Eliam approached the platoon, he saw his father waiting, already half-dressed in Philistine armor.

"Well done. Let's get you suited up," said the older man.

Together the two of them searched among the Philistine armor for the best fit. Satisfied with one that was at least a handbreadth wider than needed, but far less gory than the other options, Ahithophel helped secure the chest and back plates, then showed his son how to secure the greaves. They washed out a bloody helmet and stuffed the breastplate with linen to prevent it from wobbling on Eliam's much leaner belly.

Their newly acquired armor sufficiently fitted, the Israelites began dragging the Philistine dead from the roadway into a hole they'd prepared the night prior. The men began frantically shoveling dirt onto the dead, concealing evidence of the attack and the fate of the patrol. Fresh dirt was thrown over the pools of blood in the road and their own weapons and shields were stashed in the brush uphill from the trail and well away from the beaten path.

Jonathan looked around at the group of men.

"You all look like a bunch of uncircumcised goat-lovers," he said with a smile.

The men laughed.

"Who speaks Philistine?"

Several of them raised their hands. He looked at Ahithophel whose hand was also up.

"Sorry, what am I doing? You've got this," the prince said, taking a step back.

Ahithophel nodded and addressed the men.

"If you don't speak goat-lover, you're in the rear. We're going to mimic the same formation these guys had when we ambushed them, got it?" The men were familiar with the column formation the Philistines had been using, as it was not unlike their own used during non-combative movements. "Anyone have any questions?"

All were quiet; they'd already been briefed on the dangerous task before them.

"Seth, Agee, Jehoiada, you all take the lead and set the pace. Remember to make it look convincing but for heaven's sake, don't outrun the rest of us and try to take the fort yourselves," the captain cautioned. "Where are my archers?"

Ira, Gareb, and two others raised their hands.

"You're in the middle column, once inside, I want you to take out the guards on the wall above the gate. That is your first priority, then anyone else on the wall," Ahithophel instructed.

The archers nodded.

"Alright men. If anyone has any last-minute questions about the plan, now is the time to ask," said Ahithophel.

All of the men were silent. Several were already relieving themselves on either side of the path, preparing for the final push into the lion's den. One of the men bent over and vomited. The others stood somber. None chided him. When he finished, he stood as erect and silent as the rest.

The group formed into columns behind Seth, Agee, and Jehoiada. Once everyone was in position, Ahithophel took one last look over the formation.

"Let's move," Ahithophel shouted.

The men began marching, mimicking the Philistine column. All were quiet. Eliam was positioned third in line from the front in his squad, his father to his right in the center column. An hour later, he noticed the terrain feature that signaled their final approach to the fortress. He wasn't the only one, for their pace quickened. Eliam sensed he was not the only one anxious about the coming battle. He could feel the nervous energy of the men around him and it showed itself in their rapid pace. They were eager to get on with it. Whatever their fate may be, they wanted to meet it soon. No more waiting.

As they moved along a military crest approaching the slope that led up to the garrison, Eliam observed the patch of trees and brush that had been described by Ribai during their briefing of the terrain. He looked hard and tried to see the Israelites he knew were staged there.

Suddenly, he could see the fortress emerge over the terrain ahead of him as they marched past the trees and undergrowth. The fort's imposing walls stood high above the hill it was positioned on. Its large wooden and brass gates loomed in front of them. His heart began to pound in his ears. His breathing grew heavier. He knew he had never been more alert than he was at this very moment. He could make out the Philistine sentries on the wall above the gates now.

As the last man passed the group of trees, he heard an Israelite battle cry and saw movement to his right.

"AMBUSH!" Eliam heard his father shout in perfect Philistine dialect. "TO THE FORT!" he shouted, again in Philistine Greek.

Suddenly they were running as fast as their feet could move toward the fortress ahead. Eliam could see arrows landing just to his left, striking the dirt here and there around them. The Israelite archers to his rear were doing almost too good of a job selling the ruse. It felt real.

"OPEN THE GATE! OPEN THE GATE," Ahithophel cried out in Philistine Greek. Eliam looked up to the sentries on the wall. They were shouting down to the men behind the wall. Eliam and his men were getting closer by the second. Soon they would be at the wall. 200 cubits. 150 cubits. 100 cubits. The gates were not opening.

Would they crash against it? Would they be shot by the archers on the wall? Eliam thought to himself. What then?

Fifty cubits. Suddenly he could see light between the two gates. Almost there. He saw Seth, Agee, and Jehoiada raise their Philistine shields and plow into the gates. The rest of the patrol pushed their shields against the backs of the men in front of them and the gates flung open as they poured into the fort. They could see Philistines everywhere running to the wall. Everyone was sprinting to occupy the ramparts.

"MAN THE WALL!" Eliam could hear the Philistine commander shouting paying no attention to the infiltrators.

Fractions of a second later, they were all inside.

Seth removed the head of the Philistine commander in one swipe, then the archers went to work. Eliam saw men dropping from the wall as the four bowmen methodically picked off their targets. The rest of their century was hacking and slicing whatever Philistine targets were nearest to them. Eliam's eyes met those of a bewildered Philistine. He raised his sword and tried to defend himself as Eliam sprinted towards him. The confused man was easy prey. Save for the guards already positioned on the wall, none of the Philistines within the fort bore any armor.

They were quickly taking positions along the wall when Eliam heard the blast of his father's shofar. He threw his Philistine helmet to the ground and felt someone grab his armor from behind. He spun to swing at his attacker.

"ELIAM," he heard. It was his father.

Ahithophel pulled his son over to the gate. He removed the helmet from his head and wedged it beneath the heavy gate. The two men quickly helped remove the Philistine armor from each other's shoulders as more Israelites poured in through the open gates.

Several Israelites were shot by a Philistine archer on the wall, when suddenly the archer reeled as he was struck by an arrow. Eliam looked in the direction he'd seen the arrow come from and saw Jonathan positioned on the wall with a Philistine bow, taking aim at another archer across the fort. Yuval, not far to the prince's rear, was also sending arrows to the ramparts on the opposite side. Nearby, Seth heaved a screaming Philistine over the wall to his death below.

"Come on!" Eliam heard his father say. They ran to a nearby barracks with several other Israelites. Philistines were pouring out of the barracks like hornets from a nest. A bloody battle ensued there and throughout the open yard of the fort. Everywhere was madness. Israelites were still pouring into the fortress. Jonathan and the four other archers rained death upon the Philistines from atop the wall.

The open barracks room was quickly cleared as Israelites flooded into it.

In minutes, the fort was theirs. The din of battle quickly faded to silence as the men searched room by room for any surviving occupants.

Several moments passed quietly when the silence was broken by a shout from among the crowded courtyard.

"JONATHAN!"

The men turned to see the young Israelite soldier as he raised his sword, pointing to their prince on the wall.

"JONATHAN," he shouted again. Others joined him.

"JONATHAN! JONATHAN! JONATHAN!" they chanted raising their newly acquired weapons.

Ahithophel raised a sword pointing to the prince, high atop the wall.

Jonathan smiled, acknowledging the praise of the men, then raised his hand, pointing to the sky. He motioned to the men to quiet down.

"Do not praise me brothers! Praise the Eternal God of Israel!" he shouted.

"AHU!" they replied in unison.

"Well done men. WELL DONE AHITHOPHEL!" Jonathan shouted, looking down at the captain.

The men turned their attention to the commander.

"Alright Israelites, let's see to our wounded and check the dead. I want an aid station in the front barracks and the dead enemy piled outside the gate," shouted Ahithophel.

The men began quickly checking the fallen Philistines and tending to their own injuries, which were few. In the officers' quarters, Jonathan and Ahithophel sifted through correspondence between the garrison commanders and high-ranking Philistines stationed elsewhere. Most of the documents pertained to logistics, while a few talked of the imposition of their plans to strip the Israelites of weapons and metal. Some of the men reported that they'd located a treasure trove of farm tools and other implements in one of the rooms near the soldiers' quarters.

As Ahithophel combed through the letters, one in particular held his interest on account of a peculiar reference made in the text. Ahithophel stood silently for a moment, trying to recall the reference. Where had he heard the term before? He continued reading the letter in Philistine trying to draw more information from the context.

To Captain Rasmus, Commander of the Garrison at Geba

The King of Gath sends his greetings and the accompanying donation of the people of that city in recognition of the great service which you are doing in support of our people. News of your work has reached us from various sources. It has been a great comfort to our people. Your work will prepare the way for the extermination of our opposition and pave the way for our expansion.

As to your inquiry regarding the rumors of certain weapons of war being developed here, I can neither confirm nor deny their validity. Suffice it to say that Rapha's seed has been preserved.

*I can further assure you that if you continue to serve with such distinc-
tion, the powers that be will not overlook you and the accomplishments of
your men. There can be no doubt that such a decorated unit will be at the
top of the list when it is decided how to deploy the best and most powerful
weapons Philistia has ever possessed.*

*We wish you continued success. It is my desire to provide whatever you
or your men are in need of. Any request which is within my power to fulfill
will be done.*

General Aphek
Commander, Gath

He scanned the letter for the words again.

"Rapha's seed," he said aloud in Hebrew, hoping it would jog his
memory.

"What?" Jonathan asked.

"This reference here, Rapha's seed. I've heard the name Rapha
before, but I can't recall," Ahithophel said as he handed the letter to
Jonathan and pointed to the word.

"Rapha," Jonathan read aloud. "Years ago the Philistines had a warrior named Rapha. He was giant like Og," Jonathan said as he took the
letter and read it.

"Right, the Raphaim," Ahithophel replied.

"What do you think?" Jonathan asked. "Propaganda? No one has
seen a giant in at least two generations."

"Could be," said Ahithophel. "Could be the name of a specialized
unit," he suggested.

Their conversation was interrupted from shouts all along the western
wall of the fortress. A soldier hurriedly stuck his head into the doorway.

"There is a very large formation of Philistine chariots and mounted
infantry headed this way from the west."

The two men looked at each other.

"We can't hold here," said Jonathan, "they could starve us out. The
rest of the army doesn't even know we're here."

"We could send a runner," said Ahithophel.

"We don't know what they're bringing with them. Hades, we don't even know what provisions are here yet. That could be the garrison's resupply."

"If we're not going to hold, we need to get out of here."

Jonathan stepped outside into the courtyard and shouted to the men.

"WE'RE LEAVING! FORM UP ON THE EASTERN GATE. DON WHATEVER PHILISTINE GEAR YOU CAN!" Jonathan shouted before turning to Ahithophel. "We're going to leave in formation, maybe it won't draw as much attention if they do see us. Once we reach the thicket. Send a runner to Michmash with a report of what we've done."

Ribai and Dodo ran up to them, ready to receive further instructions.

"We're going back to Gibeah until we get further instructions. We'll push east, keeping the fort between us and them until we reach cover. Let's move!"

Both men nodded their assent, knowing there was no time for fine tuning the plan. Any plan that involved leaving the place would suffice for now.

The men closest to the gate moved to the large doors and swung them open as the last of the sentries sprinted down the stairs to the ground and filed in behind the formation.

Ahithophel and Ribai waited momentarily as the smaller team leaders confirmed their men were present. In rapid succession, the teams reported to their leaders of ten, then fifty, and up. In less than a minute, the entire division was accounted for. The wounded had already been placed on expedient litters, constructed from spear shafts rolled into large cowhide blankets the men commandeered from the barracks.

"Get those wounded in the center of the formation," shouted Ahithophel.

A few moments later the gates were flung open and the men were double timing out of the fortress. In the rear of the formation, Ahithophel and Ribai pushed the gates shut, then followed behind, guiding them to ensure they stayed concealed by the walls of the fort. By the time the last of them reached the concealment of the thicket, Ribai could see Philistines beginning to encircle the fort. No doubt their suspicions had been raised when no one answered at the gate and by the lack of guards along the wall. They were being cautious and encircling the fort to entrap any hidden enemy that lay within. The Israelite commanders breathed a sigh of relief. They'd narrowly escaped.

He dropped the Philistine armor and sprinted after his men, jumping and dodging the hundreds of Philistine breastplates, shields, and helmets the rest of the eleph had shed as they reached the concealment offered by the thicket. The sun was low on the horizon. Soon their movements would be concealed by the darkness, assuring their safe retrograde to familiar and favorable terrain.

Extremely light afoot, there were few in the army as fast over a long distance as Ribai, but he had difficulty overtaking the group. It seemed as if the men were gliding effortlessly across the land. He looked over at one of his small unit leaders. He had a resolute look about his face, focused, but at ease. Sensing the captain's gaze he turned to meet it.

"You good?"

The young leader's face lightened.

"Outstanding!"

A smile spread across the older man's face causing the young leader to follow suit along with those around him.

"EIN BREIRA!" they shouted.

They all knew the gravity of their accomplishment, the odds they'd overcome, and the coming tide it would bring. The captain felt it too. He felt the weight of the dread seem to fall from his shoulders. The first strike had been dealt and it was a decisive one. There would be no more hiding, no more cowering or backing down, no more sidestepping and politics. Now it would come down to the fight, just like their forefathers, Joshua and Caleb who'd come in to take back the land that had been given to their fathers Abraham, Isaac, and Jacob. After all of this time cowering, their mettle would finally be tested.

DEJECTED

1071 BC, Gilgal, Benjamin, Israel

He waited seven days, the time appointed by Samuel. But Samuel
did not come to Gilgal, and the people were scattering from him.
I Samuel 13:8

Jonathan entered the general's tent and stood patiently as Abner finished examining the map rolled out on the table in front of him. Finally, the general straightened.

"Good morning Jonathan."

"Good morning Abner. All was quiet during stand-to this morning. The divisions have begun training and exercising for the day until further instruction," Jonathan reported. "We lost one hundred and thirty-three more men last night."

Abner shook his head, but said nothing.

"Uncle, the men are growing impatient. We're training them constantly, but the longer we wait, the more Philistines gather. Let me take some men and scout a proper place for us to attack or probe them. We need to act, we need to... to do something."

"We're waiting for Samuel. Saul does not want to act without first receiving his blessing."

"Perhaps you could convince him that we're losing men faster than the Philistines are gaining them. The longer we stay here, the worse the situation gets. These men have families to care for. They won't sit on their hands here while their families remain unprotected at home."

"Samuel's instructions were to wait," said Abner calmly. "You know your father."

"Samuel would not have us cower in fear as our enemy grows. Is his sacrifice not as good in Ramah as it would be here? At least let me take the men on patrol. Perhaps we'll put some fear in the Philistines, make them think there are more of us than there really are. At least we'll give the men something more to do. This sitting and waiting is only filling their minds with dread," the prince pleaded.

"The order stands. Aren't you always reminding me that Gideon did more with less?" Abner responded. He didn't like it any more than Jonathan, but there was a limit to how far Saul could be pushed. "You know I don't like this any more than you do, but your father is the king. I will not usurp him. Nevertheless, I will talk to your father again."

Though his demeanor had hardly changed, Jonathan could tell his uncle was growing impatient. Still, he pressed. "But Abner..."

"You will not provoke this Jonathan. Your father's instructions are clear! We will wait for Samuel."

Jonathan knew he'd pushed his uncle too far this time. It was a rare occasion when the general felt the need to raise his voice at any man. Family or not, Abner was the General and commander of the army. Jonathan turned and exited the tent.

Yuval was already at his side as they strode away from the general's tent.

"So what is it, exactly, that you want to do anyway?" Yuval asked. "Ever since the armory was looted, there's hardly a sword or spear to be found among those of us that are left."

Jonathan cursed the deserters that had fled, taking all of the armament with them, including the weapons they'd gained from their victory at Geba. He shook his head. As angry as he was, it was difficult to find fault in what they'd done. If he had a family, waiting, unprotected while the army sat motionless for days on end, he might have done the same.

"No. Abner is right."

Yuval stopped walking, stunned at the words Jonathan had just spoken.

"It does not matter how many desert. What's important is that we wait on the Lord," Jonathan said.

"So that's it?"

"That's it. Don't worry my friend. We'll have a fight sure enough. And look at the bright side. The fewer there are of us, the more of them we get to kill."

Yuval tilted his head.

Jonathan slapped his armor bearer on the shoulder.

"And fewer to share the spoils," he said as he turned and strode towards their tent.

Yuval nodded. "Now there you have a point," he replied as he followed.

***

Abner received the morning report as the sun rose in the eastern sky. Only a fraction remained of the thousands that had come with them to Gilgal. He dismissed the formation and received the captains into his tent.

"Samuel is supposed to arrive today. Have your scouts and sentries on the lookout. We need to make sure he gets here safely. We know nothing is going to happen until he's made the sacrifice, so let's make sure that happens and happens soon. I won't insult your intelligence by telling you how dire our situation is. You know that once Saul has made a decision, there will be no turning back, so let's come up with the best course of action to present to him. Now, ideas, what have you got?"

"Respectfully, perhaps it is time we consider a withdrawal," said one of the captains. "We've been here for over a week. No doubt the Philistines have scouted out our camp, not to mention the fact that many of our men may have defected and informed them of our defenses. They are certainly well acquainted with our dwindling strength. It's only a matter of time before they seize the initiative."

One of the other captains was already shaking his head.

"Hushai, you disagree," asked Abner.

"You got that right," he replied. "Look at what we've done. Look where we've come from. How can we slither on our bellies out of the fight that lies ahead of us now?"

Abner turned to Ahithophel. "And you?"

Ahithophel nodded his agreement.

Hushai spoke up again. "What have we to lose? If we withdraw, they will surely pursue us. We would be most vulnerable to attack. Even if we were to outrun them, what then? We are in the heart of Israel and our forces have fled. If we leave, the Philistines will plunder the homes of the men we have left – which are mostly local men of Benjamin and Judah. When the rest of Israel hears how we fled, who will fight then? How will we rebuild the army? Who will be left to do so?"

"They have thirty chariot battalions, six battalions of horsemen, let alone all of the infantry. Why is this a question?" Takeo asked. Ahithophel and Hushai stood unmoved. "You would have the entire army die fighting? You would rather sacrifice yourselves and these men? For what? To what end?" Takeo asked them poignantly in his far Eastern accent. "In my country, it is known that if one's forces are ten to one, we may surround the enemy. Five to one, he may attack. Two to one, he may flank. One to one, he can avoid until he obtains a more favorable position. But if unequal in every way, the only thing to do is flee. This is the way of war. What you propose is foolishness!"

Hushai shook his head. "With due respect, King Saul has paid hand-somely for your counsel, but you do not know our people. We are as good as defeated if we flee. I say we fight. If we die, then we die." In truth, the Archite bore very little respect for this foreign adviser. He continued. "Your tactics are based solely on calculation and require little skill or courage, or dare I say, faith. Without giving you a history lesson, let's just say that your ways are not our ways."

"I am well acquainted with your history. I am paid for what I know. Your King would not pay me so "handsomely," as you say, if this were not so," the easterner said before he was cut off.

"We cannot stay *here* and fight," said Ahithophel. "We need to move to a more advantageous position. I suggest we move to the fortress at

Geba and regroup. The terrain is rougher between here and Gibeah; it will force the enemy to break into smaller elements. Their numbers won't mean as much when they are forced into smaller columns, nor will their chariots and horsemen. I suspect they will try to flank us with one or more of their infantry divisions. When they split up, we can focus our attack on one of the smaller elements."

"We have a smaller force," Takeo continued. "The terrain favors our withdrawal as you said. We can escape now and fight another day, but what you're saying is suicide, they will surround you and starve you out."

Hushai began to fire back when the flap of the tent flew open. A hush fell over the king's advisers as Saul stepped into the tent.

"Well?" Saul asked. "Let's hear it."

"We're going over the options," said Abner.

"Still nothing from Samuel? No one knows where he is," the king asked.

Abner shook his head. "I sent a party to locate him with orders to report back last night. I fear that they were intercepted."

"Or deserted more likely," Takeo responded.

"So what are the options?"

"I see only one," said Abner. "We need to move into the hill country. Between there and Gibeah we will have the most favorable terrain. Most of the men that remain are Benjaminites. We all know the land there better than the Philistines. I know Samuel's instructions were to wait seven days. We have followed his instructions and he is nowhere to be found. Perhaps he was intercepted by the Philistines. We may be waiting for something that never happens while men continue to slip away. If he has not been captured, he'll be coming from Ramah, so it's likely that we may encounter him as we head east."

"I will not act without seeking the Lord's counsel first. If the sacrifice was not necessary, he would not have troubled us to wait."

"We may be waiting for someone that never comes," insisted Abner.

"Then I will make the sacrifice myself," Saul shouted.

"Saul, you are not a Levite, but you *are* God's anointed. If you say we fight, then we fight, if you say we withdraw, we will withdraw, but

God has chosen you as King, not Samuel nor any of us for that matter," Abner responded.

Turning to the captains, Saul asked, "What say you?"

Ahithophel bowed his head slightly. "You are God's anointed and I am but a captain, not a priest. Sacrifice or not, I believe we need to act."

"We have no alternative left but to act," Hushai insisted. "What choice is there to make? We must attack or be cornered."

Takeo spoke up. "Perhaps I am not as acquainted with the ways of your people as I thought, but are you not the sovereign? In my country, the king *is* god. Do the people not call you God's anointed? His chosen one? If your prophet insists that a sacrifice be performed, who better to do so?"

Joash came to Takeo's support. "You *were* selected from all of Israel. Levites are priests by their birth and the Lord's priests are many, but there is only one King. I think you are right to pay tribute before a decision is made."

"Saul, do not trouble yourself with the sacrifice," insisted Abner. "You know there are those among us who will see it as a violation. We're soldiers, not priests."

Saul breathed heavily. He'd seen the sacrifices performed many times by the multitude of priests at his disposal.

"Have the men assemble at the altar. Bring me the burnt offerings and the offerings for peace. I will conduct the sacrifice."

Abner shook his head. The captains turned and slowly exited the tent to address what was left of their divisions. When only he and the king remained, Abner pressed him once more.

"Saul, I do not think…"

"My decision stands," Saul interrupted without looking up from the map.

The men had assembled near the ancient Israelite altar where a substantial amount of dried wood had been gathered. A fire burned hot in the center of the circle of stones. Saul stood before the men and led them in a prayer for deliverance and victory against the Philistines, then called for the sacrifices. The men responsible for sustaining the roving army selected the best specimens from among the stock and brought the animals forward. Saul had seen the rituals performed thousands of times. He knew precisely the right words and maneuvers. To the onlookers, it appeared that the ritual was performed flawlessly. The men watched as their king placed the cuts of meat onto the altar and were consumed by the flames. The aroma of cooked meat filled the air throughout the Israelite camp.

Positioned behind the large crowd stood Prince Jonathan and General Abner. They watched silently as the rituals were completed, the smoke rising from the altar under the hot sun. It was now well into the afternoon.

"Did he ask for your input on this?" the prince asked.

"He's the king. He doesn't need my advice on everything," his uncle replied as they both stared ahead at the smoking altar before them.

"I didn't think you would have supported this. Nor Ahithophel. Nor Hushai for that matter," Jonathan said, turning to his uncle. "Let me guess. This was Joash's idea?"

No response was necessary. No one knew their King better than these two men. Between them, they could anticipate nearly every move Saul made.

The ritual complete, the two men stood and watched as the smoke from the altar dissipated into the clear blue sky above. A murmur began to rise from the crowd to their right. Abner looked to see what had caused the distraction and observed a sentry attempting to push his way through the crowd.

"General Abner," he heard the man cry above the rising noise of the crowd.

Seeing he had the general's attention the man pointed back in the direction he'd just come. Looking over the men to the hillside to their west, he could see a slightly hunched figure with a large staff speedily moving down the slope, his long gray beard clearly visible even at this distance. A youthful man with brown hair and a short dark brown beard walked abreast of him.

"Samuel," Abner said.

By now, Saul had also seen the prophet headed towards him as the crowd began to part for the old man, giving him a wide path straight to the king. As it did, Samuel could see Saul at the ancient altar behind him, the fire burning brightly and trail of smoke rising from it. The old prophet stopped abruptly as the young apprentice's eyes passed from Saul to Samuel, then back again.

"Samuel!" Saul called excitedly, walking towards the prophet.

For an awkward moment, Samuel just stood and stared at the king. The men in the assembly were silent.

"Welcome!" Saul said loudly, his arms stretched wide as he walked towards the prophet.

Samuel closed his eyes, breathing in the smell of the sacrifice, hoping that his senses would not confirm his suspicions. It was not merely smoke he sensed, but the all too familiar scent of the offering. Samuel opened his eyes and glared at Saul wearing the priestly ephod.

Saul let his arms fall to his sides and stopped a short distance away from the old man.

Samuel shook his head with a look of utter disappointment, then turned on his heels and plodded back in the direction from which he'd come, violently striking the earth with his staff every other step.

Jonathan's heart sank at the sight of it. Abner placed a hand upon Jonathan's shoulder. What can this mean, he thought.

"Samuel!" Saul exclaimed. Following after the seer, he caught and pulled at the old man's shoulder.

Samuel spun around violently as Saul withdrew his hand.

"What have you done?" Samuel growled in a low voice.

Abner and Jonathan watched from a distance, unable to hear what was being said between the two men. Abner strained to listen, trying to see the prophet's mouth as he spoke, but wasn't directly facing Saul. The old man had his head turned slightly and downward as he spoke.

"Oh God, do not abandon us. Forgive us oh Lord. Do not abandon us. Forgive us," Abner heard the prince repeating in a barely audible whisper.

Saul stood trying to find the words, "The people were deserting me! You didn't come when you promised, and the Philistines are gathering at Michmash. I thought to myself, the Philistines are going to attack me here in Gilgal, and I haven't even asked the Eternal One to favor us. So I took matters into my own hands. I didn't want to, but I offered the burnt offering myself…. No one knew where you were."

"That was a foolish thing, Saul. You have not kept the commandment that the Eternal, your True God, gave to you. He was willing to establish your kingdom over Israel for all time, but now your kingdom will not last. He has found a man who seeks His will and has appointed him king over all the people because you have not kept to what the Eternal One commanded." Samuel turned and proceeded down the mountain.

Jonathan wanted to follow after him, but Abner stopped him.

"Let him go," Abner said.

Saul, standing alone and surrounded by the men, turned to see all the faces now watching him.

"Back to your posts!" he shouted.

The men slowly began to disperse as Saul began walking to his tent. When Abner joined him, Saul remained silent.

"Shall we plan our next course of action?"

Saul nodded and the two proceeded to the tent. Gathered around the rough map of the terrain their scouts had constructed on the ground the two men stood silent. Saul expected the obvious questions about what Samuel had said. Instead, Abner pointed towards a small circle of rocks on the diagram.

"That's supposed to be the fortress at Geba, is it not," the general asked.

Saul looked to the model as if waking from a trance.

"Yes, yes, that's Gibeah and that's Geba there. The scouts say the Philistines have abandoned it since their defeat. The Philistines are apparently superstitious about their dead," Saul replied.

"We can move there, the location is easily defensible. You and Jonathan would be safer there. I can remain outside with some of our forces. At least we'd have some relative safety and the terrain would force the Philistines to split their divisions."

Saul nodded. "Give the order."

***

It had been days since they'd moved through the night to the fort at Geba. Several men, struck by the brief ominous interaction between Samuel and Saul took advantage of the cover of the darkness during their movement to conceal themselves in caves and rocky crags as the army passed through familiar territory to safety.

When they'd taken the head count that morning, they'd barely had one thousand men left. Since then, a large group of men who'd been assigned watch for the night had conspired with Joash. During the night, while the others slept, they'd fled with nearly all of the few bronze weapons they still possessed.

Inside the fortress, Saul became more and more irritable and withdrawn as the days passed.

"Our scouts tell me that the Philistines have broken into three different divisions," Abner said. "One has gone to Ophrah, another to Beth-horon, and another towards the borderland near Zeboim. It seems they do not wish to attack us here. It's likely they have interrogated the defectors and expect our numbers will continue to dwindle if they wait things out."

"Mmm," Saul grunted.

"Saul," Abner said pausing to emphasize his concern. "The three divisions have been raiding our villages. They are burning homes. They are taking everything. They want to draw us out, yes, but if we wait here and do nothing, we're as good as dead. I suggest we attack the force at Michmash. They will be the most isolated."

"You mean let them draw us out? Do exactly what they want us to do?" Saul asked incredulously.

"Father, please!" Jonathan exclaimed. "Look at what the Lord has done for us. Look at what he did for us when we took this very fortress. We must have the faith to let Him go before us now. With Him, we cannot lose."

"Silence boy! You would lose my entire army to your foolish whims. Do not lecture me on faith. I, I AM GOD'S ANOINTED! ME! I will say when we fight."

"What happened up there at the altar? What did Samuel say? The men think..." Jonathan paused, trying to choose his words carefully. "The men are asking if you still have God's blessing."

"Is that a challenge?" Saul shouted as he strode menacingly towards Jonathan.

"No Father!" Jonathan said as he knelt and bowed his head. "I am your son." Lifting his eyes to his father, the prince continued. "I merely want to be of service. The men need direction. Allow me to...."

Jonathan's statement was cut short as Saul struck him across the face with an open palm.

Saul turned away and spoke sternly.

"You are no longer in command! I'm taking your eleph and placing them under Ahithophel's command. You are fortunate that you are my son. You are the reason we are in this mess. Now leave us."

Jonathan stood, dejected, then slowly turned and exited the tent. Abner departed after him, quickly catching up to the scorned prince. He placed an arm on the young man's shoulder.

"I will talk to him. I don't know what Samuel said to him, but it shook him. If something is not done soon, we'll lose the few men we have left. Just stay out of your father's sight for now, try to rally the men and get their morale up. They need you. I'll work on your father."

The dispirited prince merely nodded and walked back to his tent.

MAYBE GOD

1071 BC, Gilgal, Benjamin, Israel

"[F]or nothing can hinder the Lord from saving by many or by few."
I Samuel 14:6

As the sun set on another eventless day, Jonathan went about checking the line in the fading light as Yuval slept. He crept from each posted watch to the next until he reached the elevated position overlooking the pass near the rock called Seneh. Even in the darkness, he recognized the two veterans instantly by their outline and mannerisms, their dark bodies creating a silhouette against the lighter rock. They heard him approaching and announced the challenge, just loud enough to hear. Jonathan replied with the password.

"We weren't expecting any guests," one of the men said.

"At least not from this side of the pass," added the other.

Jonathan quietly moved to their position and laid on the rock next to the men and peered over the precipice.

"Any movement?"

"Nothing within the last few hours or so. Every once in a while, we'll hear them stirring across the pass. You'll hear a rock clamber down the slope and they'll stop for a bit. Then when they think it's safe again, we'll hear them moving again. I don't think they know we're here cause we can see the uncircumcised dogs moving from rock to rock. Last time I saw the sapper, he was right there behind that triangle-shaped one just there," Dodo said, pointing down towards the opposite slope. "They're trying to feel out our position or maybe even just put someone out forward of their lines. The way the sound travels down there, no one's going to make it up this way without being heard. We've got it in hand sir. You can rest easy."

"Well, I doubt there are two more capable men," Jonathan said.

"Tip of the spear," one man replied sarcastically.

"Why do you think they haven't attacked yet?" Agee asked.

"I suspect they don't know our numbers," Jonathan replied. "That, and we have the high ground on this side of the gorge."

"Thank God for that," Dodo replied.

The three men sat in silence for a moment. It was only a matter of time before the enemy learned how truly dire their situation was. Then, even the terrain would not prevent them from attacking.

"How are your families?" Jonathan asked.

"Growing sir," replied Agee.

"How many children do you have now?" Jonathan asked.

"Five."

"Now let's see, there's Ehud, Barrak, and Shammah? Who did I miss?"

"That's right sir. That's one hell of a memory you have. But you forgot the girls, Deborah and Jael."

"Yes! That's right! How could I forget? Your naming convention makes it easy to remember," Jonathan replied, restraining his laughter. "Five," the prince repeated, shaking his head. "That's a lot of arrows in your quiver."

"I've tried to explain what causes that," Dodo jeered, "but I think he's just a glutton for punishment. Either that or he's trying to have one child for every judge of Israel."

"What can I say?" Agee replied. "Absence makes the heart grow fonder. Perhaps we should try again for a Samson."

"What about you Dodo?"

"Just two right now. They are tight," he responded. "My youngest doesn't know the meaning of fear. I don't know if that makes him brave or crazy. Sometimes I think he is a little of both."

"That sounds a lot like his father," the prince replied.

"Dodo's just too stupid to be afraid," Agee commented.

Jonathan heard Dodo try to muffle his own laughter in the darkness.

"It must be how he got that name. If God did not love him, he'd be dead by now. His kid on the other hand. Well, he truly is fearless," Agee affirmed. "Tell him about the dog," Agee said, nudging his comrade.

Jonathan could see the warrior gleaming with pride despite the darkness.

"So there is this dog," Dodo began, "a big mean thing that our neighbor owns just over the hill, but close to a watering hole where the boys like to play. They have to pass through another neighbor's orchard to get there and back home. There is a wall around the orchard that they climb over. Now," Dodo said, pausing for emphasis, "this dog is massive. The thing looks like it was sired by a hyena. No kidding, this thing looks like the hound of hell. My sons call it 'the beast.' So when we came back from training a few months ago, I found out that my wife had just finished tanning their hides. I asked what it was about cause she usually leaves the disciplining to me.

Well, my oldest was so excited, he launches into the retelling as if he had not just gotten stripes for it. They were playing in the watering hole, which my wife had forbidden, and were sneaking back home, but as they are coming through the orchard, they see the beast ahead of them, blocking their path. They see it standing there through the trees, head down, glaring at them, snarling. My oldest takes off running, thinking that Eleazar is right behind him, but when he climbs the wall, he turns to see Eleazar just standing there with this big terebinth branch cocked back and ready. The beast barks and growls, but Eleazar just stands his ground. Finally, the beast charges, but Eleazar doesn't move. Just cubits away from the boy, when it's about to pounce, Eleazar steps towards it, swings the branch, and cracks the beast across the jaw, smashing its teeth all to hell. The dog yelped and whined and tore off back home with its tail between its legs before the boy could get another swing at it. It hasn't left the neighbor's yard since. And do you know that son of a Baal then had the gall to complain to my wife about it?" Dodo asked. "Boy did he regret that!"

"Brave kid. What did you do?" Jonathan asked.

"Well they'd already gotten their licks from my wife. Let's face it, they had disobeyed her, but later on when she wasn't around, what do you think I did? I told him how proud I was; not for disobeying their mother of course, but showing the courage to stand his ground."

The seasoned warrior grew quiet for a moment, then cleared his throat.

"When I got done talking to them, Eleazar reached into his pocket and handed this to me," Dodo said as he rolled onto his side and pulled a lanyard from over his head and handed it to Jonathan. "Look here," he said, handing a small object to the prince.

Jonathan took it in his hand and examined it in the moonlight. Three large dog's teeth, with holes bored through their top, hung from a thin leather cord made to be worn around the neck.

"My boy made that for me. He said he made it for me because I taught him to be brave," Dodo said.

Jonathan gazed at the small keepsake. He felt his throat tense and was unable to speak, surprised by how moved he was by the small gesture.

A muffled grunt was the best the prince could muster as he handed the small talisman back to the veteran.

"Got that right sir," Dodo replied, his voice cracking slightly.

Jonathan silently nodded as the three men sat quietly, unable to speak and thankful for the darkness that concealed their eyes.

There in the darkness, outnumbered and ill-equipped for the coming battle, Jonathan felt nothing but a confident peace about him. They would win, Jonathan thought. Somehow, they would win and Israel would survive because of men like this and their posterity in the generations to come. Men like this and their sons were the reason why God blessed and preserved Israel.

"So, sir, what's the plan? I can't remember a time when we've ever been outnumbered like this," Agee finally asked, breaking the silence.

"We're working on something," Jonathan said, regretting that he could not be completely forthcoming with these men.

"If you don't mind my asking," Agee said, "what happened with Samuel?"

Jonathan thought for a moment. Most Israelites knew that Levites were required to make sacrifices, but the fact of the matter is that he too was in the dark about what had been said between his father and the prophet. Why worry these men with conjectures?

"The truth is, I'm not sure," Jonathan replied. "I would tell you if I knew, but there are things the king does not even tell his son. I understand your concern and I hope you don't think I'm withholding anything from you."

The two sentries were silent.

"I'm going to keep checking in on the men down the line. Is there anything you need? Are you getting enough rest?"

"I was just about to get some shut-eye before you got here," said Dodo as he rolled onto his back and Agee took up his position overlooking the precipice.

"We've got things covered here Jonathan. Nothing will make it up that slope without us knowing."

"I believe it," Jonathan replied. "Good night."

As the prince departed for the next pair of sentries, he feared he may have lost some of the trust he'd gained with the two veterans. He considered what else he could have said to put the men at ease, but there was no putting them at ease. Their situation was growing worse by the day. Something would have to be done.

***

Rumors had spread about the apparent conflict between Saul and Samuel. It seemed that no one was sure what had been said between the two, but since nearly everyone had seen the confrontation, theories abounded. The men were growing increasingly impatient with the waiting, but no one more so than the prince.

"I have a wife and children at home, a farm, my prince," one man had complained. "I don't mind serving, to die even if the Eternal should require, but this... this waiting and sitting while the Philistines go about unchallenged..."

"What will we find when we return home?" several of the men asked.

"I know where you're coming from brothers," he assured them. "I'm sure we'll have some action soon," was Jonathan's standard reply.

Back at his tent, Jonathan paced.

"Can you calm down? You're driving me crazy," said Yuval.

Jonathan shook his head as he strode around the tent tapping the shaft of an arrow to his forehead.

"What can be done?" Yuval asked. "If your father has lost favor with your God, do you think it wise to go into battle? Besides, didn't you say Abner was right to wait?"

"We've waited!" Jonathan responded. "Samuel has come and gone, Father may have lost favor with the Lord, but I still feel the Eternal is with us. Is it not for Him and His glory that we are in this predicament? Over and over, does he not tell us, 'be strong and courageous?'" The prince was beside himself. He could not bear this waiting any longer. Some Israelites had actually defected to the Philistines, others hid in the surrounding countryside. How long before they were completely abandoned, he wondered.

"When Gideon went against the Midianites he had only 300 and prevailed over more than 120,000. Samson alone killed 1000 Philistines when the spirit of the Lord came upon him."

Yuval shook his head. "Do you really believe that stuff?"

"After all we've done already, after all we've been through, you still doubt?" Jonathan asked incredulously. "The Lord promised our ancestors that if we walked in His statutes and observe His commands, that five should chase a hundred, and a hundred shall chase ten thousand, and our enemies would fall before us."

"Well, too bad there's only two of us," Yuval replied.

Jonathan abruptly stopped his pacing.

"I've had enough. Come on! Let's go down to the Philistines. We'll have a fight one way or another."

Yuval sat up and watched as Jonathan grabbed his quiver and slung it over his shoulder. He tightened the leather strap around his chest, then grabbed his bow and exited the tent.

Yuval stood to his feet grabbing his own bow and quiver as he exited the tent.

"Here we go," Yuval said to himself as he ran to catch up to the prince. "Ok, what's the plan?"

"We'll go over to these uncircumcised. Maybe the Eternal One will fight for us. If He wants to save us, then no force is too big" motioning to the section of Philistines perched on the small outcropping across the crag, "or too small," he said, turning to Yuval and pounding his fist on the armor bearer's chest.

They approached the last Israelite sentry, who stood as they drew near.

"My Lord," said the guard, acknowledging the prince.

"Shalom and good morning! As you were," Jonathan said as they passed at a jog. The sentry, unsure what to do, looked at Yuval curiously, expecting some answer or explanation.

Yuval shrugged and motioned to Jonathan as they passed and said nothing.

Standing at the top of the southern edge of the large void that separated them from the Philistines, they peered across the canyon. They could see the small Philistine section pitched as an over-watch on a half-acre piece of flat ground to the eastern flank of the Philistine's main body. Like their own overwatch, these Philistines were positioned to warn the larger force lower on the slope of any Israelite movements on their flank. Out of bowshot, the Philistines had taunted the Israelite watchmen across the gorge for the past few days.

Jonathan turned to Yuval. "Are you with me?"

Yuval sighed. "Do as you wish. As always, I am with you heart and soul. You know that."

"We'll cross over to the men and we'll show ourselves to them. If they say to us, 'Wait until we come to you,' then we will stand still in our place, and we will not go up to them, but if they say, 'Come up to us,' then we will go up, for the Lord has given them into our hand and this shall be the sign to us."

Yuval stared blankly back at the prince. He knew that his demeanor conveyed what he was thinking about this so-called plan.

Jonathan stared back, his face a picture of quiet determination.

Jonathan's words rang in Yuval's mind, "If the Lord is with us, what have we to fear?" He remembered the lion in the thicket so many years earlier. It was clear, as then, that Jonathan had made up his mind to go with or without him. This would not end without bloodshed.

"Alright," Yuval replied.

Jonathan turned and entered a narrow crevasse that led down into the gorge, concealing their movement from the larger enemy position opposite them. Half sliding, half climbing, they made their way to the bottom and came to a large boulder downhill from the Israelite position. They paused, catching their breath. It was the last covered position within the gorge. Jonathan's eyes were set on the Philistine position above them. At the bottom of the chasm, they could see only one Philistine's feathered helmet over the rocks and terrain above. Jonathan looked at Yuval. A small shelf of rocky ground about halfway up the slope would conceal them entirely until they reached it.

The armor bearer knew there was no turning him back now. Life before Jonathan had plucked him from his wretched existence had been no life at all. He'd resolved long ago that come what may, he would share Jonathan's fate. He owed the prince that much. If this is the end, let it come quickly, Yuval thought to himself. He gave the nod of approval he knew the prince was waiting for.

This was all the affirmation Jonathan required, for he immediately stepped out from behind the boulder and shouted loudly at the Philistine high above them. The man's head jerked in their direction, taken off guard as he was. He stood immediately on seeing the Israelites below and bobbed his head, looking to either side of them to confirm their number and searching the surrounding rocks for anyone concealed there.

The man called back to his fellow soldiers behind.

"Look, the Hebrews are coming out of the holes where they've hidden themselves," the Philistine watchman shouted.

"Well, you've got their attention now," Yuval said.

Several others joined the watchman at the edge of the precipice. Glaring down at them, the men began shouting insults at the two Israelites.

"Hey there, why don't you two come on up here, we've got something to show you," one of the men said, making a lewd gesture. Several others stood on top of the small rock wall they'd stacked around their position and lifted their pteruges, exposing themselves to the men below.

Jonathan and Yuval looked at one another then back to the Philistines above.

"We'll be right up!" Jonathan shouted and began making his way through the vegetation that lined the bottom of the wadi with Yuval on his heels.

As they started up the steep slope, they came upon a thin sheep or game path traversing zigzag up the steep incline. Yuval struggled on, breathing heavily, but quieted by the realization of the fate that awaited them up the slope. If this was to be their last battle, there was but one thing he could do to repay the life given him by the prince. He would draw the Philistine's attention away from Jonathan if at all possible. He had to be the first to reach the Philistine position.

At first, the Philistines stood in amazed disbelief as the two Israelites climbed towards them up the seemingly impossible slope, partially, if not fully concealed by the rocky terrain between them.

"Go check the eastern slope," their commander ordered several of his men. "It could be a diversion."

The two Israelites seemed to be racing up towards them. Jonathan held his bow in his left hand as he made his way up the jagged pass, at times climbing with his hands and feet, his sword sheathed and his shield slung over his back. Yuval climbed as quickly as his burning muscles would allow, trying to overtake the prince and be the first to meet the Philistines on the small hilltop above them.

Yuval kept looking up at the men above them as they climbed, though he was almost as concerned of falling to his death as he was about the enemy overhead. Suddenly, he saw an archer step forward. Yuval quickly took aim and fired an arrow at the man as he drew down on the prince slightly further uphill. The archer's aim was foiled as Yuval's arrow entered his shoulder, sending the enemy's arrow down into the rocks below.

Jonathan strung an arrow and took aim as Yuval climbed on, passing him. The prince shot one of the men through the torso as he and several others began hurling rocks down at their attackers. The slope of the wadi was so littered with large white rocks and stones jutting out of it that most of the enemy's projectiles were deflected off course or stopped altogether before they reached their intended targets. Yuval narrowly dodged several tumbling rocks as he strung another arrow while Jonathan resumed bounding and climbing up the slope.

Rocks were crashing and tumbling all around them. Yuval released his arrow as a second Philistine archer emerged. The arrow narrowly missed the Philistine's face. The man drew back his bow and took aim. Yuval shouted a warning to Jonathan as he nocked another arrow and laid behind a rock too small to conceal his large frame. Concerned for the prince, Yuval raised himself to his knees and fired wildly at the archer. The Philistine loosed an arrow before Yuval could conceal himself behind the rock again. He felt the arrow slice his left triceps before he sprang from behind the rock and began clambering up the crevasse as fast as his powerful limbs would allow, hoping simply to draw the enemy's focus.

He watched as the archer took aim once again, but was struck by Jonathan's arrow. Yuval wrenched another arrow from over his shoulder, then stopped and knelt behind the largest rock he could find, nocking the arrow as he saw Jonathan renew the offensive. They were nearly upon the Philistines and more were coming forward to join the fight above them.

Several arrows sang over Yuval's head as he ducked and returned his own projectiles as quickly as possible. He saw one of Jonathan's arrows strike another Philistine as the man attempted to throw a spear. Yuval sprinted forward again. An arrow swished by his face so close that he felt the feather fletching graze his left ear as he saw the Philistine archer disappear behind the defilade above, struck by another of Jonathan's arrows. He stopped again and began loosing arrows as fast as his fatigued muscles would allow. The Philistines were within fifty cubits now. The rock throwers had given up and now crouched behind cover. As they continued climbing, the enemy began to spread out along the crest. One Philistine, having thrown his spear, turned to reach for another, but was struck in the back by the prince's arrow.

Finally, Yuval saw his opening and made the last rush to where the jagged rocky slope evened out to flat ground. Jonathan sprinted past him as Yuval released another arrow, striking a Philistine whose spear dropped to the ground mid-throw. Jonathan swooped down and grabbed the spear as he passed the man, while Yuval sprinted forward as several Philistines moved to engage the prince.

Jonathan threw the spear into the chest of the closest attacker, then drew his sword as Yuval flung his bow at the second, striking the man in the upper arm as he raised it to protect himself. Jonathan sunk his sword deep into the man's stomach. Yuval, now completely unarmed, ran to grab the man's sword as Jonathan fended off the next attacker. They were fighting side by side now, hacking and slicing as the Philistines attempted to flank them, forcing them back closer and closer to the precipice. Yuval sliced off the hand of one man who turned and fled colliding with another as he did. The approaching attacker leapt to his feet and sprinted after the wounded man.

Yuval parried a spear thrust and grabbed the shaft with his left hand. Wrenching it rearward, he hacked the man's arm with his newly acquired sword. Another swung his blade wildly at Jonathan. The prince ducked as the man's sword sliced through the air over his bent torso. Jonathan stepped into the man and wrapped his left arm under the man's thigh. He heaved upwards and arched his back sending the Philistine tumbling headlong into the jagged white rocks below. Yuval threw his sword at an approaching Philistine. It sunk deep into the man's abdomen as Yuval grabbed a spear from the ground and swung it like a staff at several attackers attempting to flank them. The closest jumped into his fellow as he tried to avoid the blow, causing both men to fall.

The third attacker knocked the spear from Yuval's grip. He seized the Philistine around the waist and heaved the man upwards driving him into the men behind him. A spear flew past his head and struck the Philistine's chest. Yuval turned to see Jonathan strike down the Philistine who'd thrown the spear as the man attempted to draw his sword. Yuval wrenched the spear from the enemy's chest and fended off a blow from one of the others as they regained their footing.

The four remaining Philistines maneuvered to encircle the two Israelites. Time was not their ally. These men could simply wait out the two Israelites while others arrived. Jonathan drew back and threw his sword at one of the Philistines; the man tried to shield his face and torso, but the sword was thrown low and sliced deep into his shin and calf. No sooner than the sword left his hand did Jonathan launch his assault on one of the other Philistines as the man tried to thrust his spear at Jonathan. The point grazed Jonathan's flank as he turned and seized the shaft of the weapon. He spun and tried to fling the Philistine into one of the others.

Yuval watched as the eyes of the nearest Philistine shifted to Jonathan. The split-second distraction was enough. Yuval thrust his spear, impaling the enemy's lower abdomen just below the breastplate. The fourth came at Yuval while his spear was still lodged in the other man's belly. He ducked under the Philistine's sword and, releasing the spear, punched upward at the man's jaw. No sooner than the Philistine struck the dirt was Yuval on top of him, pressing him to the ground. Grabbing the man's wrist with both hands, he pulled it across the dirt towards his shoulder with the Philistine still clinging to the sword in his hand. Reaching under the man's arm with his left hand, Yuval grasped his own wrist and began rotating the Philistine's elbow upward while pinning the enemy's shoulder and wrist to the ground. The Philistine writhed and punched at Yuval's ribs with his free hand, unable to reach his sword. Yuval wrenched the Philistine's elbow up and heard the grinding crunch and pop of the Philistine's shoulder as it dislocated, tearing the tendons and sinew. The man screamed in agony as the sword slipped from his grasp.

Yuval released his grip and grabbed the sword as he rolled off of the man. Before he could strike the injured man, the Philistine was on his feet. Sprinting in the direction of the Philistine camp below, the man stumbled over the chalky rocks as he attempted to flee, clutching his limp right arm as he ran. Yuval turned to see Jonathan on top of one of the other Philistines pressing the shaft of a spear down on the man's neck with the full weight of his body. Yuval sprinted after the fleeing Philistine and flung the short sword, sending it end over end through the air before it pierced the Philistine's back. The man toppled face first into a small boulder, leaving a spatter of red on the white rocks that covered the hilltop.

Yuval scanned the small patch of earth for any enemy still breathing. Looking back to Jonathan, he could see that the Philistine beneath him was no longer struggling. Yuval located his own bow and snatched it up then pulled several of his own arrows from Philistine corpses. Looking down to the goat path where the Philistine had tried to escape, he waited with an arrow drawn to meet any reinforcements. As one ascended the slope into view, Yuval loosed the arrow, striking the Philistine directly in the right side of his chest. Another with him came into view almost simultaneously. Yuval began to nock another arrow as the man was struck in the abdomen by a Philistine spear. Yuval turned to see Jonathan searching the ground for another enemy weapon.

The two Israelites stood among the dead Philistine section, breathing heavily, muscles tensed and ready. They glanced at each other briefly. Movement near the path caught both men's eyes. One of the badly injured and bloody Philistines had gotten to his feet and was hurrying down the path away from them. Yuval realized that his aim with the Philistine sword had not been as well placed as he'd assumed. The man half slid and half ran down the steep rise to the Philistine camp below as Yuval drew down on him.

Yuval's chest still heaved with each breath. He drew in a long slow breath and exhaled slowly, lowering the bow slightly to his target as the air escaped his lungs. As the injured man hobbled towards the Philistine camp, alerting those closest to him, several stood and ran over to receive him just as Yuval's arrow pierced his back. The mass of Philistines closest to them was now alerted to their presence on the hilltop above.

Jonathan searched the ground for his own bow and located it. Pulling arrows from the men that lay around him and several more from Philistine quivers, he ran over to the precipice where Yuval watched the Philistine army below them. They'd created quite a stir among the enemy camp below.

Yuval saw Jonathan stretch an arrow back as far as his bow could bend. He loosed it at the vast mob of Philistine soldiers below. Yuval quickly followed suit. Protected by the slope of the high ground they occupied, the two men sent several projectiles into the Philistine camp below as quickly as they could draw the strings of their bows. In the Philistine camp, men sought cover, running into their bewildered colleagues as arrows rained down on them from their own friendly overwatch position above.

***

From his perch in the acacia tree overlooking the gorge and the enemy camp in the natural amphitheater formed by the bend of the deep wadi, Eliam could see the multitude of Philistines stirring below. He stood and pushed branches out of his way trying to focus his eyes in an attempt to get a better look. Whatever was going on, something had caused quite a fuss. He could see a few Philistines launching arrows from behind shield bearers up towards a steep incline above them where he knew there to be a Philistine contingent positioned as overwatch. To his amazement, from behind a short wall of white boulders, he saw arrows raining down in quick succession on the multitude below. Eliam reported his observations to the runner on the ground below who quickly disappeared in search of their captain.

***

Jonathan and Yuval could see the commotion their actions had created among the Philistines. Arrows had ceased coming up from the camp below as they sent arrow after arrow into the mass of those closest to their elevated position. The two Israelites were quickly running out of projectiles though they'd seized every Philistine arrow they could find among the men they'd just slain.

"They'll realize any minute now that it's just the two of us!" Yuval shouted as Jonathan loosed the last of the arrows.

"That's it," he said, looking down to the enemy below. "Do you see any coming?"

Yuval ran over to the precipice and looked down at the path that led up to the overwatch from the Philistine camp.

"Nothing," he shouted back. He then ran further north along the spur that formed their elevated position and leapt upon a large creamy white rock. Turning back to Jonathan, Yuval shook his head.

Below, Jonathan could see the Philistines closest to them fleeing from within bowshot into the troops to their west along the line of battle, where men had begun forming into ranks.

***

As arrows struck down several Philistines on their eastern flank nearest the overwatch, many attempted to withdraw to safety, fleeing into the ranks of men behind and to their west. Those in the rear and along the line quickly took up a defensive posture with their shields pressed together forming a tight wall. Angrily, those who'd fled from within bowshot began to curse and strike those preventing them from withdrawing to safety. Many, in their haste, had left armor and shield where they lay.

Unbeknownst to the two Israelites, word of how they'd infiltrated the fort at Geba disguised as Philistines had rapidly circulated among the enemy in the preceding days. So it was, with arrows raining down from their friendly overwatch and the numbers of men fleeing to the rear, that many along the front assumed that the Israelites had once again disguised themselves.

"INFILTRATORS!" shouted one man in the midst of the confusion.

"IMPOSTERS!" shouted another.

The enemy began to form a defensive wall and started to repel those fleeing into their midst. In some areas, they began to advance on their sister units as others attempted to withdraw to safety. What had begun with an attempt to flee, was perceived as an infiltration of masquerading Israelites. The few bearded and unarmored Israelites that had joined the Philistine ranks quickly formed into small pockets to defend themselves against the panicked Philistines that surrounded them.

***

As Ahithophel approached the king, he could see that other reports were already filtering in. Abner saw the captain approaching and waved him toward the large pomegranate tree where Saul stood talking with several others.

"The Philistines are either fighting one another or some friendly force has taken the Philistine overwatch."

Saul looked to Abner and Ahithophel as they approached.

"Did either of you send someone out?" Saul questioned.

Abner and Ahithophel confirmed they had not.

"Count and see who has gone from us," Saul ordered.

Due to the commotion in the Philistine camp, many of the commanders had already begun to do so.

"All of my men are accounted for," Ahithophel reported.

Several others reported the same.

"Where is Jonathan?" Saul asked. Seconds later, Jehoiada, the ranking man of Jonathan's division arrived.

"That answers that question," Abner said before as he turned to Saul.

"Where is Jonathan?" Saul demanded.

"The men report that he left the perimeter near the cliff. Jonathan and Yuval have taken the overwatch on the other side," Jehoiada reported.

Saul cursed and turned to Ahijah the priest.

"Bring the Ark of God!"

Ahijah motioned to the Levite chest-bearers and the Ark of the Covenant was brought forth from within the tent of meeting.

"How many are with them?" Abner asked. "Are they holding the position?"

"Just the two of them sir, by God alone," Jehoiada reported, "they are holding the position, but it's just the two of them."

Saul watched as the Levite chest-bearers set the Ark before him. The commotion from the Philistine camp had become so loud that they could hear it from well within the Israelite camp.

Abner was growing impatient. The reports of the men forward of the line were clear. Given their predicament of the past few days, the window of opportunity that now presented itself could not go unmet.

"Saul, we should attack now without delay. If we stall, we may lose the initiative," Abner pressed.

Saul ignored him as he watched the priests kneel and pray. Ahijah unfastened the stone-covered pouch on his ephod.

"Saul, Jonathan is out there," Abner said sternly.

"Withdraw your hand!" Saul shouted to Ahijah as he reached into the pouch that contained the sacred Urim. Saul turned to Abner. "Prepare the attack!"

The commanders quickly dispersed to their companies where their men waited eagerly for orders, roused by the loud commotion coming from the Philistine camp.

Jehoiada shouted to the rest of Jonathan's men, who'd already begun to assemble near the northern perimeter of the camp.

"Jonathan has carved the way for us! They need us now! Find your courage men and let us not disappoint him!"

The men shouted and pumped their wooden spear shafts into the air as they filed into the line of battle left of Jehoiada.

The rest of the Israelite army formed into ranks as Saul donned his helmet and stepped ahead of the men.

"Today we have revenge on these uncircumcised Philistines! A curse on anyone who stops to eat before evening comes, and I have revenge on my enemies!" At this, he turned and raised his sword toward the Philistine camp. "ATTACK!"

***

Watching the turmoil from above, the two Israelites tried to make sense of the situation below.

"You think they've turned on the Israelite defectors?" Jonathan asked as Yuval strapped a Philistine sword and scabbard around his waist.

Yuval was silent for a moment, watching the chaos below.

"No," he replied. "They're fighting each other! Look! That group there is attacking the ones that were firing their arrows at us! They're all mixed up!"

Jonathan moved to a different vantage point. He could see the entire line of Philistines below them engrossed in battle.

"Look! Look!" Yuval shouted.

Jonathan turned his attention as Yuval pointed to the southern crest of the gorge to their west. A wave of Israelites crested the ridge and descended down the slope and up the lower side opposite the Israelite position. They watched as the wave of Israelites smashed through the already disrupted Philistine line like a tsunami. With their backs already turned, those along the front were hewn down with ease.

"EXCELLENT," Jonathan shouted as he drew his sword.

"Well, I'll be a…" Yuval's sentence was cut short by a slap on his shoulder.

"Come on!" Jonathan shouted as he sprinted towards the path that led down to the Philistine camp.

Yuval shook his head in amazement as he rushed after the prince.

Moments later, Jonathan and Yuval sprinted into the Philistine camp, bounding over slain Philistines as they ran to join their fellow Israelites. Soon, they were amidst their own men, surrounded by fighting on all sides.

Yuval struggled to remain in sight of the prince as they fought their way forward to the front of the battle. Coming to a small formation of Philistines, several Israelites smashed into their shields and were skewered by Philistine spears.

"FORM THE LINE," Jonathan shouted. Immediately the Israelites closest to him gathered shoulder to shoulder at his left and right, Yuval, several arm lengths to his right. The men raised their shields into a tight barrier, with their spears resting in the grove along the top edge. Those in the second line pressed their shields between the backs of the men ahead. Those in the third held their shields above the heads of themselves and the men in front of them. Israelites continued to pour in line behind them.

"FOR-WARD!" Jonathan called. Yuval began a cadence, shouting "OOH SHAAH, OOH SHAAH, OOH SHAAH" to which the men thrust their spears with each forward step of the left leg. The men brought their right legs up in unison as the spears were retracted and re-cocked. They moved slowly but menacingly forward, smashing the Philistine line as more Israelites maneuvered to flank the defensive formation.

Arrows passed overhead from behind the front line of Philistine shields, striking and sticking to the wood and leather Israelite shields overhead. They closed in on the Philistine line, which stood sturdy, but unmoving. Wood and stone Israelite spear tips clanged against metal Philistine shields. As they battered the front line of Philistines, the sound was deafening. The metal points of the Philistine spears embedded in the wood of the Israelite shields making them difficult to withdraw, while Israelite spears deflected off of the metal enemy shields or found their mark in human flesh.

The Philistine leader was either dead or frozen with fear, for they simply stood, buttoned up in their defensive formation as the Israelites smashed their line with each call of Yuval's cadence.

"OOH SHAAH, OOH SHAAH, OOH SHAAH."

The wall of Philistine shields was beginning to buckle. Gaps in the enemy line formed as Philistines fell, exposing the soldier to his right and left.

The war machine trudged on as the Israelite spears plunged forward again and again. Philistines in the rear of the formation began to lose heart and fled as the front began to crumble under the onslaught. When the line finally gave way, Jonathan shouted the order to break formation and pursue the fleeing Philistines.

The melee of the battle spread for over a mile of ground as small groups of Philistines held their positions, some acting out of discipline,

LION OF JUDAH

others by necessity, while most fled and were pursued by the attacking Israelites.

The rugged terrain made a hasty retreat difficult. Here and there small groups of Philistines scattered and hid or held whatever temporarily defensible positions they could find. Jonathan with Yuval ever at his side, strove to stay at the front of the scattered Israelite line. Better to kill these men now while they ran, than to fight them some later day when their courage and discipline returned. They continued to meet light resistance, clashing along the front as the Philistines withdrew and formed defensive lines again and again, each time getting weaker and weaker. The enemy was slowing the Israelite advance, allowing the majority of their forces to retreat to safety and live to fight another day.

Seeing they were getting too dispersed to effectively support each other, Jonathan called to the men ahead of him to slow their attack. The men at the forefront, seeing they were far from their fellows, slowed their advance so that the others could catch up. As evidence of the Philistine encampment was still everywhere about them, Jonathan realized they'd merely punched a hole through the Philistine line. He looked left and right constantly to ensure they were not being enveloped, climbing upon any rock or tree that might give him some better vantage. As they advanced, the vegetation grew thicker, making coordination with fellow Israelites or observation of a potential enemy ambush more difficult. If there were Philistines to either side of him, he thought, they would have just as much difficulty observing the Israelite advance. Perhaps more to their advantage, the enemy would have difficulty ascertaining just how small the Israelite numbers were.

Jonathan ordered the men to halt the advance and regroup to their location and that of their fellow Israelites. Sending runners to the rear, he ordered the rest of the men to catch their breath and replenish their strength. He was exhausted and had not paused to drink or eat since he'd been leading the attack.

Climbing upon a rock, Jonathan heard an odd humming. He quickly located the source of the noise and came upon a tree growing out of a crevasse in the rock. He approached it, seeing the drones of a honeybee hive coming and going from a large hole in the tree. Thick golden honey oozed from the hive and ran down the smooth bark of the tree. Yuval tossed a Philistine staff up to him and with it, Jonathan reached out and carefully freed some of the comb from the hive. The men around him watched with envy as he hopped down to the ground and walked a short distance away from the hive, flicking away several bees still stuck to the sticky comb.

Jonathan offered the comb to Yuval, who shook his head.

"You first," he replied. "I'm going to find some water."

Jonathan turned to those nearest him and offered it.

The men around him surprisingly shook their heads and refused the offer.

"Suit yourselves," Jonathan said as he raised the comb to his mouth and bit a large chunk from the comb and chewed. His eyes widened with delight as he tasted the sweet nectar.

Jonathan again offered some of the comb to the men around him.

Strangely, they refused.

Jonathan spat the wax from his mouth and took another bite from the comb, sucking the honey from within and replenishing his weary body.

One of the men nearest him leaned his head against a tree, his body shaking with fatigue. His hamstrings cramping and seizing as he tried to massage the muscles.

"Here," Jonathan insisted. "Take some of this honey. It will help."

Again, the man refused despite his condition.

Jonathan turned, examining the faces of the men around him.

"What is the matter with you all?" he asked.

One of the exhausted men, an officer, finally spoke up between labored breaths.

"Prince Jonathan, your father bound the army under a strict oath, saying 'cursed be anyone who eats food today!' That is why the men are faint."

Mortified, Jonathan shook his head. He looked at the remaining comb in his hand and let it fall to the ground. Seeing Yuval sifting among the Philistine belongings strewn all around them, he called to him.

"Yuval, stop what you are doing. Come here." Turning back to the officer, Jonathan instructed him to inform Yuval of the king's oath. Shaking his head again, Jonathan bent down and took a water skin from a dead Philistine and washed the sticky honey from his hand.

"My father has made trouble for the land," he said in frustration. "See how my eyes are brightened when I tasted a little of this honey. How much better it would have been if the men had eaten today of the spoil of their enemies that they found. Would not the slaughter of the Philistines have been even greater?"

Jonathan stood, contemplating their next move. Why had his father made such a thoughtless oath? He wondered. Now that the men had a moment for their hearts to calm in the wake of the intense fighting, fatigue had begun to set in. Many were without water and all were in need of nourishment. Several men had already seized up with cramping and could push their bodies no further.

"Jonathan," he heard Yuval say in a low voice.

He turned to see Yuval pointing to an approaching force of Israelites led by the king. Jonathan moved his foot nonchalantly to smother the honeycomb into the dirt.

"Father, we pursued the Philistines to this point. They're staggering their withdrawal. We've met opposition the entire way, but we've got them on the run. Apparently, there has been significant infighting among them. Those Philistines there were dead before we arrived," Jonathan said pointing to a group of enemy dead. "I ordered the men to halt here. They are spent. They need water and food."

"Nonsense, I passed several streams already. Certainly there is water here among the dead as well. We'll eat when the Philistines are crushed completely."

"Many can no longer go forward. Their bodies are failing and cannot continue in this state."

Ignoring his son's reply, Saul ordered the men to seize whatever water could be found among the Philistine corpses. They renewed the attack with Jonathan leading on the left flank, Saul in command of the center, and Abner on the right.

Skirmish after bloody skirmish, the Israelites continued to press the enemy until the sun sank in the western sky. Exhausted men were rotated from the front to the reserves in the rear, continuing their pursuit after the slowly withdrawing enemy forces. The reserve forces following in the rear were met with occasional resistance as groups of bypassed Philistines attacked along the Israelite flanks.

As the sun disappeared on the horizon, one exhausted Israelite came upon a goat, his body cramping, muscles freezing from fatigue and lack of nutrients, he seized the animal by the horn and slit its throat, then pressed the wound to his parched dry mouth. The man began ravenously cutting chunks of meat from the animal and eating. Seeing this, several others followed suit, seizing whatever animals they could find among the Philistine provisions that had been left behind.

On rotation with the men in reserve, Ahithophel observed the macabre scene.

"Stop that!" he tried to shout, though he'd grown so weak and fatigued, his call was barely more than a whisper. The men continued as if they hadn't heard him. He seized one of the men. "You're Israelites! We're in the middle of a battle. Do not defile yourselves!"

Of those who heard him, few responded. He could hardly blame them since he too was on the verge of collapse from the day's fighting. Calling for his runner, he ordered the man to locate the king and report to him immediately. Ahithophel attempted to make his way to the front in search of King Saul.

Moments later, Saul emerged from the mass of Israelites ahead.

"My King…" Ahithophel managed to say, raising a shaky hand, "the men… exhausted… sunset… they're eating blood."

Saul looked in the direction of Ahithophel's shaking finger, then back at the young messenger.

"What's he talking about?" Saul asked.

"My King, he's trying to say that the men are sinning against the Lord by eating meat that has blood in it," the young runner was almost in tears from exhaustion.

Moved by the captain's exhaustion, Saul strode quickly towards the closest group of men he could find.

"STOP," he shouted to them. "You have broken faith!"

Saul turned to Raanan.

"Gather some men and roll a large stone over here at once. Get a fire started."

Raanan immediately turned and went to work.

Nearby, the priests were seeing to the wounded and administering aid, praying over them and taking lasts requests and recording the wishes of dying men. Ahijah was just finishing a prayer with a wounded Israelite when he saw the king. He stood and joined Saul as the king walked the beleaguered captain to a fallen tree and instructed him to sit down.

"Catch your breath," the king instructed Ahithophel. Turning to the runner, Ahijah the priest, and those around them, he ordered, "Go out among the men and tell them, 'each of you bring me your cattle and sheep, and slaughter them here and eat them. Do not sin against the Lord by eating meat with blood still in it.'"

The men immediately dispersed to deliver the message and soon a roaring fire was made.

The slaughtered animals were barely more than field-dressed and skinned before being placed on a pole and held to the flames. Men crowded around and stuck quartered legs and shoulders on whatever they could find, putting the meat into the flames for a perfunctory cooking before consuming the seared portions down to the bone.

Saul ordered the men who'd eaten to immediately replace those on the line as quickly as possible. Before long, Ahijah the priest was covered nearly head to toe in gore. The ground around the stone altar was drenched with blood. As the battle pressed on, Raanan brought a well-cooked piece of beef to Saul, who took it graciously and after confirming the man had himself eaten, consumed the steak. Feeling strengthened by the meal, Saul rallied the men around him and called for a report from the captains along the front. No reinforcements had been observed from the flanks. It was evident that the Philistines were losing ground and steadily waning in numbers.

In spite of the optimistic reports, the commanders appeared uncharacteristically reserved and weary.

"We have them where we want them! Let us go down and pursue the Philistines by night and plunder them till dawn," Saul shouted. "Let us not leave one of them alive," he exclaimed excitedly. "What say you?"

"Sir, I've just come from the line," one man began before pausing to catch his breath. "The men," he paused again and corrected himself. "I mean *we* are spent. My own hand is frozen to my spear. I know these men. They will do as you command if it requires every drop of blood we have left, but I fear they will die of exhaustion if we continue to press them."

Hushai listened with admiration for the young commander before speaking. "We are prepared to see this to the end if that is what you require. Every man here has done his share today, but most are near the point of collapsing. Many are unable to stand or walk my Lord, but do whatever seems best to you, my King."

Seeing an opportunity to intervene and loathe to see another man die in his arms, Ahijah the priest stepped forward.

"My King, let us inquire of God here, now, and see if *He* will have us continue the pursuit."

"So be it," Saul replied.

Ahijah withdrew the Urim and Thummim from the ephod. Saul called the captains together around as Ahijah prayed to the Lord, thanking Him for His provision and victory over the Philistines. He asked forgiveness for the transgressions of some by consuming blood.

As Ahijah prepared the Urim and Thummim, Saul prayed.

"Shall I go down and pursue the Philistines? Will you give them into Israel's hand? If so, give Urim and if not, give Thummim."

Ahijah cast the Urim and Thummim, but could discern no clear answer from either.

Again, he cast them. Time after time, Ahijah repeated the ritual, but could not interpret any identifiable answer.

Saul was becoming more and more agitated with each indiscernible outcome.

"What does this mean?" Saul asked the priest.

"There is something wrong," Ahijah explained. "The Lord is not a God of confusion."

Furious, Saul turned to the officers around him. "Go and tell your captains to report to me here. All of them! I want every officer here! Go now."

Saul paced back and forth while Ahijah continued seeking an answer from the Lord.

All of the leaders of the army presented themselves to Saul. The men had been fighting most of the previous day and all throughout the night though the battle had waned significantly along with the men's strength and willingness to continue the pursuit. Many had collapsed on the way and had to be carried as their limbs seized and cramped from the extreme exertion.

"Come here, all you who are leaders of the army, and let us find out what sin has been committed today. As surely as the Lord who rescues Israel lives, even if the guilt lies with my son Jonathan, he must die."

Though several of those present knew Jonathan had tasted the honey, not one of them said a word.

"You all stand over there. I and Jonathan, my son, will stand over here."

As before, Hushai responded, "Do what seems best to you."

Standing before the officers, Saul raised his eyes and palms to heaven, his arms outstretched. He prayed aloud for everyone to hear, "Lord, God of Israel, why have you not answered your servant today? If the fault is in me or my son Jonathan, respond with Urim, but if the men of Israel are at fault, respond with Thummim."

Ahijah cast the stones and held a torch over them as he observed the first discernible answer he'd seen all night.

"It is Urim my King."

Saul was standing over the priest and had seen the answer himself. Wide-eyed, he looked to Jonathan, then shouted to Ahijah, "Cast the lot between me and Jonathan, my son," so that all this present could hear. "Urim for me and Thummim for Jonathan."

Jonathan stood motionless as all eyes watched the priest. Ahijah breathed heavily as he cast the stones again.

Saul's eyes passed from the stones to Jonathan.

"Tell me what you have done," he said in a tone that sent a chill through the priest's spine.

Jonathan shook his head as he looked at the ground. This was lunacy, he thought. He looked up again and returned his father's contemptuous gaze.

"I tasted a little honey with the end of my staff! And now, I must die! Surely such a breach as this requires my head," Jonathan shouted, his words dripping with sarcasm.

"May God deal with me," Saul said sternly, "be it ever so severely, if you do not die, Jonathan." Saul seized his spear from Raanan and moved menacingly towards Jonathan.

"He did not know!" Yuval shouted. "I was there, we had no knowledge of the order," Yuval pleaded as he stepped in front of the prince.

Immediately, the others nearest Jonathan joined the armor-bearer. Nearly every soldier in the small gathering spoke up, as Ahithophel and Hushai moved simultaneously to place themselves between the king and Jonathan, their hands open to show they meant no harm. Others pulled Jonathan rearwards into the safety of the crowd.

Ahithophel dropped to his knees before the king with his head bowed and palms open to him.

"Should Jonathan die?" Ahithophel asked. "He who has brought about this great deliverance in Israel," he asked, speaking more to the crowd than to the king.

"NEVER," the men responded in unison.

"As surely as the Lord lives, not a hair of his head will fall to the ground, for he did this today with God's help," Hushai proclaimed.

Abner and the other leaders nodded their affirmation.

"It is true, he and Yuval took the overwatch!" one of the men exclaimed.

Saul looked at the men around him, each of them echoing their agreement.

"Surely he should not die," a man shouted.

"Surely God was with him today," exclaimed another.

"Saul," Abner said, "Jonathan was ignorant of your command since he was not with the army. It was by his actions that the enemy was thrown into confusion. He is innocent since he did not hear your command."

Saul sank to his knees and raised his arms to heaven, "Forgive me Lord, for I pronounced the sentence before I had heard the matter." Saul bowed his head and drew his arms in. "Forgive me, my son," Saul said, his voice trembling. "Forgive me."

The men about them looked from Saul to Jonathan.

The prince stepped forward and lifted his father, though inwardly indignant at the rashness his father had now displayed for the second time in less than a day. Saul grabbed his son's shoulders and pulled Jonathan close, his massive arms curled around his son's body and pulled him in tightly. Jonathan returned his father's embrace.

A moment later Saul released him.

"Halt the advance!" he shouted.

The fighting along the forward line had already waned and nearly ceased altogether as the Philistines had become more and more dispersed. The groups of men still in pursuit were hailed back by the long and unmistakable call of the shofar, which was echoed and carried along by horn bearers along the front. Saul retreated to a secluded area to rest, accompanied only by a small contingent of royal guards.

Abner ordered the army to consolidate for a brief rest and prepare to retrograde back in the direction they'd come, gathering enemy weapons, armor, and other spoils along the way. He caught a glimpse of one man sizing the enemy's armor as he stripped several enemy dead. He held a chest plate up, checking it for fit, and was instantly chastised by several others nearby.

"Don't be a fool. You'll curse us all," they shouted at him.

As the men continued to regroup and gather about their position, Ahithophel approached the general.

"General Abner sir, with permission, should we not keep some of the weapons and armor? The men need swords and spears, helmets, chest plates and shields. Surely the priests could purify them somehow, could they not?"

Abner was already formulating his conversation with Saul. He rubbed his brow, irritated by his own lack of authority to do what was necessary.

"Consolidate everything you can for now. I'll do what I can," he replied.

It didn't take someone of the General's intellect to see the trouble boiling among the men.

Abner greeted Saul's guards as he approached.

"He's resting," the guard informed the general.

"Wake him up," Abner instructed.

One of the guards announced his arrival and Saul sat up on the Philistine cot where he'd been sleeping. He leaned forward with his elbows on his knees and waved Abner over to him. His eyes were strained and bloodshot with exhaustion. Not long earlier, it seemed as if he were the only one not overcome by the day's exertions. Now, however, the day's events had caught up with him and Abner could see from Saul's countenance that he had not yet recovered from his earlier rebuke by the men over so foolish a dispute.

"Saul, there is something we need to address here and now. It cannot wait."

"Very well, what is it?"

"Please consider, we *need* weaponry and armor," Abner pleaded. "We need iron and steel. Why not let the men take what they can unless Samuel tells us otherwise?"

Saul stood quietly contemplating the matter. "We've always offered the spoils to God before and He has taken care of us thus far, even now."

Saul's response was more receptive than Abner had hoped. He pressed further.

"Yes, but those were the first-fruits of your leadership. Never has He required everything from us save a portion, a tenth. Joshua did not withhold spoils from his men unless the Lord specifically demanded it. Why not let the men take back what was taken away from them? Most of these men have no iron implements, no tools, much less weapons

353

to defend their families with. They'd merely be taking back what was stolen. I'm no priest or prophet, but I don't think the Lord would have His people remain in the age of stone when our enemies have moved from bronze to iron."

"Mmm," Saul grunted, his typical response when challenged on matters of faith.

"I don't think it is His will that our people be continually subjected to the will of the enemy, nor that we remain primitive while our enemies advance. Please hear me on this cousin. If necessary, take a tenth of the spoil and devote it to God for destruction or give it to the priests, but allow these men to recoup their losses. We cannot pay them. We cannot restore what has been lost to them. This is the only opportunity to reward those who stayed and fought."

"I will consider it, but I won't give the final word until Samuel has weighed in on the matter."

Despite Abner's inward frustration over another delayed decision, family or not, Abner knew he'd reached the limits of how far Saul could be pushed. He turned and exited the tent where his advisors and other officers waited. The sky was beginning to lighten, though the sun could not yet be seen on the horizon.

"Send runners to find Samuel. I don't care how many. Find a horse and bring him as soon as possible if he is willing. I'll go to him if necessary. I'm not waiting. By the time he arrives, half of the enemy will be stripped and Saul will...." Abner caught himself before letting the words out. He was livid over his cousin's recent behavior, even so, he refused to let the men see it. "I'll be waiting under that terebinth tree," he said pointing up to a small but easily identified hill. "Do you see it there?"

The soldier acknowledged his orders and departed without a word.

Several hours later, the man returned to the hill on an exhausted and sweat-drenched Philistine horse to find the general sleeping soundly with his back to the tree. He hesitated for a moment, wondering if he should rouse the respected leader. He knew the man had hardly slept at all in the past three days.

"Abner," he said softly to the general.

Abner opened his eyes, squinting in the bright midday sun. Seeing the sergeant, squared next to him and holding the reins to two horses.

"Where is he?" Abner asked.

"At Ramah," the sergeant replied.

As Abner started to his feet, the sergeant cleared his throat.

"Ah, sir, I went ahead and asked the seer about what we should do."

As the general lifted his eyes and stared back, the messenger continued.

"He said to devote a tenth of the spoils to the priests and the Levites and do whatever seemed right with the rest."

Abner smiled. "Very well! Thank you. Why don't you get some rest now? I'll make sure you're taken care of," Abner said as he started down the hill to Saul's location.

As he walked, Abner thought to himself about why he'd not just asked the man to do as he'd done. Why had he thought it necessary to go and speak with Samuel in person? Was it fatigue or had Saul's brand of centralized leadership infected himself as well? He resolved to put up as many buffers to this as possible. Thank God for smart freethinking soldiers like that man, Abner thought. Thank God for Jonathan.

By the time he'd reached the king's location, a strategy had already formed in his head as to how he'd address the matter, knowing Saul was not one to place much faith in secondhand hearsay.

Already, piles of Philistine bodies had begun to accumulate at various locations. Weeping Philistine civilians were loading them on wagons and litters towed behind mules and donkeys. The Israelite soldiers had already been stripped of armor, weapons, and whatever other valuables could be found before moving the bodies to collection points. The civilians weren't allowed to touch anyone or anything not yet stripped of iron or other valuables.

Finally, Abner located the tall silhouette of the king on a hillock overlooking a piece of flat ground they'd covered the day before in their pursuit of the fleeing Philistines.

Saul noticed him approaching.

"Good afternoon cousin," Saul said with a smile. "Any word of Samuel's whereabouts?"

"We found him at Ramah." Abner responded. "He said we are to set aside a tenth for the priests and the tribe of Levi. The rest can be used as we see fit."

Saul looked surprised. "He's not coming?"

"No. He is, after all, an old man. I thought it best to spare him the journey."

"You heard this yourself?" Saul asked.

"With my own ears," Abner offered.

"Very well then," Saul said.

"I will oversee the matter and make sure it's done to the letter," Abner said, hoping to avoid further inquiry about Samuel's specific instructions.

"Thank you," was Saul's only response.

Abner turned and proceeded to locate his captains. "Thank God," Abner said under his breath as he left the king's presence. After today's battle, they would have enough weaponry and armor to outfit the entire Israelite army several times over. The enemy armor and weapons greatly outnumbered the dead since so many had discarded the heavy equipment while fleeing the attack.

Abner gave orders for the army to collect the dead and wounded Israelites and move them to Gibeah. Further instructions were given to collect weaponry, shields, armor, and anything else of use to the army at Gibeah, where the loot would be amassed and dispersed accordingly.

Israel's army would now be equipped with every necessity. As Abner walked the ground scattered with enemy dead, he quickly came to the realization that each man would now have armor, a sword, a spear, a first aid kit, and for most of them, more than a year's worth of income taken from the enemy dead. Even artillery such as slings, sling stones, bows, and throwing sticks or clubs were amassed among the spoils.

Reflecting back on the previous forty-eight hours, Abner could not help but marvel at the outcome. This feeling of awe was further strengthened when he began combing through the intelligence captured from the Philistine command tent. Pouring over the maps and correspondence, he realized just how dire their situation had been. There were indications that reinforcements would have arrived today in order to envelop their position and cut off any escape. A letter dated just three days earlier from a General Demeter referenced the special Philistine contingent that would be joining them from Jezebel for this very purpose.

If Jonathan had not acted precisely when he did, today would likely have seen the death of Israel's entire army, its king, and his most promising successor, resulting in the enslavement of their people. Looking up from the letters spread out before him, Abner could see the position where the battle had begun, the elevated piece of ground where Jonathan and Yuval had taken the enemy overwatch.

The young man's aggressive and audacious actions had won the day. Jonathan possessed that unique quality that was so seldom found in most men, a combination of courage and daring coupled with exceptional skill and physical ability. The same actions performed by most men would have sent them to an early grave. Jonathan had, on more than one occasion now, acted with a sort of calculated recklessness that blurred the lines between selflessness and suicide, genius and insanity.

How was it that Jonathan was so different from his father? From anyone for that matter? Oh to just have ten more men like this, Abner thought, men that needed to be reined in instead of being prodded forward.

One of the staff officers interrupted his thoughts.

"Sir?" he heard the man say.

"How can I help you?" Abner responded.

"We counted twenty Philistines on the overwatch position. Jonathan and Yuval killed twenty men up there. I confirmed it."

Abner contemplated the number, the terrain. It just didn't make sense.

"Let me ask you something," he said to the officer. "What sets Jonathan apart from the other men of this army? Six-hundred men were brave enough to stay when they could have fled. They stayed despite lacking swords or armor. Most of these men have faced challenges and over-come hardships far beyond any struggle that Jonathan has encountered as a prince. So why do you think Jonathan is our most valiant warrior?"

The man looked around as if to confirm he and the general were alone.

"Speak freely man," Abner said. "Let's have it."

"Honestly sir," the veteran spoke in a low raspy voice, "what Jonathan and Yuval did took courage and skill. Regarding this, there is no doubt, but as you said, there are many brave men among us and yet, even the king's own son was nearly killed for disobeying a..." he paused as if to choose his next words carefully, "a foolish order." He continued, "there are men here who would gladly give their lives for Israel and for the Lord, but there are few who would give their lives for a king who cares so little about their welfare as to forbid that they eat on the day of battle. If any other man had eaten, no matter how bravely he'd performed, no matter how many Philistines he killed, he would've been slaughtered like an animal. There are Israelites lying in the field as we speak who would not be there if they'd been allowed to strengthen themselves by eating yesterday."

Abner nodded his affirmation of the officer's assessment.

"You're not wrong," Abner conceded. He appreciated the man's candor, but the truth of the matter stung. Saul no longer resembled the man he'd grown up with and loved. Serving under Saul's rule, while difficult, was necessary to provide whatever insulation he could for the men. To the extent he was able, Abner determined to instill trust in the men and grant them as much freedom to act as could be allowed. If there were any way that he could protect the men, it would require that he remain close to Saul.

AFTERWORD

Iron sharpeneth iron;
so a man sharpeneth the
countenance of his friend.
Proverbs 27:17

B ecause I have seen the great and wonderful things that my Lord and Savior has done and was always willing to do in and through me, I have chosen to follow His lead by writing this book. At the age of 21, as a new officer in the Marine Corps, another close friend and fellow Marine officer, Christopher Young, inspired me to read the books of Samuel and Kings. I am ashamed to say that while I professed myself to be a believer, I had never read the Bible from cover to cover. Because I had grown up in church, I thought I knew all of the stories contained within it.

Reading 1 and 2 Samuel set my life on a new course. I realized how little I truly knew of the life of David. Being the third of four brothers, the trio of Joab, Abishai, and Asahel specifically stood out to me. These were men I'd never heard of in church. I thought to myself, what else have I been missing?

The stories of these men and others contained in the books of 1 and 2 Samuel sparked my first endeavor to read the Bible from cover to cover. As I proceeded to do so, my life began to conform to the higher calling which I'd so long confessed to believe in, but failed to live out. Slowly, my personal struggles with sin, shame, and self-doubt faded as my actions and behavior conformed to my beliefs. I am proof of the life-changing power of scripture.

I have prayed that I would be a conduit through which God would reveal truth about the lives of these great men and women who, like us, were flawed. Their faith faltered, they made mistakes, but never once did God abandon those who were willing to repent and turn to Him. While the names and characters change throughout history, the characteristics of God never do. He is merciful. He is kind. He is GOOD.

I have written this book because I wholeheartedly believe in the truth of the events contained in scripture. Though I have taken license to add stories and experiences so that I might flesh out the individuals, using many of my own experiences, it has been my goal to never once deviate from scripture. I hope the reader will forgive me if I have failed in this. While I have used extra-Biblical sources to help inform my knowledge of the events, people, times, and places, when or wherever those sources contradicted the Bible, the Word prevailed. My primary goal is to inspire the reader to search the scripture for themselves and discover what lies there, waiting to be discovered between the lines on the pages. Thank you for your interest. Thank you for your time. Thank you for your prayers. Keep digging!

*The Lord bless you and keep you; the Lord make his face
to shine upon you and be gracious to you; the Lord lift
up his countenance upon you and give you peace.*
Numbers 6:24-26

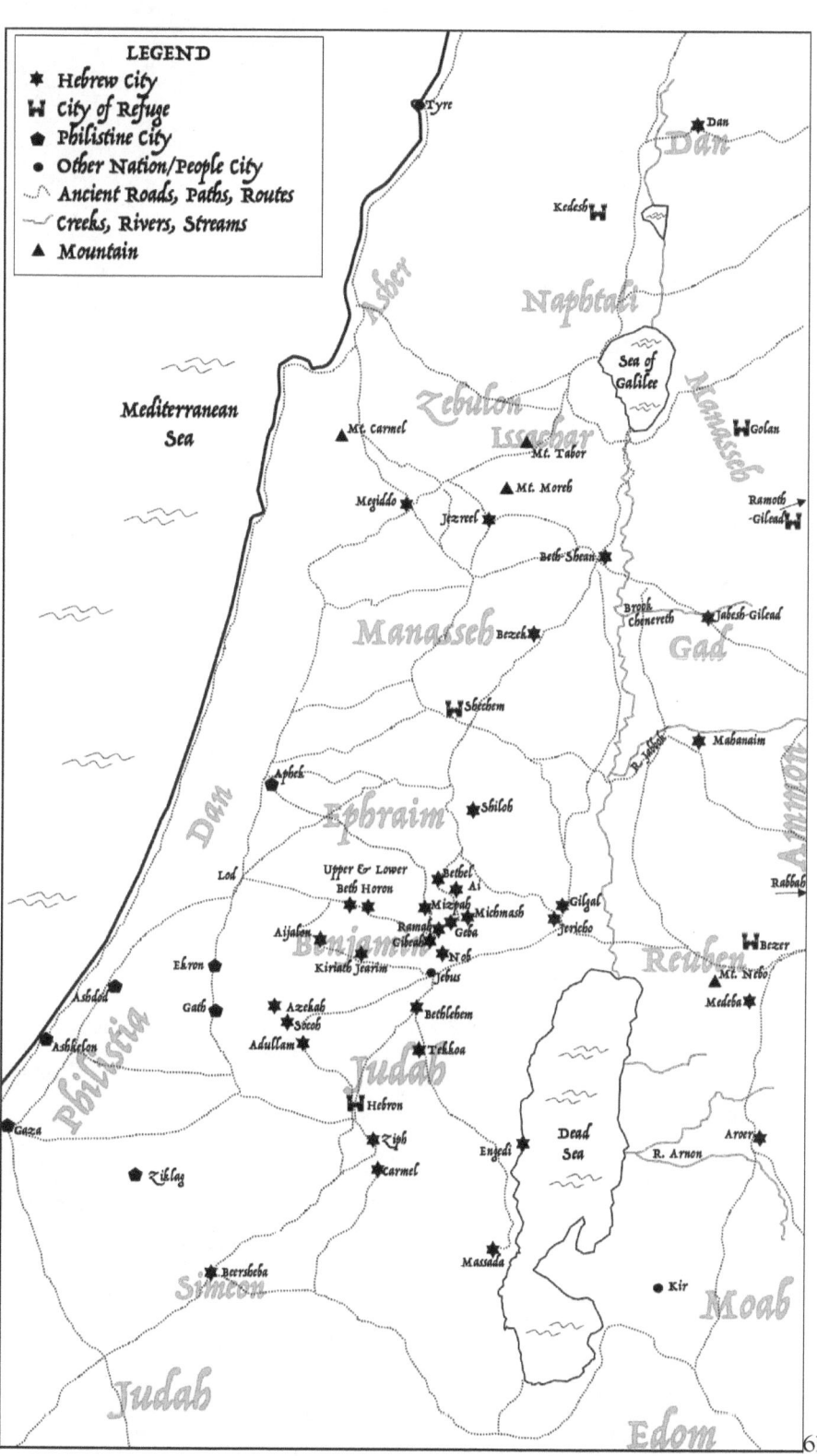

LEGEND

★ Hebrew City
Ⱨ City of Refuge
⬠ Philistine City
● Other Nation/People City
⋯ Ancient Roads, Paths, Routes
⁓ Creeks, Rivers, Streams
▲ Mountain

Mediterranean Sea

Tyre

Dan

Dan

Kedesh

Naphtali

Sea of Galilee

Manasseh

Golan

Asher

Zebulon

Mt. Carmel

Issachar

Mt. Tabor

Ramoth-Gilead

Megiddo

Jezreel

Mt. Moreh

Beth-Shean

Brook Chenereth

Jabesh-Gilead

Manasseh

Bezek

Gad

Shechem

Mahanaim

Aphek

Ephraim

Shiloh

Ammon

Lod

Upper & Lower Beth Horon

Bethel

Ai

Mizpah

Michmash

Gilgal

Rabbah

Aijalon

Ramah

Geba

Gibeah

Jericho

Benjamin

Kiriath Jearim

Nob

Ekron

Jebus

Bezer

Reuben

Ashdod

Gath

Azekah

Socoh

Bethlehem

Mt. Nebo

Medeba

Ashkelon

Adullam

Tekhoa

Judah

Philistia

Hebron

Gaza

Ziph

Engedi

Dead Sea

Aroer

R. Arnon

Ziklag

Carmel

Massada

Kir

Moab

Beersheba

Simeon

Judah

Edom

www.ingramcontent.com/pod-product-compliance
Lightning Source LLC
Chambersburg PA
CBHW050510110726
47899CB00005B/1400